A LONELY BROADCAST

BOOK ONE

KEL BYRON

CONTENT WARNING
This book contains depictions of blood, gore, substance abuse, emotional trauma, vague references to suicide, and body horror.
There will be no sexual violence or pet death.

Copyright © 2023 by Kel Byron.

All rights reserved.

No part of this publication may be reproduced, distributed, or transmitted in any form or by any means, including photocopying, recording, or other electronic or mechanical methods, without the prior written permission of the publisher, except as permitted by U.S. copyright law.

The story, all names, characters, and incidents portrayed in this production are fictitious. The use of song titles or musical artists featured on the fictional radio program is protected under Fair Use.

Book Cover and Illustrations by Kel Byron.

This book is dedicated to the tumor that tried to kill me and to the people who stood by me when it failed.
Thank you. I love you.

Unless you're the tumor.

- Kel B.

CHAPTER ONE: FOG DAY
Evelyn

Every time I came home, the world changed.

If you've ever lived in a small town, you might know the feeling; you leave for a year, come back, and everything goes tits up. Your favorite ice cream shop is a hair salon now. They opened up a chain restaurant no one asked for and the water tower has a fresh coat of paint, but the color makes your eyes sting. Your old neighbors are gone. Strangers moved in. That's what it was like the first time I came home, right after graduating from college. But now? The second time, Pinehaven just seemed smaller than before.

The trees rushed by in a blur of autumn colors, hugging the edge of a winding road. I made myself dizzy just trying to watch them. It reminded me of the last time I traveled these roads, sick and cold while huddled in the back of a taxi, just trying not to vomit all over the seats. Do you have to pay extra if you do?

Back then, the sickness was different. It was a hangover and three nights without sleep. It was from the cold air, rain-soaked clothes, and infection trapped in my lungs. This time around, that storm brewing in my stomach didn't make much sense to me. I just knew, for one reason or another, I didn't want to go home.

Pinehaven was the smallest it had ever been that day.

My name is Evelyn McKinnon, and I'm the newest host of 104.6 FM. There are plenty of things around here that shouldn't exist, and this radio station is one of them.

The driver that had brought me back into town was already pulling away by the time I got my backpack on. I didn't have a tip to give him, but he didn't wait around. In the haze of early morning,

I found myself gaping at the far, open sea of pine, birch, and oak. The first brown leaves of fall had begun to litter the forest floor, and above the horizon of green was a gray, lifeless sky full of billowing clouds. It wasn't raining yet, but it would soon. There was that familiar aroma in the air of an incoming September storm – the kind that chills you deep down to your bones.

At my feet was a gravel driveway that led through the woods and back to the road, just long enough to feel truly abandoned but with that tiny, subtle hope of finding civilization at the end of the path. I was all alone here, hidden in the forest with a rickety tower of wood and metal standing before me. And as the wind blew, it groaned and whined like an old, aching beast. My sore back could sympathize.

The radio station had been seated in what used to be an old fire watch tower, now fitted with a few extensions and updates. Wires and pipes stretched down to the ground, bending and wrapping around the beams while the cords that connected to the mast swung dangerously in the wind. Even the tower's concrete base didn't give me any comfort. I imagined the bolts coming loose and the whole damn thing toppling down during a strong wind. Wouldn't that just be my luck? *Here lies Evelyn: burning in hell after being crushed to death on her first day of work.*

The head of the network left a message attached to one of the wooden beams. "To the new recruit of 104.6 FM", it said. Now, most people would say that FM stations don't *have* even numbers. And yet, every time I rode in the car as a child, it always showed up: 104.6 FM, the only station that could reach us in the valley between the deep green mountains—the only voice for miles and miles.

As a kid, I never questioned why that voice changed every few months.

The letter was still waiting for me, held to the wood with a single tack. A frigid breeze made it flutter, so I grabbed it before the wind stole it away. As I began my journey up the zig-zagging metal steps, I read the message:

Evelyn,
Welcome to your first day at 104.6 FM. Regrettably, I won't

be able to join you to give you a tour, but I hope we'll have a chance to talk very soon. There's plenty to discuss. In the meantime, I've written your instructions next to the computers.

Extra keys are in a box in the utility closet. Please follow the instructions very carefully. Don't forget to check the automation tools each night. We'll be interviewing for a part-time position next week, but until then, you'll be working alone. Your groceries will be delivered every Friday.

Please make yourself comfortable.

Good luck.

A. J.

I shoved the letter in the pocket of my flannel, folded lazily in half. The stairs were long, feeling slightly unstable against the wind. I counted each step as I rose to the top, wondering why that final *'good luck'* made the hair on the back of my neck stand on end.

The door was just as noisy as the steps. Immediately, the stale aroma of dust and old wood caught my nose, as if the place hadn't had the stench aired out in a good, long while. I was surprised there weren't any bats. The only thing I could see in the cramped space was the dull glow of two computer screens, continuing the broadcast even while no one else was there. A lone machine singing to itself.

I turned on the lights and gazed out of the massive lookout window that faced the woods. From here, I could see everything. The green and orange trees rolled in waves until they were lost in the mist that swirled atop the mountain peaks. I could see the glimmer of light from Pinehaven just getting ready to start the day. It was so close, and yet, that mile between us felt almost endless. It was lonely, quiet, and daunting up here at the top of the world.

One way or another, I would have to get used to it. The radio was all mine for the next few weeks, and the employee apartment in the back would be my home until I could afford a real mailing address. From the looks of things, the 'apartment' was more like a closet, but I wasn't picky. It wasn't even the worst place I had laid my head.

I put down the backpack holding all of my worldly possessions and made the short walk over to my seat. There, the dusty computer desk held a ring of keys and a piece of laminated paper.

"Okay, pal, what's your deal?" I whispered with my tongue sticking out between my teeth, leaning against the edge of the desk and cracking my back.

> *Rule #1: Take care of the equipment. Tools, spare parts, and a generator can be found in the shed.*
> *Rule #2: Record all listener calls. Report any calls that are suspicious in nature.*
> *Rule #3: Never let the broadcast go quiet. When no Operator is present, make use of the automation tools.*
> *Rule #4: If the fog rolls in, issue an emergency broadcast. Keep the radio on. Lock the doors. Do not leave the tower. If the signal is down, activate The Bell.*

The final rule made my skin tingle with a fresh set of goosebumps. I had no idea what the good-golly-fuck 'The Bell' was, but I *did* have the faintest memory of the fog. For the briefest moment, I could imagine a crackling radio and the view of my mother closing all the curtains in the house one by one. I remembered the way her hands trembled and the hollow sound the basement stairs made when we rushed down into the dark. I remembered asking about dad every time. No matter how hard I strained my mind, I could not recall what came next, but trying to think about it made my stomach sick all over again.

Maybe those memories were a dream. Fog was just fog, and the vast mountainside was easy to get lost in. I wasn't a brave woman, sure, but I knew I wasn't afraid of some goddamn *clouds*.

I put the list down on the desk, settling myself into one of the chairs. It squeaked as my full weight fell against it, the well-worn cushion sinking down with a hiss of air. I had everything I needed. On the screen, the automation tools were hard at work choosing music to play—mostly folk-rock and oldies that my parents probably grew up with.

I grabbed myself a cup of coffee in a mug that apparently

came from a zoo gift shop somewhere in Kentucky—it had a kickass image of a tiger on it and everything. The drink tasted bitter and burnt, mixed with the aged flavor that came with the bottom of a very old coffee pot. I probably should have washed it first, huh? I sat down at my desk, headphones situated on my ears, microphone on. It was eight o'clock on a Monday morning when I made my very first broadcast.

"Good morning, this is Evelyn McKinnon with 104.6 Pinehaven Radio: your local station for news, weather, and more. I'm looking forward to joining you every day to liven up that work week. Today's forecast is mostly cloudy and gloomy with a high of 47 degrees Fahrenheit. Tonight, look for rain and freezing temperatures, and make sure to drive safely if you're going down the mountain path. I'll have more weather updates this afternoon. But for now, we're kickin' off thirty minutes of uninterrupted music here on 104.6 FM, Pinehaven Radio."

The microphone was off and Eagles took over the airwaves. I breathed a sigh of relief. Was it normal to feel stage fright when no one was watching? Looking out over the trees and at the tiny village, I wondered how many of them still listened to the radio. Perhaps my voice was simply a whisper unheard in a void of dead, ghostly broadcasts.

I had thirty minutes of audio in place before I had to speak again, and another thirty minutes before the next advertisement. I leaned back in my chair, sipping that dreadful coffee and wincing whenever the sour taste hit the back of my tongue. I couldn't tell if the taste was from some nasty beans or nasty water. If it was the latter, I didn't want to know.

Morning became afternoon, but the cloudy sky was far too thick to watch the sun's great migration. Time seemed to move slower. I was the queen of my own shitty, colorless domain, wearing a crown of headphones while I sat upon a throne with squeaky wheels: the queen of weather forecasts and 70s classic rock for dads.

But that quiet daydream didn't last. A loud smack against the glass broke me out of my drifting thoughts. It was too quick for me to see, but I jumped with an undignified shriek. The window straight ahead trembled from the force like a shockwave, and all that was left was a spot of thick, deep blood on the outside.

I got out of my seat and pushed the chair in, headphones clattering against the top of the desk. My nose crinkled in slight disgust as I stepped forward, watching the stain begin to drip.

My face was pressed against the glass, my forehead cold and wet from condensation as I tried to peer down at the forest floor beneath me. It was so far away, I thought ... and then another loud *bang* made me jump straight out of my skin.

"Jesus—*fuck*!"

I watched as a particularly stupid bird hit the window, cracking its bones against the glass and adding to the grotesque graffiti. With a heavy breath, I clutched at my chest. God, the poor thing ... I could see its mangled body as it fell, twisted up like a crescent moon. What were the odds it would happen twice in the exact same spot?

Three times, as it turned out. As I stood there with a hand over my heart, a distant blackbird flew closer and closer, flapping its wings erratically as if it were spiraling out of control. And then, *smack*. Again. Blood and bone. A stain on the window. My heart: still racing.

And again. *Smack*. Once more. *Bang*. Each time, I took a step away from the window until an absurd thought popped into my head. Were they coming after me? It was stupid to think, I know. Why would some birds be after my blood? What did *I* do?

I think I could kick a bird's ass. I could kick *several* birds' asses, in fact.

My eyes followed the falling body of the sixth bird, which crumpled against the window and then plopped into the dry grass with all the rest. Maybe it was just the way its bones snapped, but it looked as if it had a second beak.

"Fantastic ..." I sneered, not looking forward to the mess I had to clean.

I decided to at least wait until it had dried and the blood no longer smelled fresh and hot against the window. Briefly, my eyes took in the metal fire escape that I would have to trust; I didn't like the looks of it already. No sir, no ma'am.

Thankfully, that was the end of it. No other woodland creatures, flying or otherwise, decided to tempt fate and rush head-first into the glass after their fallen brethren. It left the rest of my afternoon in a state of stale, empty boredom. There were no calls, no requests, and probably no listeners. I entertained myself by rolling my chair around, juggling paper balls badly, and occasionally lying face-down on the floor and pretending to be dead.

As the sun began to set, I was lounging with my legs over the side of my chair and my headphones limply hanging off one ear, half-asleep. It was then that I heard an unfamiliar sound.

The phone was ringing.

At first, I thought I was in a dream. I flailed like a spider in water, all my limbs moving at once and getting me nowhere at all. I shoved my headphones back on, eyes darting over the console to find the button I needed.

"Hello, you've reached 104.6 Pinehaven Radio, this is Evelyn McKinnon. What can I do for you this evening?"

I waited a moment. Silence. Then, I heard a sound like the parting of dry lips, followed by a wheeze. It tickled my ear in a repulsive way, like a cold breath whispering against my face or *tendrils* reaching out from the phone and exploring the inside of my head. Inhale ... exhale. Each was more labored than the last. And then, they hung up. I was alone again, feeling this spine-tingling sensation that crawled up my arms and left goosebumps alongside the freckles. Even in the silence, I didn't feel alone anymore. I felt as if that eerie breath was closer than ever. Was someone watching me? Spying on me?

Was this why the last radio DJ quit?

"Shit."

I looked at the console, realizing I had forgotten one of the very important rules left for me: recording all of the listener calls. No one would know, right?

Whatever the case, I let the next song play. It was an older song, something for the geriatrics of Pinehaven to enjoy and reminisce about their younger days. I leaned back with my legs on the chair next to me, one boot untied, all while letting the sweet tones of 'Unchained Melody' play for several minutes ... several very, very long minutes.

The lightbulb above my head popped and the room was plunged into darkness, only the light of the screen shining in my face. The next song never played. Instead, the Righteous Brothers were back at it again as the track looped for a second time. I leaned forward, squinting at the screen as I tried to spot where I had gone wrong. There was no button I had pressed on accident, no setting that I had fucked up. The music was seamless, like a single track that wouldn't end, going on and on and on.

I tried desperately to change the song, but when I did, the program froze and refused to budge. The screen started changing colors, red and purple and toxic green. And still, the song played ... and played ... and *played*.

I still knew every word. It played at my high school senior prom. I remembered dancing with a tall, blonde girl who smelled like vanilla and cinnamon. I wore black and she wore dusty pink. I stepped on her toes so many times that night.

Eventually, I gave up. There was nothing I could do but stop the radio entirely, and I had a sneaking suspicion that breaking the first rule would do me fewer favors than clogging the airwaves with a 1960s love song.

Two hours passed. Two entire hours and that same song played over and over while I bonked my head against the desk. No one called, no one complained. My controls were all frozen, but the computer screens were glowing red the whole time. I heard a rumble from below and a clanking sound from the bathroom as if the pipes were settling. And finally, at the stroke of nine o'clock exactly, it all stopped. A tune from The Doors began to play and I felt a relief I hadn't felt in ages. *Finally, oh sweet release.*

There was a blinking light; a call was coming in. I exhaled slowly before clearing my throat and answering, putting on a fake smile for what I was almost certain was going to be a complaint about the music.

"Hello, you've reached 104.6 Pinehaven Ra—"

Before I could finish speaking, I heard it again: that rough, raspy breath I knew so well. It breathed in, then out again, like a shriveled mouth full of sawdust. And then, for the first and only time, I heard the labored voice of an old, weak man croaking through dry lips.

"Thank ... you ..."

That was all he said before hanging up the phone, leaving me in emptiness once again. Two simple words, and they managed to chill me to the bone.

I took off my headphones, unnerved by the sound of my own pulse hammering in my ears. There was a low gurgle from behind me, coming from the kitchen sink. It was a voice ... Music. Music, coming from the pipes. It was there for a moment, and then it was gone, but it stayed just long enough for me to catch a few words.

The same lyrics I had heard all evening.

I didn't say anything on air for the rest of the night, simply letting the music play and keeping my headphones off. All the while, that old man's voice played over and over in my head, along with a dreadful presence that was still all around me in that bleak, empty room. My little kingdom was small, like sitting inside a shoebox, but I felt more exposed than ever.

Sometimes I thought I saw a shadow in the corner of the room. Sometimes I felt a tickle on the back of my neck like the touch of cold fingers running along my spine. I know I should have changed that lightbulb, but the unease had paralyzed me and I found myself sitting in one spot for hours, just staring dead-eyed at the screen until my head began to pound. It didn't help that the utility closet in the corner was open just a crack.

I didn't remember leaving it open.

⊶⊶||⊷⊶|⊧|⊧||⊧|⊧⊷⊷||⊷⊷

That night, I hardly slept. I didn't like the way the trees creaked at night, how their limbs would scrape against the windows. I felt exposed, lying on a stale-smelling mattress in an old janitor's closet and staring at the ceiling. For hours, I listened to the rattle of the windows and the distant howling of wolves from the mountainside. Their voices were strained, suffering, like the whine of a beast in pain. A screech owl was wailing nearby, a rabbit squealed in the night as if plucked from the ground by a predator. Now and again, somebody whistled.

And when morning came, my tower felt just as oppressive as before.

All the cupboard doors were open when I finally rolled my ass out of the closet. I tried not to think about it—it was way too early for this poltergeist bullshit. While my coffee brewed and the automated system played on, I finally fixed that lightbulb and then took a bucket and a sponge out to the fire escape to clean off the dried blood. A turkey vulture was already circling, having pecked at the carrion through the night.

Cleaning the window was disgusting work. The sponge took on a rotten, metallic smell as it soaked up the dark red stain. I winced each time I had to shove my hand into the ruddy water, but when it was done I was relieved; now, I simply had to hope for no more suicidal birds.

I emptied the water bucket in the soil, grabbing the dead birds one at a time and tossing them into the woods like nasty, blood-caked frisbees. A little treat for the coyotes and bobcats. As I stood at the tree line, I heard the crunch of twigs. It didn't bother me at the time as I imagined all the little beasts that could have been curiously lingering near the tower. I stomped back up the stairs when it was done, all the while hoping that the chill on the back of my neck was just from having nasty, dirty hands.

But as I blew the hair away from my face and glanced out to the open expanse of woodland, I saw it. Far over the wave of trees, like an ocean of green pines and dying leaves, something was moving on the horizon. It was the fog bank, drifting over treetops and swallowing them whole. The way it moved raised goosebumps on my arms. The wind seemed to change direction in an instant, brushing against my face and whistling through the pines like an eerie, lonesome song.

Rule #4: If the fog rolls in, issue an emergency broadcast.

"Shit, shit, shit ..."
I quickly dropped the wet sponge into the bucket with a

grotesque 'splat'. I grimaced, teeth bared as it tipped and rolled away from the metal platform. The bucket bounced all the way to the bottom of the stairs, one obnoxious and sharp clang at a time.

Quickly, I scampered back into the building, closing the door behind me with a slam that shook the walls. Through the glass, I could see it all. The forest was being swallowed, bit by bit, tree by tree. Distantly, I could hear the caw of blackbirds. They hushed, going absolutely silent the moment the fog reached them as if they too were swallowed beneath its weight.

Closer and closer, it rolled in. I could see the way it pushed itself along. Fog didn't do that. It wasn't a solid mass, moving through the trees like snakes weaving a path through sand, and yet that's exactly what it did. The fog *slithered*. It was like its own beast, racing toward the radio tower with purpose and folding over itself as it went, tumbling and rolling like a stormy sea.

I stepped back slowly, afraid to tear my eyes away as I became aware of something else: it was so eerily quiet in here.

I heard a ring. It was the landline.

I broke my eyes away from the fog and jumped for the wall-mounted phone, holding it up to my ear.

"Hel—"

"McKinnon, what the *fuck* are you doing?!" The voice of a man came through, panicked and furious. "Run the emergency broadcast. Turn the radio back on *now!*"

"I'm sorry, I just—"

"I said *now!*" And with that, he hung up with a click. I flinched, a shaky hand placing the phone back in its cradle. The fog was closer now, nearly breaking the edge of the forest. In moments, it would reach the clearing where I sat, enveloping everything in a world of gray.

My heart was racing. Why was it racing? It was just *weather.*

I rushed to the computer desk, adjusting the microphone arm until it was right in front of my face.

"This is Evelyn McKinnon with 104.6 FM, issuing a fog warning for Pinehaven Village. I repeat, there is a fog warning for

Pinehaven Village."

As I spoke, my eyes glanced at the button on the wall. The Bell. It had been so expertly placed out of the way, off on its own where it couldn't be missed. I didn't know what it did, I didn't ask. It was so tempting to press, but just as I wrestled with the thought of marching over there and smacking it with the palm of my hand just to see what would happen, my ears were filled with sound. The music was back on.

There was only one rule left to follow: staying inside, away from the fog bank.

It was easy enough to do. In those few moments, all visibility from outside the window glass was gone. I got up out of my chair and slowly inched forward, my hand touching the cold surface. The world on the other side was simply a vortex of swirling gray clouds. And, if I looked hard enough, I could see shapes weaving and undulating deep inside the mist.

It groaned. I heard it with my own ears. Something in the fog was lamenting in pain like a wounded animal dragging itself to its den to die. The sound of a low voice was behind it, reminding me of a whale in deep water. I narrowed my eyes into the gloom, feeling that brief rush of adrenaline that urged me to step outside and see for myself. But then, I would catch sight of a large, dark shape moving through the mist, scraping claws and tentacles against the glass. It changed my mind pretty effectively.

For a long time, I stared at my own hand against the surface. It was so cold, and yet I felt a strange ... vibration. A dark shape, formless and impossible to make out, danced behind the layers of mist and began to follow the motions of my hand. When I slid my palm up, it followed. When I slid my palm down, it met my touch there too. It could have almost been a fun game if it wasn't the weirdest fucking thing I had ever seen in my life.

Moments passed, and nothing happened. But then, I noticed the shape of the trees coming into view once more. Slowly, gently, the fog was clearing. It was as if it were pushing back in the same direction from which it came, easing away inch by inch. I could see the tree line again. And as the fog rolled back up the mountainside, the pines shivered in its wake before falling still and silent in their places once more.

The fog was gone, and all it left behind was my racing heart-beat and a scattered collection of broken, snapped branches at the edge of the forest.

But as I looked closer, I could see something else: a cluster of dead, mangled blackbirds scattered across the fire escape. Their necks were broken. One of them had two beaks.

How did they get back into the clearing?

I poured myself another cup of coffee and sat in my seat, staring out the window while the music played on. A frown formed on my face as I looked into my cup, my appetite disappearing.

It tasted like gasoline. It probably *was* gasoline.

My ears caught a sharp tap at the glass. On the fire escape, I saw a small bird perched on the rusted metal, its beak pecking at the window. It went completely still, and that's when I noticed that it had a pair of distinctly human eyes.

CHAPTER TWO: PART-TIMER
Evelyn

It took a week, but finally, the network found me a co-host.

His name is Daniel Esperanza. He's about thirty years old, has a degree in performing arts, and within just a few hours of working at the radio station, he was already lying on the floor in a pool of his own blood.

But perhaps, we should go back to where it started: at the break of dawn on a Monday morning.

During my time alone at the station, things got progressively stranger every day. It started with the fog and a weird bird on the fire escape. By the second day, ghostly voices were coming out of the kitchen sink and a fox was standing by the tree line on its hind legs for almost an hour. By the end of the week, I awoke to find that everything on my desk had been turned around to face the opposite direction, a mysterious black residue left behind. It was hell to clean, but by then I had stopped questioning things. I was too tired.

So tired, in fact, that when a representative from the network arrived to introduce the new part-timer, she visibly grimaced at the first sight of me. I hadn't combed my hair in ages, I was wearing a hoodie with a giant hole in one elbow, and I had a bruise on my forehead from falling down the stairs the day before. My new co-host, however, pretended not to notice.

The first thing I learned about Daniel was that he had more energy than a puppy on his first trip to the park. He moved fast, he talked fast, and he was always waving his hands in dramatic gestures as he spoke. When we first met, I tried to go in for a quick fist bump, but instead, he shook my hand with enough force to make my knuckles crack. This fella was loud, chatty, and way too happy to be here.

But the worst thing about Daniel? The thing that really cracked my nuts? He was actually kind. You know, nothing ruins a good mood like trying to dislike someone who is a genuinely decent person. And he knew what he was doing. Like me, he had some experience with radio, but unlike me, he *loved* the sound of his own voice. I let him take over the morning news, and he did so with great pleasure.

"Goooood morning, *beautiful* people of Pinehaven," he said at the start of his broadcast. This guy had too much energy at the ass-crack of dawn. While I was still half-asleep and struggling to untangle the bird's nest growing out of my head, Daniel was busy trying to single-handedly charm all of Pinehaven with his dulcet tones. Shit, man, between the two of us, he just might succeed.

By noon, his constant sunshine still hadn't waned.

"You know this is a small village, right?" I giggled, stirring more sugar into my cup of caffeinated bog water. "I appreciate the energy, pal, but you don't need to broadcast like a city DJ. There's, like ... ten people listening *tops.*"

Daniel shrugged, leaning back in his seat casually with one Oxford shoe against the desk. "Maybe one of those ten people needs a good pick-me-up," he said, turning his shit-eating grin toward me. "Is it you? Are you the tenth person?"

"Oh, piss off," I snickered at him from behind my drink. The cup of the day was a yellow-tinted antique from some charity tractor pull in 1989. "I don't need a pick-me-up, I'm in perfectly good spirits."

"Yeah, like a haunted house."

Daniel didn't miss a beat. He *never* missed a beat, the rat bastard. All day long, no matter how vulgar I was, he just smiled and laughed while thriving off of this back-and-forth bullshit. I think it was starting to turn into some sort of game.

We made a strange pair. While he was wearing a pair of suspenders and a color-coordinated bowtie, I was wearing a moth-bitten camouflage t-shirt with two warm granola bars in my hoodie. I didn't even know how they got there. Daniel was mostly leg, wearing high-waisted trousers that made him look like someone's grandpa about to have a night on the town. He had a big smile with a prominent gap in his teeth, warm brown skin, and dark curls that somehow looked wild and purposeful at the same time. In a way, I felt bad for him – he was a good-natured, hard-working guy who didn't belong here. He could have been doing anything else.

And as far as first days go, Daniel had an extremely weird one.

Around noon, we took bets about what kind of poison had been slipped into our coffee and why it tasted like stale rat piss. At one o'clock, I let him do a live weather broadcast, but it rained for approximately three seconds just to keep him on his toes. Not long after, that bird with human eyes showed up again and sat on the fire escape, staring at him through the glass. I had to explain that it had been hanging around for a few days and probably wasn't up to anything. It was just ugly.

An hour later, Daniel came out of the bathroom with a distraught look on his face. He seemed shaken, some of the color drained from his cheeks.

"What's wrong with your sink?" he asked, pointing at the bathroom door.

I had been spinning in my chair, bored out of my mind as I watched the clock tick backwards. "Hm?"

"The sink," he repeated. "I heard something down there. Somebody crying."

I didn't know whether to be comforted or disappointed that he heard it too. It meant that it was real. I stopped spinning, tapping one foot against the floor and biting my bottom lip.

"It does that sometimes," I said with a dry, awkward chuckle. "This place is old; it makes all sorts of noises. I think we're on, like, a magnetic field or something. Or maybe it's haunted."

"It's *definitely* haunted," Daniel said with certainty as he sat back down at the desk. Then he leaned in, speaking quietly as if telling me a secret. "My great aunt saw a ghost once, you know. Maybe we should try sending a recorder down there to see if we catch anything. We could do a show about it, like ... like a ghost story hour. Yeah?"

I had to laugh. These last few days spent alone up here had

felt like a little house of horrors and Daniel was just soaking it up.

"Sure, you can talk about *whatever* you want if it gives me a break from gabbin' about the weather." I leaned back, stretching my arms. "Just keep in mind, ghostly crying from the sink does *not* excuse you from washing your hands."

Daniel didn't get a chance to tell his little ghost story on-air. At four o'clock, exactly on the hour, we got a caller. Days had gone by without a single ring from the phone; I almost started to forget people lived here. I stared at the screen for the longest time before hitting the record button and answering the incoming call.

"Hello, this is Evelyn from 104.6 FM, we've got you on the air."

The line was quiet for a moment, but then a voice came through. It was an older woman, and as far as I could tell, this one was real.

"Yes, Evelyn. Hello, dear," she said in a soft, quivering voice. I assumed the tremble in her throat was from nerves. "My name is Rose. I had something I'd like to tell you if you have the time."

"Of course, Rose. What's on your mind today?" I asked.

Daniel slipped his headphones on and I gave him a lazy thumbs-up, signifying that all was fine and normal.

"Well," Rose continued, "I've had a lot of strange dreams, dear, and I'm wondering if anyone else has had the same. You see, last night, I had a dream in which the forest split in two. It was like the parting of the Red Sea, my dear. I *do* hope you know the story of Moses. Don't you?"

I spared another glance at my co-host, who was wearing a restrained smile. Judging from the look on his face, he was just happy that I was the one who picked up the phone instead of him. I suppose it was only a matter of time before we had our first religious messenger.

"Um … sure I do, ma'am. What happened next?" I asked politely, swatting Daniel on the arm when he stifled an audible laugh at my expense.

"Well, the ground was open and something was rising out of it." As Rose continued, the tremble in her voice disappeared. She spoke with confidence and certainty. "It blocked out the whole sky, you see. I can't even truly describe it! A great fog, I suppose, but it was made of something new ... something that's never existed before. Soon it covered everything, all that my eyes could see. The town, the sun, the trees ... and, oh, the sound that it made. My dear. It was a fearsome bellow that shook the whole earth."

There was a long pause between the two of us. I didn't know what to say. Rose took a deep, shivering breath before she sighed and spoke again, her words coming out as a soft, slow whisper.

"Do you think that God lives in the forest?"

Her words sent a shiver up my spine that I couldn't quite understand. I went silent and looked over at Daniel, catching an uncomfortable glance. He seemed to understand the plea, and did the merciful thing—he turned on his mic and answered in my place.

"Good afternoon, Rose. Daniel here. That's an interesting dream! But I think that if God lived in the forest, he wouldn't be giving you nightmares like that." He laughed, but his jovial tone was cut off by a snap from the woman on the other end.

"We're *meant* to be afraid of God, my dear." She enunciated the last two words in such a sharp way that it took all the affection out of them. The sweet, calm voice from before turned into more of a slither, venomous and rotten. "Besides ... I wasn't talking to you."

Daniel and I shared a sideways glance, smiles gone and grimaces taking their place. There was an obvious discomfort in the air shared between the two of us and a furious wickedness from the other end of the phone. All I knew was that I didn't want this conversation to continue any longer. I was done with Rose and her dreams.

"Sorry, Rose, but it's time for the weather. We're going to have to let you go." I apologized as kindly as I could, my finger already itching to hang up the line. "Thank you for calling, ma'am, and have a wonderful afternoon."

I hung up the phone before she had a chance to respond with any more cryptic bullshit, mouthing the words 'block that number' to Daniel as I did.

But Rose wasn't the last.
Moments later, we had another call. Another dream.

A man from the village said that for the last week, he had been having vicious nightmares about being dragged into a mine shaft in the forest where he was surrounded by piles of bones. And every night, he would sense that there was something in the tunnels looking for him. Chasing him.

"At the end of the path, there's a purple glowing light," he said. "Somethin' about it don't sit right with me, but it's the only way to go."

A guy who works at the corner store deli called in shortly after. He's an avid hunter—likes to sell his own home-dried jerky, that kind of thing. He told us that he had a dream just last night about taking his rifle up the mountain and chasing after something big ... something he had never *seen* before. He said it had six eyes and the head of an elk but the claws of a wolf. He said it stood on two legs and became taller than the trees, and when it opened its mouth, he saw dead human faces peering out from inside its throat.

A mother of three called soon after and said that she dreams about a man wearing a mask made of tree bark. He walks up to her kitchen window and stares at her for hours, all while the fear of looking away keeps her frozen on the spot. As Daniel spoke to her, she started to cry, saying, "I can't look away. If I do, it will take my children. One by one, it will take them."

By the time the sun had started to go down, we had listened to dozens of stories and dozens of dreams. All of them could be written off as the nightmares of superstitious town folk who just wanted someone to talk to, but the last one we received sent an icy shiver through my entire body.

"Good evening, this is Evelyn at Pinehaven Radio. What's on your mind?"

There was silence on the other side of the phone at first, then a shaky breath. It was a young woman, no older than me. Something about her voice was familiar.

"I saw a bird with human eyes," she said flatly, a quiver in her throat.

My heart gave a small jump as I looked up at the fire escape, half-expecting to see our own visitor waiting for me to meet its gaze.

It wasn't there.

"In a dream?" I asked.

"No," she answered, then took a sharp intake of breath. "I don't dream. M-my doctors—they put me on sleeping pills, but they don't work. I don't sleep anymore since it started sitting outside my windows. All of them, even windows that weren't there before."

It sounded crazy, right? But the panic in her voice made my blood turn to ice. I looked over at Daniel, my hands growing cold and pale as I pulled the microphone a little closer to my lips.

"Listen, if you need help—"

"I'm sorry," she said frailly. "I ... I shouldn't have called. Goodbye, Lynny."

I opened my mouth to respond, but it was too late. She had already hung up. I felt a lot of difficult emotions all at once: regret, concern, fear. I wished I had gotten her name. I wished I could have helped somehow or given her a piece of advice that would have made it better. Mostly I just hoped she was doing alright out there, and that she figured out where all those extra windows came from.

But why did she call me *Lynny?*

"I think I need a break," I told Daniel, slipping off my headphones and taking a deep breath. My hands were shaking from a mixture of unease and low blood sugar. It took me the whole damn day to realize that I hadn't eaten. Sometimes I forget about the delicate nature of the human form.

"I'm going to make a sandwich. Need anything?" I asked.

"Yeah, get me some of whatever Rose was smoking," Daniel joked in response, breaking the tension. Then he went back to sipping his coffee, which he had drowned in sugar and cream just to make it palatable.

After I got out of my seat, Daniel had a call. I heard him answer it with his usual cheer and sweetness, then go oddly quiet. Moments ticked by. I finished slapping together my peanut butter sandwich and then peered around the counter, about to ask if everything was alright.

Then I felt a tremble below us. The dishes and cups in the kitchen rattled and the wooden beams beneath us creaked. An earthquake? No, this was something else. I immediately felt a chill go down my spine, that all-familiar sense of dread coming back in full force.

As soon as I took a step into the broadcast room, I witnessed my co-host ripping the headphones off his ears with a desperate shriek, tossing them to the ground, and staggering back with both hands against his head. His eyes were wide and impossibly bloodshot. Veins were popping in his forehead and neck. His hair was stuck to his skin amongst a glimmer of sweat and a dark drip of blood was falling from his nose and over his top lip. He fell to his knees, hands held over his ears as he clenched his jaw and hollered out in pain.

I dropped my sandwich and voiced a few choice cuss words on my way across the room, then fell to my knees next to him. My heart was pounding and I was in a panic, unsure of what to do.

"Holy shit, what *happened?*" I grabbed one of his wrists, trying to pull his hand away to see the damage. "Daniel? Let me see."

I noticed blood pooling beneath his palm and seeping out between his shivering fingers. It was streaming out of his *ears*. He smacked me away, looking down in horror at the crimson droplets now gathering on the floor, dripping down his arms, staining his clothes. As soon as he saw it, he began to hyperventilate, looking nauseous and light-headed.

"Hey, buddy, calm down, take a breath. Can you hear me? *Look at me,*" I frantically called out to him, but he didn't answer. His eyes scanned over my face, watching the movement of my mouth. A dark cloud of sadness fell over him. God ... he couldn't hear *anything*.

The call was still recording, broadcasting live over the air. I made the decision to keep the rest of this moment private and I marched across the room to turn our microphones off and let the music take over. I briefly glanced at the console. There was another call coming in from a hidden number.

I ignored it, leaving a stain of blood on the keyboard as I left.

Daniel had decided to lay down on the floor, plunked over onto his side with his hands still cupped over his ears. He was breathing heavily, his body shivering every once in a while with quiet sobs. I rushed over to the wall-mounted phone and called 9-1-1, already dreading what they would tell me. We were alone between these mountains, after all. No hospital, no help for miles and miles—just that sea of pines stretching over the rolling peaks and endless twisting roads.

"Yes, hello?" I spoke into the receiver and heard a far-away voice answer me, muffled by a crackling signal. I took in a deep breath, still shaking from head to toe. "This is Evelyn up at the 104.6 FM station. I-it's about a quarter-mile inside Pinehaven Forest, just a few minutes out of town. My coworker has a head injury, I think. H-he, um, he's bleeding and needs to go to a hospital."

After a short exchange, someone from the Pinehaven police department told me they were contacting the next town over; an ambulance would be circling the mountain before nightfall. It was the best they could do. In the meantime, it was up to me to keep Daniel comfortable.

I returned to his side and sat across from him, all the while trying to calm the shiver in my hands. The smell of blood was making my stomach turn and the sight of his wide, traumatized eyes was chilling, like looking into the face of a ghost.

"Someone's coming," I told him, mouthing my words slowly. "They'll be here in a little while. What do you need?"

He tried to mouth a few words at me, but I couldn't make out what he was saying.

"Can you repeat that, pal?"

Before he had a chance to respond, his eyes rolled back and he fell into a dead faint, his blood-stained hands dropping to the floor. With a sympathetic sigh, I put my fingers underneath his nose to make sure he was still breathing. He was. I watched him sleep and memorized the pattern of his breath, occasionally checking his pulse. It was slow, but not too slow. I just hoped he wasn't going into shock.

On the other side of the room, my abandoned peanut butter sandwich still sat on the floor. I watched as a group of very fortunate ants circled it, probably thinking that some merciful god had taken pity on their little souls. That's when I found the half-melted granola bar still crumpled up in my front pocket. Maybe I was my own merciful god. I looked down at it in disgust, however, tossing it in the trash and then wiping the sticky residue on my pants.

After a while, Daniel finally started to stir. He was alarmed, gasping for breath as if waking up from a terrible nightmare. His eyes darted around the dark room in fear and paranoia until he noticed me in the space across from him, getting on my hands and knees to be closer to his level.

I laid down on my stomach, face-to-face with him so he could read my lips. There we were, two losers at the shittiest slumber party ever without even one pillow to share.

"Your face is all bloody. Think you can get to the bathroom?" I asked, speaking slowly.

Daniel nodded in silence.

"Good. Do you wanna lay on an actual mattress?"

He hesitated a moment, then nodded again. I gave him a tiny, lopsided smile. Sleeping it off wasn't going to make it better, but at least he wouldn't be resting his head in a puddle of his own ear blood.

I stood up first and offered him a hand, supporting his weight gently as he struggled to get to his feet. I could only imagine that the whole world around him was tilting and turning with each step that he took, like being drunk on a boat. When we got to the tiny, cramped bathroom in the corner of the tower, I sat him down on the toilet seat while I gently dabbed warm water on his head and neck. I wanted to get rid of all the blood before he had a chance to see it for himself. The last thing I needed was for him to faint again.

"Can you hear me at all?" I asked, creating a pile of blood-stained cotton balls in the sink.

It took a moment before Daniel spoke, his voice a dry whisper that was so quiet he probably couldn't hear it himself.

"Barely," he said. "You're friendlier when I can't hear you well."

Had it been any other time, I probably would have slugged him one. But I felt bad for the guy. Between the two of us, his first day on the job was certainly worse than mine. Even if he was a little aggravating and a bit too extroverted for my tastes, he didn't deserve it. So, I just snickered and gave him a friendly pat on his arm.

"Alright, smartass," I said, tossing the last cotton ball in the sink. I'd clean it up later. "Let's get you to bed."

Cleaned up and exhausted, Daniel followed me to the 'employee apartment' that I called home. It wasn't much to offer. In the tiny, windowless room, there was a mattress big enough for one and some plastic shelves holding various janitorial supplies—a hint of what the space had been originally meant for.

"Go ahead, lay down," I told him, crouching next to the mattress while he settled in. "I'll let you get some rest, okay? Just knock on the wall if you need anything—I'll be right outside the door. Promise."

I was just about to stand up, but I felt a tug on the edge of my sweater. Daniel grabbed me before I could get too far. He was looking up at me, his dark eyes wide with anxiety and sweat collecting near his temples.

"I heard it," he mumbled, the volume of his voice fluctuating and trembling with a touch of fear. He looked clammy as if he had a fever. "God in the woods ... like Rose said."

I furrowed my brow and turned away, grabbing a thin blanket from a pile of clean linens and shaking it out before draping it over Daniel's body. I shook my head.

"That wasn't God, Daniel. It was just something really, *really* fucked up with your headset. You can tell me about it later. Ok, man? For now, just get some rest."

Daniel didn't say anything else. He just looked at me, forlorn and lost in a nightmare that I didn't understand. I waited to leave until he finally closed his eyes, drifting off to sleep. That mattress is where he stayed for the rest of the evening. I checked on him every once in a while, sometimes to try forcing water in his mouth and other times to put a fresh towel under his head to soak up a stray trickle of blood.

It was strange. I had never been a nurturing person, but watching over him felt somewhat cathartic. Memories came flooding back during those quiet moments. I recalled some of my darkest days, stuck in bed with a hangover that wouldn't end or sleeping off a cocktail of pills I couldn't even name. When I woke up, *she* was always there. Worried. Tired. Disappointed. I had never been on the other side until now: the side that watched the minutes tick by.

It took the ambulance hours to get there and only minutes to take Daniel away. The paramedics couldn't get a stretcher up the stairs, so they walked him down one careful step at a time. I watched from the top landing as they loaded him up in the back of the truck and disappeared down that curving path.

Amazing how I went from being annoyed by Daniel's voice to missing it in a matter of hours. He was gone, the only evidence of his presence taking the form of a bloodstain on the floor and an abandoned pair of headphones. I thought for sure I'd never meet him again. We were just two transient souls passing by like ships in the night, only we were both off-course and about to crash.

I sat at my desk for the longest time, even though I didn't need to. The broadcast was continuing on its own—this trustworthy machine that could survive without me for the night. I left my headset off, choosing instead to listen to the sound of the wind and the pitiful cries of distant animals that lurked in the darkest parts of the forest.

Sure, I lied to Daniel. We both knew this. It wasn't something malfunctioning with his headset and it wasn't just an accident. There was something deeply, impossibly wrong; I felt it in the wind's chill, the rumbling of the soil, the eerie creak of the wood. I heard it in those pained cries from the forest, coming from the mouths of animals I couldn't even name.

The clock struck midnight, and I noticed the console light up. A call was coming in. I stared at it for a long moment, then moved my finger over the button, and blocked the number.

As the night grew late, it was just me, the wind, and the glimmering human eyes of that strange bird still sitting at the edge of the window. I noticed that it didn't blink.

CHAPTER THREE: STONE
Evelyn

O n Tuesday morning, I got a call from Daniel's mother. Lovely woman, by the way. She was more than happy to inform me that while her son's hearing couldn't be restored in one of his ears, a hearing aid for the second ear could give him a better semblance of the life he knew before. It was terrifying to imagine how such tiny, cramped caverns of bone and tissue could be so easily ruined. The part that surprised me, though? He didn't quit his job.

Despite everything, Daniel was coming back in a few days.

"That's great," I sighed. "Do they, um ... do they know what happened?"

She was quiet for a moment. I could almost hear the gears in her head turning as she searched her mind for an answer that might satisfy the question we both had.

"No, not really," she answered. I could tell she was disappointed. "Daniel said he heard something over the phone before it happened. Doctor said it was probably a harmful frequency ... but we don't know. Danny wouldn't describe it to me. He said he didn't want to think about it."

We don't know. That was the theme, wasn't it? Things just happened and each passing day brought us no closer to understanding it. It was amazing in a terrible way how something as mysterious and inconsequential as a phone call was able to decimate this man's hearing for life.

Speaking of, Mrs. Esperanza talked my ear off for a good half-hour after that. She gossiped about Daniel's youngest sister getting into her dream college, told me all about the deer she saw crossing the road on her way to the hospital, and even invited me to her niece's wedding later that year.

"*You seem like a sweetheart,*" she said. "*My Danny has only said nice things about you.*"

I tried to hold back a snort, very tempted to tell her that Daniel must have been talking about someone else. Instead, I thanked her for the invitation and told her that I would check my schedule.

Finally, she said her goodbyes, but not before I heard Daniel shouting in the background, "*Mamá, tell Evelyn I'm not done being a nuisance yet!*"

It was good to hear that some of that spirit still remained somewhere behind the bandages and the painkillers.

So, I still had my obnoxious part-timer—a part-timer who was taking a very early, very medicated vacation.

While Daniel was gone, I was stuck spending my time at the radio tower alone once more, just as it all started. But goddammit, that fucking bird would not *leave!*

I noticed something while looking out the window after giving the first forecast of the day. It was building a nest. That little shit-piece, with its creepy-ass eyes and its incessant tapping, was building a nest in the tree right in front of where I sat all day long. I used to like birds, you know. I like all wildlife, so long as it's not trying to run away with a body part of mine. But the last thing that I wanted to see was this little prick laying eggs and making multiple versions of itself, following me from room to room for the rest of my days.

I decided that when Daniel got back, I would leave the station long enough to move the nest into the woods where that thing would follow. Maybe if I took it far enough, that stupid bird would never come back and I'd finally get a little peace. It could stick to its side of the forest and I could stick to mine, alone. There simply wasn't enough room in this clearing for the two of us.

God. I fucking hate that bird.

When I cleaned myself up in the bathroom, the sink was quiet for a change. The voice of a woman crying from down in the pipes was the first strange thing that both Daniel and I experienced together. At first, it was easy to say that it was simply the isolation of being up here by myself, making me hear things that weren't really there. But he heard it too.

That day, I didn't hear anything. It was just me and that stupid, ugly bird, left alone in an endless staring contest while the rest of the radio station was as quiet and as still as the grave. At this point, I would almost prefer the sobbing in the pipes.

I had a brief idea that when Daniel got back, maybe I'd try to convince him that it was actually a colony of mole people living down in the plumbing system. If shit was going to keep being weird, the very least we could do was find a way to laugh about it. Did I think it was a ghost? A real person? I didn't know, nor did I care. So long as it remained only a sound and nothing else, it didn't matter to me where it came from.

As the morning went on, I forgot about it. I didn't think about the strange noises, I didn't think about the fog, I even tried to not think about that *got-damn* bird. The skies were blue and clear that day. The air was chilly but the breeze was light, dancing between the blue asters and the phlox. All in all, things were peaceful and boring. I suppose I could use a boring day after watching my co-worker's eardrums simultaneously rupture without warning.

I sat down, putting my headphones back on and waiting for the track to end so that I could catch folks up on the news of the day. There was a line of 'get well soon' cards lined up across the consoles from friends and strangers alike.

Word got out quickly about Daniel's 'accident', and I imagined that the gossip had a lot to do with the fact that most of it had happened live on the air. His agonized screams and my panicked yelling probably made for the most interesting night in radio that this town had heard in quite a while. At least ten different people sent cards straight to the station with the early morning mail, wishing Daniel a speedy recovery.

I guess I was right about him. He charmed the whole town real quick.

Markus—this gangly guy about nineteen years old—usually just honked his horn when he arrived with the groceries. This time, though, he brought the box all the way up the stairs and knocked on the door instead.

"Hey, thanks," I said with a polite smile as I took the box from him. "Let me grab you a few bucks for that 'get well' card. Did you find it?"

"Yeah, I've got it right here," he said, reaching into his jacket. It was in a pink envelope. "So, uh ... really crazy what happened, right? I heard it on the radio. I was doin' a delivery for Salvador's Diner at the time. You know the place?"

I snickered, sifting through my wallet. "Yeah, I know it. Still the only one in town?"

"Yeah, it is." Markus grinned with crooked teeth and stuck his hands in his pockets, rocking back and forth. "We should, uh ... we should go sometime if you want to. You can tell me about how creepy this place is."

I wore an awkward smile that was more like a grimace, adding a couple extra dollars to the stack in my hand. "Thanks, I'll, um ... I'll check my schedule. I'm pretty busy right now, actually."

"Cool, cool." He nodded and glanced around the room as if looking for a new conversation starter. "*Sooo*, is it haunted or somethin'? I used to try breaking in here all the time back in high school, but police were always hangin' around. I know someone got decapitated here about two months ago, though."

Well, *that* was tonal whiplash. The impact of that news hit me so quickly that my brain rattled in my skull like a maraca.

"No one told *me* about that," I said, feeling my face flush. "Christ on a bike ..."

"It was big news," Markus chuckled. "Anyway, my number's on the receipt in case you change your mind about the diner. See you next Friday, okay?"

I gave a slow nod, silently handing over his tip and taking the card in exchange. It wasn't until after he left that I realized he had accidentally grabbed a 'Happy Birthday, Grandma' card instead of 'Get Well Soon', but after that lovely conversation, I wasn't too eager to call him and ask for a replacement.

So, I signed it and put it up with the rest.

"Good morning, this is Evelyn McKinnon with 104.6 FM," I spoke into the microphone, trying to hold back a sleepy yawn. "I hope everyone is enjoying the sunny skies today. My co-host, Daniel Esperanza, will not be joining me this morning, but we would like to thank everyone for their kind well-wishes while he recovers from his injury. Stay tuned for the morning news and the five-day forecast at nine-thirty, but until then, here's 'Sweet Caroline' to start your day."

As the music began, I leaned back in my seat and wasted most of the morning away in a lazy, bored haze. The problem with small towns like these was that there wasn't usually much to talk about, so the news I caught up on mostly included sales going on at the local meat market or someone's prize-winning pumpkin patch.

Halloween was coming up, I realized. I should have remembered when I saw the falling leaves and felt the chill in the wind. Once upon a time, I used to enjoy the holidays. I used to enjoy a lot of things.

I was back in college again. I remembered how cold I was, wearing my Halloween costume with no coat overtop. I was dressed as a pirate. Jennifer was dressed as a fairy. She had glitter on her eyelids and her cheeks, little butterfly clips in her hair. She spent all night bopping me on the head with a magic wand, the kind that had a star on the end and streamers hanging off of it. She danced with a lot of different people, but she always came back to me when they played one of her favorite songs.

I remembered watching her dance in the strobe lights. She would raise her hands above her head, waving them back and forth with no particular rhythm. She didn't need rhythm. She was just dancing to her own beat, singing along to a song that no one else could hear. The body glitter on her shoulders and her face always caught the light in just the right way.

I got so drunk at the party that she had to help carry me home. I remembered her grabbing my arms and putting me piggyback on her shoulders, reminding me time and time again not to let go or else she'd drop me on the pavement and I'd bust my head open.

Her pink tutu was rough against my knees, but she was warm. Her hair was freshly washed—smooth and blonde—and soft against my cheek. She smelled like vanilla and cinnamon.

"Don't let go, I'll drop you," she scolded me again.
The sound of her laugh warmed me like a favorite song.
I would never let go.

At some point, I must have gotten lazy and put my head down on the desk, because I was looking at my screen one moment and then being jarred awake the next. In a panic, I looked at the time. It was noon. The music line-up was still going. What had woken me up, however, was the sound of the phone. We had a caller.

I took a moment to sip some water and get the dry scratch out of my throat before I answered, recording the call but leaving it off air. Probably a song request, I thought.

"This is Evelyn at 104.6 FM, what can I do for y—?"

There was a loud gasp on the other end of the phone, then a shaking, shivering sob. A woman was struggling to breathe through a stuffy nose. I recognized this sound. I knew this pattern of whimpers and sniffles ... It was the same voice I heard from inside the sink every day on a loop.

I felt a chill run up my body, like the sudden gust of wind you feel after walking out into a blustery winter's night. Every pore and freckle on my body was like a stinging pin-prick, each nerve on edge.

And then, I heard words begin to come through.

"You have to stop." She was still sobbing as she tried to get the words out.

"Ma'am, are you al—?"

"Listen to me!" she shouted back. "God damn you, you never *listen!* I'm so tired. So, so tired ... This is my h-home. I wanted to help you, b-but you just won't let me! *It's like you won't even try!*"

I was confused. Speechless. Was she talking to me? It was as if I were listening to only one half of a conversation, like a recording that only caught one side. Something about the voice sounded familiar to me—enough to make my stomach flip and my heart flutter with dread. I knew this conversation, and it wasn't just the sink ...

"Please," she said after a long sob. "Please, just let me help. You h-haven't been sober a *single day* since gradua—"

All at once, I ripped the headphones off of my ears, pushing my chair back and leaving the device dangling on its cord like a pendulum off the side of the desk. It wasn't for any lack of reason. I felt the most intense nausea suddenly erupt in my stomach, guts churning and mouth watering. There was no time to calm the sickness before I rushed myself to the bathroom with the call still recording. I could hear the voice wailing into the open air even as I left the room and slammed the bathroom door behind me.

A wave of vertigo struck as soon as I entered, making those two measly steps to the toilet feel as if I were walking in a bright, spinning carnival tunnel. I thought for sure I would fall on my face, but my knees buckled and I went crashing down right in front of the toilet, white knuckles gripping the edge of the seat. I dragged myself toward it, just in time for that nausea to turn into something else. I wasn't sick anymore, I was *choking*. Something large and solid was stuck at the base of my throat, making my lungs burn. I couldn't breathe. If ever there was a time to have a co-host, this was it.

Vibrant colors took over my vision. Sparkling lights crept into the edges of my eyes, dancing around like the kind of fireworks that fall in a shower of gold. I suspected it would be the last thing I saw before I lost consciousness.

But then, with a single desperate cough, I felt a sharp pain in the back of my throat. Something dislodged itself and was coming up. It hit the back of my teeth on the way out and clattered to the floor, heavy and solid.

My dizzy head hit the tile with a loud thud and I found myself staring directly at the thing that had somehow gotten inside of my body. It was a stone. Just a stone. It was a brown, speckled one like the kind you'd find out in the woods, maybe on a hike, maybe from a river bed. It certainly wasn't the kind of thing you expected to be your lunch, though.

I pushed myself up, arms trembling as the blood rushed back into my head. I grabbed the stone in my pale fist and tossed it into the toilet, flushing it down immediately. It was then that I heard a sound—a small sniffle coming from the pipes under the bathroom sink. It was her again.

"You can have it back," I sneered and wiped my face with my

sleeve.

Once I finally got to my feet, I washed my hands thoroughly, scrubbing the grime from under my short, chewed fingernails. I only spared the tiniest glimpse in the mirror, hardly recognizing the ghostly, hollow eyes that looked back. I returned to my desk, woozy and sore with a pounding headache that wouldn't go away.

The headphones were still dangling off the edge of the table, swinging back and forth slowly, just waiting for me. I shoved them back on my head as if nothing ever happened. I was greeted with a dial tone on the other end. The crying woman had hung up the phone.

I tried to play back the recording. I wanted to hear it again, to see if I could put the pieces of this puzzle together in my mind. She wasn't there. All the recording managed to pick up was my own voice and a constant stream of white noise that drowned out the rest. It was as if she was never there at all.

The discomfort hadn't left. That *bird* hadn't left. The worst part is, I saw it clicking its beak against the window again, looking straight at me the entire time. It wanted to come in. I know how crazy that sounds, acting as if I know what a bird wants and thinks, but the expression on its face was so ... obvious. Pleading, yearning, demanding eyes were constantly pointed my way, only leaving occasionally to fill its nest with more leaves.

I was never going to let it in.

I knew there was a fog advisory for Thursday. All week, I found myself staring across the forest, expecting to see the mountains begin to move. I expected to see them burst open, tendrils of fog reaching up to the sky above.

I imagined it, drifting up from beneath the ground, rising into the air and covering the town and the forest and the sun. It would cover all that my eyes could see.

And the sound it might make: a fearsome bellow that shakes the whole earth.

Maybe I shouldn't have blocked Rose's phone number after all.

I stared out the window for so long that I hardly noticed

36

something sitting at the edge of the fire escape, just outside the window. It was a brown, speckled stone with white paint on one side, spelling the words, "Class of 2019". I don't know how it got there. More importantly, I don't know who on earth fished that thing out of the goddamn toilet.

CHAPTER FOUR: THE SLEEPWALKER
Evelyn

I can honestly say I've never dreaded a Thursday the way I did that week. I mean, it's a perfectly fine day of the week, right? Rarely do you ever hear people complaining about Thursdays. There are no *"Is Thursday Over Yet?"* mugs out there next to the Monday ones at gift shops and gas stations.

However, as my week slowly drifted by, all I could think about was the constant warning of another foggy day on the horizon. It crept into my mind every time I looked up from my desk and out into the endless trees that encircled me. At any moment, the fog could skulk over the horizon again like a great white beast stomping over the mountainside.

On top of it all, my morning started with a bit of bad news. The paper read, *"Jennifer Cook, 26, Still Missing After Three Days"*. She was a known sleepwalker who would leave her house in the middle of the night. This time, her boyfriend didn't catch her. A search party was already out looking for her in the woods, but they had found nothing.

When I read the article and saw her face looking up at me in blurry black and white, all the breath was stolen from my lungs. I knew her. We used to be friends. We used to be roommates. It all seemed like a lifetime ago, but now, it was all flooding back.

I summarized the article on the air during my morning news segment, but even countless rehearsals couldn't stop me from choking through it. When it was done, I tossed the paper in the trash so that I didn't have to look at it again. You know, I thought I would cry. I was tempted to. But no matter how long I sat there in misery or how many guilty thoughts came to mind, I couldn't make the tears happen even if I wanted to.

Somewhere deep in my heart, I hoped she wasn't out there between those trees. Instead, I imagined that she had left town in the night to escape this small-town life and find something new. Something *exciting*.

One good thing happened that day. Daniel decided that resting at home was boring as hell and he made the decision to return one day earlier than expected, still recovering but plenty well enough to pester the everloving shit out of me. I almost hated to admit it, but I think I missed the guy a little. I suppose it's true that you don't always realize what you've got until it's gone. Bickering with *him* was much better than arguing with a bird, and far less embarrassing for everyone involved.

"*Happy Birthday, Grandma?*" Daniel laughed as he picked up the card I had put out for him, opening it to find no kind words, just my signature and a doodle of him with two Beethoven-inspired ear trumpets duct taped to his head. What can I say? I was really bored. "Thanks, Evelyn. You were always my favorite grandchild."

After the morning weather forecast, at which time Daniel joined to announce his return to the radio station, we turned off our microphones during an ad-free music hour to simply catch up for a while. It hardly needs saying that 'catching up' for us didn't only involve the mundane.

Daniel told me all about his procedures in vivid, disgusting detail, almost excitedly so. And to be honest, I was completely enthralled the whole time. Delicately, he tilted his head from one side to the other to show off the scars behind his ears and the surgical dressing that was still stuffed inside. It was no wonder he kept reading my lips more often than not—even without the damage to his eardrums, he couldn't hear shit with all that cotton stuffed in there. I started getting in the habit of speaking a little louder, a little clearer, and being patient when he asked me to repeat myself. We had a little notepad sitting between us just in case.

He showed me a few words in American Sign Language, which he had been picking up since his time in the hospital. I asked him how to say *fuck you, ugly stupid bird* but he calmly told me that he hadn't gotten to that lesson yet.

Eventually, we grew tired of talking about scalpels and stitches. Daniel asked me what he had missed during his break, and I didn't even know where to start.

"Well, the sinks are still acting up."

"Sinks? Plural?" he asked.

"Oh, yeah," I laughed. "Toilet too. The pipes were a little bit rusty the other day, though, so I think that was making it a bit *weepier* than usual. Water tasted *extra* bad if you can believe it, like raw sewage with a touch of graveyard dirt."

"Mm, delicious," Daniel snickered. "Did you get any calls?"

I hesitated for a moment, trying not to look too unwilling to answer the questions. Rather, I pretended that I was deep in thought, scrunching my lips to the side and humming softly under my breath.

"Um, not really," I lied. "Just a couple of music requests. Heh, some guy in town has the biggest crush on Nina Simone."

Daniel's eyes were stuck on my face. He knew that I was hiding something. The fact that I kept looking away from him didn't help. I don't know why I wanted so badly to keep secrets from him: the call, the stone, the voices. All I knew was that the bottom of that rabbit hole was a dark, unpleasant place and I didn't want to go there yet.

"Why do you think the network wants us to keep all these recordings?" Daniel asked.

I was relieved that he changed the subject.

"Maybe they're studying us," I said. "Oh! Maybe the government is doing experiments up here. You know how there are some areas where folks see tons of UFO's? Mothman? That kind of stuff? Maybe it's like that."

Daniel chuckled. "You say that as a joke, but folks around here seem a little ... you know."

"No, I don't know." I smirked and crossed my arms over my chest, giving Daniel an accusatory squint. "Please, do elaborate. Folks around here are a little what?"

Daniel held up his hands in defense, grimacing as he considered his words very carefully. "Ehh, I'm just saying, you're a bit superstitious. Eccentric. That's all."

"Oh, so we're eccentric," I put a hand to my chest in a dramatic display of mock offense. "Okay, big city boy, I see how it is. You're not without your quirks either, you know. By the way, you never did tell me where you came from."

"Couple hours from here," Daniel answered.

He was heading to the kitchenette, empty cup in hand, giving it a rinse and filling it with water. When he noticed the ruddy color in the mug, he poured it down the drain and went digging around for bottled water instead. "I lived in Beckley. A place called Thurston Heights—it was an apartment building. We were right across from this kickass pizzeria called Antonio's. They had breadsticks big as your arms."

"Wait, no shit!" I stood up, giving one quick glance to the computer monitors before I abandoned the desk to help Daniel in his search for clean water. "I know that place. My mom and I lived in Beckley for a while. I went to college there. Class of 2019."

I found the bottled water in a cupboard underneath the sink and I tossed one to him, which he fumbled with. He wore a huge grin as he straightened up, taking a sip while leaning against the wall as if it never happened.

"2017 right here, baby!" He pointed to his chest with pride.

It was a small world, I realized. Daniel and I could have passed one another in the halls a hundred times, we may have even had classes together. I wouldn't know, honestly. I always slept through lectures.

It got me thinking about the way things tend to come full circle, and about life's little surprises, twists, and turns. Sometimes, those long, winding roads lead you back to where it all began.

We stood there and talked for a while. I'll admit, it wasn't too bad. Now that we found a little common ground, Daniel and I actually had something to discuss rather than just bouncing jokes back and forth like two improv actors who didn't know when to quit. We learned a few things about each other—stupid, inconsequential things, like the fact that he wore reading glasses and I had a birthmark on my hip that looks a bit like Michigan. We both liked extra mushrooms on our pizza, campy horror movies from the 70's, and big, fluffy dogs. All of that stopped me from thinking about

41

Jennifer, the forest, and those search parties, if only for a little while.

But by the time we got back to the desk, things started happening again. A phone call came in from an unknown number; it was a man speaking backwards, but in a different language. I recorded the call and sent it to the network.

Things only got sillier from there. Daniel stepped out to grab lunch and came back in a panic.

"There was something ... in ... my car," he gasped for breath, scratches on his hands and a takeout bag clenched in one fist. "Big. Hairy. It kicked my ass."

"A 'squatch?" I asked, wincing at the scrapes. There was a bit of blood trickling over his knuckles. I was already heading toward the closet to grab a first aid kit. "What did you see?"

"I don't know. It happened so fast." He sat down and put a hand over his heart. "I-it was like ... a giant rat. Brown and with creepy little hands and a long tail and these giant teeth—"

"Sounds like you've been bedeviled by a muskrat, my guy," I chuckled and sat on the edge of the desk, smoothing some ointment over Daniel's hands. "It was probably just scared and stuck."

"No, I think it was trying to steal my car," he said, wincing in pain as I began to wrap a bandage around his wrist. "I gave it a french fry and it ran away. D-do you think I'm gonna get rabies now?"

"Mmhmm, yeah, for sure."

"Oh man, I don't wanna die ..."

"I'm joking, dingus, you're not going to die," I laughed and closed up the first aid kit. "That's not how it works. If you get bitten by a muskrat, you turn *into* one—I thought everyone knew that."

Daniel gave me a toothy grin and flicked me painfully on the elbow, calling me a 'dumbass' under his breath as he did.

"I think you'll be fine," I continued. "Just don't itch it, okay?"

"But can I *scratch* it?" he teased. I didn't answer him. Instead, I shoved the box back into the closet, wiping my hands on my jeans. All the while, I kept my eyes on the mountaintop, waiting for that fog advisory that I knew was coming. This time around, I'd be prepared.

We got quite a startle when the signal started to falter right in the middle of a live ad-read. We pulled the plug on the advertisement, both of us scrambling to find the source of the lost connection. It didn't take long. That stupid, ugly bird was outside the window, pecking at one of the cables that connected us to the mast.

"Oh shit, he's gonna get electrocuted," Daniel said, horrified. He got up and rushed over to pound his fist against the window. The little bastard didn't budge.

"I'll shoo him away," I groaned, kicking off the edge of the desk and rolling across the floor. "He's probably trying to take the cord back to his nest. *Speaking of,* I gotta move that fuckin' thing."

When I jumped out of my chair and stomped across the room, Daniel gave me a quizzical look.

"What, you don't like the nest?" he asked. "I think it's kinda sweet."

"It's gonna have all its creepy-looking babies right in front of our broadcast room, *Daniel.*"

I put my hands up to the glass with a groan of frustration. But even when I knocked my fist roughly against the cold surface, that shitty little bird did not leave. It just stared straight up at me, its face turned so that one human eye followed my every move. I think that if its beak had the ability to move in a grin, it almost surely would have been smiling at me. Jerk.

"... I'm getting rid of that little shit."

"Wait, wait," Daniel put out a hand to keep me in place. "I know it's weird-looking, but you're not going to kill a bird—"

"No, I'm not killing it," I corrected, turning toward him and enunciating my words very clearly. "I'm going out on the fire escape, grabbing the nest, and then I'm taking that shit out into the woods. I won't hurt your bird. I'm just putting its nest in a different spot so that Bitchass McGee out there finds a new place to have its weird alien babies."

Daniel looked at me with a tired stare and I could just see the thought passing through his mind: *"This is my life, this is my job."* Finally, he gave a great, big sigh and nodded his head, as if he knew that there was nothing he could do to dissuade me from making this

43

ridiculous little journey.

All he needed to do was get the music back up and running. The plan was simple, effective, and would end in the celebration of us finally having our radio tower back from the clutches of this Area 51 escapee. I still couldn't wrap my head around that feeling of urgency, I just knew that I needed to get rid of that damn nest and it needed to happen *immediately.*

I turned off the emergency exit alarm and crept out onto the fire escape, the rusted metal beneath my feet creaking and scraping as I did. It felt unsteady out there, like one wrong step would send it all falling down like a house of cards. Daniel was watching me through the window and I just knew he was keeping his fingers crossed under the desk, hoping I didn't fall and break my neck. Then he'd have to run this place on his own, I guess.

When I stood out there, I felt a sense of ... immense insignificance. The world around me felt so big and I felt small, suffocating somewhere in the middle of all that vast and limitless space. It all just went on forever: the mountains, the trees, the clouds. It was the first time in a week that I had felt the wind on my face, but it didn't feel like freedom to me. It felt like a violation. I felt seen, like a newborn exposed to the world, caught in the eyes of something much bigger than me. This air tasted hopeless.

I tried to make this job as quick as possible. I took off my flannel and tied it around my waist, holding onto the edge of the building as I climbed up onto the metal bars that surrounded the top of the fire escape. As my feet wobbled, I looked down. That distance to the ground formed a gnarled ball in my stomach, sitting there like a stone. I didn't need one of those in my guts again.

"Okay, you feathered *fuck.*"

I leaned far over the edge, waving my hand to shoo the bird away. It took a few tries, but finally, the damn thing left. A moment later, I came to the uncomfortable and disappointing realization that it hadn't gone far. It just hopped to another branch to perch and watch me struggle as if saying, *"I'm only moving because I want to."*

I reached a little further, my fingers grabbing the edge of the nest and plucking it off the branch. I had it in my grasp at long last. As much as I hated this bird, I couldn't bring it upon myself to be rough with its nest, so I brought it toward my chest with the utmost care. I looked down into the circular web of twigs, leaves, and animal fur, expecting to see a little group of eggs.

There were no eggs, but the nest wasn't empty.

I let out a sudden shriek, a chill rushing through my body as I shuddered and dropped the nest at my feet. All my limbs wiggled and shivered in disgust. I wiped my hands frantically on my shirt and kicked that thing away from me, watching it fly off somewhere into the woods. My stomach was sick again.

Inside that nest, tucked into the center like beloved, delicate little eggs, were four human fingers chewed off at the knuckle. They were young and slim, the nails sporting partially-chipped red polish.

I was catching my breath, a hand to my chest when I heard something behind me. It slid against the metal stairs, heavy, wet, and sickening. I turned, ready to lock eyes with whatever creature had crawled its way out of the woods and up the stairs, only to see thick, thorn-covered vines gripping the railing of the fire escape.

I had seen a bird with human eyes and a sink with a human voice, but god forbid would this plant start gaining sentience too. Eager to get off that fire escape and back inside the building, I rushed toward the door with hands outreached, only to feel a sharp pressure around my right ankle. One of the vines had taken a tight grip around my leg and was pulling me, one tug at a time, toward the stairs.

I was dreaming. This wasn't *real*. At any moment, I expected that the impact of my head and elbows against the fire escape would wake me up, but instead it just left bruises.

Through the window, I saw Daniel's eyes peer up and widen with fear before I was dragged away, my back hitting the rusted metal with a sharp 'twang'. I was pulled, one step at a time, down the zig-zagging stairs, the back of my head making a hard impact with the metal each time until I started to feel dizzy. These vines had incomprehensible strength. Even as I reached for the railing, my hands weren't strong enough to hold on. The whole time, I was screaming, but above me, I could hear the sounds of the door shaking and rattling—Daniel was trying to get out, but had locked himself in. *Something* had locked him in.

I felt like a ragdoll, being tossed one way and then another. Finally, the vines let go of my ankle, but only so that they could throw me over the edge. You know that feeling you get when you dream of falling? All the blood rushes to your head and your heart jumps in your chest right before you hit the ground. I started to feel that way until I flailed enough to turn myself over and fall chest-first onto the railing below.

The air was knocked out of me, arms gripping the metal bar as pain erupted in my shoulders and elbows. I was crumpled over the railing, all four limbs wrapped around it to keep from being pulled away again. It was then that I lifted my head, looking up to see that I was at the bottom of the stairs with a sea of green ahead of me. The vines were coming from the woods, covering the forest floor beneath us like a pit of vipers.

Everything changed when I saw a new movement on the horizon. It was that undulating, swirling, thick cloud of fog slowly creeping toward the radio tower. And this time, I heard a groan in the wind louder than before. It wasn't quite a rumble, like one would expect from thunder, but the low moan one might hear echoing from the ocean floor. The fog was making that sound, like a living thing with a voice of its own.

I used all my strength to pull myself up onto the landing, dragging my aching body across the rusted metal until I could half-run, half-crawl up the stairs. I felt the platform tremble underneath me as vines gripped the bars and aggressively shook them side to side. One of them tried to grab me again, snagging my flannel shirt on its thorns. I let it slide off my waist and left it behind, not bothering to go back for it.

I stumbled up the remaining steps until I got to the top, avoiding the slithering masses under my feet all the way. More and more plants were bursting out of the ground, surrounding the radio tower and making the old metal creak and groan, as if trying to push it over.

The door was still locked shut, roots and miniature trees growing over its surface and keeping it stuck in place. I was face-to-face with Daniel's terrified expression as the crawling bark and twigs obscured him more and more from the other side of the glass like a wall forming between us. He couldn't hear me. Soon, he wouldn't be able to see me either.

My hands ripped at the saplings, but thorns bit into my skin until the leaves were red with blood. Every bit of greenery that I tore away just grew back in an instant, stronger and tougher than before.

"GET! IN! THERE!" I screamed at Daniel through the glass, pointing at the desk behind him. "TURN THE RADIO BACK ON!"

The lights began to flicker inside the station as those slithering vines wrapped around the wires and cables that led to the mast.

The distant groan of the forest was closer now as wisps of fog surrounded my ankles. In moments, the mist had rolled out from the mountains and over the trees, covering everything. It was here. I pounded on the glass until the fog was so thick I couldn't see anything at all except for the brief flicker of lights from inside the building. Eventually, even those were gone.

There was an eerie, terrible silence as I stood there in the gray void. The air was freezing cold against my skin, forming goosebumps up my arms below the sleeves of my t-shirt. I turned around, the metal beneath my feet whining in protest. I couldn't tell which way was forward, which way was back. Everything disappeared except for the pale, swirling clouds that had now engulfed the radio station entirely. I was cradled in it, caught like a blind fly in a spider's web.

I don't think I had ever experienced that kind of silence. That kind of pure isolation. I reached my hands out in front of me and I didn't feel the door. I didn't feel anything. I could only taste cold, wet soil in the air. My fingers were just reaching out, floating in some endless waste. It was a void of cold, heavy air that tickled every single hair on my body and left me feeling like a ghost.

Then I heard it again. That deep, whale-like groan came out of the fog, but this time it moved around me. It was circling. The sound was followed by a strange series of clicks, like a tongue against teeth rapidly popping with no real pattern. The voice was alien and strange. Unnatural. I heard a low grunt and a cold puff of foul-smelling breath hit the back of my neck.

I wasn't prepared when it *touched* me.

I closed my lips so tightly, trying desperately to keep from making a sound while something sharp and thin grazed the flesh on the back of my arm. I stood completely still as another joined the first, like impossibly long fingers or the legs of a giant spider. It toyed with my hair, plucking strands out of my braid as if it were ... playing with me. Inspecting me. This thing was like a warden patrolling the fog, trying to figure out what I was and what it would *do* with me. I held my breath and pretended like it wasn't real. Maybe if I didn't move, it would lose interest. Maybe it would just walk away.

I was waiting for fangs and claws to rip into my flesh, but it didn't happen. The creature just touched the back of my head, the sides of my face, my chin. At this point, I was trembling in absolute terror while still holding my breath, just trying not to scream or cry or run ... I was going to die, I thought. I was about to be eaten alive, bones and all, by something I would never get the chance to see and my last act on this earth would have been *harassing a goddamn bird.*

My teeth chattered as I waited for a fate that was certainly grim. And so, I was surprised when I felt the presence around me suddenly back away. The ground beneath me shook once, twice, and then the world went still again. There was a terrible ringing in my ears, but the groaning was getting quieter and quieter ...

I could see green grass, brown and yellow leaves. I could see the swirling gray clouds in front of me slowly begin to clear away and crawl back into the forest. And beneath my feet, I could see vines start to sink back into the earth, their thorns scraping through the soil as they went.

My feet were on the ground now, standing right at the edge of the tree line. How the hell did I *get* there?

With aching lungs, I finally let out a long and painful breath. Against all odds, I was alive.

Up until this day, I don't think I had ever rushed up a set of stairs so quickly in my life. Pure adrenaline got me to the top of the building in what seemed like an instant, where I found Daniel sitting at the console with a microphone situated in front of him and the radio back on track. It was better late than never, I suppose. I slammed the door behind me and slumped against the wall, holding my aching ribs and coughing out the cold, wet air.

Through the window, I could still see my flannel shirt. It was waving in the wind like a flag of surrender, ripped by the thorns that caught it. If I had moved any slower, that probably would have been my flesh.

At that moment, I made a solemn oath that should I ever see a bird's nest near the fire escape again, it can stay. Hell, I'd throw it a damn welcome party if that would keep this from ever happening again. My war with birds? Over.

I sat on the floor for a long time, inspecting the bruises under my t-shirt. The fall down the fire escape had left me with a nasty pattern of purple and green marks that spread from my shoulder all the way down to the bottom of my ribs. I must say, it hurt like a bitch.

"Evelyn? You okay?" Daniel asked, getting out of his seat to come check on me. "Jesus Christ, you look like a mess. We should get you to the hospital." He offered me a hand and I took it, letting him help me to my feet.

"No, I'm fine. I'm totally fine," I told him, gritting my teeth. Falling down the stairs kind of sucked—imagine that. I looked at the puncture wounds on my arms and the strange patterns left by the winding vines. I had no idea what happened to me out there or what to even call all of *that*.

"How about you, are you okay?" I asked. "Did we lose power?"

Daniel shook his head 'no', but pointed outside at the radio tower that reached up into the sky.

"Not quite, but that thing's a bit tilted. We'll have to watch it." He took a deep breath and I could tell he was jittery, nervous. I'd be shocked if he wasn't. "I saw something big moving around out there, inside the fog. I felt it too. The floor was shaking, like an earthquake."

I wish I had words to comfort him. But how on earth could I explain something that I couldn't even wrap my head around? With a sympathetic frown, I patted him on one shoulder and nodded in solidarity.

"I know. It does that. I-I think it always has."

What else could I say? There was no diagnosis for this, no wisdom or special insight that I had as a local. It just ... happened.

Everything in Pinehaven just fucking *happened.*

We sat at our desks for a while in silence, looking at one another every once in a blue moon but otherwise just staring out at the horizon. The fog was still there. It was off in the distance, looming over the furthest trees at the top of the mountain peaks. Watching us.

"It was trying to bring down the building, wasn't it?" Daniel broke the silence, his voice cracking as a dry throat tends to do if you haven't spoken in a while. "Why would it do that?"

My hands were trembling. I hated not having answers, I hated *not knowing anything.* I just shook my head and refused to look at my co-host, eyes glued to the tree line. The furthest pines were moving and swaying in a heavy gust of wind that hadn't reached us yet, but I watched the wind travel down the path one row of trees at a time.

"I don't know, man," I finally answered, a bitter bubble of anger forming in my throat. "No one told me about this when I got the job."

Daniel huffed through his nose.

"Yeah. Me neither."

···‖‖··‖‖‖‖‖‖‖‖··‖‖···

The phone line was on fire all afternoon. First, we got an angry call from the owner of the network, who claims that it took us far too long to sound the announcement for the people in town. The fog had started to reach the streets, he said. Everyone was scared. *Yeah, no shit.*

Next, we got a call about a breaking news story of a married couple who had been last seen taking a walk near the woods before the fog arrived. When it dissipated, they were gone. They just vanished, and they haven't been seen since. We made an announcement immediately to the surrounding area so that everyone could keep an eye out. Before the day was done, police were already out looking for clues at every edge of the forest, including ours.

They found the fingers too.

When they came up to question us about what we had seen,

if anything, they concluded that the fingers were probably bitten off by some kind of animal. That was the story they were running with until they learned something new. The missing girl, Jennifer Cook, probably died of exposure and coyotes got to her, they said

Why they ended up in a bird's nest, we didn't know. I didn't ask and they didn't clarify, but I don't think any of us wanted to think too hard about it. That bird was still hanging outside of the broadcast room, and I didn't want to know what else it might have started storing in its little collection.

They took the fingers as evidence, much to my relief. We didn't know if they belonged to Jennifer and I sincerely hoped they didn't ... but I suppose they would find out soon enough. Apparently, the word around town was that she had been taking a new sleeping pill that made her wander at night. I guess, this time she just wandered too far in the wrong direction.

Before they left, the police asked for copies of our caller recordings from that week. We were more than happy to oblige, so long as they understood that some of them would be intelligible. For some reason, they seemed to expect as much, and took them regardless. There was something weird about the files, though. All of the recordings were there, except for one: the day that Daniel's ears burst open. That entire recording was completely gone.

When the police left, I felt relieved. Sure, I didn't do anything. Neither of us *did* anything. But, I still couldn't shake this eerie feeling that Daniel and I were involved in something way too big for us to handle...Like we were sticking our noses in where they didn't belong, and it would come back to bite us on our asses if we weren't careful.

"Maybe there's a serial killer on the loose," I said to Daniel after the police had left, chuckling to myself. It wasn't funny, but I laughed anyway. "That would be simpler to deal with, wouldn't it?"

"On top of everything else?" Daniel shook his head while he grabbed his jacket, putting his arms in one at a time. "No, ma'am. Nuh-uh. Not for me."

We were both tired. I could feel that stale energy in the air; just two people exhausted, finding it hard to cobble together two brain cells to make a thought. I didn't even have that many brain cells to begin with, most likely. I leaned against the wall, feeling a throbbing pain in my shoulder as I did, all while watching Daniel get his things together. He was leaving for the night, going back to his apartment in town while I stayed up here as I always did.

He paused after he put his messenger bag on his shoulder, looking my way. There was a gentle look in his eyes, compassionate and worried. I saw his eyes briefly travel to my bruised shoulder.

"Will you be alright while I'm gone?" he asked softly. It was the first time he had done this ... the first time he had asked if I was okay by myself. The answer was a complicated one. "I can stay if you want me to. I mean, I don't need to go home, it's not like—"

"No. Daniel," I put a hand up, chuckling. He had just been in the middle of slipping his bag off his shoulder. "No, I want you to go home. Get some rest. I'll still be here in the morning."

"You better be," he said, digging his keys out of the pocket of a brown leather jacket. He dressed like a dad. I kind of liked that about him. "I don't wanna be stuck working here by myself. But listen, if you need anything—"

"I don't. I *won't*. Go get some sleep." I urged him toward the door before he could hesitate again. "I've got your phone number, just get your ass outta' here. I'll see you tomorrow, part-timer."

Daniel reluctantly left. I watched from the window as his old station wagon slowly pulled away down the gravel road, turning at the stop sign. He put his turn signal on even though he didn't need to. There was no one else on the road that night. But as he drove off toward the village to settle himself in his own bed for the night, I found myself thinking too much. Too deeply.

All of the records of our previous calls were still there on the console. One of the recordings we passed over to the police was a call between myself and a young woman from town who couldn't sleep because of birds outside her windows.

She started a new sleeping pill, she said.

It gave me an idea. For the first time, I paid attention to the actual numbers that came through on these calls, digging through the contact history until I could see for myself whose phone had dialed in that night. I dug around in my bag of old belongings—mostly clothes and sentiments I hadn't touched since I moved back to town.

My cell phone was in there, long dead and with a cracked screen, several generations behind the newest model. I let it charge for a few moments, hoping and praying that it wasn't totally destroyed.

The screen lit up. I quickly scrolled through my tiny list of contacts. My mom, an old doctor's office ... and there was Jennifer. She was still listed as 'Jenny' with pink heart emoji next to her name. God, how long had it been since we spoke? Six months? More?

I gave a deep sigh and put the phone face-down on the table. I saw the number. It was the same. Jennifer had called the station that night, but that wasn't even the most shocking thing I noticed. She had called *twice*. The first time, it was to tell us about the bird, but the second?

It was the day I coughed up that stone. The day Daniel was gone, recovering from surgery. The day the crying woman called me. The day the sink went quiet.

Jenny ... I'm so sorry.

While I sat there, numb and cold from the inside out, my phone vibrated against the desk. I saw the screen light up, glowing around the edges. With a sick feeling in my stomach, I picked it up and turned it my way, almost blinded by the light of the screen in a darkened room.

I had a text message waiting for me. A message from Jenny.

Come find me.

Maybe it's time to take a walk in the woods.

CHAPTER FIVE: DO THEY KNOW?
Daniel

There was a time when I used to like listening to the radio in the car. I loved the feeling of driving for miles and miles, the stations changing across state lines. You'd find yourself in a new place with new music, new voices, stations you've never heard of before, genres you didn't expect. Then I started working at Pinehaven Radio, and now I couldn't even hear the music if I wanted to.

I was getting my hearing aid in the morning. Sure, it would undo just a little bit of the damage that had been done, but I didn't imagine it would restore the desire to listen.

Rain pattered against the window as I entered town. Immediately, I noticed the little hints of a passing disaster still left behind after the fog. There were downed trees, a snapped power line, mailboxes that had been beheaded and were now dangling off their poles. There were lawns wrecked and plants uprooted, as if a tornado had ripped through the village earlier that day.

At a certain point, right after the first stop sign met the corner of the little general store, the damage simply stopped, leaving the business district untouched. Maintenance workers were already out trying to clean up the mess, and I briefly wondered: did they know?

Before going back to my apartment, I stopped at the only grocery store in town to pick up a few items, twenty bucks in my pocket to spend. As I was grabbing a box of pancake mix from the top shelf, I saw two women standing with their heads together, speaking close with secretive, shifting eyes. I couldn't hear their voices, but I could read a few words on their lips.

Something about a husband and wife, a storm, missing people ...

I felt breathless, chest tightening as my heart began to pound. It was so tempting to tell everyone the truth, to march back to the radio station and announce over the airwaves that it was never about a storm. It was about so much more, so much that we weren't being told. We were all being lied to, every single one of us, but by whom? And why?

I would sound insane, wouldn't I? I didn't have any proof. I didn't have any answers. Here I was, burdened with the curse of half-knowledge, aware that something was wrong but unable to put my finger on it yet.

Then again, I was a stranger here. Maybe they *did* know. Maybe I was the lone out-of-towner left in the dark, gathering pitiful glances as the folks of Pinehaven asked the same question about me: *does he know?*

I paid for my items and stepped back out into the streets, the rain falling heavier now. Before I traversed the wet pavement and all of the puddles that littered the parking lot, I noticed a glimpse of paper rustling in the wind. There were dozens of signs plastered all over the brick wall outside the grocery store: advertisements, businesses that were hiring, a poster for a play going on at the local high school. They were doing West Side Story. I was halfway down the page, smiling as I recalled my own illustrious career as a melodramatic, bisexual theater kid. Not to brag, of course, but I made a *fantastic* Tony.

Sadly, that fond memory didn't last. Next to the poster was a black and white photograph, and another, and another, and another after that. The eyes of missing villagers were staring back at me, their faces warped by the rain. The ink was running, turning them into melted ghosts. Some of them were children, some were elderly, some were the same age as me.

Their stories didn't differ too much. A married couple disappeared while taking a walk near the woods. A teenage boy ran into the trees, chasing after his dog, but the dog came back without him.

A little girl had been playing by the tree line and disappeared without a trace, and her mother went missing the very next day. They were swallowed by those pines, each and every one of them, added to the list of others who simply never came out.

This town couldn't have had more than six hundred people living in its limits at most. How many of them were in graves?

I tilted my umbrella to watch strangers pass. Some of them regarded the wall with a quiet glance and others avoided it altogether. They didn't want to think about it. Thinking about it too much would make it real.

It felt weird, going home. When I marched up to the second floor of the apartment building and bumped open the sticking door with my shoulder, the dark space that greeted me felt like it belonged to someone else.

I wasn't used to this new silence yet. I wasn't used to not being able to listen to music, not being able to hear the neighbors talk between the paper-thin walls. Every sound that made its way into my ears was muffled and distorted, like listening to another language while submerged in water. I thought about turning on the television, but squinting at the captions on a tiny, long-outdated screen just made me feel depressed. Very briefly, I considered the radio. As much as I would love to hear Evelyn's husky, tired voice trying not to yawn through another weather forecast, it wouldn't do me any good.

I didn't have her phone number, but she had mine. She would send me a text if something went wrong, right? I threw my legs over the side of the couch, my head resting against one of the cushions as I scrolled through the messages on my phone. Two of my sisters had texted me. Elisa was asking if I felt any better and Isabel sent me a video of her boyfriend's new puppy learning to howl. I didn't have the heart to tell her that I wouldn't be able to hear it, but I was sure it was cute.

My mother was blowing up my phone as usual.

Mijo, are you sure you're ready to go back to work?
You can come home if you want to.
The convenience store down the road is hiring.
We have a spare bedroom.

You're so far away.

Sometimes I wondered if she still thought I was sixteen years old, but then I remembered the way she fussed over my little sisters too. She was just like that. I calmly texted her back, telling her that my first day returning to the radio station went just fine. I didn't mention the fog. I didn't mention the vines. She lived two hours away from here, far enough that she'd never have to look out her window and see those billowing clouds and the violence they brought with them.

I loved my family. I wanted to tell them everything, and usually I did. But this? They didn't need to know about any of this. I didn't need to see their critical eyes as they asked me yet again, *"What have you gotten yourself into this time, Danny?"*

I had a dream about the fog that night. It crept into my apartment, sneaking through the open window like a thief. I was trapped, the door jammed shut and the windows refusing to open more than an inch. From below me, I could hear screams. As the fog began to fill the room, it choked me like poisonous smoke until I couldn't breathe. I was wheezing and gasping for breath, watching as my bedroom became clouded in a sea of gray that devoured everything around me. I couldn't tell what was up and what was down.

Something was in the room with me, but I couldn't see it. I could just feel it. It had cold breath that smelled like rotten flesh, moss, and wet soil. Long claws were toying with my hair and scraping along the skin on the back of my arms. I knew it was going to tear me open, spilling my guts all over the carpet, and I found myself bracing for the pain as the mist continued to suffocate me.

When I awoke, I had my face shoved into the pillow, lips and nose smothered in the soft cotton. I jolted up and took a deep, painful breath, a stain of sweat left behind on the sheets.

⸱⸱⸱�\|⸱⸱⸱\|⸱\|⸱\|\|\|⸱\|⸱\|⸱⸱⸱\|\|⸱⸱⸱

That day, something funny happened. After leaving the doctor's office in the late afternoon with my new hearing aid, Evelyn's voice happened to be the first I heard. I breathed out a sigh, a refreshing sort of comfort washing over me as I began to experience clear, intelligible sound again.

"Expect rain off and on until seven o'clock tonight, when we'll finally get a peek at a clear, starry sky. The forecast is looking cloudy yet dry for Halloween night, but remember to wear your jacket while trick-or-treating when we hit those evening lows. Stay tuned in a half-hour for more updates on how you can enter the 104.6 FM pumpkin carving contest, but for now, here's Fleetwood Mac."

I grinned when she hit the sign-off right before the lyrics, wondering how long it took her to rehearse that timing. That grin on my face started to disappear when I reached the winding road that took me out of town, however. It was amazing how quickly Pinehaven ended. Once you passed the sign, the view ahead was nothing but pine trees and a long stretch of curving road, the only speck on the horizon being that familiar tower perched against an overcast sky. I could see the red blink, rhythmic and dull behind the blur of rain falling down the windshield.

I thought about my mother's messages again. The convenience store *was* hiring. And as tempting as it was to just keep driving down that lonely winding road and never come back, something was telling me I had to stay. I followed the blink of the radio tower like a lighthouse, pulling into the gravel driveway and watching the trees fly by. I'd give this place one more shot.

It's like they say on the stage: the show must go on.

A cold wind caught the back of my neck as I climbed to the top of the tower, weaving back and forth on the zig-zagging staircase. I didn't like looking up at the tree line, turning my eyes down to watch my feet instead. Every time those pines came into view, I worried that I would see something I didn't want to see—something strange and impossible, something that looked back at me too.

But as it turned out, the only strange thing I saw when I arrived was my co-worker. When I cracked the door open to our cramped little workspace, I saw her pacing back and forth from one side of the room to the other, tapping at a cracked cell phone with more speed and energy than I had ever seen before. The door closed behind me with a heavy click and Evelyn looked up, finally slowing to a stop and giving me a half-smile. It was one of those shitty, polite smiles where you just stretch your mouth in a straight line across your face -- the kind you'd give to someone who waved to you in traffic.

"Hey, part-timer," she said, slipping the phone back in her pocket. "How's the new earpiece workin' out?"

"So far, so good." I took off my jacket and put it on a hook by the door. "It's not perfect, but it helps a little. I tested it out by listening to your riveting forecast this afternoon. And you know the best part? If I'm super bored, I can just turn it off."

Evelyn cracked a lopsided smile. "What about WiFi? Does that thing connect to Bluetooth?"

I shook my head sadly. "Nah, no Bluetooth. But if I stand real still, I think I can hear old reruns of Sesame Street."

She giggled and let out a snort, but it was forced and tired. I wondered if she slept at all last night. Leaning against the wall, fishing her phone out of her pocket, she tilted her head to one side and gave me that polite, awkward half-smile again. "I'm glad you're back," she said simply. No follow up, no reason.

"Yeah. Me too." I sat down at my desk, considering putting on my headset but ultimately deciding against it. "So, did I miss anything exciting? Is your bird still out there?"

Evelyn sputtered, stuffing her phone in her pocket again. I wondered why she kept checking it.

"*My* bird?" she sneered. "Ugh, no. Well, yes, actually. He's still out there. I saw him sitting at the tree line, just screaming his ugly little head off, but he hasn't been back up on the fire escape."

I narrowed my eyes, watching her lips while she spoke so I could keep up. "What's he screaming about?"

"I don't know, I didn't ask." Evelyn shrugged, tapping her phone again. She grimaced, seemingly disappointed by whatever was—or wasn't—on the screen. "You love him so much, why don't *you* ask him why he's havin' a conniption? Anywho ..." She shoved her phone back into her pocket for about the tenth time, crossing her arms. She was still wearing that ratty old flannel shirt she tore on the fire escape, but it looked like she had tried to hand-sew a few holes shut. "There was music coming out of the sink last night.

Pretty loud, too. Stuff from the '50s. We must have had some wind too, because the fire escape was just covered in twigs and leaves this morning. And maggots."

She made wiggly motions with her fingers while I shuddered, making an over-the-top disgusted sound and sticking my tongue out.

"Jesus, please tell me you didn't touch them. I hate maggots."

Evelyn had that shit-eating grin again, as if learning one of my weaknesses filled her with a dark, wicked power.

"Mmhmm, oh yeah, I touched 'em all, for sure. In fact, I invited 'em inside and let them crawl all over your desk and your chair and—"

"Ew, stop!"

" —and all over the bathroom and the kitchen—"

"Ugh, gross, gross, *gross*!"

I fiddled with my hearing aid and took it completely out, welcoming the silence instead of listening to Evelyn get another word out. At least I knew my maneuver actually worked because moments later she was holding her stomach and laughing, but I could hardly hear a peep of it. Finally, I saw her mouth the word 'sorry', and was more than pleased when she didn't continue that grotesque, skin-crawling conversation.

While I put my hearing aid back in and adjusted it to a comfortable volume, Evelyn was getting seated and adjusting her microphone arm in time for the next announcement, clearing the gunk out of her throat just as the audio bed began to play. She casually tossed me a clipboard with the evening's schedule hastily scribbled in blue pen, an arrow pointing to the next news segment with the words 'your turn' written beside it. She started after counting down on her fingers. 3, 2, 1 ...

"We're bringing the workday to an end here at 104.6 FM, and my co-host has just joined me for the evening. Daniel, how the heck are ya'?"

"Not too bad, Lyn, just enjoying this gentle rain we're getting today. Mind if I call you Lyn?"

"Yes, I do." Evelyn's voice was cheerful and smooth, a fake-sounding giggle in the back of her throat, but the smile on her face was menacing.

"Ha! *Allllright,* well, fair enough. Listen, everyone, a quick announcement from one of our favorite sponsors tonight. Looks like Salvador's Diner down Main Street has reopened the lobby after that sinkhole incident. Go show 'em some support and let them know Dan sent you if you want a half-off breakfast coupon. Anyway, next up is thirty minutes of uninterrupted music here on Pinehaven Radio. Remember, the request line is *always* open. Have a safe drive home."

Microphones were off. Music was on. While I put my headphones back over the arm, Evelyn was a few steps away, tinkering around with something in the kitchenette. A few moments later, she came back with a cup of coffee and handed it to me. It smelled slightly burnt from sitting in the pot too long, but at least the mug had a really cool picture of an eagle on it.

"A peace offering. No bugs, I swear," she said with a hand to her chest. "I put extra sugar in it for ya'."

"Why, are the pipes extra rusty today?" I asked, taking a test sip. It was certainly sweet, that was for sure—thankfully, I liked it that way.

"*Ohhh* yeah," Evelyn said, putting the dry creamer on the shelf. When her back was turned to me, it was a little harder to hear her, but luckily she didn't get far. "Rusty, a little bit brown, and very talkative. But don't worry, I've been drinking it all night and I haven't died yet."

Somehow, that didn't give me much confidence. Evelyn always looked like she was about ready to die at any moment. I'm not saying she was bad-looking, mind you. She was cute in an unkempt sort of way, with long red hair and freckles all over. But she also had this sickly pallor and big, sunken eyes that reminded me of a fading Victorian child getting ready to meet her ancestors in the next life. Right now, still littered with bruises and scrapes from the prior day's shenanigans, she looked sorrier than ever.

"What do you mean, 'all night'?" I asked, spinning in my chair slowly just to have a reason to move. "Didn't you sleep?"

Evelyn's expression started to drop. She was fiddling with her phone again, checking the screen as if waiting for something, all while her shoulders began to sink and her face wilted into a worrisome frown.

"No," she said honestly, "I just had too much on my mind."

I stared at her for a long time, and she seemed to be actively trying not to look me in the eyes. We hadn't worked together for very long, but I liked to think that the reality-shifting horrors we had already experienced together meant I was a little bit deserving of her honesty, at least. So, I decided to pry, but only a little.

"Gonna tell me about it?" I asked, watching the computer screen as a pre-recorded ad began to play.

Evelyn bit her bottom lip in thought, looking down at her phone before turning her eyes up to me at long last. They were big and blue, round like an owl and circled with sleepless, purple bags from her insomnia. She took in a little tremble of breath before she spoke, all the sass melting away.

"The fingers in the nest ... the missing girl," she began, hunching her shoulders against the wall as if trying to shrink down. "I knew her. I think she's out there in the woods somewhere, waiting for someone to find her."

Something about the way she said it made the hair on the back of my neck stand on end. It sounded like a ghost story, this image of a wounded and tattered figure wandering the trees and calling out to be found.

"The fingers, though ..." I said quietly, my jaw clenched as I tip-toed delicately around the subject. "I mean, if she's hurt and if something bit her fingers off, we don't know if she's still—"

"I know," Evelyn interrupted with a snap to her voice. She was glaring at me now, the light from her phone making the bottom half of her face glow in the shadow of a corner. That sharpness faded slowly and she softened her posture, looking through the lookout window at the tree line below. "I know. But, I have a feeling that she's waiting out there for me. Maybe it's stupid."

I shook my head. "No, no. It's not stupid. It's just ..." I paused, watching Evelyn's expression turn suspicious and tense. "There's already a search party. I'm sure they've got it covered."

Evelyn crinkled her nose in annoyance, marching across the room and standing behind her usual seat. As she folded one arm on the back of her chair, she took out her cell phone and tapped at the screen, the light flooding the bottom half of her face.

"They don't know where to look," she said bluntly.

I raised my brows. "And you do?"

"Yes," she said immediately, giving me a harsh side-eye. There was a heaviness in the air as her glower pierced straight into me, the expression on her face dark and determined. "She told me herself."

CHAPTER SIX: EMPTY EYES
Evelyn

"So, here's the thing," Daniel started, already giving me a tone. "It's dark out, the forest is apparently alive and trying to *kill us,* and you want to go frolic around in the pines looking for a dead body?"

Daniel hadn't been here very long and already he was giving me an attitude. I shot him a look, eyes narrowed and my frown cold and bitter as I tightened the laces of my boots.

"First of all, no one said she was *dead.* If those fingers are the only part she's missing, the rest of her might still be okay. And second of all, I would have gone during the daylight if I didn't have to watch the broadcast. That's why I need your help." I shook my head with a low chuckle. "*Frolic,* he says ..."

I was already getting my jacket on, slipping my arms into the musty-smelling, aged denim sleeves. I would be the first to admit that I was ill-equipped. A first-aid kit that I found in a cabinet and a dusty flashlight were all I had to arm myself with for a walk into the woods, but it was going to be fine. There was no fog on the horizon, no oddities at the tree line waiting for me. The evening was still and quiet.

Daniel, however, didn't want to let me leave. He stood in the doorway, blocking it completely so that I couldn't march down the stairs.

"I don't want you going out there alone," he said, heavy brows lowered in frustration. "What if you don't come back? What am I supposed to do then?"

I gave a big, dramatic shrug.

"Congrats on your full-time position, I suppose?" I said

with a sarcastic, dark chuckle. Daniel did not laugh. "You'll figure it out, buddy. Now come on, little to the left."

"No. I'm going with you."

I shot Daniel a look of impatience. "Uh, no you're not." At the moment, I thought I sounded demanding, but my part-timer didn't nudge even a bit. Instead, he just scowled at me, unconvinced and unmovable from the spot. "Daniel, listen, we can't leave the station empty, you *know* that. Who's going to monitor the broadcast while we're gone? The weird-ass bird? The toilet ghost?"

"Excuse you, it's the *sink*, not the toilet." Daniel snapped back at me with an insistence that made me laugh on the spot. "Besides, I think I have an idea."

I huffed out a breath and pinched the bridge of my nose, feeling a headache begin to form. I already knew I wasn't getting out of this.

"Alright, what's your idea?"

Daniel pointed a finger at his palm, listing off his plan one step at a time.

"So, here's what we do," he started. "We record the evening weather, the ten o'clock news, the last couple of advertisements, and then we pre-record a 'goodnight' message to make it sound like we're still here. Then, we put those recordings in the line-up with the rest of the music and no one will even know!"

"And what if the radio starts acting up?" I asked.

"It won't." Daniel sounded certain. "There's no fog tonight. Everything's quiet. It *will* work."

His plan was simple. It was *obvious*. But that simplicity was what convinced me to give him a chance. After all, he was right; there was no fog. The radio had been behaving all day. Just this once, perhaps leaving it unwatched wouldn't tempt the mechanical beast to start making its own decisions.

We sat down and recorded everything one by one, wasting precious time behind a microphone as the sun began to set. The darker the sky became, the more anxious I was about walking into those pines. I had to admit, I was glad that I wouldn't be doing it alone.

"I'm supposed to leave at ten," Daniel reminded me. "You don't think I'll get overtime if anyone finds out we were just dicking around in the woods, do you?"

"There'll be no *dicking,*" I groaned. "But I'll pay the grocery guy extra to bring you some doughnuts if you require compensation for your valiant efforts."

Daniel was staring at the screen, his tongue between his teeth as he focused on moving a bumper into place between one of our ads and the next song. Quietly, he said under his breath in a low and serious tone, "Secure me some raspberry filling and you've got a deal, baby."

I couldn't believe I was actually going to do this. I couldn't believe I was letting *Daniel* do this. Honestly, I didn't know what scared me more: the thought of walking into the woods at night and leaving the station abandoned, or the thought of going alone and leaving Daniel with the responsibility of taking my place. He was nice enough, sure, but was he competent? Was *I* competent? Sometimes, I wondered if a rabid badger from the woods could run across the console and do a better job than us.

"There's another flashlight in the closet," I told Daniel as I double-checked my coat pockets for batteries and a first-aid kit. I hoped we wouldn't need to re-attach any of our fingers on our journey, but the previous day's grim discovery had brought that possibility up a level from 'not worth mentioning' to 'unlikely but could happen'.

I wasn't paying attention to where Daniel was going, too busy making sure I had my keys and my phone. A moment later, when I heard the squeak of an old door hinge, my chest grew tight and fluttered with brand-new anxiety.

Daniel opened the wrong door. He was standing next to the twin-sized mattress, reaching above his head to grab the pull chain for the hanging bulb that sat above my head while I slept. That tiny storage closet held everything I owned in the world: a ratty old backpack, a couple of threadbare shirts and jeans, some old things that used to belong to my dad. I stood in an uneasy silence as he looked down at the mattress, then up at me, concern written between his eyebrows.

"I almost forgot about this," he said softly. "I was so out of it when the ambulance came for me, I almost thought I imagined it. Do they make you sleep in here?" *Do they make me?* It was such an innocent question, assuming the responsibility in the exact wrong place.

I shuffled from foot to foot, suddenly feeling half my size. I shook my head, teeth chewing on my chapped bottom lip.

"No," I said quietly. Daniel was watching my lips. "I asked them if I could."

A second later, he seemed to get the message. Daniel turned off the light, side-stepping to avoid touching anything as he shut the door and left the room the way he found it. Suddenly, we were both looking down, finding it difficult to meet eyes when the air was so thick with unpleasant tension.

"Hey, uh, listen, Evelyn. If you want to talk about it—"

"I don't."

Daniel nodded his head, breathing out a slow sigh and popping his lips. "Right. Okay, yeah, that's fine." He cleared his throat, quickly pacing to the other side of the room and swinging open the *real* closet doors. He couldn't find the flashlight quick enough. "Got it. Ready to go?"

If there was one thing I could thank Daniel for, it was the fact that he moved on quickly. I knew he meant well. He always did. But, some things were just meant to be tucked away.

My second trip out into the fresh air didn't feel as daunting as the first. Maybe it was because the fog wasn't set to roll in for a few days. Maybe having an important goal and a sense of purpose drowned out that feeling of heavy, immense insignificance. I fished my phone out of my pocket again, looking at the minuscule number of bars in the corner. Out here, with a wall of trees all around us and a seemingly endless forest stretching all the way up the mountain-side, it was dangerous not to have some kind of connection to the outside world.

I briefly wondered a very dark and unsettling thought. If we got lost out there, how long would our bones sit under the shadow of the pines, waiting to be found? Weeks? Months? As we crossed the tree line, I watched the bars disappear, wet leaves squeaking underneath our shoes.

"I don't know much about hiking in the woods," Daniel said, shining his light up into the trees. "I'm a city slicker, remember? Unlike you."

I snorted. "Oh, and what am I? The country bumpkin?"

"Yes," he answered without hesitation, shining the light on his own face and giving me an evil grin. "But that's good! If we get lost, you'll be the one to get us out."

"With what? My innate tracking skills?"

"What, you don't have those?" He smirked. "Man ... I don't think I've ever been out here. It's creepy at night."

"It's creepy during the day, too," I said.

Daniel was flashing his light on the ground, then turning it up to the trees at his eye level. God, I *hated* when he did that. I had some deep, visceral fear that he'd shine the light up and illuminate something ghastly that neither of us wanted to see.

"You, uh ... you *do* know your way around up here, don't you?" he asked.

I was grasping at memories. I had left town so young and stayed away for so long that any recollection of playing in the woods was lost to me at this point. If I focused really hard, I could picture the tree line in my mind, seen from the height of a child. I could almost feel my father's hand holding mine, clasping it tightly and pulling me away from the woods. I wasn't allowed in here, I don't think, but it was all such a blur.

The last two years had not been kind to my memories. Those bits and pieces seemed to melt, as if thoughts of Pinehaven ran straight out of my brain like water.

"I was here a couple of summers ago, but I didn't stop to memorize the paths. It's not as if we can't see the radio tower from miles away, though. Just look for the flashing red light."

When I turned back, I could see it blinking between the branches. The light was dim and small, but it stood out against the black and cloudy sky. Daniel looked too. I saw him linger on the shape of our metal and wooden sanctuary as it loomed above us like a solitary figure: cold, still, seeing everything for miles.

I kept my flashlight off to preserve the batteries. Daniel, on the other hand, was moving his back and forth to look at everything at once: the station, my face, every sound, every creaking branch. I had to admit, his constant tomfoolery with that damn thing was starting to get on my very last nerve.

"Will you stop that?" I asked, nudging him on the elbow to get his attention.

"What?" He pointed the light at his own face, dumbfounded.

"Stop dicking around with the flashlight."

"... What about the flashlight?"

I raised my voice for him, remembering he couldn't hear my hoarse whispers. "I said, *stop dicking around with—*"

Before I could finish that thought, a sound erupted from the bushes in front of us, loud enough to even make Daniel jump. It was the groan of an animal, either aggressive or in defense of its territory, followed by an impatient huff through a beastly snout. Daniel whipped back around, his flashlight pointed straight toward the source. We both stopped in our tracks, holding completely still. I didn't even want to breathe.

It was an elk, enormous in size with eyes glowing white at us in the darkness. Three eyes—one on the left, one on the right, one in the center of its forehead. There was no way this giant thing would have gone unheard, leaving me to believe that it had been standing there watching us all this time.

Its antlers clacked against the surrounding trees as it shook its head in a show of aggression, stomping its front hooves into the dirt and stones. Those heavy footfalls made the soil tremble under my boots. Daniel and I both backed up several feet. The animal didn't charge at us. Rather, once it was finished with its noisy tantrum, it turned and stared straight at us for the longest time. Those eyes were like reflective orbs, but when it blinked, its eyelids met vertically like those of a reptile.

Then, with a heavy grunt and a hot, misty breath through its nose, it bounded away further into the pines. I noticed, between instances of wondering how close I had been to shitting my pants just now, that it ran with a very odd gallop. It had three back legs—one on one side, two on the other.

It was a seriously fucked-up looking elk.

"Is there anything out here that doesn't look like an abomination of God?" Daniel asked in a hoarse whisper, his flashlight slowly scanning in a search for anything else that might have been hiding in the overgrowth. There was nothing, not even a sound. After a few hesitant moments, we were on the move again, though I decided that raising my voice again probably wasn't going to do us any favors.

I didn't answer Daniel. I was looking down at my cell phone, watching the bars in the corner. I wouldn't have expected to get any signal out here, but strangely, one single little bar kept flashing and then disappearing. It was as if we were getting close to a connection. I had no explanation for it, but I didn't think about it too much—of all the weird horseshit I had already seen out here, a cell phone signal was the most mundane of curiosities. All I cared about was that I might be able to make a call if I only had one more bar.

"How do you know her?" Daniel broke the silence after a few more steps, once we were sure that giant, mutated elk wasn't still stomping around. "The missing girl, I mean. You seem to have history."

"You're real nosy, aren't you?" I asked, giving Daniel the tiniest smirk out of the corner of my mouth. He clammed up a little bit, embarrassed. "It's okay. We were best friends. Grew up together, went to college together, shared a dorm. She moved back here after graduation and ... well, eventually I did too. She was generous when I needed a place to stay."

"... And now you live in a radio station?"

I turned my eyes down to my phone, shrugging my shoulders. I was acting nonchalant, like I didn't give two shits. I actually gave quite a considerable amount of shits.

"She, um ..." I hesitated. "She didn't want me there anymore."

I could feel the question in the air. I didn't even have to look at Daniel to know what he was thinking or how badly he wanted to ask why a kind, generous best friend would kick someone out of their home. Luckily, before he had a chance to speak and before I needed to grasp a new conversation topic, I saw it: two little bars on my phone, springing to life and defying all odds against this wild and uninhabitable mountain. I raised my phone up in victory, stopping exactly where I stood in fear of losing that meager connection.

"*Yes!* We have it. We have a signal!" I said, feet planted firmly. "Don't move."

Daniel gave me a confused stare before I had a chance to explain. I was tapping away at my phone, looking for Jennifer's phone number among my minuscule list of contacts.

"I'm calling her," I clarified. "If she's nearby, she can help us find her, assuming she also has a signal and battery life."

"And assuming she's *alive*," Daniel said hoarsely, a glimmer of fear in his eyes. While I held the phone up to my ear, he was shining his light up into the trees, watching owls and bats fly from their perches and flutter overhead.

I didn't answer. I whispered a hoarse 'shh!' as the phone began to ring in my ear. It rang once, then twice, then ... suddenly, I heard it in both of my ears. Her tone, a basic selection from the library of sounds, was distant but audible in my one exposed ear. I lowered my own device, listening to the sound echo from further in the trees. It was faint, but it was *here.* Daniel turned to the direction of my gaze, his light scanning along the ground to find a path of broken twigs and flattered grass that railed off deep into the brush.

It didn't look like the path of an animal. It looked like drag marks.

"Evelyn? What are you—?"

"Her phone."

That was all I said before I reached into my coat and pulled out my own flashlight, smacking it once and watching it flicker to life. The tone stopped ringing, and so I called it again, desperately hoping that this wasn't just a trick of the ears. I couldn't help but feel some level of paranoia, knowing that this forest could be drawing us further into a devious trap. Anything could be an illusion, anything could be a lie. Perhaps that's exactly what it did to Jennifer.

I felt a sense of familiarity with the forest then. Suddenly, I *knew* this path. I almost felt sick the moment some old, buried memory started to resurface. It wasn't trauma, no, the nausea was a *part* of the memory. I could see a campfire, roaring high in the center of a clearing, one person's distinct voice warning that it would burn the trees down if it got any bigger. I remembered tripping over beer bottles and the sound of shitty guitar music, some drunk idiot singing off-key. Shit ... now that I think about it, maybe *I* was the drunk idiot singing off-key. I could hear Jenny's voice, minging with the crackling fire and the terrible music, saying, *"Evelyn, lay off, you've had enough. Hey! Don't you scream at me! You're such an ass ..."*

I remembered feeling dizzy. I remembered getting over-whelmed, deciding I needed to take a walk to clear my head. I re-membered ... something moving between the bushes.

And to think, that graduation party was the last time I had ever seen this place until now.

Damn. Why did I ever come back?

I was going too fast, my feet unable to keep up with the fallen logs and the roots below. The toe of my boot caught a bit of rotten wood and I went tumbling down, my face buried in a pile of dead, wet leaves. The soil carried an awful, sickening smell that made my stomach churn and bubble. And as I reached out for my flashlight, I felt something cold and wet instead; it was sticky against my palm.

"¡Mierda!" I heard Daniel gasp, horrified, before I caught sight of what he had found. And god, I wish I hadn't seen it. I found my flashlight and gave it another good smack as it illuminated the grass below. There was blood soaking every inch of the forest floor ahead, bits of cloth and who *knows* what else strewn about the soil and fallen leaves.

And just inches from where I had fallen, there laid a man. The top half of him, at least. His face was wrinkled from the sun and stretched into a horrified grimace, pieces of his flesh torn away by birds and scavengers while maggots took up residence. His mouth was open. Flies were crawling around on his dead, swollen tongue. Nearby, I saw the bottom half of his body, dressed in khaki pants and a pair of walking shoes. He had been separated messily across the middle as if ripped in two by sheer force. His entrails had spilled across the forest floor, dragged around and picked at by wildlife.

And he wasn't the only one.

Fuck, I shouldn't have looked up. I shouldn't have turned my light to the trees, but the sound of creaking branches tempted me. My light followed the trunk, stained all the way up with streaks of dark red blood, until it fell upon another body that was ripped in half just like the first. The pieces were stuck in the branches by their clothes and their limbs, as if tossed into the air and catching wherever they fell. The second body was that of a woman, but it wasn't Jennifer. Her white, empty eyes were staring down in an expression of frozen horror, her gray hair limply waving in a slight wind. Her mouth was still open in a silent, permanent scream.

Daniel was getting sick in the bushes behind me. I felt as if I was a moment away from joining him. All of the shadows and shapes were swirling around in my vision, the pungent smells not only in my nose but on my tongue as the full wave of that terrible scent hit me. I gagged, but before I could turn away from the scene, my light caught something else: the glow of eyes from the trunk of a nearby hollow tree.

I've seen uncomfortable things in my life. I've seen unforgettable shit just working out here in these woods, not only gruesome and terrifying things but *unsettling* too. *Unusual* things. But as of right now, what I saw in that tree takes the cake.

We found Jennifer. She was in one piece, as far as I could tell, aside from a hand missing every finger except for the middle one. I'd like to think that perhaps that was some final joke from whatever murdered her, but that's probably just wishful thinking.

Her body was stuffed into the tree, her limbs twisted and cracked to roll her into a human ball inside the hollow trunk with her stark-white face peering out through the hole. Her eyes were open wide and staring forward, round and bright like the ghostly eyes of an owl. It almost looked like she could see me, like she was staring right at me. Her mouth was open, jaw unhinged and filled with dry grass and twigs ... like a bird's nest.

Her other hand was sticking out, the arm broken at the

elbow. It was tilted, palm pointed to the sky and her cell phone sitting in the center. She was offering it to me. I was trembling from head to toe as I picked it up, my fingers briefly grazing her cold, wet flesh with a sensation that made my bones quake. The phone was flashing "10% battery", along with two missed calls from me. My name was on the screen: "Lynny", followed by an alien emoji. She hadn't changed it since the last time we met.

There's not a single damn person on this planet who could convince me that she wasn't positioned that way on purpose.

We weren't even friends anymore. But *shit,* man. I really failed her one last time, didn't I? At least, in the end I was consistent.

My chest was tight, my heart was racing, every inch of my body was shaking from head to toe. I dropped the phone and crouched down, knees up to my chin and curled as small as I could be. You know, I wanted to cry. I really did. But I couldn't. I was numb and frozen when I heard the crunch of footsteps behind me. Daniel tentatively came over to my side, kneeling down beside me with a hand over his nose and mouth. He was rocking back and forth, struggling to catch his breath.

His free hand rested carefully on the center of my back. He trembled just as much as I did, but the light touch was warm and I didn't shove him away. Instead, we rocked together.

"We can't stay," he said breathlessly. "I-I think we need to go."

He was right. Not only was it a fucking nightmare to behold, but the smell from the blood and the bodies surrounding us was making both of us sick. That's a smell you don't really forget, I don't think. It wasn't until we both stood to leave that I wondered if the killer was still out here somewhere, still watching the scene of its gruesome act. Did it know we were there? Was it human? Did it *matter?*

We turned back to leave, completely silent. We had nothing to say, no comforts to share and no energy to even talk about our fears or our disgust. I kept my light on the ground as we walked, but every now and again I would hear the shuffle of an animal's steps or the squeak of a bat in the trees above us. The distant bugle of an elk made my spine tingle. Once, I thought I saw the briefest glimpse of a bare human foot stepping behind a tall berry bush. Daniel didn't notice, and I pretended I didn't see it.

We were halfway back to the radio tower before Daniel spoke again, his voice cracking as if he hadn't used it in days.

"You know," he started with a sniffle, "I-I wanted this job because I thought it would be right up my alley. I thought I'd be *good* at it, maybe make some people laugh, meet interesting folks, be part of a community and really get my career off the ground. I didn't think it would be like this."

I felt a twinge of guilt. I knew that hiring Daniel had been none of my responsibility, but I still felt as if this was all a mistake. He meant well and his heart had always been in the right place, but he was suffering for it. He had the chance to leave, but he chose to come back time and time again even when that long open road stood before him. He didn't need to be here. He didn't need to be *out here* in the forest with me. Sometimes, I wondered if he stayed because this bizarre tower of horrors was the only exciting thing he had to look forward to.

But now? He was in too deep. We both were.

"Hey, Daniel?" I asked softly, shining the light on my own face so that he could read my lips.

"Yeah?"

"So ... your mom invited me to a wedding in the summer. Still looking for a plus-one?"

He laughed, but it was strained and tearful.

"Yeah, I'd like that," he said with a weary smile. "Matching tuxedos?"

I nodded decidedly. "With plaid bow ties."

The rest of the walk was quiet. It was well after midnight when we got back to the tower, everything just as calm and as quiet as we left it. I looked up at the blinking red light while Daniel lingered near his old station wagon, his breath hitching as he tried to think of the right words to say.

"I can stay for a bit if you want me to," he finally offered, picking the twigs and leaves off his jacket. "J-just, you know, if you're feeling anxious or if you want to talk."

I shook my head.

"Go home," I told him softly, wearing a sad half-smile. "I'll be fine. You should go get some sleep."

"Are you sure?" he asked. And for the first time, I saw a glimpse of something I never noticed before—something I wasn't used to. It was genuine care. Sometimes, it was far too easy to forget that some people were just kind and selfless without expectations.

"Yeah, bud, I'm sure," I joined him next to the vehicle, hesitantly offering a hand. He looked down at my palm and then shook it, his fingers still trembling. I could have been emotional about the whole thing, thanking him for saving my life in the fog or for insisting on coming with me to find Jennifer. I kept those thoughts to myself. But still, I could not ignore the fact that I had been sort of a dick to him ever since he arrived.

"Listen, Dan ..." I started, scratching the back of my neck. "You remember earlier, when we were on the air? I was just fuckin' with you, actually. You can call me Lyn if you really want to. I think we're there."

He wore a satisfied little smile, nodding his head. "Good to know." He shoved his hands in his pockets, breathing in the scent of the chill night air. "I'll see you in the afternoon then. Sleep tight, Lyn."

"You drive safe," I replied, giving his arm a friendly bump with my fist. "And I want you to show up tomorrow in one piece, okay? Two pieces at most, but only if it's a small loss."

Daniel laughed, pointing to his more damaged ear and saying, "I've already made my blood sacrifice."

I stood in the gravel driveway and watched him pull away, the wind chilling my bones as the isolation wrapped around me like an icy blanket. When his lights disappeared down the winding road, it was just me and the whistle of a breeze between the branches.

Going up those stairs felt like an eternity, and opening the door to see a dark room with two glowing screens reminded me of the day I first arrived. I could still smell the dust in the air, the stale scent of burnt coffee at the bottom of a pot that was left on too long.

I settled in slowly. The automated system was working just fine, as we had hoped it would. I took my time, seeing no need to rush back to the console or even to the old, lumpy mattress where I laid my head at night.

I spent a long, long time just sitting cross-legged in my chair and looking out at the window. I had my headphones on, listening to the music, watching the trees sway while dark clouds slowly covered a sliver of moonlight. I almost wanted to turn on my microphone and ask who was out there listening with me, but I'd be too disappointed if nobody answered.

Once again, I was at the top of the world, looking down on a silent kingdom that didn't even know I was there. And all night, the image of her face was burned into my mind—the broken limbs, the white blind eyes, the nest stuffed into her open mouth. I remembered the last time we ever spoke face-to-face and all of the cruel, angry things I said as I packed my belongings and left the apartment for good.

She cried the whole time. I never even apologized.

It was two o'clock in the morning when I decided to turn on my microphone and interrupt the music. Softly, I spoke into the night, preaching to a sleeping audience.

"This is Evelyn at 104.6 FM. If anyone's still awake out there, I have some advice. Don't treat your friends like shit."

CHAPTER SEVEN: BODY IN THE WOODS
Finn

None of us ever wanted 'forest duty'.

It was dirty business. Down here, set in the valley between the wide green mountains, it was far too common for folks from this little shitheap of a town to go missing after wandering into the pines after dark. Sometimes they came back in one piece. Sometimes they came back in several pieces. Most often, they didn't come back at all. This town's weird, rotten energy took many hands to be properly contained, and one of those great honors was 'forest duty'.

My name is Finn. I'll leave it to the imagination whether that's my first name or my last. I've been on the Pinehaven police force for five years now, and one thing I've learned in that time is that nothing ever really gets old. It doesn't matter how many times you have to trudge into the woods to collect bodies, it doesn't matter how many calls you get about animals with two heads or people with upside-down faces. It never becomes normal. It never gets boring.

But goddamn, did I wish it got boring.

The forest that surrounds Pinehaven is a border between our own world and one that is vicious and feral. In the last year, I had been involved in more wild cases than I could count. These are just a few.

February: White female, 78 years old, called the station to report a wild coyote pacing back and forth at the tree line near her property. This normally wouldn't be an issue, except for the fact that the coyote in question was apparently wearing the bottom half of her husband's face. Her husband, who had been dead for a year, was supposedly buried in a family plot near the edge of the woods. The dirt above the grave was frozen solid, but when it was exhumed in the spring, the old man's body was gone and a tunnel had been dug beneath the empty casket.

April: Black female, 13 years old, was hanging out in the old Pinehaven Elementary School playground after school with a few friends when she noticed a vaguely humanoid shape standing between the trees. She described his face as 'wooden, like a mask made of tree bark', and said that he was trying to lure her into the forest. When asked what he said to lure her, she told my fellow officer, "He didn't say anything. He just stared at me, and I knew he wanted me to follow him."

June: White female, 26 years old, was revived by paramedics on the floor of her apartment bathroom after attempting to drown herself in the tub. The situation seemed ordinary enough until she was rushed to the hospital, where she told the nurse about a mountain lion who was wearing her father's face. Blood alcohol levels were dangerously high. Once sober, the patient did not remember this conversation.

August: White male, 54 years old, calls the station to complain that something got into his barn in the middle of the night and slaughtered all of his livestock. He went on to describe a gruesome scene, involving every animal missing its limbs and eyes but the torsos being left unharmed. Three days later, the same man called the station again, telling us that he had 'found' the limbs but refused to elaborate. He was found dead in his own pickup truck later that night, parked near the old church with the motor still running.

October: Latino male, 30 years old, had both eardrums rupture due to a malfunctioning piece of audio equipment. Moments after his coworker called 9-1-1, another call came in from a different number. An elderly woman said, and I quote, "God has given him deaf ears to better see his glory." The woman never gave her name, and the number could not be traced.

I wish I could explain why things were like this, why they had *always* been like this. Unfortunately, solving mysteries of the unknown was a bit above my pay grade. The most I could do was keep people out of the woods, keep a gun pointed at the tree line, and occasionally join the rangers on 'forest duty'.

That's what we were tasked with on a cold, wet October day after a set of severed human fingers had been found outside the old broadcast tower a mile out of town. A man had called in with an anonymous tip at seven o'clock, telling us that the rest of the corpse was stuffed into a hollow tree. My partner, Nancy, and I took a K9 out at ten o'clock in the morning, following the scent of the recently identified woman.

"Jennifer Cook, huh?" Nancy asked, tightening the laces on her boots on the edge of a hollow log. "Her prints were already in the system. She got a record?"

"Small one," I answered, my eyes following a sound from up above. It was just a hawk leaving its nest, circling nearby in search of food. "Back in the spring, she was brought in for a domestic disturbance involving her roommate. No charges, though. Just a screaming match."

Nancy had only been here for a few weeks. She was a transfer from a city precinct, taking over after we lost two officers in one night (to resignations, thankfully). Nancy was good: level-headed, no-nonsense, and with fifteen years of experience to show. But even I don't think fifteen years on the other side of the mountain could prepare her for her first day on forest duty.

"What are we thinkin'?" she asked. "Coyotes? Wolves? You got wolves up here, Finn?"

"Sure we do," I answered, tightening my grip on the K9's leash as he sniffed at a nearby thorn bush. "Wolves wouldn't stuff her body inside a *tree,* though. That's what the witness said. I'm just hopin' she hasn't gotten too far away."

Nancy laughed. It was a loud, boisterous laugh, followed by the smack of her hand against a nearby tree trunk.

"If she's dead, it ain't like she's getting up and walking, is it?"

I didn't answer her. Trying to explain the way the forest worked while out in the thick of it felt like I might pull its attention toward me, like a curse just waiting to happen. I'm not an overly superstitious man. It took me years of growing up around these parts to finally start accepting that not everything has a scientific answer. But when it came to the woods around Pinehaven, I knew better than to taunt it. I knew better than to challenge a beast far bigger and more vicious than myself.

"Do you feel dizzy out here or is it just me?" Nancy asked, putting a hand to her forehead as she scanned the view.

"You get used to it," I said. "Out here, it's hard to tell when you're going up and when you're going down. It's no wonder people get lost so often."

"People like Gordon and Pamela Richmond?" Nancy gave me a look, her eyebrows raised.

"Yeah, like them." I voiced a low sigh. The search parties were still out for those two after they disappeared during the last fog warning. It was a terrible time to go out for a walk, if you ask me. Then again, those damn fog days had a way of sneaking up on us ... Maybe if the new recruits up at the broadcast station had been a little more competent, we wouldn't have lost three people in one week.

It was a shame, really. Of all the people tasked with keeping Pinehaven safe, the Operators were always the first to go. I couldn't help but wonder how long the new ones would last.

Our K9 caught the scent of something toward the west. He began to sniff at the ground, digging aggressively, pulling on his leash to get further into the thick cluster of pine and oak. Nancy and I followed after him closely, a couple of rangers behind us, trying to keep up.

We noticed the flies first. There were hundreds of them, buzzing in circles at the edge of a big clearing. The sound was nothing compared to the smell. I lifted my arm, putting my sleeve over my nose and mouth to shield from the terrible stench of decay. It smelled like mold, rot, and human waste, all wrapped together in a horrible concoction that had been baking in the sunlight for days.

Beneath our feet, the dead leaves were stained with blood. I could see the movement of wriggling maggots crawling across the ground, circling a mass of flesh and torn fabric a few feet away from where we stood. It was Gordon Richmond. Or, at least, it was the top half of him. He had been sliced through the middle, a pair of legs lying a few steps away and his organs scattered around in the soil and the dying autumn grass. There was blood trailing away to a nearby tree, splattered up the trunk all the way to a branch ten feet high.

A pair of crows were picking at the branch, a bit of torn flesh caught on a twig.

"Jesus *Christ* ..." Nancy backed up a step, covering her nose and mouth with a hand. "We've got a sick fuck on our hands, Finn ... God, he's only been gone a few *days*. Smells like he's been rotting for weeks."

Our K9 was following a path of flattened grass that stretched through the grisly scene; it looked as if something had been dragged, sliding through the soil and wet leaves.

Whatever used to be at the end of the trail wasn't there anymore. Instead, a large oak stood soaked in dark, dripping sap that was leaking from the hollow in its center. I stepped closer, that terrible smell stronger with each step. It wasn't sap. It was blood, thick and dark and pooled inside of the tree by the quarts. It was surrounded by loose twigs, leaves, and strands of long blonde hair.

While two of our rangers pulled out a stretcher for Gordon's remains, Nancy and I circled the tree. It was exactly as the man on the phone had described it, right down to the drag marks and the nearby thorn bushes, but the distinct lack of a body was ... distressing.

"Shit. If Jennifer was here, she ain't here now." I said softly, shining a flashlight into the tree. Floating in the pool of foul-smelling blood was a tangled mess of dead grass and leaves, but no sign of a corpse.

"Think she's been moved?" Nancy asked with a grimace, stepping back to take photos of the scene. "Taken by whoever put her there?"

I shook my head, squinting up into the branches above us. Crows were circling, waiting to take their piece of the scraps left behind. I wondered if something *else* had already been here to take its own pieces. But why would it leave Gordon Richmond?

"No, I don't think that's what we're dealing with." I stopped to listen. The forest was quiet that day, the wind calm and still. The smell of blood and decay should have been attracting the attention of scavengers of all types, but it felt lonelier than a tomb out there. "I think Jennifer's on the move already."

Nancy voiced an incredulous scoff, but it was delayed and

uncertain. In her eyes, there was a glimmer of anxiety behind the doubt.

"You're kidding," she said, almost as if she were trying to convince herself more than me. "We'll talk about your ghost stories later, Finn. We've got a bigger problem here."

She was kneeling down, a pair of rubber gloves on her hands while she brushed through a pile of wet leaves. Between her fingers, she gingerly picked up a cell phone. It was damp, cracked, and stained with blood, but the screen still lit up when she pressed the center button.

"I take that back," Nancy said. "We have *two* problems."

"Let me see." I crouched next to her, craning my neck over her shoulder. The phone battery was almost dead and the screen was dim, but we could both see Jennifer's most recent activity front and center. There were two missed calls, and the name 'Evelyn' was assigned to both.

"One of your new broadcast employees is named Evelyn, right?" Nancy said quietly, looking over her shoulder to make sure that the rangers were occupied. "You took the anonymous tip this morning. Did he sound familiar at all?"

"... Ah, shit." I dug around in my front pocket for a pack of cigarettes. There was only one left, but this was a good time for it. As I lit it up, carefully holding it away from the crime scene, I grimaced at the cracked glass and thought back to that early morning phone call. Maybe if I listened to the radio more often, I would have recognized him right away. "... They're not supposed to be out *here*."

Nancy sighed. "You know how this looks, Finn." Her voice was low and disappointed. "McKinnon knew the victim and never thought to tell us? She had her *fingers*."

I wasn't comfortable with this, but not for the same reason Nancy was. While she eyed the phone with suspicion, her mind probably cobbling together all sorts of theories about why one of these young women might try to kill the other, I was thinking of the *last* radio DJ to sit in that tower. He didn't keep a cool head either. It took days to scrub the blood and guts off the staircase.

"I'll talk to her later, get the full scoop," I said, wiping my brow with a gloved hand. "Sure she's got a reason for this."

"I dunno, man. I don't like the fact that those two chuckle-fucks have unrestricted access to this area, and one just so happens to tell us where to find the body? A search party has *been* through here before." Nancy's eyes squinted out between the trees, watching the wind rattle the branches and knock loose a few dead oak leaves. "It just screams 'plant' to me. I think McKinnon knows something, and maybe her co-worker is helping her keep it quiet."

If we were anywhere else in this big, wide world, I would probably agree with her. But here? The situation was a bit different, and I wasn't so sure I was the right person to tell our new recruit that. My biggest concern was up in that tower. After losing our twenty-seventh broadcaster, we could not afford to lose another so soon ... even if they were a couple of incompetent slackers.

Nancy and I both turned to a new sound of disgust from one of the Pinehaven forest rangers. Two of them had been attempting to move Gordon's torso onto a stretcher, but they couldn't get him off the ground. I watched as they gave the corpse a heavy tug, his body pulled back into place by a series of roots that were growing *into* his spine.

His body was being invaded. Roots and vines were digging into the places where his organs would be, leaving the bones and skin as a rotting shell. The smell that rose from Gordon's body cavity was powerful and thick—one of the rangers staggered back and began gagging as soon as they managed to pull him up. It wouldn't have been the first time a seasoned ranger lost their breakfast out here after seeing something that Pinehaven Forest had never done before.

"Looks like we'll have to cut h-h-*hurh*—" One of the rangers said as he turned his back, escaping the smell by walking a few paces away and putting his hands on his knees. I pulled my jacket up to cover my nose and mouth before approaching, kneeling down to inspect the body for myself.

Almost as soon as my hand touched him, Gordon began to move in a series of twitches. An unearthly, guttural groan left his mouth. When he stretched his dead, cracked lips, opening his jaw wide, we could see the twists and curls of branches moving around inside of his throat. They were wiggling on the ground as well, circling around his body to hold him tight to the earth. All at once, the roots pulled him back against the forest floor until he was flat on the dirt, the plant life wriggling into his empty body cavity as if his corpse had become its home.

We could have believed that the breath he took was an automatic response of some sort, perhaps one last release of gas from his old, dead lungs. That didn't explain his next trick.

His eyes were wide open, white with blue veins pale on the surface. He made an agonizing croak as his head leaned back and something started to dig its way out of his throat. A set of human fingers, blue and bloated, crawled out of his mouth one inch at a time like a fat, fleshy spider's legs. We saw his faded irises moving from side to side, inspecting each face surrounding him. He looked at me. He looked at Nancy. He began to let out a low, inhuman groan and then—

BANG!

He didn't make another sound. Nancy had pulled her gun from its holster in an instant and shot him straight between the eyes point blank, sending bits of his skull flying. It was a panic response, sure, but I already knew we'd both be getting into trouble for this later.

"Did you have to go and do that?!" I shouted at her, my ears ringing from the sudden gunshot next to my head. "Now look, you done fucked up his face!"

"As if it wasn't already?!" Nancy's voice broke. She sounded confused, scared, just trying to put herself back together. Nearby, one of the rangers was brushing a bit of rotten brain matter off of her jacket while another was preparing a large knife to cut through the roots. Nancy backed up against a tree, clutching her chest. "Finn, what the *hell* did we just see?"

"Welcome to forest duty," I said, stepping away to let the rangers get Gordon into the sling. I didn't want to stand too close for two reasons: first was the smell, second was the fact that the roots *screamed* as they were being cut.

The torso and the legs were both covered in a white sheet, transported back to the tree line near the old broadcast tower. I was making a mental note to have a conversation with the Operator who had shown up on Jennifer's abandoned cell phone. But before we had a chance to head back, our K9 began to make a low, guttural growling sound with his nose pointed up into the trees. I felt a tug from his leash as he ran for the trunk, putting his front paws against it and barking up at something unseen. All of the hair on his back bristled and he was baring his teeth as if threatened.

And for a split second, I swore I heard something growl back. That, and the momentary glimmer of something between the dark branches: a collection of gray human fingers, sliding back into the shadow of the pines, paired with at least five glowing white eyes that all blinked at the same time. The dog tucked his tail and backed away—if he was startled, it was a good time to leave.

I wasn't going to bother trying to speculate about what our K9 may have been looking at. There's good logic for this: all my life here in Pinehaven, I've learned two distinct things. First of all, you never know what you'll come across. Second of all, you'll never, *ever* be prepared for it even if you do.

There's a reason we don't take kindly to outsiders here. There's a reason we try to keep people away. This place is a nightmare on its worst days and it radiates a general unease on its best. So for any travelers out there, I only have one piece of advice.

If you're driving down a long mountain pass, looking for something to listen to on the radio, give a quick scan for 104.6 FM. If you find it, that's a very good sign to turn around and go right back the way you came.

The forest doesn't need to grow.

CHAPTER EIGHT: FOLLOW THE RULES
Evelyn

It was early afternoon by the time they brought the body out of the woods. Headphones on, I watched from the lookout window as a pair of police officers led a group of rangers in green uniforms into the clearing, a stretcher behind them. Just *one* stretcher. I waited for them to go back in for the other two, but they never did.

"Did you tell them about the couple in the tree?" I asked, looking over at Daniel while Billie Holiday crooned in my ears. He was sitting at his side of the desk, munching on some stale potato chips and fiddling around with something on the screen. When he glanced up at me, I saw the dark circles under his eyes.

He shook his head. "No, I didn't. I described Jennifer to them, but they started asking questions and I got nervous a-and I couldn't breathe so ... well, I hung up. I probably should have been more thorough, you think?"

"Probably, yeah." I slowly trudged over to the desk, sitting down on the corner with one foot propped up in my chair. "Looks like they only found the one. How the fuck did they miss the other two?"

Daniel made an exhausted sputtering sound between his lips and shrugged. He was quieter than usual since he arrived, clocking in an hour and a half earlier than expected. He told me he didn't want to be alone, and it didn't take a genius to figure out why. This *Stand By Me* bullshit hit him hard.

We both felt it. I couldn't close my eyes without seeing Jennifer's face. The horror was still fresh, but I felt numb as if the reality of what we saw out there hadn't really settled yet.

"Munchies? Hm?" Daniel held out the half-eaten bag of potato chips. When I ignored it the first time, he shook it at me aggressively, making a loud and annoying sound. "You've gotta eat somethin', bud. You're gonna waste away."

I pushed the bag out of my face.

"How can you eat that?" I asked.

"Easy, I use my mouth." He gave me that shitty little grin again.

"That's not what I meant," I whined, leaning my head back with an exasperated sound. "I mean ... after everything that happened yesterday. I swear, I can still smell the bodies, like it's stuck in my nose. I can taste it on my tongue, it's—"

"Lyn. Stop." Daniel looked up at me sternly, a deep and uncomfortable frown on his face. "We don't have to keep talking about it. I don't *want* to, not right now. Let's just try to have a normal day, alright?"

I could see the dim expression in his eyes, the way his clothes looked a little wrinkled and his hair seemed limp and unwashed. He probably hadn't slept. Daniel was just as upset and traumatized as I was, he just so happened to be a better actor.

"What is a normal day?" I asked with a slight smirk, finally reaching into the bag of chips and grabbing a handful. I was licking salt and grease off my thumb when Daniel responded.

"I dunno. Blood in the sink, a haunted coffee maker, maybe Jimmy Hoffa's ghost will call the station this time."

I scoffed. "If you see Sasquatch, let me know. I've been trying to get a picture."

"Try the bathroom mirror," Daniel said without missing a beat. I flicked him on the forehead, leaving a greasy stain on his skin, much to his distress. I watched him get out of his seat, stomping over to the tiny kitchenette to grab a paper towel for his poor, sullied face. While he was gone, I stared at the screen, listening as Billie Holiday's voice faded and made way for some Bob Dylan. So far, things hadn't been too strange. No birds were flying into the window, no strange plant life was trying to creep up the fire escape, no five-legged elk stomped around by the trees.

Most notably, however, the sink had been completely silent

ever since we found Jennifer. It was almost as if she had said all she needed to say.

Somehow, none of that normalcy brought me any comfort. Things felt wrong. I felt a creeping dread washing over this whole place, as if this was just the calm before a storm. As we watched the forest rangers packing up their gear and preparing to transport the corpse, something *real* and visceral was sitting in my stomach. I was afraid of what would happen next. I was afraid of what this all meant, and of what in the unholy fuck we had gotten ourselves into this time.

"I think we've got company coming," Daniel said. I finally noticed that he had been standing near the lookout window, watching a pair of figures make their way toward the stairs. He had both of his hands on the glass, his breath making a fog against the surface. He looked back at me, nervous and unprepared.

"It'll be fine," I assured him. "We didn't *do* anything. They probably just wanna ask us what we saw."

That may have been the truth, but it didn't stop me from feeling some amount of anxiety building up. It started as a flutter in my chest and quickly turned to fidgeting fingers and a foot that wouldn't stop tapping against the floor. Daniel was pacing. Watching him stomp back and forth was making me even more anxious, especially when the sound of his footsteps began to match the heavy boots we heard marching up the stairs.

"What do we tell them?" he asked me, hands in his pockets. "If they know we were out there, th-they might ask *why* we were looking and I don't think they'll believe that a ghost told you to—"

"Dan, relax." I took a deep breath as an example. "We don't have to tell them we were out there. Okay? That's not important. We didn't *do anything*. We were up here, doing our jobs, we didn't see anyone go in or out of the forest. You went home at ten. Got it?"

Why did we want to lie? Why did we feel like we *had* to lie? I understood why Daniel was afraid. He was an upright kind of guy, probably never got in trouble once in his whole life. But here in Pinehaven, he was a strange new face in a community of old families whose roots ran as deep as the trees. Suddenly being tossed into the middle of a triple homicide case probably felt like walking on broken glass. But I was nervous too. Sure, I didn't know anything about the other two people we found in the forest, but Jennifer? She was a special case.

I'd never hurt her, not in a million years. I wished to God that I could bring her back just to say 'I'm sorry' one last time, but to the eyes of an outsider, I probably would have looked like the person who hated her most. But I didn't. I just hated the way things had to end between us. I hated the way we never made it right.

A knock on the door startled us both. I was holding my breath as Daniel did the honors of opening the door just a crack at first. I couldn't see who was on the other side, but I heard a woman's voice: stern, older, but calm. *Rehearsed.*

"Nancy Bell, Pinehaven police. This is my partner, Finn. Mind if we talk for a minute?"

"Uh—yeah, sure." Daniel spared an anxious glance toward me. It was almost apologetic in nature as he let the door swing open, stepping back as two officers in uniform joined us in the broadcast room. The woman was square-faced, her black hair pulled back into a tight, slick bun. The man next to her was so broad that he looked as if he could have snapped Daniel in half like a twig and tossed him into the woods with no effort.

The man, Finn, gave me a pointed stare and gestured for me to approach. Reluctantly, I pulled off my headphones and joined my coworker, just as Nancy was pulling something out of her pocket. It was a little plastic bag, a blood-stained cell phone inside. *Ah, shit.*

"Evelyn McKinnon, is that right?" she asked, and I nodded silently in response. "We've got a warrant to check your cell phone. We have reason to believe you've been in contact with Jennifer Cook, and until we figure out where she is, those phone calls are evidence."

What did she mean, *where she is?* I think they both saw the confusion written on my face as I looked between the two of them, feeling my blood run cold. That single stretcher they pulled out of the forest ...it wasn't *her*? I stared at the phone in the bag. Jennifer's body was gone, but that single piece of evidence had been left behind as if someone *wanted* the police to find it. And somehow, that phone had held its battery just long enough to reveal its rotten secrets. It should have been dead. Why wasn't it *dead?*

The only thing more terrifying than wondering what put Jennifer in the tree was wondering what the hell took her out of it. For a brief, sickening moment, I pictured her dragging herself out of the tree: broken limbs, all tangled in a pretzel as she crawled down onto the forest floor. Impossible as it was, the image gave me the shivers.

"This would go a lot quicker and easier for both of you if you cooperated with us," Finn said.

I felt Daniel give me a nudge to the elbow, snapping me back to reality.

"Uh, yeah, sure thing," I said shakily, unlocking my own cell phone and handing it over. "I-I did try calling her. We used to be friends. I didn't expect her to pick up—"

"Did she?" Nancy asked, taking the phone out of my hand. She and Finn shared a glance, and I could see the light of the screen shine against the lady officer's chin as she scrolled through my messages.

I took a deep breath, shaking my head. "No. She didn't."

A moment later, my stomach plummeted as Nancy looked through my text message history.

"You texted her too," she said. "A few times."

When she turned the screen around to show me what she saw, my blood ran cold. The message from Jennifer was gone. I clearly remembered staring at it for hours, trying to make sense of what she meant when she said *'come find me',* but now all trace of that message had disappeared. On the screen, it was just me, carrying on a one-sided conversation with a dead woman. Talking to myself.

"I-I guess ... I guess I was just thinking about her," I said. It was true.

Nancy and Finn went on to ask us all sorts of questions, and we were completely useless for most of them. *Did anyone stop by the station in the last two days, did you see anything suspicious outside, have either of you had contact with any of the victims?* Luckily, the answer to all of those questions was 'no'.

But when they started questioning Daniel, things got more complicated.

"We received an anonymous call early this morning," Finn said, leaning against the wall by the door. He stuck a toothpick in his mouth, chewing on it like a nervous habit. "The voice was a little familiar. Know anything about that?"

Daniel was gnawing on his bottom lip. I hadn't expected him to lie, and I was right. He quietly gave a nod and murmured under his breath, fidgeting slightly from side to side.

"I called it in, yeah," he admitted. "I, um ... I found the body out on a walk last night after my shift."

The son of a bitch took the fall. I didn't ask him to, I didn't *want* him to, but he did. He looked over at me and I glared back at him, my brow heavy while he gave me the softest and most pitiful smile, both apologetic and kind. He had a heart of gold, this one, but I had never known a bigger idiot.

"And what time was that?" Finn asked, taking notes on a small pad of paper.

"About ... ten o'clock? Eleven at the latest?" Daniel voiced a sharp intake of breath. "I-I lost track of time, I couldn't tell you exactly."

Watching Daniel get backed into a metaphorical corner was painful, like watching a small animal get eaten alive. Finn scratched his beard with the end of his pen and gave Daniel a dark, suspicious scowl. "That's a bit late for a walk in the woods, don't you think? Especially with three people missing from the area ..."

Daniel stammered, struggling to come up with an excuse. I was fully prepared to set things straight, but before I could even open my mouth to argue, I felt a small tug to the edge of my collar. Nancy had noticed the bruises poking up from the neck of my shirt.

"May I?" she asked, gingerly pulling the fabric down just a couple of inches to reveal a portion of the long, dark marks that stretched all the way to the bottom of my ribcage. It still hurt like a bitch, and the story that went along with it was impossible to explain. They wouldn't believe it anyway, would they?

"Where'd you get these?" she asked, her thumb brushing one of the painful spots by accident.

"I fell down the fire escape," I said. It wasn't a lie—not *technically.* "When I rolled down the stairs, I hit myself pretty hard on one of the handrails. It was an accident."

She didn't press further about the bruises, but it didn't mean I felt any better. It was uncomfortable, watching how intently the officers glared as they took in every single detail, even the things that weren't important. I knew it was all just a part of their job, but I suddenly felt as if I was in trouble for things I had never even *done.*

Finn put his notepad away, glancing out the window at the rangers who were already slowly driving down the long, gravel road with a corpse in the back of the car. He and Nancy shared a quiet, stern glance, and I watched as Nancy's hand began to hover near the handcuffs at her waist.

"We'd like to ask you more questions, Miss McKinnon, but it would be better if we waited until we got you to the station," she said slowly, accurately. "If you don't argue, then—"

"If I don't argue, you won't cuff me?" I asked, eyes following the motion of the woman's hand. She gave me a tight-lipped stare and nodded her head.

Daniel's mouth was slightly agape, as if he struggled to find the right words. When we locked eyes, I saw fear. It wasn't that same type of fear we had known before, faced with impossible things. This was a very realistic dread with no room for disbelief.

"Follow the rules. Okay?" I said softly, before grabbing my jacket off the coat rack. Daniel just stood, the wheels turning in his mind, and in that moment I couldn't tell if he was more afraid of me getting thrown in jail or if he was afraid of the mere thought of running this place on his own. He'd have to get used to it.

Sorry, buddy. 104.6 FM is yours now. Welcome to your full-time promotion.

As we stepped out into the chilly October air, Nancy walked ahead of me while Finn followed behind. I took one last glance out over the trees, watching the way the wind brushed through the pines and the gnarled oaks. They creaked and whined, as deep as a low cry of pain. I thought about her again. I remembered her face, gaping wide and stuffed with a bird's nest, her eyes like two white marbles. I wondered if she could see me looking back at her.

I wondered where she was now.

    I ducked as Finn pushed me into the back seat of the vehicle, closing the door behind me. You know, it's almost funny how things ended up. I hadn't been to town in so long, stuck up here in a rickety piece of shit on stilts at the top of the world. At last, I finally get a chance to stretch my legs and it's at the police station, getting questioned for a murder case.

    As we pulled out of the long gravel drive, I spared a last look up at the tower. Sometimes I forgot just how big and menacing it could look when you were right below it. Finn had the radio on—it was quiet and low, muffled by the seats in front of me. Still, I could clearly hear Daniel's voice as he recited the news forecast we had pre-recorded earlier that day.

    Rain tomorrow. A chance of fog in the evening. A good night to stay indoors, a bad night for a walk.

    Remember your training, part-timer. Radio on, doors closed, and never forget to sound the emergency broadcast.

CHAPTER NINE: THE VISITOR
Daniel

Evelyn had dropped off the face of the earth.

I had been handling the radio station on my own for two days before any news came my way. Things were oddly quiet on the first morning. There was no crying coming from the sink, no freaky-looking bird outside the window, no fog. Despite it all, I was still uneasy, mostly because the police were almost always present in their never-ending search for that girl in the woods. The fact that they couldn't find it, even in the light of day with a scent to follow, gave me this sinking feeling that Jennifer was out there hidden in some secret, far-away place. Maybe something ate her, leaving nothing behind. Maybe her body wasn't even in there anymore.

In mid-afternoon, I saw the same officer from the day before standing outside by the tree line, speaking into a walkie-talkie. She looked just as stern and unfriendly as before. After finishing a quick news update about a bit of road construction outside town, I abandoned the desk long enough to run down to the clearing and see how close I could get to the yellow tape.

I simply asked her when—and *if*—she expected Evelyn to be done doing her part in this case. I was hoping that my role as the 'concerned trainee' would convince her to give me an estimate on when I might see her again, but guilt-tripping a cop isn't something I would advise. It didn't work for me.

"Can't be sure of that," she said, blunt and matter-of-fact. "Depends on how well she cooperates. We can't question her yet, though ... Had to let her go in for medical treatment first."

She refused to elaborate any further.

I shouldn't have been too surprised, but I was. Evelyn didn't look healthy by any means, but I somehow doubted she would have agreed to a hospital stay in the middle of all this mess. This was the same woman I had never even seen drink *water* before. I felt like there was something more going on, something that no one was telling me.

That curiosity was gnawing at me all day. I kept thinking about Evelyn and her secrets, her moody silence, her ever-present raincloud. So, between recording an ad for a pumpkin patch down the road and answering phone calls asking about all the police vehicles in the area, I decided to do a little digging. Thankfully, Evelyn didn't think to give her computer a very original password. It was just 'password'.

I know that snooping through someone's computer is a quick way to make an enemy out of a friend. It wasn't polite to do and it probably wasn't right. But, now I know she was hiding a few things from me. *More* than a few things, really. Evelyn's thoughts were scattered through notes and documents, half-written accounts filled with revisions all about her daily experiences.

The stone, the crying woman on the phone, that *thing* in the fog ... I almost couldn't believe how much she hadn't told me. Yet, I couldn't shake the feeling that too much of this was personal. I should have stopped there, respecting her privacy and never mentioning it again. But it was then that the screen began to flicker. Pages upon pages of opened tabs appeared, tracing a path of Evelyn's internet history.

Most of it was the product of boredom: clickbait articles, dumb quizzes, a google search for mountain birds. But she had a social media page too. There were tons of unchecked notifications waiting for her, so many that it seemed as if she hadn't read through them in weeks. She posted even less.

I noticed right away that almost all of the content on her profile belonged to other people. Some relative of hers, maybe an aunt, asked, *"How have you been?"* and she never responded. A young man tagged her in a post with several others, calling for the old D&D group to get together again, which she didn't react to either. Then, there was an entire library of tagged photos that other people had taken.

Most of them were posted near the end of last summer. As

I scrolled through, I have to admit that some of the pictures made me smile. Evelyn's hair was shorter and she had a sunburn across her nose mixing in with dark clusters of freckles. She was smiling widely, grinning with all her teeth as she posed with friends from college in their caps and gowns. I saw her next to a familiar woman, making faces at the camera.

It was Jennifer. The sight of her face made my blood run cold as I remembered that ungodly mask of terror that she wore the night we found her corpse in the woods: her eyes were milky white, her bones snapped, her skin was like wrinkled paper. But here in the past, she was rosy-cheeked and happy. I saw her a lot more often, mostly in photos she herself had taken of her and Evelyn together.

"Lyn and I went hiking today," one post said. *"Moving day with Lynny!"* *"Evelyn and Jen: couch-lifting champions"*.

They were arm-in-arm on Halloween, covered in glitter. Jennifer was kissing Evelyn's cheek under the mistletoe at a Christmas party. They were posing in front of a scenic sunset over the Blue Ridge Mountains.

Then, there was a dark and blurry photo. It was the first of many. These final pictures were part of an album that tagged Evelyn and at least fifteen other people. My smile began to disappear when I recognized those trees. Seeing that forest and the dim faces of strangers, most of them drunk or lost in clouds of smoke, make those photos seem ghostly.

I saw her again. Evelyn was standing in the background of a few photos, sometimes so small that I had to pay an awful lot of attention to see her. She was smiling in one, her arm around Jennifer while she clutched a red cup in her free hand. In another, she was sitting next to a man playing an acoustic guitar.

Then, she disappeared. I saw Jennifer, talking and laughing and dancing with friends, but Evelyn wasn't there anymore. That is, until I found her again, standing in the background in one particular photo that chilled me right to my very core.

I saw her between the trees, half-hidden in shadows, the flash of the camera illuminated a wide-eyed and terrified look on her face. One of her hands was against the trunk of an old oak as if holding it for stability. She was like a ghost, staring straight into the screen with a stark white expression devoid of all color. In the next photo, she stood at the edge of a group, as if someone had pulled into the photo while she was passing by. Her face was stuck in that grim look of terror, and I realized very quickly that *something* had happened. Evelyn had seen something that she didn't want to see.

I couldn't get away from the photo fast enough. The way her eyes burned into the screen, round and bright in the camera flash, felt like a curse. It reminded me of Jennifer's white, soulless eyes reflecting the flashlight. Evelyn was in almost every picture, holding a cup in her hand each time, and I watched as that scared, traumatized expression on her face transformed into near-unconsciousness. Two friends were holding her up by the arms. Either she was drugged, completely wasted, or both. Then, both her and Jennifer disappeared from the remaining photos, leaving no trace behind.

I regret lingering so long on those photos because my online status—or rather, Evelyn's online status—had caught someone's attention. I saw the blip of a private message, the chat automatically popping up in the corner of the screen. Reading her messages was the ultimate betrayal of any kind of privacy she had left, but it was just *there* right in front of my eyes.

I sincerely hope, if Evelyn ever finds out about what I've done, that she doesn't murder me for this.

Scrolling up the chat, I saw a one-sided conversation between Evelyn and a person I hadn't seen on her page until now. The tiny profile picture displayed in the corner had a familiar face, though— it was Jennifer, standing cheek-to-cheek next to a young man with light brown hair. His name was Elijah, and he made his purpose as a go-between very clear through a flood of at least twenty unanswered messages he had sent over the last few months.

August 5th: Lyn, can we talk?

August 18th: Where are you staying? Are you still getting help?

August 25th: Jen has been asking about you a lot. She really wishes that you would unblock her. You two need to talk.

September 2nd: Evelyn, please.

And as I sat there, on a cloudy and cold October day, he messaged again, simply saying, **Lyn? Hello?**

As I scrolled upward, I found the first message that started it all. It was from mid-June, the very first message he had ever sent to her.

Hey, Evelyn. Jen told me about what happened. I hope you get well soon, but please take it easy from now on. She can't babysit you just to make sure you don't drown yourself. You know if you need some help, they've got programs for that sort of thing, right? You should look into it. Jen cares about you, but she liked you a lot more when you were sober.

Another red bubble. Another message. I was hesitant but still curious as I scrolled back down, finding that Elijah had left a handful of short, aggressive messages in the span of seconds.

Answer me. Where's Jennifer? You know something, don't you?

Lyn, I know you're reading this.

I can see you.

My blood ran cold as he continued to type, putting down a sentence that made the hair stand up on my arms and the back of my neck.

They all die on that mountain. Every single one.

I closed out the browser and turned off the screen as quickly as I possibly could. Elijah's words struck me instantly with this sudden fear that if I had stayed on that page, I would have seen and read far more than I wanted to. *They all die,* he said. Who is 'they'? Hikers? Climbers? People who worked here before? I wasn't sure if his words were a threat or a concern.

I'm no detective, but I'm worried that nothing here is co-incidental. I can't pretend that all of this doesn't somehow fit to-gether like a puzzle that I just can't figure out. The fog, the bodies, the vines, that sound I heard over the phone: they're like clues to a mystery, but I don't even know the question yet. Evelyn, if you ever read this, I'm sorry.

And I hope that one day, you can remember what you saw that night in the woods.

Sitting alone up here all day and night has made me realize

the full weight of this isolation. It's boring, yes, but there's a constant tension that has been keeping me on edge. There's an eerie, consuming, *penetrating* silence that is only comparable to how I felt before getting my new hearing aid. Through my headphones, I can hear the soft music playing and the occasional jingle of a pre-recorded ad, but the rest is just ... empty, dead air.

The phone didn't ring. I couldn't hear the traffic from the road. Even the birds were silent.

At five o'clock, I gave the evening news.

"It's the end of another workday, and we're going to celebrate with thirty minutes of uninterrupted music here on 104.6 FM. But first, here's the word around town." I picked up my clipboard, reading off the list that I had typed up earlier. "Just as a reminder, the rest stop at the corner of Smith and Saint Arbor is still closed for maintenance. But if you and the kids are looking for something to do on an October afternoon, Phil Goldman's hayrides are open from 2 p.m. to 5 p.m. every day. And lastly ..." My breath was stolen from me as I read the final line in my head before speaking it. "... Lastly, expect rainy weather and fog from the mountains later tonight."

My head was spinning. It was becoming harder to breathe. I had been trying so hard to forget that day when the fog rolled in, but here it was again. Sometimes, when I was trying to sleep late at night, I could still see Evelyn's pale and terrified face as she was ripped away from the window and pulled down the stairs. I remembered the shadows that I saw dancing in the fog, formless creatures surrounding the tower and pressing their rotten hands against the windows.

I remembered my dream. That smell. Rotten, mold-spotted flesh and wet moss ...

Evelyn wasn't here this time. The sun was going down. I was stuck here on my own, at the mercy of an enemy that I didn't even understand.

But I knew the rules. Radio on. Doors shut. Sound the emergency broadcast.

At five thirty, I made myself a sandwich, picking apart pieces of bread that were growing little bits of mold. It was Friday. Evelyn said someone arrived with groceries every Friday, but I hadn't seen them yet.

Radio on. Doors shut. Sound the emergency broadcast.

At six, I played some Jackson 5 on the radio and tried to distract myself by making a game out of counting the birds that had gathered at the tree line. Eleven, twelve, thirteen, fourteen ... or did that last one just have an extra set of wings?

Radio on. Doors shut. Sound the emergency broadcast.

At six-thirty, I cleaned up some of the trash that had accumulated in Evelyn's closet. I felt sick when I found what seemed to be a clump of long, blonde hair on her pillow. Lyn didn't have blonde hair.

Radio on. Doors shut. Sound the emergency broadcast.

At seven, I bagged up the trash, finding that the can was full of live maggots. I rushed down the stairs to throw it in the dumpster, my spine tingling with disgust the whole way, and found that a blue sedan was parked in the gravel drive. No one came to the door. No one knocked. I glanced in the passenger's side window and found the vehicle completely empty.

"Hello?" I called out, squinting into the soft light of dusk as my feet crunched against the stones. There was a bitter chill in the air, as if the wind that passed through the trees was a whistling breath on the back of my neck. "Hello!"

Something rustled between the bushes. I saw a quick flurry of movement—animals were scattering. The birds that had gathered at the tree line suddenly took off with the flutter of many wings, fleeing back up into the mountains. I thought, for the briefest moment, that I heard a whisper, not from my ears but inside my head. But then the breeze whistled through the branches again like the quiet whine of a ghost, barely audible.

The wind changed directions. It was cold and sharp against my face. It brushed my neck like icy fingers as dead, dry leaves rolled over the toes of my shoes. As I stood there in the dark driveway, the red blinking light from the radio tower shining down in rhythmic pulses, I saw someone standing at the edge of the clearing. He was faced away from me, back to the tower and staring silently into the pines, swaying slowly back and forth in some sort of daze. It was a young man, holding a large cardboard box of groceries.

"Markus?" I called out, taking a few steps toward the silent man. "Hey, Mark! Listen, Evelyn's not here, but I can help you carry those up to the tower if you like."

He didn't answer me. I watched him intently, hoping he wasn't about to take another step into those woods. In the back of my head, the last words that Jennifer's boyfriend said to Evelyn rang out again: *They all die on that mountain.*

Every. Single. One.

Three people had died in the woods in just as many days. I didn't want to witness one more person getting lost and being pulled out in a body bag. Without even thinking of the radio and whether or not the next song was set to play, I began to close the distance between the delivery man and myself, just as his absent-minded swaying stopped and he took his first steps into the dark, oppressive cluster of trees. He dropped his cardboard box, leaving items spread across the ground in a mess of rotten food, maggots, and dead leaves.

I stood at the edge, yelling at him to come back, but he didn't even register that I was there. I watched his figure disappear between the pines until all traces of him were completely gone—no sound, no sight, not even the movement of branches. It was as if the forest had eaten him alive, leaving nothing behind.

You know, I've got plenty of things to dislike about myself. One of the worst things, though? I can't leave well enough alone. Going into the forest, day or night, was a brainless thing to do but I couldn't handle the shame of not doing anything.

I pushed through the overgrowth, sticky pokers attaching to my pants. As soon as I entered the woods, the air around me already felt colder. Darker, sicker. I called out for Markus again as I weaved around the pines and the birch trees, tripping over complicated systems of above-ground roots. There was no sight of him, no sound that my ears could pick up.

But something was moving out there. I could see it in the shadows, quick and graceless as it stumbled along the wild forest floor. Maybe it was our grocery boy, realizing his terrible mistake and turning back. Maybe he had awoken from his trance to find himself lost and feeling foolish. The closer I crept, the more certain I was. I saw a shock of shaggy blonde hair and a red t-shirt. Markus, however, was not alone.

Almost as soon as he came into view, I spotted rotten hands gripping his head and digging fingernails into his skin. Markus was already dead, his mouth hanging open and his eyes rolled back, neck broken and limp to one side. Those hands reached around his face. With one sickeningly loud crack, I watched them tear the top of his head away from the jaw, ripping the corners of his lips in a gruesome smile until his tongue was hanging loosely from an exposed throat. The sound of his flesh tearing was one I won't forget, nor will I forget the blank look in his eyes as the top half of his head rolled toward my feet.

The rest of his body was thrown to the ground. I could see what killed him: a ragged collection of human parts, staggering through the long grass. It was Jennifer. I'm not even sure 'staggering' was the right word. The way she moved was so much more ... *impossible* and complex than that. Her neck was broken, her back was curved, and her legs were snapped in directions that made my skin crawl. Her joints were clicking in and out of the sockets as she weaved back and forth one step at a time.

One arm was twisted backwards at the shoulder, her wrist dangling so loosely that I thought it might fall off. She *shambled* in the truest sense of the word, putting weight on whatever parts of her legs would support her, like a dirt-covered marionette with tangled strings. There were twigs, dead leaves, and bits of long grass sticking out of her hair and stuffed into her open, unhinged, crooked mouth. =And the sound that she made ... it was unnatural, like wheezing and gasping mixed with these low, guttural groans and frog-like croaks. I couldn't even tell if she was looking at me. Her eyes were milky white and her head rolled back and forth loosely on her snapped neck.

That was the scariest part. She shouldn't have been able to move, but she *did*. She broke every law of the human body just to get to me.

Without even thinking, I abandoned Markus' body and began to run. I couldn't help him anymore. I stumbled toward the clearing, practically throwing myself into the long grass just in time to see a thin layer of mist forming around my ankles. I turned to look back for just a moment. It was a terrible mistake on my part. Jennifer was *running* now, using her feet and her knees and her hands all at once to support her weight as she broke into a clumsy sprint on all fours. She looked like a ruined, tattered animal that shouldn't exist.

And she was gaining on me. I didn't know how she managed to move so fast and I honestly didn't give a *fuck*. I raced through the clearing and up the stairs, pure fear and adrenaline pushing me to the top without so much as a second to pause and look back. But I could hear her the entire time: her dry death rattle, her croaks and gasps, those hints of a voice muffled behind a mouth full of grass.

When I got to the top, I threw the door open and slammed it behind me, locking it with shivering fingers. I shouldn't have looked through the tiny glass window, but I did. She was there, an inch from the glass, the fog slowly enveloping her body until all I could see were those dead, white, hollow eyes. I could still smell her: the rot, the damp soil. I could still hear her, not in my ears but in my mind.

I didn't care about the grocery kid anymore. Just being locked up in the broadcast room was all I wanted, that and the comforting sunlight. It was still so many, many hours from morning. I put a chair in front of the door, barricading myself in as the handle began to jiggle. Backing away as far from the door as I could, I avoided the windows for fear that I would see her again. Her face ... I can't stop thinking about *her face.*

It had only been minutes since I left the broadcast station, and in that time, the radio had stopped. I looked at the frozen screen, the timeline empty and every track of music and audio gone. In hindsight, I should have known. When the sink whispered and the clocks ran backward, why wouldn't the computers also make decisions on their own? The fog had only just arrived—I had time. I grabbed the first song I could find and let it play, sitting in front of the screen and shivering as I placed the microphone in front of my face and prepared to go live with an emergency announcement.

The fog hadn't reached the town yet. Everything was under control. I had to remind myself of that.

"This is a fog warning for the village of Pinehaven. Please remain indoors. Please keep your windows shut. I repeat, this is a fog warning for the village of Pinehaven."

I listened to the music, trying to focus on it rather than on the sound of scraping fingernails and claws against the windows and the door. 'Unchained Melody' was playing, muffled through the headphones I refused to put on. And still, I could hear her ... Jennifer was wheezing and groaning in pain from the other side of the door.

I took out my hearing aid, letting it clatter onto the table. Even in the silence, I could still remember the vivid sound of her terrible, inhuman, *impossible* voice, and the way she coughed on dried leaves and twigs.

The fog left slowly. I watched it drift back into the forest, taking the nightmares with it as it lingered within its boundary. There were no calls, no complaints—this time, it never reached the road. But as the hours ticked by, uneventful and quiet, I never felt safe. The way the mist collected near the tree line felt like a hovering mass that was watching me from afar, waiting for me to make another mistake. I couldn't imagine how Evelyn felt, living here all day and night, so very alone but haunted all the same.

It was almost midnight when I got a call on my personal cell phone. I had never been so happy or relieved to hear someone else's voice. I popped my hearing aid back in and picked up the phone.

"Hello?"

"Daniel? You there?"

My heart skipped a beat. It was Evelyn. She sounded tired, but even that grumpy voice was a joy to hear.

"Where are you?" I asked, skipping all the pleasantries and getting straight to the point. I think she heard the panic when I spoke. "Please, please, *please* tell me you're not in jail. I cannot run this place on my own if you're—"

"They didn't arrest me. You can breathe, *compadre,*" she said, and I heard a light chuckle in the back of her throat. "I'm coming back in the morning. I'll be there before six, that's all I can promise. I'll catch you up to speed when I see you."

Evelyn must have heard me let out the biggest sigh of relief because her next words sounded concerned.

"Dan? What's wrong?"

"Nothing, I'm fine." It was a lie, but my nerves weren't ready to have that discussion. "Just ... be careful. Get here safe."

"I will," she agreed softly, but I could tell she didn't call just to tell me that she was alive. Even over the phone, there was a heaviness in her tone that told me she had so much on her mind that she couldn't tell me just yet. "Listen, when I get back, we have a lot to talk about. Just hold the fort for a few more hours, okay? Don't do any dumb shit, don't go outside. Hold tight. Can you do that for me, part-timer?"

I had to laugh. She had no idea that I had already broken all of her rules, but she would be more than happy to know that I had zero intention of doing it a second time.

"Yeah, I think I can handle that. I'll see you soon, boss."

"Never call me 'boss' again." She laughed over the phone, weary and low. For a moment, we sat quietly, unwilling to end the call but unsure of what to say. My mind was everywhere. I was stuck on this impossible pressure to keep this place running, and I still didn't know *why* this godforsaken radio station was the center of every weird thing happening in these mountains. All of a sudden, I had a feeling that I hadn't really digested until just now. I realized just how much this job—this *place*—had changed my life.

I didn't want to hang up yet. I sat on the floor by the window and we talked about anything that came to mind, eating up the minutes just to feel less alone. Eventually, I laid my back against the hardwood and stared up at the ceiling, pretending I was anywhere else.

"Hey, Lyn?"

"Yeah?"

I sat up and spared a glance to the window, relieved to see that the fog was higher up the mountain now. However, I did see a subtle and unnerving sight that wasn't there before. A pile of twigs, long grass, bits of dead leaves, and long blonde hair littered the fire escape and made a path down the stairs.

How long was she standing there, watching me?

I let out a shaky breath. "As soon as we get a couple more part-timers, you and I are taking a vacation."

CHAPTER TEN: RESPONSIBILITY
Evelyn

I felt like a jackass sitting in the back of a police cruiser, sinking low in my seat so no one on the street could see me. I was never put in handcuffs, I was never put in a cell. But when we arrived at the police station and Finn dragged me back into a set of small, isolated rooms, he didn't want me out of his sights for even a moment.

Before I was questioned, however, they inspected me a bit too thoroughly for my liking. As a woman in blue gloves shined a flashlight in front of my eyes, I immediately had my suspicions.

"I'm not shooting up at the radio station, if that's what you're wondering," I said bitterly, and the woman just shot me a slightly annoyed look out of the corner of her eye. "I'll take a drug test. I don't care."

"You can discuss this with the sheriff later, Miss McKinnon. But for now, I need you to strip down. Shoes and socks too. We'll make it quick."

I wore a scrunched-up scowl as I followed her directions, using my hands to cover whatever part of my body I could until the woman pulled my arms to the sides with heavy, forceful hands. I could tell by the way her lips were formed into a tight line that she was already done with my fidgety bullshit.

She checked my bruises and made note of any scratches or wounds. She counted all my fingers and toes, my eyes and ears ... I didn't know what she was looking for, but I was relieved when she finally told me that I could put my clothes back on. Before the medical examiner left, she took a few swabs and a sample of my blood, putting it all on a rolling cart and leaving me to sit alone on a metal table in a cold, dark room.

I sat there for over an hour, trying to listen to vague bits of conversation through the door. I could hear a voice, somewhat familiar, speaking sternly to the others. Where had I heard this man before? While I couldn't make out much of the conversation, a few words stuck out to me: they were talking about the tower, something called an 'amalgamate', and the number twenty-eight.

It was late in the evening by the time I was put into a private room, where I sat at a long empty table. When the door creaked open, a middle-aged man with dark skin and a neatly-trimmed gray beard stepped in and regarded me with a look of quiet patience. He was dressed in a gray uniform, with patches and medals hanging off his shirt.

"Listen, I'm not a junkie," I told him, a tired whine in my voice. "I thought we were here to talk about my friend."

"We are."

He sat down at the other side of the table. In contrast to my bitterness, he seemed calm. He was concerned and watchful, not flinching even once at my grumpy attitude.

"I'm Sheriff Andre Jacobs, we've spoken on the phone before. I apologize for what you've gone through today, but due to your exposure, we needed to have a full medical exam before anything else. We're glad to see you're still in one piece, McKinnon."

"Why wouldn't I be?" I asked. "And what *exposure?* If there's radiation or-or a gas leak or something poisonous in the water out there, I deserve to know. Daniel deserves to know."

The sheriff shook his head, putting up a calm hand to silence me. "It's nothing like that." He folded his hands on the table as he continued, leaning in slightly. "We have learned to be very thorough when it comes to making sure that anyone who spends a considerable amount of time in the woods is safe … and intact."

I squeezed my lips together, feeling them twitch in anger. Safe, he said. Yeah, they were doing a great job of that so far, weren't they?

"Safe like Jennifer?" I asked, chin trembling. "It's a great use of your time, shoving swabs up my asshole when instead we could be talking about *my friend* who was *fucking murdered.*"

It was probably in bad taste to cuss at the sheriff, sure. I knew that. But I was furious. I was angry and confused, I was heartbroken and scared. So much was being hidden from me; so much that I wanted desperately to know but hadn't been trusted to understand.

He opened a folder, licking the tip of his thumb before flipping through the pages and files. There were images, but I didn't want to look at them. Out of the corner of my eyes, I could see the harsh flashes of bloody, messy crime scene photos that I did not want to see a second time.

"Evelyn Faye McKinnon." He wasn't asking, but clarifying. As he continued to sort through the stack of papers, I found myself growing impatient. "You were arrested twice in the last twelve months. DUI's both times. You and your roommate—"

"Former roommate," I corrected.

The sheriff gave me a brief glare before he cleared his throat. "You and your *former* roommate, Jennifer Cook, were fined one time for a domestic disturbance at your apartment building."

"We had a purely verbal argument," I explained. "I had just gotten out of the hospital and she was lecturing me about—"

"*My point is ...*" The sheriff spoke with such a piercing tone that I shut my mouth immediately. "... we had your fingerprints. And we matched them to a set of prints on Jennifer Cook's cell phone, which we found a half-mile away from your workplace next to a tree filled with her blood."

I had opened my mouth to speak, but his choice of words gave me sudden pause.

"Filled?" I asked. "Wh-when Daniel and I found Jennifer, she was *in* the tree. All of her. So what does that *mean?*"

"It means, the tree was oozing several quarts of her blood, but the body was not there."

He was giving me an icy stare and I was waiting for that shoe to drop. I was waiting to somehow be blamed, to be asked the clear and concrete question: *did you kill Jennifer Cook?*

"I didn't have anything to do with her death," I said. "She was my friend. We weren't on good terms, *sure,* but I would never kill her."

The sheriff's next words surprised me. He held up his hand,

quieting me before he continued in a soft, almost comforting tone of voice. It was the kind of calm, level-headedness I would have expected from my own father.

"Nobody thinks you were the one to hurt her," he said, "but we need to know what you saw in the forest last night. Now, when we received the anonymous tip from Mr. Esperanza, we were expecting to find the body of a young woman. You can imagine our surprise when we found the body of a man instead." He leaned a little further across the table, hands folded together tightly. "Evelyn, I need you to describe the scene to me. The *real* scene, every single detail of it."

The urgency in his voice shocked me. I imagined Jennifer's family would want her remains, but the way he looked at me was desperate. It was as if finding her body was just the tip of something far more important.

"Jennifer was ... in the tree," I explained. I knew it would sound strange, but I was starting with what I knew best—the thing I remembered most clearly. "She was stuffed into it. I-I don't even know how she *fit,* but her head and one arm were sticking out. She was dead. Her mouth was stuffed with what looked like a bird's nest and her eyes were open like she was staring at me. They were white, cloudy. She was holding the phone in her hand. I-it looked like she was *presenting* it to me, but whoever pulled her out must have dropped it and left it there on the ground."

"You think she was posed?" the sheriff asked.

I nodded my head. "Yeah. Yeah, I do. I mean, there's no way she got in there by herself, right? And the other two bodies—they were just *thrown around.* There was no rhyme or reason to it, but with Jenny, it was deliberate."

"... Two?" Sheriff Jacobs stared me directly in the eyes. He was frozen, his expression dropping into a look of perplexed discomfort. "There was a third body? Your friend didn't mention that."

I grimaced, a sensation of guilt and unease taking over. *God, Daniel, why didn't you say something?*

"There were, um ... there were two other bodies, yes. A man and a woman. They were both split in half, only the woman's body was tossed up into the tree ... just hanging here, stuck on the branches. Dangling."

110

The sheriff was flipping through his papers again, pulling out photographs and files. I caught a glimpse as he sorted through them, recognizing the forest floor, the grass covered in blood and torn fabric strewn about near a singular, mutilated corpse. He pulled out a trio of photos and set them in front of me on the table. I grimaced when I saw them. It looked worse in the daylight.

I felt sick as I recognized the man's body, his face pointed to the sky and his mouth hanging open as if stuck in an eternal scream or one last gasp of breath. His legs weren't far away, half-hidden in the bushes.

But then I saw the tree, now empty where Jennifer's body would have been. Blood was running down the bark, dripping from the hole leading to its hollow center like red sap. That tree wasn't the only one that was bare. The limbs of the second oak were bloody and stained, but the corpse that we had seen thrown into its branches was gone. There was no sign of that woman's face, her crooked limbs, her limp hair swaying like Spanish moss in the breeze. She had been taken, just like Jen.

"They were there," I said, shaken. "I-I saw Jennifer in that tree, and there was an older woman up in those branches, sh-she was split at the waist. I could describe her, I could draw you a picture, I could—"

As I rattled on, Sheriff Jacobs was standing and fishing a cell phone from out of his pocket, dialing a number quickly and turning away from me. He spoke in a hushed tone, but his voice was urgent. Anxious.

"It wasn't just her. There's another. Pamela Richmond, probably." His free hand was rubbing at his forehead. He squinted his eyes shut in distress and pinched the bridge of his nose. "Something may have just moved them. If not, then it's too late. They're a part of it now."

With a heavy, discouraged sigh, he hung up the phone and shoved it back into his pocket. Before he even turned back to me, I tapped my hands against the table in annoyance.

"What's going on?" I demanded. "They're a part of *what?* Listen, I should know what's going on out there, I work there!"

I watched the sheriff sit back down, waiting for my outburst to end. His brow wrinkled with confusion.

"You really don't know?" he asked, dissatisfied. "I thought Frank would have told you everything. Your father was a ranger, a volunteer. He spent time in that tower, same as you. When I saw your name on that application, I assumed—"

"You assumed I was ready for this?" I asked, my heart aching. "I wasn't. I'm *still* not. You know, maybe my father would have told me about all this if he didn't die before he got the chance. He died working for *you.*"

"I realize that," Jacobs said calmly. "And I regret what happened. Frank was a good man—a courageous, stubborn man. Evelyn, I know you're angry and you *should* be angry. So, now that we can finally meet face-to-face, I will answer anything you want to know. We can have the conversation we should have had on day one."

I only had so much energy left for anger. Truly, I wanted to hate this man. A small part of me wanted nothing more than to stomp out of this room and hitchhike my way out of this fucking mountain, but where would I go? What would I do? What would Daniel do?

"Alright," I agreed, sniffing and wiping my face. "You can start by telling me what in God's good name is *wrong* with this place."

The sheriff gave me a nod of understanding and took a deep breath.

"People go missing," he said, "several, sometimes dozens a year, on that mountain. Sometimes their bodies are found and sometimes they aren't, but they never return as themselves. And it's not just people. You see, we hire rangers to collect any dead animals they find and get them out of those woods, but far too often, those rangers don't come back either."

I was silent for a long time, processing his words. "What happens to them?" I asked.

"A variety of things we can't explain," he continued in a hoarse whisper. "People see strange things out here, you know that already. Someone might go for a walk in the woods and say that they saw a rabbit with one human ear, or maybe human hands growing on the end of a tree branch instead of twigs. A few weeks ago, an elderly woman nearly scared her son to death because she tried to coax a deer out of the woods, saying it had her husband's eyes. Her husband collapsed on a woodland trail one month earlier. When we found him, his eyes were *torn out*. Do you understand?"

I felt sick, thinking of those human eyes. I didn't need to imagine it. I had seen it. That bird. That damn, shitty little bird sitting on the fire escape every day ... I started to wonder whose eyes those were after all.

"So things die and mutate together?" I asked, fear and disgust written on my face. My stomach felt sick. "Why?"

The sheriff continued. "We don't know. All we know is that when the fog comes around, it gets worse. People go missing. Those *creatures* you see moving in the mist? They're always devouring one another, always growing in size and adding new parts, turning into amalgamations of dead skin, plants, *anything* they can find. We think the fog is how it travels. It's always trying to get to us, to spread as far as it can. We've been studying it for a century and we're not a step closer to figuring out why our little village is the way that it is, only that sound has been our best weapon against it. This is why we built 104.6."

He leaned closer across the table, and I didn't even try to say a word. I just stared, breathing shakily through parted lips, as he looked me straight in the eyes with an expression that was absolutely dire.

"One thing we do know?" he said. "... So far, we've hired twenty-seven different people to speak over that radio. Twenty-seven Operators watching the tree line, sounding the emergency broadcast, keeping the sound alive. You and Mr. Esperanza? You're Twenty-Eight and Twenty-Nine."

At that moment, I felt like my heart wasn't in my chest anymore. It had sunk so low that I felt every bit of confidence and courage in my body disappear all at once. One thing was bothering me though. One little thing was in my head, and I had been trying to piece it together all the while.

"The people in the village don't know?"

He didn't avoid the question, but he took a good, long moment to answer. Finally, he nodded his head and sank back down into his chair across from me, closing up the folder.

"Some know and some don't. The radio station is a comforting mask," he said. "People trust you. They'll tell you things they wouldn't say to a police officer. And while we're collecting that information, the signal keeps those creatures in the woods where they belong. A few get through from time to time, yes, but no plan is perfect. People around here feel a lot safer when they just think about the music, and that's what we're trying to do: keep everyone calm until we know how to get rid of this problem forever. The rangers, the fire department ... I hired them all to keep this place safe. I hired you, too."

"So it's a cover," I said. It was making more sense to me now, why the station was so high off the ground and why it was in the middle of the forest. It was a watchtower. The broadcast station was our first line of protection and Daniel and I were its guards.

I finally remembered why I knew the sheriff's voice. He was the one to call and tell me that I had been chosen for the job. He was the one who scolded me when the fog rolled in. It was so obvious and I never knew ...

"Why didn't you *tell me* how bad this would get?" I asked with a trembling lip, tears of panic stinging in my eyes. "All this time, you knew what I was getting into and *nobody* said a goddamn thing? You just ... assumed I already knew? What about Daniel, he's not even *from* here!"

The look on the sheriff's face was one of regret and hesitance. "Miss McKinnon, if I told you all of this on your very first day, would you have stayed? Would *anyone* stay?"

I tightened my lips as a tear rolled down my cheek. I angrily wiped it away with the sleeve of my shirt, sniffing loudly. "So you didn't hire me because I was the best for the job, did you?" I asked. "You hired me because I was *desperate* and I had nowhere else to go—no one to look for me if I disappeared."

Finally, I saw a glimmer of kindness in the sheriff's eyes. It was soft and guilty, and I knew right away that he had probably had this conversation many times before.

"It was never my intention to make you feel that way," he said. "Your father was never disposable to us and neither are you. Our Operators are the *blood* of Pinehaven. It's a heavy responsibility to put on just one person, but your father took it with grace and dignity. He took it *willingly*. I knew I could trust that the same loyalty ran through your veins too."

I scoffed with tears in my eyes. "I'm not like him."

That time, Sheriff Jacobs didn't respond.

"What would happen if the broadcast stopped for good? If no one was there?"

He shrugged and gave a heavy sigh, then looked at me with an expression made of steel. "We don't know, and we never want to find out," he answered. "The fog has reached us before and as a result, Pinehaven has been rebuilt more than once. We think, if left unchecked, this problem would keep spreading as far as we let it. You've seen what it does, McKinnon. That married couple? The ones you saw in the forest? The fog took them, and the next time it comes around, we may be seeing Mrs. Richmond a second time."

He stood up from his seat, walking around the table and giving me a heavy pat on the shoulder. I just sat there, my brain gone to mush and my mouth turning dry.

"You'd better get back to your station ... Number Twenty-Eight."

ᴵᴵᴵ·ᴵᴵ·ᴵᴵᴵᴵᴵᴵᴵᴵᴵ·ᴵᴵ·ᴵᴵᴵ

I stayed in a motel that night, but I didn't sleep. I checked in with only the clothes on my back and my phone in my pocket, finally returned to me after they had scrubbed it for any little bit of evidence. They didn't find anything worthwhile, I don't think. When I unlocked the door to room seven at the Heritage Motel, I found peeling walls and a lumpy bed waiting for me. I couldn't really complain. I mean, I lived in a fucking closet.

I took a shower, standing under the hot water for so long that it started to turn cold. Wrapped in a white towel, I sat on the edge of the bed and heard it squeak under my weight with a grating sound that made my teeth hurt. It was late. The sky had been dark for a while, but I still decided to try giving Daniel a call just to let him know that he wouldn't be alone much longer.

He sounded anxious on the phone. Jittery. I guess he had plenty of reasons to be after the last two days, but he just sounded so relieved to have someone to talk to. He didn't tell me what happened, *if* anything happened.

I told him that I wasn't getting arrested and that I'd be back in the morning before sunrise. I had so much to tell him, but I didn't even know where to start. How could I condense, in just a few sentences, that everything we thought we knew about this place was wrong? How could I explain to my coworker that we had accidentally signed ourselves up for a war against the unknown?

I couldn't. So I didn't say anything, not yet. I'd take the night to think it over, to let it settle in my mind before I broke the news. I just hoped that Daniel could get a little rest before dawn, because he'd need it.

"As soon as we get a couple more part-timers, you and I are taking a vacation," he said.

I smirked, picking underneath my fingernails. "That sounds like a great idea."

We sat on the phone for a while, not talking about much. I think Daniel just wanted to hear someone else's voice. I told him about the motel room and how I was already grabbing anything I could steal: little soaps, shampoo, a washcloth no one would miss. This room had the same yellow walls of a dorm I had in college, I said. We compared experiences. I went to school for journalism, he went because he wanted to be an actor. We were polar opposites, him and I. Oil and water.

"You should try to sleep," I said, watching the little finger on the clock strike 'two'. "Take the mattress in the back. Your feet might dangle off the end, but good news: that closet is so small, no demons could fit in there to bite your toes off anyway."

Daniel chuckled. "Joke's on you, maybe I'm into that."

"Well, if I see any toe-biting demons here on the west side of town, I'll send 'em your way," I teased, letting my eyes scan the window across from me. The motel was right against the tree line. Seeing those dark pines and gnarled oak branches made my stomach flip. "I think I'm gonna dry my hair and go to bed. But I'll be up there in a few hours, okay? Hold down the fort for me."

"Consider it held," Daniel said, but there was a sigh of disappointment in his voice. He wanted to go home so badly, I could tell. "Goodnight, Lyn."

"Good morning, Dan."

At 5:45 a.m., I hitched a ride back to the radio station before the sun came up. But before I did, I made one brief stop along the way. In those early hours of dawn, I had the driver wait for me as I quietly made my way up the stairs of the apartment building where Jennifer used to live. It was the same one she kicked me out of, and the same place where her boyfriend Elijah was probably still living without her.

I didn't knock or ring the doorbell, but I did slip a small piece of paper underneath the door. It was the only printed photo I had of Jennifer, carried around in my wallet next to a photo of my parents. And now, it was his.

As the car pulled up to the radio tower and I tipped the driver, it felt as if I had been gone for weeks. It was hard to believe it had only been a couple of days. The lights were on up in the broadcast room—I could see them in the windows, along with a shadow pacing back and forth in the cramped space. Daniel was starting his day early, or perhaps it never ended.

My first hint that something was wrong came in the form of yellow tape that hadn't been there before. The police had been in the forest sometime last night ... but *why*?

When I got to the top, a little breathless from the cold air and the absurd amount of steps, my co-worker was happy to see me. I almost expected him to have his coat on, ready to go home and sleep in his own bed, but he was just sitting at his desk with a mug in his hand and a weary smile on his face.

"Welcome back, boss," he said, pulling out the chair next to him. "So, how was prison? Get any cool tattoos?"

I smirked as I sat down. The chair was slightly warm, probably because of Daniel's habit of using it as a footrest whenever I left it unoccupied.

"Oh yeah, tons of 'em," I said. "Got a big ol' tiger on my back. Oh, and a spider on my left ass cheek. Wanna see?"

"No, thanks," he teased. "I'll take your word for it." All at once, I felt like things were going back to normal already; our weird, creepy little definition of 'normal'.

After a little time settling in and eating bagels for breakfast—getting crumbs everywhere in the process, of course—I finally decided that maybe it was time to start explaining some things to Daniel. And this time, I didn't want to hide anything from him. He had a right to know just as much as I did.

So, I told him everything. I told him about Sheriff Jacobs, about how this tower was somehow connected to the town government, about how many broadcasters had been hired before us and lost to the forest. I told him about how anything that goes in there is destined to come back *changed,* mutated and combined with the other beasts of the forest. It was a lot for him to digest.

"So, the people who hired us ..." Daniel started.

"Not really a network," I finished the idea. "It's some branch of town government, I guess. He called us 'Operators'."

Daniel brushed a few crumbs off his side of the desk, dark eyes distant and lost in thought. "You know, it's obvious when you think about it. I always knew something was weird about our job up here ... the location, the demands, the strict scheduling, the outdated tools. It's not like other radio stations. I just didn't think we were on some kind of monster defense squad."

"Yeah," I said uneasily. "Yeah, I hate it when that happens."

I tried to laugh it off, but it wasn't funny. It was rarely funny. Daniel went quiet for a moment, but I could see the way his gaze stuck to the fire escape. He was thinking about something, remembering something.

"I saw her again," he said. "Your friend? Jennifer? She was here when the fog rolled in."

I could see the goosebumps raise on my arms. For a moment, I stopped breathing. When I looked up at Dan's face, I wanted to believe that it was a sick joke, but the look in his eyes was deadly serious.

"What do you mean?" I asked, voice full of air. "Like, you saw a ghost or—?"

"No," Daniel shook his head, swallowing hard. "I-I saw her body. Her corpse. She came out of the forest, straight-up *Night of the Living Dead*, twitching and stumbling. *Groaning*. She killed Markus."

"Wha—the grocery kid?"

"I tried to help, but she got to him first," Daniel clutched at his chest. "So I ran, and she chased after me like some kind of wild animal. And when the fog disappeared, she must have gone with it. B-but I still felt like she was watching me."

He was staring at the trees. I wondered what he had seen out there, moving around all night in the dark: shadows, eyes, limbs ... things trying to break the boundary. My hair stood on end when I remembered Sheriff Jacobs saying, '*no plan is perfect*'.

"It's just like the sheriff told me," I murmured, words slurred and tired. "Anything that dies out there comes back changed. I don't think that was Jennifer anymore. I hope it wasn't."

We were both silent for a long time, our eyes both stuck on the trees. They were swaying in the wind, a heavy gust brushing through the pine needles and making them shiver. The wind reached us too. I could hear the creak of the stilts beneath us and a rattle in the glass windows. A storm was brewing.

"What happened to them?" Dan's voice was weak. "The other broadcasters ... Did they quit?"

I met his gaze at last, seeing the glistening dread in his eyes and the way his brows crinkled with worry.

"I don't think they quit, Dan."

We didn't say it, but we were both thinking the same thing. How long would we last? Which one of us would be the first to go?

A rumble of thunder made the ceiling tremble. Both of us turned our attention to the window where heavy clouds were rolling in against a gray sky. The furthest trees were swaying violently back and forth in a gust that hadn't reached us yet. A flash of lightning cracked over Pinehaven, a wall of rain appearing up the mountainside. It was coming our way.

And through the drafty walls of our little sanctuary on stilts, I could hear something other than thunder: a deep bellow, like the roar of an angry god. Something in the forest was waking up.

"Lyn? This place has a generator, doesn't it?" Daniel asked as the lights began to flicker for the first time. My heart stopped as the radio skipped to static for just a split second, rain pattering on the windows quietly at first and then loudly as the storm rushed in.

"Yes," I said coldly.

"Where is it?"

I frowned, giving him an apologetic look.

"Out there."

CHAPTER ELEVEN: THE AMALGAMATE
Evelyn

The forest was alive.

Even without the fog, we could see the way the pines shivered, moving in waves as gust after gust of wind blew in from the north. It was a cold, bitter air that made the windows tremble and my bones ache. I won't beat around the bush. We were scared. Daniel had seen enough to know that we wouldn't be safe if this got any worse. As the rain poured down and the cables swayed from side to side off the edge of the tower, we were afraid for not only our safety but everyone else's.

This tower was keeping the town alive somehow. *We* were keeping the town alive. It's almost funny. An alcoholic and a failed actor. Who knew?

"It's not too bad yet," Daniel said as he stood near the window. While I was watching our computer screens, listening to Bruce Springsteen through the speakers, he was pacing back and forth nervously with his eyes stuck on the tree line. "The lightning is still up in the mountains. It might pass us, I can't tell yet."

I curled my legs up, sitting cross-legged in my rolling chair and fidgeting with my braid.

"Those dark clouds don't give me any confidence," I said. "How's the town look?"

I could see the way his face turned, his eyes squinting. He was looking over the tree line and off into the distance, a mile away where the village of Pinehaven was sitting quietly between the mountains.

"Fine," he said. "Power is on. Maybe we should sound an alert, just in case?"

I was thinking the same thing. As I slipped my headphones back on, Daniel joined me at his side of the desk, adjusting his microphone while I counted off before going live with a brief announcement. 3 ... 2 ... 1 ...

"This is Evelyn at 104.6 FM. A heavy storm is on the way, bringing in some cold air from the north with high winds and a chance of flooding."

"It's a good afternoon to stay indoors and avoid the roads." Daniel took over, squinting at his screen as he pulled up a full weather forecast. "Expect low visibility, lightning, and make sure you've got your generators on hand in case of emergencies. We'll be keeping Pinehaven up to date every hour with more information."

The microphones were off. The bumper led into the next track of music, playing softly through our headphones until I chose to set mine down on the edge of the desk. I sat back in my chair limply, breathing out a heavy sigh as I watched those dark clouds move closer.

"You would've made a good weather man," I told Dan. "You've got the voice for it."

A moment passed, and my companion was oddly quiet. Finally, he cracked a little smile and exhaled heavily through his nose. "You wanna know what I did before this?" he asked. I knew he'd tell me anyway, but I still nodded. "After I graduated with a master's degree from art school—*a master's degree*—the only acting job I could get was recording a commercial for some plumbing service. I recorded some lines in a studio, talking about toilets for twenty takes, putting on the stupidest voices. And you know the worst part?"

He laughed, looking over at me with this crooked, dumb smile. I could see a hint of disappointment in those eyes, though.

"They didn't even pick mine," he said. "I got paid for it, sure. Then I heard the commercial on the radio while I was in my car and it was someone else completely. And I sat there and I thought, 'are you really gonna let yourself get *upset* that you weren't chosen as the voice of shit-clogged toilets'?"

That actually made me laugh, even if it was a bittersweet moment. I shrugged my shoulders, passing Daniel a glance that was both nonchalant and a little apologetic.

"Figures you'd get fucked by the radio *twice,*" I gestured to the room around us and Daniel gave a quick, sharp laugh.

"If I knew it'd be like this, maybe I would have stuck to toilets," he said. "You know, that's part of the reason why I came here ... They always say, once you get a foot in the door, that's all it takes. I was so relieved when I got the call. After years and years of rejection, someone was finally taking a chance on me instead of passing me up for someone else. They always said I didn't have the right look, or I didn't have the voice, the right body, *whatever.* And here I was, thinking being a radio DJ would be *easy.*"

"You and me both, my good man ..." I crossed my arms, tearing my eyes away from the tree line. "If it's any consolation, you're a really, *really* good radio DJ."

He gave me a sad smile, thankful in his own subtle way. I turned back to the window, my gaze stuck on the storm. While the music played softly through our headphones and the wind whistled between rickety wooden walls, I could feel Daniel's eyes on me. He didn't say anything for a while, as if afraid to ask until he finally made up his mind.

"What about you?" he asked softly. "What did you do before this?"

It wasn't a big question. It wasn't an *unusual* question, either. And still, I found it so difficult to answer. How far back did he want me to go? I could tell him about living with my mom, the little retail jobs I had here and there, or the time spent writing articles that went nowhere and receiving enough rejection letters to wallpaper my old apartment.

But, none of that mattered. None of that led me *here.*

"I was in rehab," I said honestly, "for a second time. It was a short stay, not as long as the first. The first time it was Jennifer's idea. I didn't wanna go, but I almost died in the bathtub and she gave me an ultimatum: either get help or get out. You know, I don't even think I did it on *purpose.* I felt like ass and I wanted to take a bath, but I was so shitfaced that I passed out almost the second I got in. Jennifer found me after I flipped face-down. She thought I died. When the police got there, they said it was a suicide. Then one of them managed to get my heart started again and they found that I was *still* just as hammered as I was when I went in."

I laughed but Daniel didn't. I knew it wasn't funny, but I was so desperate to grab at straws just to find a reason to take it lightly. But when I looked over at my coworker and saw the severity of the frown on his face, my smile disappeared. Suddenly, I regretted everything I said, like a child being scolded by a parent.

"How long have you been sober?" Dan asked.

I felt a tightness in my throat and the breath I took in next was shaky and rough. When the facts were all laid out on the table, it was hard not to feel pathetic. It was hard not to feel ashamed.

"My ... my first sober day was that day I came into work," I admitted. I had to bite my bottom lip to keep from letting it tremble. You know, putting it into perspective felt humiliating, reminding me of just how fresh this really was. "The only reason I'm not drunk right now is because the goddamn grocery guy wouldn't bring me anything but bottled water and cheap, shitty iced tea."

That time, we both laughed, but it wasn't happy. It didn't last, either. In a split second, my amusement turned to tears and I unwillingly felt a sob escape me, both of my hands covering my face as if hiding could make that regret go away. With eyes squeezed shut, I could only hear the sound of chair wheels squeaking and a gentle, quiet shush from the man sitting next to me. I felt Dan's hand resting between my shoulders, but he didn't say anything at first. He didn't move. He just stayed with me until I uncovered my face.

"You have to start somewhere," he finally said. "I'm really proud of you, Lyn."

"I'm glad someone is."

I refused to let myself cry out loud. Those feelings were pushed back down as my eyes returned to the stormy sky and the mist at the top of the mountain ridge. I watched it move and swirl, making lively and erratic shapes against a dark horizon as it waited eagerly to make its move. We were so close to the tree line. Too close.

A familiar pair of eyes stared back at us then. Sitting on the fire escape, balancing on one of the metal rails, was that damn bird again. I looked at it closer this time. Its eyes were hazel. The more I looked at it, I found myself wondering less about where it came from

124

and more about who those eyes used to belong to.

"You think we'll end up like that one day?" I asked with a little scoff, wondering what sort of strange life that stupid bird must live. "Trapped in the body of a little forest animal that stole our parts?"

"I hope not," Daniel said, pointing to his own face. He gave a big smile, dimples and all. "A handsome mug like this? It'd be a crime."

He was trying to lighten the mood and it worked, but the wide-eyed fear was still there. I could see it in the way his brow muscles formed a line on his forehead and the way his fingers never stopped trembling. It was all fun and games, talking about the abominations in the forest, until we heard that wind again. It was picking up now, and I was torn between going outside to get the generator running or staying up here where it was safe. Struggling to find the motivation to move, I found myself staring at that bird again. It stared back.

"I've been meaning to ask you something," Daniel said quietly, breaking my concentration. "What did you see?"

I didn't process his words at first. When I did, I glanced at him from the corner of my eyes and voiced the tiniest, 'hm?'

"At the graduation party," he continued. "... You were in the woods. You saw something, didn't you?"

That specific set of words made my blood run cold immediately, like hearing something foul and forbidden. The pain I felt in my chest was hard and sudden. It stole my breath away and it made the hair stand up on my arms as if the icy wind from outside had found its way in.

"H-how do you know about that?" I asked, my voice frail.

Daniel hesitated, biting his lip.

"I saw the photos," he finally admitted, "on your computer? The ones your friends posted. I-I shouldn't have looked but—"

"No, you *shouldn't have,*" I spoke sternly, but my voice betrayed me with a pathetic crack. "Goddammit, Dan, I can't even leave for a day or two without you digging around in my shit?"

"I was just worried," he said, breathless and guilty. "I'm sorry. I-it was just open and when I saw those photos, I ... I knew something had happened. You don't have to tell me if you don't

125

want to, it's okay."

It was too late, really. Now those memories were coming back, creeping into the forefront of my brain where they had long been banished. I almost got rid of them, you know. For so long, they were hidden away in a little box somewhere in the back of my head, but Pandora here had to find the key. I almost wished he didn't mean well, because that meant I could stay angry.

"I forgot about the forest when I left," I said, a grimace on my face. I refused to look at Daniel and stared down at my own hands instead—dry fingers, dirty cracked nails, cuts and scrapes. "I was still a kid when my dad died and mom remarried. She hated this place and wanted to start over somewhere new, so we moved to the other side of the mountain. Then Jenny and I came back the week of graduation to go to some party with people we used to know as kids. We all knew something was wrong with the forest, but we went anyway."

Bits and pieces were still missing from my memory, but I was putting them together between pauses and vacant glances at the misty mountainside. If I tried really hard, I could remember the fog drills at school, the way my mom would always keep the radio on, the way she told me to never look out the windows at night. Pinehaven was *always* creepy, but she sheltered me from it then ...

"It was loud and I was overwhelmed. Everyone was acting like assholes, so I wandered off, just far enough away where I could still see the bonfire through the trees. I heard something. I-it was a growl at first, but the more I think about it, the more I can remember this *voice* underneath it ... A low, gravely, painful groan. An animal stepped out of the bushes and I thought for sure it was a-a cougar or a mountain lion, but its *face*. Oh God, it had this *face*. Eyes like a wild cat, but the nose and mouth were ... human."

I could still see it so clearly. My face was stuck in a grimace of pain as I recalled every detail: the wrinkles from wide smiles, bushy red eyebrows, and so many freckles. I stopped to catch my breath, my nose stuffed.

"H-he looked at me and I saw his mouth move, trying to say something, but he couldn't get it out. He just m-made this terrible wheezing sound, like it hurt to breathe. He sounded as if he was suffering, a-and it took everything he had just to say a word. So, I-I ran back to the party and I drank and I drank and I fucking *drank* until I couldn't remember that thing's face anymore. Then I'd get sober and I'd think of him again. The cycle worked for a while, but now?" I wiped my nose on my sleeve, wishing I could make myself two inches tall. "N-now, all it took was thinking about it once for that face to be stuck in my head again."

Dan gave me a frown of guilt, his hand going to my back yet again. He rubbed between my shoulders in slow circles as I furiously wiped tears from my face with the edge of my sleeve, but he never got a chance to speak. As I heard his lips part and he voiced a small, sharp intake of breath, we were both taken aback by the buzz of a faulty light.

The bulb hanging from the ceiling flickered. We heard static from the radio for only an instant before the music resumed, and each time the signal faltered, I noticed Daniel flinch and reach for his hearing aid. There was electricity in the air. I could feel it making the edges of my hair bristle.

"You okay?" I asked, noticing the way Daniel rubbed below his ear.

"Yeah, it's fine," he said, stretching out his jaw. "Just a bad ringing sound is all."

It could have been the weather. It could have been the radio signal. I was beginning to think it was a mixture of both as I squinted into the horizon, staring through the lookout window at a growing layer of fog that was collecting at the top of the mountain. It was swirling, undulating, *moving* ... It was coming for us.

"It's still far away," Daniel said, but his chest was heaving with quick, anxious breaths. "We ... we should run the emergency broadcast before it gets here, just in case."

I knew what he meant by *'just in case'*. A strong wind whipped past, rattling the walls of our structure and making the wooden floorboards whine beneath our feet. I felt unsteady as if the old stilts holding us up would give in and we'd crash into the trees below. The rumble in the floor reminded me of a deep, rattling breath before the building settled back into place. I thought about the distance between us and the ground and I couldn't decide what would be worse: the long drop or being exposed to the open woods if we somehow survived the fall.

Daniel rushed to the desk, microphone pulled toward his face as he recited a crackling emergency message over the air. I busied myself by rummaging around in the little closet near the staircase entrance, looking for a flashlight and the keys to the generator shed. All of these supplies made more sense to me now: backpacks, flares, first aid kits, fire starters ... I imagined the people who came before us being seasoned rangers and survivalists, and that thought made it all the more upsetting when I remembered they were gone.

If they couldn't make it, how could we?

While knocking things out of my way in search of the keys, I found a pack of walkie-talkies. They were old and worn, but they still had batteries. I turned one on and found that it buzzed to life.

When Daniel was done with his announcement, he joined me next to the closet and began sifting through boxes while I shoved them out of the way.

"What are we looking for?" he asked.

"The keys to the shed," I told him with a heavy, disgruntled sigh. "We gotta get the generator ready in case we lose power. I'll pull it out, get it plugged in. Shouldn't take me too long. *Ah!* Here it is ..." I found a little tin box, and pulled it open to find a ring of old, ruddy-looking keys. One of them had to go to the shed.

Dan spotted the walkie-talkies sitting on the floor, set off to the side. He picked one up, and I could see the gears turning in his head as he thought the exact same thing I was thinking: one of us would have to go out there. *Only* one of us.

We couldn't risk both of our lives. The station needed someone to take over the responsibility.

"Music going?" I asked, standing up and curling my fingers around the ring of keys.

Daniel nodded.

"It's going," he said, but there was a distinct lack of confidence in his voice. The lights flickered overhead, the wind still rattled the windows and the fragile walls. Every now and again, I would hear a crackle of static from one of our abandoned pairs of headphones.

128

The radio was running *now,* but for how long?

The fog, meanwhile, had moved. It bounded through the trees and engulfed the entire woodland, eventually stopping to rest at the tree line. I had never seen it *pause* like this before, almost as if it waited for permission to cross the boundary. It was waiting for the radio to die. And when it did, that wild and terrible world would finally be free to infect the town and everything beyond it. All it took was one wire to snap, one cord to break. Then every ounce of security we had would come crashing down.

I could see it in my mind's eye already. Those shapes in the fog—hundreds of eyes, mismatched arms, dead and rotting bodies— eager to crawl out of the forest and rip us to pieces. I could already see them at the forest's edge. There were dark shapes hidden in the mist, some large and some small, but all of them pacing back and forth impatiently.

We had to make a split decision. Any moment now, we could be plunged into a dark, thick silence and it would be too late.

"Let me see the keys," Daniel said, reaching out and grabbing them from my hand before I could even react. A flash of lightning made us both flinch. "I'll let you know when I'm about to plug the generator in."

"No," I said flatly, standing up on my toes. I swatted at the keys, but Daniel held them just out of my reach like the tall, stupid bastard that he was.

"You need to stay in here so you can turn everything back on if the power goes out," he argued with me.

"I said *no,*" I argued back, an annoyed frown pulling at the edges of my lips and a sharp glare in my eyes. "Dan, you've already gotten hurt once. I didn't help you then, and I didn't—" my voice broke. "I-I didn't save Jenny either. Please, let me do *this.*"

We stared at one another for almost too long, the lights flickering above our heads. The radio crackled, and through the static, I could hear it again: 'Unchained Melody', playing slightly distorted and out of key. The sound of those first few words was starting to make my spine tingle every time.

Finally, Daniel dropped his arm to his side. He looked at my outstretched hand, palm exposed, and placed the ring of keys gently in the center. His hand cupped over mine for a brief moment, giving it a supportive and determined squeeze.

Daniel, if you're reading this, you snooping piece of shit: *thank you.*

The door took a heavy push. I burst through with my shoulder, taking loud and quick steps down the clanging metal stairs that circled round and round like a spiral underneath the building. My eyes were following a series of cords, connecting one after the other in different colored extensions that snaked down the scaffolding.

The rain was already soaking my hair and my clothes even underneath the safety of the tower. Violent winds from the north pushed against the old, trembling wood and rocked me from side to side. As I grabbed hold of the railing, recalling the pain of falling chest-first onto the fire escape, I thought about the distance between the tower and the generator. How heavy *was* this thing? The wall of fog was waiting just beyond the shed, swirling and rolling over itself as if hitting an invisible forcefield. I remembered how fast it moved.

I wondered if it knew I was there.

When I stumbled to the bottom of the stairs, I reached for the extension cord and pulled it along with me, feet hitting the wet and muddy soil. The cold chill shocked my ankles as deep puddles soaked the frayed ends of my jeans. It was a horrible view. The mist reached the tops of the tallest trees, and the sound that came from within the fog was maddening to hear. The amalgamates were suffering inside of themselves, parasites eating off of one another and groaning in constant, agonizing pain. The ones who didn't cry out in anguish were voicing aggressive growls or rattling breaths as they paced back and forth, hungrily searching for another living thing to tear apart and add to their collection of stolen pieces.

As I rushed to the shed, slipping in the mud on my way, my flashlight caught sight of milky white eyes within the fog. Sometimes, I could see the slick shine of rain-soaked fur and rotten skin, or the glint of gnashing teeth.

My hands began to shake as I fumbled with the keys, rattling the old rusted padlock. The first key didn't work, the second one was a bust. As I struggled with the third, my fingers cold and shivering,

I watched the lights flicker in the tower above. The third key wasn't right either.

I heard a crackle of noise from the walkie-talkie. It was Dan's voice, but he was distorted and hard to hear. I held it up to my face, trying to speak as loudly and as clearly as I could.

"Say that again," I told him.

"Did you get in yet?" he asked. I could hear the panic in his voice. "The lights are acting up. Th-the sink is making noise, the radio's been playing *backward,* I-I think it's—"

"Dan, calm down," I snapped, my fear turning to aggression. "I'm at the shed now, j-just chill the fuck out. I've got it—"

As it happened, there was plenty of reason *not* to chill the fuck out. As I spoke, a bright flash lit up the clearing and a deafening crack made my ears sting, followed by an eerie electric buzz. Lightning had struck the radio mast, and I watched as sparks flew and cords snapped. In an instant, everything went dark. The lights were out, the red flicker from the tower had turned black, and a cold, wriggling layer of mist was forming at my feet.

The fourth key was the one. I jammed it into the padlock, my hands struggling to crack apart the old, rusted metal pieces. I made the grave mistake of looking to my left, seeing a woman's face staring up at me with dead, pale blue eyes. She was dragging herself by the arms, her legs missing and her spine ending in curls of roots that formed a heavy, twisted tail of exposed nerves and rotten muscle tissue. A second head was starting to grow out of her shoulder, warped and malformed.

The worst part of it all was how pleadingly she wailed, almost as if the human part of her was begging for a way out. Her suffering didn't pull on my heartstrings, not when her hands swiped toward me with filthy, boney fingers looking to rip at my flesh. I knew that wide, open mouth and that thin, gray hair. The last time I saw Pamela Richmond, she was draped over the branch of a tree and sliced in half.

It seemed as if she had crawled her way down, after all.

I tore the door open and slammed it behind me with a loud crack. The wood was weak, splintered, and thin. Within seconds, I could hear the scratch of nails and the pounding of weight from the other side. Underneath the door, the mist was beginning to seep in, swirling around my ankles. I tugged at the extension cord and held it tightly as I dragged it to the generator, hoping and praying that the old thing still worked.

My flashlight scanned the walls, the floors, and a solitary window that was cracked in one corner. Outside of my frail sanctuary, strange and rotten figures were pressed against the glass. Heavy footsteps shook the ground. I could see the face of a man, his head half-encased in tree bark, insects burrowing inside of the moss-covered wood and maggots under his eyelids. When he opened his mouth to scream, he spat living flies from his throat. Within seconds, however, he was gone. In a flurry of fur, blood, and bone, he was ripped away from the glass by the claws of something much larger. He shrieked as he disappeared into the fog, and what followed was the stomach-turning sound of cracking bone and tearing flesh.

My hands were shaking as I tore open the cap to the generator and searched for a can of fuel in the dark. I spilled some of it on my pants and my jacket, shivering from head to toe. I managed to get most of it into the machine, but I wasn't alone.

I heard heavy grunts and stomps of feet, hooves digging into the dirt. I could hear a woman shriek, but the sound of her voice was mixed with an almost avian call. The cry she gave was pained and tortured, and all at once, it was gone. Those heavy steps came again, one after another until they began to shake the floor beneath my feet. The mist was thicker now. The forest was quieter. When I glanced at the window, everything had *scattered* ... until I spotted a glimpse of bloodied brown fur, mixed with rot and moss. Something large was circling, scraping claws against the side of the shed.

It knew I was in here. It knew I couldn't stay in here forever.

I didn't have time to drag the generator out into the clearing. If this shed caught on fire, it caught on fire. I flipped the switch, preparing to pull the rope that would bring the whole thing to life. Walkie-talkie up to my lips, I called out for Daniel in a trembling, broken voice.

"Dan? Are you there?" I felt my heart pounding as moments

passed and he didn't answer. "Dan!"

"I'm here," he finally responded. "Th-there's something on the fire escape. Dead things. P-people, I think, but they're—"

"I know," I interrupted, my pulse racing out of control, "I'm about to get the generator going, but you have to switch everything off first or it's gonna overload itself. And—" As I spoke, an enormous thump made the ceiling shake. Something huge and heavy was on the roof, hooves pounding and sending bits of dust falling onto my head. "A-and make it *quick.*"

Daniel said nothing, and I could only hope he was doing as I said. The four walls of the shed were trembling under the weight of the beast above me. I could hear the thing's horrible, tremendous voice. It gave a spine-chilling roar and cracked through the roof with a clawed hand, beginning to swipe at the air above my head. I flattened myself against the floor, taking in a glimpse of this *thing*. It was massive, covered in rotten, peeling flesh and patches of matted fur. Its eyes—six of them, at least—were pale, flecked with jaundiced yellow, and peering through gaps in the ceiling. Enormous, twisting antlers clacked against the wood as it pounded its head on the roof, trying to break through. And its hands ... those long, clawed fingers reminded me of a spider's limbs.

All at once, I remembered my first time stuck in the fog. I remembered standing blind, feeling the sharp tips of long, curved fingers scraping the back of my neck and tangling in my hair.

I could smell it. From the end of its elk-like snout, the amalgamated beast let out a rattling breath that carried the scent of blood and death. Endless hunger. A broken and twisted body filled with rot and decay. As the beast continued to swipe at me, desperate and starving, I heard a crackle from the walkie-talkie.

"I found the breaker," Daniel said, panting for breath.

I didn't waste any time. I pulled the rope, hearing the generator wheeze as it struggled to start. With each useless pull, my heart sank further and further, until finally—

"I got it!" I yelled into the walkie-talkie, the generator finally rumbling to life. It jumped and sputtered, rattling dangerously a few times before I jammed the extension cord into the plug. "Dan, flip the switch and get the radio started. *Now!"*

Another crack above my head, another set of claws swiping through the air. Dust and dirt and splinters of wood fell from the ceiling and into my hair, broken pieces scattered across the floor. The window beside me shattered as rotten, withered hands reached in and began to paw desperately for something to grab. Even the shards of glass sticking into their arms didn't stop them from reaching for me; some of them were human hands, some had extra fingers, some weren't human at all.

I pressed my back against the wall, knowing that even if I didn't survive in this collapsing hunk of old, rotten wood, maybe the tower would still stand. Maybe Daniel had a chance.

I heard it before I saw it: the lights buzzed to life, the radio tower blinking red in the darkness and the dirty yellow glow of the tower suddenly shining down from above. Streams of light flooded through the cracks in the walls as if the sun had come out in an instant. That's when I heard my device crackle again, Dan's voice speaking hurriedly on the other side.

"I can't get the radio started," he said with shivering terror. "Th-there's not enough power to run it! It won't come back on!"

It seemed like a failure at first. This was how it all ended, with him stuck in a 50-foot death trap and me about to be eaten alive by a giant made of mismatched corpses. But then I remembered that stupid, laminated piece of paper I had been staring at on the edge of the desk since my very first day.

Rule #4: If the signal is down, activate The Bell.

My only regret was that Daniel would get to push the button before I did.

"Dan, see that button on the wall? The one behind the case?" I shouted sternly. "Push it. Don't hesitate, *just push it!*"

I could hear him on the other end, fiddling with the case before he did exactly as I said. The next thing I heard was surprising.

Nothing. I didn't hear a single goddamn thing. No siren blared, no great and terrible horn echoed through the mountain-side. Moments later, Daniel let out a pained yell. A small, mechanical whine and a clatter followed as if something had been thrown at his feet.

The creatures outside didn't disappear. Rather, they became noisy and agitated in their pain, collapsing and dragging themselves along the ground. One of the faces at the window let out a scream of agony, its once-human ears bursting in a spray of dark, rotten blood. They gave up their pursuit of violence one at a time, the hulking beast on the roof being the last to tear itself away.

Those six pale eyes disappeared and antlers scraped the wall of the half-collapsed shed, and finally, I could see a glimpse of the stormy sky above. The fog was lifting. The Amalgamate was retreating back to the forest.

Something bothered them. A drone, perhaps too high or too low for my ears to hear, drove them off with cries of anguish and tortured shrieks. But even those hair-raising sounds soon became quiet and distant. I laid down on the floor, staring up at the caved-in ceiling and watching the mist sink away. My heart was still pounding. My lungs were on fire. But the moment I saw the pale light of the moon peering behind a storm cloud and the red blink of the radio tower against a black sky, I felt the relief of a life spared.

It took all the energy I had to get up off the floor and out into the cold air again. When I tell you that the fresh air tasted different, I mean it. I took a deep, freezing breath, rain still pouring down and soaking my hair and my clothes. It was the greatest feeling in the world. And in the dark of the storm, I saw only the briefest glimpse of a blood-stained hoof disappearing into the tree line with a heavy, ground-shaking stomp.

Daniel had propped open the fire escape. While I took slow, aching steps across the muddy clearing, he was already racing down the stairs, tripping over his long, stupid legs on the way down. The first thing he did was pull me into a sudden hug, lifting me several inches off the ground with a force that could have snapped my ribs.

"Lyn," he said breathlessly. "You smell like gasoline."

No profound words. No wisdom, no thoughtfulness. And you know what? I think I preferred it that way.

Daniel didn't go home that night. We could see the emergency lights from town and we could hear the police sirens. I think Daniel knew that things would be bad—I didn't blame him for not wanting to see it for himself.

The next day, the sink stopped crying altogether. We got lots of calls, lots of reports about missing people, and complaints about dead birds in peoples' yards. One man called in to describe hoof prints on his property that were the size of dinner plates. Things only got weirder from there. It rained *pebbles* after the storm, and I told Daniel I was pissed off that he didn't collect any for me like a baby otter.

We're starting to think that things will always be unpredictable up here at 104.6 FM. There will always be a story to tell, but right now, our main focus is avoiding the same fate as Operators one through twenty-seven.

And in case you're still wondering, that bird made it through the storm too. He's still out there, pecking at the window and shrieking at me from the other side of the glass. Daniel has decided to name him Bartholomew.

I fucking hate Bartholomew.

CHAPTER TWELVE: AFTERMATH
Finn

This wasn't the first time that a storm had rocked Pinehaven into disrepair. Years ago when I was a much younger man, I remembered a snowstorm so terrible and so devastating that the hospital around the mountain was filled shoulder-to-shoulder with injured villagers. They were all in a panic, babbling about monsters from the woods and loved ones who had been torn to pieces.

We lost our Operator then. I still remember him: brand new guy, used to be a police officer, good head on his shoulders. He took the job eagerly, expecting it to be easier than working forest duty with me. He only lasted four days in the tower. We found him in a snowbank three days later. All four limbs were torn off and his headphones were still on.

It was right after Halloween when we did the final count. Seven people had gone missing from Pinehaven on the night of the storm. Driving around the village was like witnessing an image of grief itself—people were silent, families were hanging up posters, and there were candles and vigils placed in front of their homes. But all of that paled in comparison to the horror of the first morning.

McKinnon and Esperanza didn't see it, thankfully. When the sun rose on the 1st of November, there were trails of blood on the road and doors hanging off their hinges. I was in a police cruiser when it all happened, circling the perimeter of Pinehaven and doing my best to keep people in their homes. But when the fog swallowed us all, there was little to do but keep my pistol loaded and pray that I hit the right target.

When it was all over, we got more calls in one morning than we had gotten in months.

A young woman called the station in hysterics, screaming and crying in total distress. Her sister had gone out that night to grab a pack of cigarettes from the gas station. When the fog crept back up the mountain, the caller stepped out her door and found her sister's torso draped over the fence. Her bottom half was missing completely, but her head was found a block away in someone else's yard.

A man two streets down didn't have any missing family members, but his property was no stranger to death. He found two dozen dead birds surrounding his house, all of them near the windows and with broken, crooked necks. Their tiny, brittle bones were sticking out and their spines were shattered as if they hit the glass at full speed. Two of our forest rangers were dispatched to clean up the mess, and when they did, they found that all of the birds were malformed. One had four legs, another had a third eye on the top of its head. One had a human mouth full of baby teeth.

Just before I left after a twelve-hour shift, I answered one last call. A young man, fresh out of college, told me that his mother lives in Pinehaven and called him up during the storm.

"She was standing at the door," he said over the line, "and I could hear the thunder and the rain. She told me, 'your sister's come home. She's standing by the gate'. Emily went missing on a hike three years ago, but I thought maybe—just *maybe*—she actually found her way home! Right? So I drove all the way back around the mountain. I'm here now at my mom's house, but she's not here. Neither of them are. But the door's wide open and there's blood on the carpet. Handprints on the ceiling, the-they're *everywhere*. And hoof prints ..."

Nancy and I went out to the house. We never found the missing lady and we never found her daughter, but we did find a human tongue on the floor. You never realize just how long a tongue is until you see the whole thing, ripped out in its entirety. It's still being examined, but I can hazard a guess as to who it used to belong to.

The forest is growing. It's *changing*. Almost every day, there's a new oddity, a new sighting of something unexplained, a new tragedy that Pinehaven is all too accustomed to. We're losing people so often that I'm starting to think a majority of our population lives between the pines.

I knew I wouldn't sleep well after the storm. When I went back home to my family's old farmhouse, there was a shift in the wind that didn't sit right with me. It murmured through the leaves of my grandfather's apple trees, one of the fruits falling loose and rolling into the long grass. The hay field across the road was rippling in deep waves and the dogs were howling, agitated by something I couldn't see.

This place held a lot of memories, stories of my parents and grandparents carved into the chipped paint and the old barn doors. I couldn't find it in my heart to leave it, but sitting so close to the tree line was an endless nightmare. I knew that even if I couldn't see what was lurking in the dark beyond those trees, they could probably see me just fine.

"Alright, settle down, old girl," I reached to pat the head of a German Shepherd. Her name's Ripley. Her brother, Sergeant, was pacing back and forth at the fence and baring his teeth toward the woods, snarling with his ears lying flat. Last time he growled like that, drool dripping from his fangs and lips pulled back, he was having a proper Wild West stand-off with a young black bear. This was different.

I could see something moving out there. When I blinked into the gloom, I could barely make out the shape of something dangling from the tree. It looked like a trio of legs, gray and rotten, swaying ever-so-slightly in the breeze. They were thin and petite, toes pointed to the ground, all of them converging into one body at the top. It wasn't a human body, I don't think. It was hard to tell in the dark. But I heard whispers, soft and hoarse, paired with the glow of at least a dozen white eyes, all blinking at different times.

Whatever it was, my dogs didn't like it. I liked to think they were a pretty good judge of character.

I stayed up late, sitting in an armchair near the wood stove, tossing bits of kindling in and thinking about the nights my grandpa would sit in this very same spot and pluck the strings of his guitar. I thought about my mother, reciting old stories about the forest that her Cherokee parents used to tell her. The dogs settled down and decided to fall asleep on the rug near my feet.

I would doze a little now and again, but something always woke me up: the wind and rain, the cry of an animal, the sound of someone whistling outside my house. I didn't investigate. I knew better. In the light of early morning, I stepped outside to see an empty tree line and a yard littered with tiny pebbles. They were all over the roof, too, as if they had just fallen from the sky. Folks around here would call that downright 'biblical'.

···||┃··|┃|┃┃|┃|··┃|···

I didn't want to go back to work. I didn't want to hear more stories, more tragedy, more misfortunes that I would have to go investigate. But as soon as I got there, my day was already planned for me.

"Finn," the sheriff pointed me out as soon as I arrived, carrying a folder under one arm. "I've got something for you. I'm gonna need you to go to the west side of town, talk to a family that lives over by the doctor's office. Know the one?"

"Yeah, I know it," I told him, taking the folder from his hands. My rough, calloused fingertips flipped through the pages. "What's goin' on over there?"

Sheriff Jacobs shook his head regretfully. "Young boy just went missing. Eight years old. Still don't know if it's a human problem or a *wilderness* problem, but we've been seeing way too many of these lately. I need you to go talk to the parents, see what they have to say."

"Damn, another missing kid?" I got to a black and white poster of the child's face. He was missing one of his front teeth. His name was Aiden. I could remember seeing a few of these posters plastered around town already, stapled to telephone poles and taped to windows. "I'll see what I can do. You know I'm not a people person, though."

I offered the tiniest smirk, but the sheriff just nodded knowingly, eyebrows raised.

"I know that," he said, "but if I'm being honest with you,

I just want you to get away from the phones for a while. Get away from your desk. You need it."

I wasn't sure which was worse, honestly. Chasing after stories and hearing call after call from panicked villagers was no walk in the park, but missing kids? The sheriff was right. This *had* been happening way too goddamn often.

"Yeah, I'll take care of it," I said, not even bothering to sit down. "Want me to ask Nancy to come with?"

The sheriff's face went grim for a brief moment, his heavy, square jaw becoming tense. He shook his head. "No, no, she's taking a little time off. My idea. The storm was a big shock for her."

It was her first one. It made sense. Briefly, I wondered if I'd ever see her again, or if she'd follow in the footsteps of the last two officers who just didn't know how to handle this place. Could you blame them?

When I arrived at the home of Aiden's parents, Nathan and Lydia Price were waiting on the couch already. Lydia was just hanging up the phone, saying very tired goodbyes to a friend while her husband answered the door. Their faces looked like ones I had seen many times: weary and depleted, older in heartbreak than in years.

They offered me iced tea. I refused it politely and sat down on the other side of the living room set, a notepad on my lap.

"When exactly did you realize that Aiden was gone?" I asked, watching Mr. and Mrs. Price share a careful glance and squeeze one another's hands gently.

"Middle of the night," Nathan said. "He went to bed without a fuss, asked me to leave the door cracked a little and his nightlight was on. H-he's still a little afraid of the dark. I settled him in early because he had school in the morning." Mr. Price squeezed his eyes shut and steadied himself with a deep, full breath. "At about three o'clock, I stepped into the hall and noticed his light wasn't on anymore. A cold chill came from his room. That's when I saw the window was open and he was gone."

"Any sign of force?" I asked.

The mother, Lydia, shook her head. "No," she sounded defeated. "No, the screen wasn't cut, there was no damage ... We didn't even hear a thing."

"*You* didn't," Nathan suddenly spoke with a venomous tone of voice, his fist clenched. "I've heard the whispering ... I've heard Aiden talking to someone in the woods—whoever was out there *took* our son. And you said I was being paranoid."

I pointed my pen between the two of them.

"What about the woods?" I asked. "Was your son playing out there?"

"No. Well, yes, sort of," Lydia said, exasperated. "Aiden would play near the trees, but we didn't want him going any further than that. It's so dark in there. Recently, we've heard him ... talking to someone or something right at the edge. I'm convinced it was just an imaginary friend or maybe he was talking to a little critter he saw in the grass."

Nathan was shaking his head more violently now, grumbling in frustration.

"No, it wasn't that," he said. "You know *damn well* it wasn't that. Aiden's friends at school have seen it, those missing kids saw it, and now our *son* has seen it too—that monster in the woods."

Lydia's breath hitched and I could see goosebumps form on her arms. She went quiet, tightening her lips as her eyes blinked away the mist of fresh tears.

"Tell me more about the monster in the woods," I said, my pen ignored. I wasn't taking notes any longer. This story was starting to sound familiar to me, matching up with tales I had heard from other children in the area.

Mr. and Mrs. Price shared a hesitant glance before Nathan finally spoke, voice trembling behind a shivering, sharp breath.

"The man in the wooden mask," he said slowly. "Other children on the playground have seen him. Aiden's friends were gossiping about him, like an urban legend. Some ... big man with roots around his head, standing between the trees, gesturing for the children to walk with him. Aiden himself was afraid he'd see him one day."

I had heard the stories already. There was something out there, vaguely but not entirely human, taking kids from the playground and the homes that bordered the woods. A few children and teens had been wise enough to run away, but they weren't all spared. It was becoming a problem. You see, amalgamated creatures and vicious predators were one thing. They were predictable. They had fangs and claws. When the fog rolled in, they hunted for anyone and anything they could overpower like starving animals. But this?

This was new territory for us. We had been researching the root-faced man for months, and yet our rangers were no closer to recognizing *how* the forest had figured out these new tricks. How did it learn to lay traps, to speak, to think like a human being? Worst of all, we had no idea how to stop it yet.

The Price family believed their son had been abducted from his bed, either by man, monster, or something in-between. They weren't too far off, I believe. More than likely, Aiden went willingly with that thing from the forest, drawn to the trees like biting flies were drawn to livestock. He wasn't the first. I was hoping he would be the last.

"He was wearing a pair of blue pajamas with, um ... with yellow stars on them," Lydia said, wringing her hands. "If you find anything—"

"We've already got rangers searching the woods," I explained, closing up my notebook. "I'll pass these clues along. As soon as we find something, you'll be the first to know, alright?"

"Yes, sir," Lydia nodded, wiping at her face with the sleeve of her shirt. "Thank you."

Don't thank me yet, I thought to myself. This whole case made me feel cold, drained, and exhausted from that same old disappointment time and time again. In just a few short years, I had seen so many heartbroken families and so many torn homes that the horror of Pinehaven was beginning to turn worn and wearisome.

With every missing kid who never came home, I was one step closer to handing in my badge for good.

⸱⸱‖⸱⸱‖⸱‖⸱‖‖⸱‖⸱⸱‖⸱⸱‖‖⸱⸱

The rangers didn't usually go out after dark. They used to,

especially when missing kids were involved, but too many good folks weren't coming back. By the last light of day, I watched a half-dozen men and women in green coats emerge from the pines, empty-handed and stone-faced. One of them was injured, limping and being supported by another.

While they got her into the back of the van, I sat on the edge of the cargo space while her friend inspected a series of puncture wounds just below her knee.

"Have a rough one out there, Santos?" I asked, pulling a cigarette from the pack and placing it between my teeth.

"Guess you could say that," she said. She groaned and straightened the leg out. "Got too close to one of the old mines. Something grabbed me by the leg, tried to pull me down. The fellas managed to cut me loose and get a piece of the bastard. Hey, mind if I bum one?"

"Where's the piece now?" I asked while I handed her a cigarette from the pack. She stuck it between her teeth while I lit the end for her.

Santos took a slow breath before answering me. "Back of Neil's truck," she said. "I'll warn you, though … it's not pretty, my friend."

"Never is," I chuckled, giving her a rough pat on the shoulder. "Heal up, alright? No more flirtin' with danger out there."

"Oh, but it's *so* much fun," she exhaled a puff of smoke through her nostrils. "I'll try my best, Finn. You take it easy."

While Santos was getting her wounds cleaned and wrapped, I jumped down from the van and made the small trip over to the back of a dark green truck. In the bed, there was a tarp laid down already, covered in bits of dirt and dead leaves that had collected over time. And in the center, there was a grotesque sight that made the hair on my arms stand on end.

I smelled it before I saw it. The ranger had brought back what looked like an arm, but it was deformed beyond recognition. It was twice the size of a human arm with gray, putrid skin that was bloated like a water-logged corpse. It had more fingers than it should have, with bumps and pustules all up the forearm.

At one point, I thought it had been human. It was probably

more than *one* human, but I didn't want to think too long about who may have been included in that collection.

"Is this what grabbed Santos?" I asked, slipping on a glove and poking at the thing. It was cold and it wriggled slightly at the touch.

"Yep," Neil said with a heavy sigh. "Not what we were lookin' for though. No sign of a man with tree bark for a face, just this fleshy bastard livin' in the mines. We're losin' light though. We'll have to come back tomorrow and look again."

Out of curiosity, I poked at one of the large bumps along the creature's arm. To my surprise, it wasn't a pustule at all. Its lids opened and one big, green eye began to dart around, making a wet noise when it blinked. Disgusted, I drew my hand away and wiped my finger on the side of my coat. The eye was still looking at me as I began to step away.

I thought back to all the missing people from the town. I wondered if any of them had green eyes.

⠂⠄⠆⠇⠿⠸⠇⠿⠇⠇⠿⠇⠂⠄⠆⠂

I parked my cruiser in the lot next to the old elementary school that night. The view was terrible. As I stared into the woods, sipping from a cold travel mug, it reminded me too much of the sleepless nights back home when my eyes couldn't leave the trees.

It was after midnight. The swingset chains would jingle in the wind and the merry-go-round was spinning slowly on its own as if ridden by ghosts. I don't know how long I sat there in silence, watching the sway of the branches while a light rain pattered against the windshield.

First, I felt that familiar tingle. It ran from the base of my spine all the way up to the back of my neck where it lingered, cold and sharp. As I got out of my car, I never stopped looking into the trees, scanning beneath the thick pines for any sign of movement. At first, I didn't see anything. I stood in the cold air, shoulders growing damp from the rain as I listened to the subtle crack of twigs and the rustle of wet leaves.

A whistle. That was the first thing I heard. It was shrill and sudden, echoing into the night. As I squinted my eyes into the trees, I could see the faintest outline of something standing between the shadows of two pines, its head cocked to the side and posture stiff. It twitched a little as if a shiver passed through it, reminding me of how brittle twigs might move in a breeze. I didn't have eyes. It didn't have a *face*.

But as I stepped closer, I could smell the scent of fresh rot and I could hear a heavy rasp as if the creature was struggling to breathe. I flashed a light at its face, and all at once the thing dipped away and hid behind the trees. For only an instant, I saw it—a glimpse of twisted roots and tree bark forming a new head atop a rotten human neck.

I didn't hesitate. I took chase, gun pulled and tightly wrapped in my fist as I rushed into the forest and began to follow the crunching twigs. The sound grew faster and quieter. It was gaining speed, running erratically in zig-zagging motions with an uneven gait. At any moment, I was prepared to draw my pistol and shoot at the first thing that I saw, but this beast traveled as if it knew this path by heart.

The forests were thick and overgrown. The vines at my feet were wriggling like serpents and the branches groaned as they reached out to grab me. My light caught the trunk of a tree, where I saw a twisted and pale face sinking into the bark as if trying to escape. Some of the twigs that caught my jacket were fingers, others were sharp, curled claws. As I reached a dark canopy that even the rain couldn't reach, I saw dozens of glowing white eyes peer out between the fronds and I remembered the dangling, rotten legs I had seen outside my farmhouse. I remembered the whistle I heard that night.

My gun was pointed at the thing, my hands steady. I took a deep breath, waiting to see it move, when all of a sudden, from behind me, I heard a crack.

Then I heard a cry.

It was the voice of a child. He sobbed and whimpered, but the sound was muffled as if choked with a mouthful of dirt. Ignoring the sick feeling in the pit of my stomach, I turned and saw two milk-white eyes staring at me from the darkness.

My light was shining on the forest floor, illuminating a pair of gray, wrinkled feet and black toenails. I kept it there, not wanting to look up. I didn't want to see him. He choked again and I watched maggots and worms falling to the ground between his bare toes. Above his ankles, I could see a pair of filthy, mud-soaked pajama bottoms: blue with yellow stars.

And in an instant, he was pulled away. With a muffled shriek, the boy disappeared as if plucked from the ground and pulled upwards. I heard the whistle again, paired with the sound of creaking branches and groaning wood. I popped off two rounds, aiming into the darkness. I heard a low moan of pain, but on the third shot, I didn't hit anything at all. The beast was moving again, crunching through the dried grass and twigs.

It was too dark. The trees were too thick. As much as I wanted to find that thing and blast it to pieces, it had the upper hand now. I could hear something chasing me through the dense foliage and the screams of that child never stopped. He wasn't the only one. A chorus of voices, all of them wailing in agony, rang out in my ears as my feet pounded on the soil.

I got out alive. I breached the tree line and practically fell into the grass, panting for breath with a pistol still in my hand. I was just outside the playground, swings still jingling in the wind. The merry-go-round was still twirling on its own. And those cries and shrieks from the forest were distant but still calling for me more desperately than before.

That night, I made a decision.

•••||•••||•||·||•||•••||••·

"What's this?" Sheriff Jacobs looked down at the stack I was building on his desk: my badge, radio, taser. It was early morning and he hadn't even gotten settled into his office yet.

"I can't keep doing this," I said hurriedly. "I'm sorry, Andre, you *know* how much this work means to me, but I can't keep being the one to—"

"Finn. Settle down. *Breathe*," he stood up, rounding the table to push against my shoulder. He urged me to sit down and I did, slowly sinking into the leather seat. "You've got time. Tell me what's going on."

My teeth were gritted, my jaw was clenched. For the first time, I realized I could hardly breathe and my heart was pounding so fiercely as if I was running out of time. Andre gave me that *look*. His stern face, speckled with a gray and black beard, was firmly fixed on me with patience and control.

"I went out to the woods last night," I explained. "The story of the Price family bothered me and I couldn't let it rest, so I went looking for Aiden myself. I found him."

I didn't need to explain any further. Sheriff Jacobs sat down on the edge of his desk, straightening his tie. He shook his head in disappointment, but it was the kind of disappointment that was expected. We both knew it was coming.

"It's the families that bother you, isn't it?" he asked. "It's funny, Finn. Your old man was the same way. He made a great investigator, but the moment you put him in front of a grieving spouse or a mother who lost her kid, he just fell to pieces."

I chuckled quietly. "Yeah, well, it runs in the family."

Andre crossed his arms, standing straight in front of me now. He was thinking, I could tell—his eyes were fixed on the floor, his dark brows were scrunched together.

"You're a good officer," he said. "I'd hate to lose you. We've got a position open, but you'll probably stick your nose up at it."

I sputtered a bit, trying to hold back a laugh. "Listen, I can't imagine anything worse than what I've already been dealing with. What've you got for me?"

Andre's face morphed into a smirk, twitching just at the corner of his mouth. Then, after a deep breath through his nostrils, he lifted his chin and smiled at me with confidence.

"How about I promote you to 'delivery boy' for a while?"

CHAPTER THIRTEEN: PASSING TIME
Evelyn

*O*f all the things that changed after Halloween night, Finn's arrival was probably the least terrible. The former officer showed up on a cold, blustery morning right at the first glimmer of dawn. The sight of him almost scared me out of my sweatpants, but luckily, he wasn't there to arrest my ass a second time—he was just delivering a case of groceries. The box was neatly packed and organized with careful efficiency. Unlike our last guy, rest his soul, Finn carried it up the stairs without even breaking a sweat, bringing it into the broadcast room and placing it on the counter with a heavy thump.

Daniel was off that day, visiting his parents around the mountain for the weekend. The sight of another person, as jarring as it was, hit me as a sort of relief.

"You look like shit, Twenty-Eight."

That was the first thing Finn said to me since the day of my arrest. The worst part was, he wasn't wrong. I couldn't even blame him. I had just woken up, my hair was falling out of a braid that was starting to look like a muskrat stuck to my head, and I had already spilled coffee on myself that day.

"Yeah, well, I *feel* like shit. I'm not a morning person," I said, leaning against the bathroom door as I watched Finn fiddle around with the sink. I yawned loudly. "So what's the deal? Did you draw a short straw or something? Last time I saw you, it was in a police cruiser."

"Yeah, well, that wasn't workin' out for me." Finn grunted as he got down on the floor, peeking inside the cupboards. "I told the sheriff I wanted a change of scenery, so I'll be delivering your goods and fixing the place up as I see fit. Get your laundry around, I'll take that too. Oh, and you've got a leak down here, by the way. How long has that been going on?"

I was chewing on one of the strings from my hoodie as I shrugged.

"I dunno," I said honestly, "since I got here, probably."

Finn groaned, exasperated. He was reaching for his belt, grabbing a tool to tighten up one of the rusty old pipes that had turned loose over time. "Listen, Twenty-Eight, you've gotta pay attention to this sort of thing. You let this place get any structural damage, you'll be droppin' out of the air like fleas off a cow's ass."

I shivered at the thought. I had enough nightmares about this building toppling over in the wind, I didn't want to think about it crumbling from mold and rust either.

"Fair enough," I said, crouching down to watch him work. "And my name isn't *Twenty-Eight,* by the way. You can call me Evelyn."

Finn grunted in response, finally tightening the pipe until the slow, steady drip had stopped. Then, he looked over at me with narrowed eyes and his thick brows raised. "Don't you have a job to do?"

It was six o'clock in the morning and I *did* have a job to do. It was the same goddamn job I did every day: broadcasting the news, the weather, receiving calls from townsfolk, and the occasional visit from oddities beyond my comprehension.

While Finn was checking out the damage done to the shed during the storm, I chugged enough water to get the dust out of my throat and sat down behind the microphone for another day of 'that same old shit'. I complain an awful lot, but the truth is, it felt nice to wake up in the morning and see that the world still turned. It felt nice to be a survivor.

"Good morning, this is Evelyn McKinnon and it's currently 6:15 on a beautiful Friday. The air may be cold, but that sunrise sure is spectacular, isn't it?"

And it was.

Time moves in strange, mysterious ways. The first few weeks here at 104.6 FM seemed to crawl by like a tub of molasses that had crystallized in the cold. Then suddenly, it was December. We celebrated Christmas in the broadcast room to the best of our ability, mostly because Daniel absolutely *insisted*. I bought him a framed poster from a run of *The Producers* that I found on eBay. He got me a little mini-fridge. We put up a string of lights near the lookout window, but it got distracting when they would flicker different colors in the dead of night.

We drank sparkling grape juice on New Year's Eve. Dan left for a few days during *Semana Santa,* but brought me back a metric fuck-ton of food that his mom insisted he give to me. When we had a video call so that he could show me the fireworks in Puerto Vallarta, he introduced me to his sisters and his parents as his 'friend' instead of his 'co-worker'. It felt weird, but it was kind of nice. Before we knew it, the snow had melted and the smell of spring dew was fresh on the breeze.

Finn stopped by every Friday to bring me groceries and fix anything that broke. It took him a couple of weeks, but he managed to get the shed patched up until it looked like new. Things were okay. Things were *decent*. When the fog rolled in, we handled it. When eerie voices spoke over the phone, I hung up and carried on with the news forecast. When I saw something rotten floating at the tree line or spotted eyes in the darkness, I looked away. And when that stupid fucking bird decided to show up and peck at the window, I tossed him half of a peanut butter sandwich and that usually shut him right up.

It's hard getting used to this place. I would still find myself afraid of my own shadow or having nightmares about that *thing* that tried to pull me through the roof and spill my guts on the forest floor. It'll always be like that, I think. But you know what? I'm getting the hang of this.

Besides, there are worse kinds of pain.

I've lost people dear to me. I've watched my dreams slip away as I fell into a pit of failure, but none of that holds a candle to the pain I felt on a muggy June morning when I was kicked square in the pancreas by a guy going record speeds in a rolling chair. Daniel, in all of his leggy glory, had beaten me at yet another game of 'office chair jousting'.

From my spot on the floor, upside-down with two of the wheels still spinning, I could see a pair of heavy black boots step through the doorway. Without even seeing him, I could tell it was Finn by the way he stomped around like a buffalo with something to prove.

Once a well-respected officer for the Pinehaven Police Department, he was now stuck in this podunk shit-heap I called home with the fantastic honor of being our grocery boy. I had the distinct feeling that it wasn't the kind of downgrade he was hoping for.

"Should I even *ask* what you're doing?" He wore a sneer, which looked exceedingly silly from my angle. His eyes glanced between Daniel and me while he put a crate of grocery items down on the floor.

"Keepin' ourselves entertained," Daniel answered while I was still busy gasping for breath. He got out of his chair and held his hands out to me, helping me upright while quietly whispering an apology for knocking the wind out of my lungs.

"You can entertain yourselves by doing your job," Finn pushed the cardboard box toward me with his foot. Sitting on top of a box of instant potatoes, I saw a brown package that was tightly sealed with packing tape.

"There's a fancy bit of tech in there for you," he said. "A couple more kids from town went missing last weekend and people are riled up about it. The sheriff wants you two to keep an eye out, so he sent over a couple of security cameras. We'll put 'em right near the tree line and connect them to your monitors so you can *entertain yourselves* by watching them if you get bored."

I sat cross-legged on the floor and started to scrape my fingernail against the tape. "Great, just what we need—an even better view of the woods."

Finn pinched the bridge of his nose with a sigh. "Imagine you're a six-year-old getting pulled into the forest. Now *that's* a close view you wouldn't want. Count your blessings, McKinnon."

I shuddered. The thought of being out there alone in the

dark was bad enough, but I could hardly imagine that same feeling mixed with the daunting fear of being small. I took back what I said, feeling like an asshole for complaining. "You know what? Fair," I pulled away a strip of tape and opened the box, noting all of the individually wrapped pieces of equipment, wires, and tools that were all labeled and ready to assemble. "I feel like I'm going to find a way to break all of this just by looking at it."

"I'll help you get it set up," Finn promised. "I've installed dozens of these things."

While I didn't trust my shitty little hands with hundreds of dollars worth of equipment, I still did my part as an active participant. Finn and I ventured down the tower and toward the tree line while Daniel stayed behind, recording a couple of ads for a farmer's market being organized in town. I could appreciate the way folks around here tried to have a normal life.

Stepping into the shed to grab a ladder made my stomach flip. As I looked up, I could see the varying colors of wood grain from Finn's patch job. I recalled the night of the storm and every detail of that beast that tore through the ceiling just to grab me. I could still smell it so vividly: rot, mildew, fungus from the woods. Every time I heard the scratch of tree branches in the wind, I imagined it was those antlers again.

Day by day, I felt desensitized to a certain extent, but never quite enough. Even after eight full months in this place, I didn't feel safe looking out into the woods. I didn't feel alone.

"So, missing kids, huh?" I asked, carrying the ladder while Finn looked for a good spot to screw the first camera into a tree. "Dan told me about the posters in town. So many of them ... What's the deal?"

Finn knocked his fist against a tree, finding it dense enough for his liking. He pointed to a spot and I got the ladder set down, holding it steady while he climbed up.

"Somethin' from the woods is luring them in," he said gruffly. "It's not an animal, not a person either."

"Then what the hell is it?" I asked.

Finn scrunched up his face, holding a screw between his

teeth. "*'Ere's a man wib' roobs' on 'is 'ead.*"

"… A roof on his head?"

Finn took the screw out of his mouth, smacking his lips while he secured it into the tree.

"*Roots* on his head," he corrected. "The fucker's been spotted for months now. A teenage girl saw him this week, and so did at least four kids since Friday. He was at the edge of the woods near the school. Kids said that he looked like a man, but his head and face were covered in roots like … like a helmet or a mask." He sighed, shaking his head in frustration as he dug in his pockets for a second screw. "Even though we know the majority of *his type* usually can't pass the tree line, every kid who sees him said he tried to lure them in somehow. For a while, the curfew helped. Now, we've got another rush of cases."

My frown became more of a grimace the longer I listened. The thought of seeing a demented Treebeard didn't sound like fun, but seeing any of those kids becoming one with the forest sounded even worse. My mind went to Jennifer, her body stuffed into the tree and every one of her limbs broken and twisted. I thought about her gaping mouth, caught in a silent scream and filled with twigs and grass. The only thing worse was Daniel's description of her when she came back.

"There," Finn patted the tree and gave one of the thicker branches a shake to test the camera's sturdiness. It didn't budge. "That one's all set. We'll put up another on the edge of the tower to get a full view of the clearing. Think you can check the supply closet upstairs and see if we've got a few long extension cords?"

"Aye, aye, skipper." I snapped a flattened hand to my forehead in salute, holding onto the ladder until Finn had just about gotten both feet to the ground.

He paused to glare at me with his brows scrunched low and bristly over narrowed eyes.

"Never call me that again," he said.

That was my cue to leave. I gave him a quick pair of finger guns before gladly jogging back to the tower. The days were getting warmer, the air muggier. Biting flies were out with a vengeance and the mosquitoes around here were as big as hummingbirds. It made the trip back up to the broadcast room a lot rougher on the lungs than it would usually be. I was out of breath by the time I reached the top, my bangs sticking to my forehead. I shook the bottom of my t-shirt to give the boob sweat a little fresh air. Daniel—ever the pain in the ass—snickered with a stupid, gap-toothed grin on his face.

"What, did he make you climb the tree yourself?" he chuckled, biting his lip.

"*Fuck. You.*" I put a hand against the wall as I gasped for breath. "I'm just grabbin' a few extension cords. You seen any in the closet?"

"You know I don't look in there," Dan said with a wink before he pulled his microphone closer to his mouth and began to read through the news of the day. He was always so boisterous with his live broadcasts, regardless of the subject. There was something hilarious about hearing that velvety, charismatic voice of his talking about something as mundane as an annual farmer's market and old man Luke's roadside fruit stand.

While he rattled on, I was pulling open the storage closet door and crouching down to get a closer look. There were boxes and boxes of useless junk stacked in there. I found old recording equipment, outdated tech, broken microphones and headsets, a few frayed cords. I shoved the largest box out of my way so that I could crawl in further.

That's when I noticed something I had never seen before.

"Lookin' for Narnia?" Daniel asked with a snicker right after he finished his news segment.

"Oh, hush," I said, finally emerging and wiping the dust off my hands. "Come look at this. There's something back here, like … a little door."

Daniel got out of his seat, abandoning the controls to join me on the floor instead. Without any hesitation, he was on hands and knees with his ass in the air, experiencing the full glory of cobwebs and the faint scent of mold. I grabbed a flashlight and handed it to him. When he cast its glow on the wall, he confirmed what I had suspected. Way in the back of the closet, a piece of cheap flimsy plywood was covering a spot roughly six inches long on each side. It had been nailed down, closed off tightly as if something had been hidden behind it.

"Could be a patched-up hole in the wall," Daniel said, turning the light toward me. I squinted and put my hand in front of my eyes to shield them from the glow.

"Maybe," I shrugged, "but it creeps me out."

We looked at one another, then back at the board as if waiting for someone to make the first move and start digging around for a hammer. Given enough time, I'm sure one of us would have decided to take that initiative. As it turned out, that investigation would have to be put on hold. The broadcast room door squeaked open and Finn came stomping in, his heavy boots walking a couple of paces before he stopped and stared at us in silence for just a moment.

"Seriously?" he finally said with an incredulous laugh. "Between the *two* of you idiots, you can't find an extension cord?"

I was the first to crawl out of the closet, knowing that Finn probably didn't want to have a conversation with just my ass. I smacked my head on the doorframe as I shuffled out into the light once more, pointing at the largest box that was already pulled out and sitting near Finn's feet.

"They're in there," I told him. I was getting tired of his grumpy attitude but I had a feeling he was probably tired of mine too. "We found something else back here too."

Finn was digging around in the box, pulling out a long green cord and tossing it to the side while he looked for another. His curiosity soon got the better of him and he tore his eyes away long enough to look up at me, then at the closet.

"What did you find?" he asked.

"I don't know," I answered. "It's like a little panel in the back."

Finn simply shrugged, slinging three long cords over his shoulders. "If it ain't somethin' we can use, it's not important. Now, start looking through those manuals that came with the cameras. I'm gonna get 'em fired up."

After snaking wires over every inch of the station and watching Finn run back and forth to re-adjust the cameras a few times, I actually started to forget about the little door in the back of the closet. Daniel and I set up a new monitor that would connect only to the security cameras, positioned in front of our desk so that we could always see it. As the grainy image appeared, cycling between the cameras on a loop, I felt an eerie chill traveling up and down my spine.

Right now, the only thing we could see was a view of the forest and Finn marching back and forth to collect his tools. But I knew that it was only a matter of time before something ghastly was staring back at us from beyond the tree line.

When afternoon arrived, Finn packed up his things and bid us farewell. The stillness set in again. It was just Daniel and I, sitting in our respective places at the desk, listening to some Jimi Hendrix through our headphones. Every now and then, our eyes would dart between one another and the fuzzy, pixelated images on the screens.

I already wasn't a fan. Every time I looked up, I expected to see *something:* a rotten face, some strange creature, a shambling corpse. I didn't know what it would be, only that we would soon become all too aware of what watched us from that wild, untamed border. Now, we had the honor of watching it right back.

We got a call in the late afternoon. It was a music request. A man from the edge of town by the name of Phil wanted to hear some Johnny Cash, but not before telling us all about the weird new plants that had been growing all around his farm.

"These vines, thicker'n a man's wrist, have been chokin' out my pine saplings," he said, his voice muffled by the wind as he roamed around his property. We could hear chickens, dogs, and cows. "I been tryin' to cut 'em down, but when I got the hatchet to 'em, this sticky red goo came burstin' out. Smells like pennies, made a real mess of my good work boots. If any of y'all see these, I wouldn't recommend cutting 'em. I think a strong weed killer will do just fine."

All I could think about while listening to his story was Finn's description of that man in the woods. He had roots growing all around his face, he said. I was starting to wonder how much of his human self still remained beneath the tree bark.

When Phil hung up, we played "Ring of Fire" for him, and to my great distress, Daniel knew every word and insisted on singing along. Apparently, losing most of his hearing hadn't stopped him from carrying a tune—it only made him *louder.* I got out of my seat to stretch my legs and escape the embarrassment of being serenaded, only to find myself looking at the closet once again. I had almost forgotten.

"Man, I really want to know what's in there," I said, turning to give Daniel a sideways glance.

I watched the gears turning in his head. He couldn't resist the temptation either, I knew it. I could sense it. It was just a matter of who would be the one to smash the door open.

"I'll hold the flashlight if you get a hammer," Daniel replied. It seems neither of us were very patient.

I didn't realize just how much useless shit was hidden in the back of that closet until all of it had to be removed. We tossed it all onto the broadcast room floor, creating a tripping hazard in the process. We found a dead woodrat back there too, mummified and stiff. Daniel tried to chase me around with it for a while—this boy wouldn't go near a ladybug, but he'd hold a dead rat with no problem. Finally, after giving Mr. Cheepers a proper burial, it was just the two of us, that little door, and the hammer nestled snugly inside of my fist.

Maybe it was a little *too* therapeutic smashing that piece of plywood to bits because I immediately gave up trying to pull the nails out of the wall. When the first nail didn't give way, too rusted and old to budge, I started smacking the blunt end of the hammer against it until the wood splintered and cracked down the middle.

As we pulled away bits of broken wood and old nails, we found a rusty tin box hidden right next to the insulation. We dragged it out onto the floor. It looked like a lunchbox—the kind my father would have taken to work up at the fire station. But when Dan popped it open, we found something more perplexing than a decade-old sandwich.

"Cassette tapes?" He picked one up gingerly between his fingers, blowing dust off the surface, then coughing immediately. "You ever see one of these?"

"Yeah, I had a shit-ton of 'em as a kid," I said, grabbing another. It had the number '3' written on it in permanent marker. "You know, the good stuff. Britney, TLC, Backstreet Boys, N'Sync ... Backstreet Boys were better though."

Daniel scooped up a few more tapes, putting them in order while voicing a snort of laughter under his breath. "I don't think these are the same kind of tapes, Lyn ... Though I do agree. Backstreet Boys were better."

The box was caked in dust, possibly abandoned for years in that little hole in the back of the closet. There were over a dozen cassette tapes in total, each of them with a number written on one side. We put them in order from one to sixteen, but that was where we lost one. Number fifteen was missing. Still, with a clear order in mind, we had a place to start. As Daniel cleaned up the mess we had made on the broadcast room floor, I dug out an old cassette player from a box of outdated equipment. By some miracle, it was still in working condition.

It was almost seven-thirty. Dan's shift ended in two hours, but we had nothing better to do. "Think we've got time to see if one works?" he asked. My answer was an absolute no-brainer.

The player started up with a crackle of white noise before the voice of a man came through the dusty machine. Some spots were pretty damaged, but Dan and I managed to listen to the entirety of *Tape #1.*

Today is the twentieth of November. My name is Eric. I am Operator Number Seven: the seventh person to work at the Pinehaven Emergency Broadcast Station. This morning, at approximately five-fifteen, I pulled my old climbing gear out of the shed so that I could assist the police in retrieving Number Six from the top of the radio mast. His legs are still missing from the knees down, but at least now we've found the torso.

Before I get into that, here's a little context. Before moving up to the tower, I was a member of the Pinehaven Forest Rangers. Before that, I was a Conservation Officer. I spent four years in wildlife rescue, protecting the reserves from Montana to West Virginia. I studied the mountain terrain, the deep marshland, and the rehabilitation of injured animals, mainly birds of prey. It's my hope that there won't be a need to replace me anytime soon, but I want this recording to survive whether or not I do. Perhaps, these accounts might help the next unlucky Operator.

At four-thirty this morning, I was awoken by a terrible sound. It chilled me to the bone—the sound of metal scraping and whining outside the watchtower. Just as disturbing to me was the absolute silence from inside the building itself. While I slept, the radio signal had been lost, probably due to the wind storms we sometimes get this time of year. This was my very first lesson upon arriving at the station: never let the radio go off air under any circumstances. Doing so at the wrong time would unleash horrors I didn't even want to imagine.

I tried my hand at quickly repairing the console, but after pressing every button I could get my hands on, I realized that the problem was outside the station itself.

I could still hear it. Something was climbing the radio mast, messing with the signal. I didn't think those things from the woods could get that close to the tower, but their craftiness knows no bounds.

There was no fog. The town was still safe. I grabbed a shotgun from the closet and ran to the fire escape to get a better look. The sky was still dark and it was freezing cold like you wouldn't believe. I shined a flashlight up at the metal tower while the thing rocked and swayed from side to side.

There were birds, at least a dozen of them, all picking at the wires and messing with the signal. They were huge, some with extra wings and others with beaks as long and sharp as a pair of shears. They were making the most ungodly noise as they all fought for pieces of electric cable to rip away and take with them.

They weren't alone. I saw a blob of flesh, enormous in size and made up of so many different textures and tones. It was the most grotesque thing I had seen since my arrival—the thing that stalked the station almost every night. It looked like a deer at first glance, standing on two legs, but its eyes were pure white and its fur was a dusty gray, caked in mud and rotten flesh. Giant twisted antlers smacked the metal as it thrashed its head, making a tremendous amount of noise.

The worst part about this thing was just how complex it was. If not for the antlers, I wouldn't know what it used to be. It had more than two eyes—six at least. I saw a glimpse of giant hooves, claw-like hands with long talons, and smaller limbs that weren't even necessary.

160

As enormous as it was, the beast moved in such slithering motions in the dark that I could hardly make out all the details. All I knew was that this thing should not exist.

It didn't shamble clumsily up the tower, no. This monster was crouched up high, its filthy claws holding a bundle of flesh and cloth. It was Number Six, or at least the top half of him. One arm was gone, his blood dried, his skin bloated and turning a dark, putrid blue.

I had seen this bastard before, and like with all the freakish abominations from the woods, I knew better than to fight it. These things don't die, you see. They just end up absorbed by the others, growing bigger and stronger and more dangerous.

Just then, I became aware of perhaps one of the least comforting sounds I could have possibly heard: the screech of stressed metal underneath the beast's weight. I listened as it shifted, its dead, empty eyes following my movements. It abandoned Number Six, leaving him tangled in the radio mast like a grim flag of victory as it quickly crawled its way down the tower like the strangest, most grotesque spider I had ever seen.

Just as I pulled the door open and threw myself inside, I could feel the weight of the creature landing on the fire escape. It bent the metal under its hooves, causing the entire structure to shake and tilt. The lookout window shivered as those large, gnarled antlers rammed against the glass, leaving tiny cracks and scratches with each pound of its head.

It would have braved a skull full of broken glass just to get to me, I'm sure. I did the only thing I could think to do. My hand slammed down on The Bell and the beast let out a deafening roar that made the insides of my ears sting and itch. I saw the gape of its mouth, full of rows upon rows of mismatched teeth and bits of fresh meat tangled between them. Blood and rot. I hit the button once more and it finally jumped down from the building, causing the tower to quake as dust fell from the ceiling over my head.

The creature began to stagger back to the forest, shaking its head in discomfort the whole time.

The radio is up and running now. Number Six has been retrieved from the radio mast, though no one is sure if his uncovered *parts were eaten by the beast or just ... misplaced. I suspect I'll find out soon enough if his legs pay me a visit. Something else has been bothering me though. This little mountain bird has been sitting outside the window for a long time now. It looks normal enough, but the way it taps its beak on the glass for hours on end is really getting on my nerves.*

The tape was insightful but unpleasant. When the static began to play, I shut the machine off, leaning back in my chair with a sigh of mental exhaustion. The sky was dark now. A song by Simon & Garfunkel was playing on the radio. Daniel and I shared a glance, saying nothing. Knowing that he and I were the only surviving people to have worked at the station made hearing the voice of Eric seem like a mournful experience. We both knew that at some point, somewhere and somehow, the forest had won and all that remained of Number Seven were the words on these tapes.

"You think this will be us one day?" I asked with a sly smirk, but the suggestion wasn't humorous in the least. "Reading all of our own stories on a cassette, saving them for the next Operator when we're both gone?"

I watched Dan pop the tape out of the machine, blowing the dust off of it like an old game cartridge and placing it back with the rest. One down, fourteen left to go ...

"Nah," he answered with a mock casual tone. "We'll use a flash drive instead."

CHAPTER FOURTEEN: INTRUDER
Evelyn

In the early hours of the morning, before the sun came up, I saw something I couldn't explain. It wasn't supernatural and it wasn't inhuman. I had a visitor at the broadcast tower.

Usually, at five o'clock in the morning, I would still be fast asleep, but a bathroom break had proven timely. I got a perfect view of our new stalker as they wandered around outside the radio tower, peeking into the windows of the shed and circling the clearing a few times. I could see them on the security cameras, their face obscured by a dark hoodie that covered their hair and eyes. It was clear from the way they stalked around outside the building that they weren't necessarily looking to come inside for a chat.

Now, usually, calling the police would be the natural response. This was private property. But out of some curiosity for what this mysterious little weirdo was up to, I found myself more interested in just watching them poke around outside, all the while prepared to intervene if they got too close to the forest. Their actions seemed curious, but not aggressive.

First, they marched around the perimeter, peering through gaps in the wooden walls of the shed. Then, they walked along the treeline and shuffled their feet in the dirt for a bit, kicking up clumps of soil and loose grass. I couldn't tell if they were looking for something in particular or just investigating every little detail they came across.

I left for only a minute, starting a pot of coffee and resigning myself to a very early start to the day. Fog was in the weather prediction. I knew already that I'd need all the energy I could get. While I leaned against the counter, waiting for the coffee machine to slowly drip while tapping mindlessly at my phone screen, I never took my eyes or ears completely off the lookout window. Sure, Creepus Maximus out there hadn't done anything outright malicious yet, but that presence still gave me an eerie feeling. As isolated as this place could be, sometimes it was scarier to know I wasn't alone.

I stirred sugar into my cup, dropping the spoon into the sink with a loud *clang*. Before I had a chance to step away and groggily drag my feet back to the desk, I heard a sound that was a little bit too familiar. It was a whisper, so faint but sharp in my ears. It was coming from the kitchen sink. I thought we were done with this bullshit a long time ago.

I glared down at the drain while trying to decipher quiet, mumbling bits of sound that didn't quite form full words. I didn't need to hear every word to understand it, though. It was her again. Everything about that tone of voice – the sadness, the anger, the disappointment – was all too familiar to me. Suddenly, I was remembering the day I left Jenny's apartment for the very last time. I was remembering the way I turned my back and refused to look at her, knowing it would hurt more if I did.

Bubbles rose in the basin. As if the liquid down the drain was boiling, the droplets popped and formed more in their place, splashing tiny pinpricks of dark red fluid all around the sink. A rancid smell was coming from deep down in the pipes, like metal mixed with the sickly sweetness of rotten meat. It tickled my nose, burning my eyes. Immediately, it turned me off from my coffee, which I promptly dumped down the exact same drain. Perhaps it was a bit rude, but it made the voice finally stop. She had apparently said all that she needed to say.

Even though I lost my coffee, I had gained an even stronger sense of anxiety as I shuffled my feet back to my desk, the quiet nature of the moment convincing me for a time that our visitor had finally left. I stretched my arms over my head, listening to my back crack. My eyes turned to the clock on the wall, passing the lookout window.

"Oh, shit!" I jumped back, nearly crawling out of my own skin.

My heart was racing. I grabbed my chest, every hair on

my body standing on end. That familiar hooded figure was standing directly on the other side of the glass, having climbed the fire escape just to glare at me from the other side. Both hands were in the pockets of their sweater, but I could see a human nose and a human mouth. It's difficult to describe this very specific kind of fear: seeing someone only a few feet away from you, but still very separate. I was safe, technically. And yet, I still felt a chilling sense of dread. He was real. He was alive. The fact that he wasn't a shambling, half-decayed monstrosity made him almost more threatening than the beasts from the forest.

I could get rid of monsters with the push of a single button. I couldn't get rid of this so easily. And the worst part? I couldn't even begin to imagine his motives.

Almost as soon as I spotted him, the figure turned and pulled his hood further over the features of his face. He darted down the fire escape, one metallic *clang* at a time, his steps racing away until I could no longer hear or see any trace of him. The very last glimpse I got of my stalker was a view of his feet through the grass as he turned the corner, heading into the gravel driveway.

"Fucking creep ..." I murmured under my breath, turning around quickly. As soon as I did, I was smacked in the face by another startling sight. The sink was bubbling again, only this time, it was spraying a mess of ruddy red water all over the countertops. I quickly reached for a plug and clogged it up, my hands dripping with the sticky, smelly substance.

I used the bathroom sink to clean myself up, but all the while, I still heard that voice. She was in the bathroom sink now too, her whispers cutting through the silence after the spout was turned off. I could hardly understand what she said, but I knew one thing: I heard my name, clear as day. The name she used to call me. *Lynny.*

"I'm seeing someone."

I didn't process her words at first, sleepily staring up at the ceiling while half-listening to the television. I don't even remember what show we were watching, only that it was very late and I was very drunk. Jennifer and I had gone out to a party earlier that night with a few friends she met in her photography class. I didn't like any of them and none of them particularly liked me either. After a couple of hours, Jen dragged me back to our dorm and I told her that I felt too sick to be left alone. That was a lie. It was just an excuse to lay next to her for a while.

"Hm?" I finally looked up, bonking my head against her shoulder.

"I'm seeing someone," she repeated with a little giggle in the back of her throat. "We went on a date last Friday. I thought it would just be a one-time thing, but he's a nice guy. I'm seeing him again this weekend."

The tight feeling in my chest was strange and unexpected. Jenny told me about her dates all the time – guys she met in class, mostly soft poetic types who liked her for her taste in classic literature or the pink streak in her hair. I would tell her about some stranger I kissed at an indie music gig, blinded in a cloud of smoke. Those conversations didn't mean much. This was different, though. She had this smile on her face, dreamy and distant.

"That's ... great, Jenny," I said with a forced smile. "He better treat you well."

She was glowing. She never looked at me like that before.

Even when we were together, I never once saw that same sparkle in her eyes.

I'm proud to say that eventually, I *did* call someone. I had absolutely no trouble waking Finn up at five o'clock in the morning and telling him that we had an attempted break-in at the station. I'm choosing to be optimistic here and say that his exasperated curse words and tired, angry sighs were in response to the hooded creeper and not to my phone call.

After I wiped down the kitchen counters, I decided to wait on the stairs, bare feet against the cold metal and my dad's old jean jacket wrapped around my shoulders. My ears were listening for any sign of a disturbance: footsteps in the grass, breaking twigs, voices I didn't recognize.

Thankfully, the only thing I heard was the gentle purr of an engine as our brand-new guard dog rolled into the driveway and jumped out of his vehicle. Finn rushed up the stairs, meeting me at the top with his keys already jingling in his hand. He looked breathless, tired, still wearing a pair of dark gray sweatpants. He looked like shit before his morning coffee. He took one look at me and nearly jumped out of his skin, goosebumps raising on his arms.

"Jesus *shitting* Christ, Lyn," he clutched at his chest before pushing past me, slamming the door behind us after nudging my shoulders back into the building. "I came up here looking for an intruder and instead, I see you sitting there in the dark lookin' like a goddamn ghost. You scared every last fuck right out of me. So thanks for that."

"You're welcome," I shrugged, leaning against the door while Finn paced around the room. "Thanks for getting here so quick, I—"

"Yeah, yeah, no problem," Finn interrupted, eyes scanning the tree line. Always cutting right to the chase, this one. "So you said you saw a guy out here poking around? Did he get in the building?"

"No, he didn't," I clarified, pointing at the lookout window. "He was sneaking around by the border, then near the shed, checking out the cameras. I saw him come up the fire escape—scared the piss out of me, by the way. He was scoping the place out, I think, but he ran like a chickenshit son of a bitch when he figured out I could see him."

Finn finally stopped his pacing, running a hand through his hair. He took in a deep breath, then let it out with a mixture of relief and exasperation as if he had been holding it this whole time.

"So he's not here anymore? He ran?"

I nodded, crossing my arms as I continued to stare into the vast sea of trees. It was still and peaceful out there, the red light of dawn just beginning to tickle the tops of the mountains.

"As far as I know, he's gone," I said.

Finn looked less than amused. Thick, square fingertips reached up to rub the bridge of his nose, the veins in the back of his hand prominent when he clenched them. "Evelyn. You called me about a break-in ... that never happened?" he asked, gritting his teeth. "You called me at five o'clock in the goddamn morning for an intruder who's already gone. Why the hell am I out here?"

At this point, I had seated myself in the rolling chair I claimed as my own, Daniel's seat left empty. I knew he wouldn't be here until eight o'clock, and perhaps that knowledge made me a little more willing to admit what was on my mind. I had good reason to not want to be alone.

"Because I know who it was," I said, looking up at Finn with an expression both apologetic and vulnerable, "and I was scared."

The automation systems were still running. I watched the screen, eyes crossing as a pre-recorded ad began to play. Through my abandoned headphones, I could just barely make out the sound of Daniel's voice, energetically talking about a fundraiser for the Pinehaven High School softball team.

Finn had decided to stick around a little longer, going through some recordings from our security cameras. I was still figuring out how to review the footage, but luckily, it wasn't too difficult to go back just a short amount of time. Before long, we were sitting side-by-side and staring at a paused image of the man I saw, this time from the perspective of the tree line. He was staring into the woods, standing right at the edge where the forest stopped and the clearing began.

"Who is this guy?" Finn asked as he zoomed in on the blurry, half-visible face between the dark hood. The poor quality of the night vision camera made his features look hollow and his eyes as bright as headlights in the dark. It reminded me of Jennifer's eyes: white and cold.

"His name's Elijah," I answered. "I'm almost sure that's him. He was dating my friend Jennifer before she ... you know, decided to walk into the woods and never come back."

I watched as Finn's lips curled into a thin frown of contemplation. I wasn't an investigator of any sort, but even I could put two and two together to make a story. The last time I saw Elijah, he and Jennifer were trying to stage an intervention for me. Less than a week later, I was leaving the apartment for the last time. Shit lot of good that intervention did, huh?

"Think he was out here trying to mess with you?" Finn asked.

"It's possible," I said with a shrug of the shoulders, pulling my knees up closer to my chest. I could understand why Elijah would hold a grudge. His girlfriend went missing and suddenly her severed fingers just so happened to be found at my workplace? The last memory Elijah would have had of me was the blowout fight that ended my friendship with Jenny for good. It was a brutal one too. Anyone who says that breaking up with a best friend is easy compared to breaking up with a partner doesn't know jack shit.

Still, something didn't seem to fit.

"I'm not sure though," I continued. "It almost looked to me like he was searching for something. Maybe he's still looking for her. I mean, her case was closed so abruptly, and without anything more than her fingers and some blood samples. He doesn't know the rest." I stared at the fire escape, my eyes stuck on the spot where he had been standing just an hour before. Remembering the way he glared at me from the other side of the glass still sent a shiver up my spine.

"When he came up the fire escape, I felt like he was just trying to freak me out. The door was three feet away and he never even tried to open it. He didn't want *in* the building, he just wanted me to see him."

"Or maybe he wanted to see *you*," Finn said. The dark tone of his voice made my hair stand on end and I shivered, sticking my tongue out in disgust.

"Ugh, don't say it like that," I said with a sneer, reaching over to smack the former officer on the arm. "The last thing I need is to imagine that this guy has been hanging around watching me while I work. I live here, I'll remind you."

"All the more reason to keep those cameras goin'," Finn remarked, pointing to the monitor. Currently, the cameras were slowly cycling back and forth between a view of the clearing and the dark edge of the tree line. I could see something out there, but it wasn't Elijah. It was just a deer, I think ... It was hard to tell. Its back legs were facing the wrong direction and its antlers were wiggling. I regarded it with a disgusted scrunch of the nose before tearing my eyes away and looking down at my dirty fingernails instead.

"Hey, uh ... by the way, thanks for coming all the way out here so early," I said, picking at a loose string on the edge of my sleeve. "I appreciate it. I-I would have just waited for Dan to get here, but—"

"It's alright, Evelyn," Finn said as he lit a cigarette and tossed his head back, letting out a heavy breath. "You don't have to explain yourself, it's okay to admit when you feel unsafe up here. You've got every right to. Besides, Dan's a good fella' and all, but ... well, I watched him get startled by a bumblebee the other day."

I rolled my eyes with a fond smile. "Yeah, that sounds like him," I said.

I liked Dan just fine, but his resting anxiety level made me look like the most relaxed motherfucker in the world by comparison.

"Hey, Finn? Speaking of Dan, I've got a favor to ask you."

Finn blew a cloud of smoke out of the corner of his mouth, raising one bushy eyebrow at me.

"So, we've got somewhere to be next weekend," I said with a nervous smile. "I'll split that week's paycheck with you if you take over for a bit."

The look on his face was hard to read at first. He blinked a few times, his expression cold as stone, all while I grinned at him with all the sweetness I could muster. Just as I was tapping my fingers together with an innocent pout, he finally sighed and cracked a little smile.

"Is it important?" he asked.

"Yeah, super important," I nodded. "We're going to his cousin's wedding. His mom invited me."

You would think that my answer was a joke by the way Finn suddenly spat out a laugh as if it crept up on him. I'll admit, I was a tad bit insulted when he didn't take it seriously, but between his giggles and my grumpy, wrinkled brow, he finally gave me a surprising answer.

"Sure, fine, I'll let you have your break. You look about a month overdue for one."

"The hell is that supposed to mean?"

"I'm just sayin', if we put you next to a raccoon in a hoodie, I'm not sure we could tell the difference." Finn laughed again, tapping his cigarette butt on an empty cup Dan had left on the desk the day before. Meanwhile, I was sitting up taller in my chair, holding up my palm to threaten an open-handed smack. Finn just grabbed my wrist and lowered it.

"Settle down, scout. Sheesh. I could still change my mind." His laughter died away, but he still wore that rotten smirk. "Promise me you'll dance with Dan at least once and we've got a deal. I expect photographic evidence, ya' hear?"

There wasn't much on this earth aside from shoving a hornet's nest up my ass that would make me dance. That being said, I guess we had a deal.

I smirked, licking the palm of my hand and holding it out.

"Shake on it," I said with a devilish, toothy grin.

Finn looked at my wet palm with a revolted frown. "No. You're disgusting."

"I said, *shake on it, Finn.*"

"Absolutely not."

"Shake on it or *no dance.*"

"Miss ma'am, I will throw you off this tower if you lay that filthy hand on me."

⊷⑊⊷⑊⊷⑊⑊⑊⊷⑊⊷⑊⊷

The sunrise came and went. I gave a cheerful 'good morning' to the people of Pinehaven, reporting the day's forecast with some gentle caution. "It's nearly eight o'clock and the sky is looking clear right now, but there's a fog advisory in place for the next two hours. Please stay tuned for updates, and as always, please remain indoors until the advisory has passed. This is Evelyn from 104.6 FM wishing you all a relaxing start to your day."

Finn was about to leave, yawning into his hand and probably already fantasizing about the nap he was going to take when he got home. In the middle of my broadcast, I gave him a lazy wave as he lit another cigarette and disappeared down the winding staircase. I only caught a glimpse of his boot as he closed the door quietly on his way out.

I listened to the buffer between my announcement and the next block of music, the cheerful little jingle standing out like a sore thumb against the eeriness of the fog advisory. "Coal Miner's Daughter" by Loretta Lynn began to play. Once I slid the headphones off my ears, I spared a glance at the mountaintops. The mist was up there, circling around in a slow rotation over the tallest and oldest pines in the forest. For now, it was content to stay there. How soon would it begin to travel?

Every time I watched it barrel down the hills and race toward us, I felt that same primal terror I felt the very first time I saw it. But now, things had changed. I had been here long enough to know exactly what to do, when to do it, and how to control the situation if things didn't work out the way we planned. This strange, eerie reality was mine.

The weather was getting warmer every day. A humid, sticky heat was making this box in the sky feel more like an oven, filled with the stench of mildew and whatever fast food bags we had lying around. I had a thought to open the door and let a little fresh air in while I still had a chance. You can imagine my surprise when I heard the muffled suggestion of voices—multiple voices—through the door. They sounded agitated. Angry. One person was yelling.

Curiosity got the better of me, as well as a strange territorial instinct. As much as I hated this place, it was becoming synonymous with my everyday life and if someone was causing trouble in *my* domain, I wanted to be there to defend it. There was no one on the stairwell, no shadows outside the door. I grabbed my keys and locked up before marching down the stairs one heavy step at a time, the voices growing louder as I descended to the gravel driveway below.

The first thing I heard was a loud smack and something heavy collapsing to the ground, followed by a series of angry yells. What I didn't expect next was to almost get hit by a flying body, as whatever argument had ensued didn't stay verbal for very long. I got a split-second view of a dark sweatshirt as Finn threw his assailant onto the ground, knocking the wind out a very red-faced and breathless Elijah. He was back now, in full daylight and looking just as furious as ever.

"What the fuck happened?" I backed up as Elijah tried to wrestle away, Finn's knee holding him tight to the ground. He had him under control. It was only then that I noticed the crumpled heap on the ground had been Daniel, who was already trying to get back to his feet after collapsing next to his car. He was holding his hands over his face, his eyes beginning to water.

"He got me good," he said, his voice nasally. I rushed over and grabbed him by the elbow, helping him to his feet while he pinched the bridge of his nose with a hiss of pain.

"Did he break your nose?" I asked, reaching up to grab Dan's chin and tilt back his head. "Let go, let me see."

"Ah! Don't touch it ..."

"I won't," I promised before Daniel finally dropped his hands to let me get a peek. He had a scuff on his nose and one on his cheek, a small spot of blood coming from one nostril. The rest was just swollen and red but didn't look broken. "I think you'll live, hoss."

My co-host carefully wiped the blood away, gritting his teeth in discomfort the whole time. "I-I don't even know this guy," he said. "He was yelling and I told him to settle down an-and he *punched* me."

"I'll fill you in later." I looked over my shoulder. Elijah was now only putting up a mild struggle as his cheek was pushed painfully into the loose stone. He huffed in frustration as Finn reached into his back pockets, pulling out a wallet and a folding knife. He opened the knife, which glimmered in the sunlight.

"What were you planning on doing with this?" he asked, waving it in front of his face.

"Nothing," Elijah argued. It wasn't a good enough answer. Finn twisted his arm behind his back, coaxing a pained yell from the other man until he conceded. "Ow, fuck! Stop! ... Okay, I-I wasn't gonna use it, it was just for show!"

Finn folded the knife back up and tossed it several feet away, where it disappeared into the tall grass near the forest's edge.

"So you're trying to tell me that you were just here to fuck around and then leave?" he asked with a skeptical chuckle.

This time, Elijah turned his head to the side to glare daggers up at the man above him. "Isn't that what you did?" he asked in a hoarse, seething voice. "I watch the news, you know. You assholes searched for Jennifer for maybe a whole hour before you gave up and closed the case. You didn't even try. No one tried. Everyone was so willing to say she was dead, but we can't even bury her because you left her body out there to *rot!*"

Finn's gaze, as stern as ever, fixed itself on him first and then up to me. All this was starting to make sense now. Elijah didn't have a murderer to blame for his girlfriend's death, so the closest he could get was blaming the ones who failed to save her—the ones who failed to bring her home.

The silence between us was tense and heavy, a moment of understanding passing between our faces. Finally, Finn loosened his hold on Elijah's arm, letting him lie face down on the ground with his limbs resting limply at his sides. Although it was summer, I felt a chill in the air like a tickling wind, just cold enough to raise goosebumps on my skin. That breeze made the leaves rustle and the grass blow in a new direction. My ears itched as I heard the creak of the heavy wooden stakes that held up our tower—it sounded like a weak old animal, groaning in pain as it settled.

That eerie feeling made my pulse pick up speed. I didn't want to be out here anymore.

"Elijah," I spoke softly, crouching down to see him face-to-face. "You should go home."

Even when Finn stood and released the weight from Elijah's back, he still took his time sitting up with sluggish, aching movements. He rubbed the back of his neck, something cracking as he stretched. When I offered him a hand to help him to his feet, he looked at my palm and ignored it with a grimace of disgust as if I were contagious.

"You don't get it," he told me, his expression weary and lips pulled into a frown. "You don't have to live surrounded by her things every single day."

The shitty thing was, he was right. I didn't have to live where she lived. But how could I possibly begin to explain to Elijah that Jennifer haunted me in a completely different, more literal way? I may not have been surrounded by memories of her life, but I was certainly surrounded by the reality of her gruesome, terrible death.

The wind hit me again, loose strands of hair tickling my face and neck like a spider's legs. The branches near the tree line began to creak and sway, rattling together like bones. A dark cloud was passing over the sun, turning the air colder and the day darker. It brought another groan from the woods, this time more ... vocal. Dan had long since stopped nursing his swollen nose and was shifting where he stood, dark eyes darting from side to side. I knew he felt it too: the too-familiar agitation of a skipping heartbeat at the sudden desire to get somewhere safe.

It was time to go.

CHAPTER FIFTEEN: DEVOUR
Evelyn

"I guess I never noticed how tall the trees were from down here," Daniel said, his gaze flicking down to my face. All at once, the color began to run from his cheeks. He was touching his arm, feeling the prickle of goosebumps on his skin. We had a brand new problem now, something far worse than petty arguments or a busted nose. I heard another whine from the tower. No ... not the tower. The *woods*.

I never realized how little we could see when we weren't in the air.

"Fog day. Everyone upstairs. You too." I pointed to Elijah, who seemed to be the only person who didn't understand our urgency. Finn tugged on the back of his sweater like a mother cat picking up her kittens by the scruff. Daniel and I rushed ahead, trusting that the two of them could get up the stairs without us holding their hands.

Daniel patted my shoulder, pushing me forward to the front of the line. Finn was right on my heels, heavy boots stomping up the winding staircase one loud metallic clang at a time. My hands were fumbling when I reached the top of the stairs, panting for breath. I was looking for the right key to unlock the broadcast room, but inside my pockets were nothing but lint and a few sticky old gum wrappers. I cursed under my breath when I realized I must have dropped my keys, and that my co-host was no longer right behind me.

"Elijah, hurry up! We have to get inside!" Daniel was yelling at the bottom of the stairs while our guest was wandering out into the center of the clearing. From up top, I could see those swirling clouds of gray start to inch toward us, swimming through the pines.

"Dan!" Yelling down the entire length of the stairs made my throat burn. "Dan, I need your keys! I need your keys!"

He looked up at me briefly, but his expression didn't register any understanding. I was out of his range and too far away for him to read my lips. I swore an oath that I'd start using my spare time to improve my American Sign Language, all while I pushed past Finn to stomp back down the stairs and grab the keys for myself. Once I got to the bottom, I tugged on Dan's sleeve, breathless and clutching at my pounding heart.

"Dan, I need your ..."

When I took a deep breath, I noticed he wasn't looking at me anymore. I followed his gaze, our eyes collectively drawn to the tree line, where those billowing clouds had slithered their way into our section of the forest. Elijah was standing out there, his back facing us and his posture as still as the dead.

Let him go. Let him get swallowed. The thought was tempting but cruel. I had more to worry about than one man standing outside in the fog like a moron, but I couldn't do it. I couldn't let him just disappear. It was our job to make sure no one else ended up like all those missing people, like the delivery man, or like Jennifer Cook.

"What are you doing?! Get in here!" I yelled as I raced into the field of long grass and bushes. Daniel reached Elijah before I did, immediately grabbing hold of one of his arms. It was quickly swatted away. He never looked at us, he didn't speak. His eyes were glazed over in a trance-like state as he stared unblinkingly at the mist. He watched dark, impossible shapes move within the clouds as the fog billowed upwards, snaking through the branches as it spread. At first, it looked as though it had hit an invisible wall.

That hope was quickly snuffed out. The fog began to crawl across the ground, the grass beneath it quivering as if coming to life. But Elijah wasn't looking at any of that. His stare was fixed completely on the many pairs of eyes glowing white between the trees. They were staring straight at us with purpose—with hunger.

"She's in there," Elijah whispered hoarsely, his jaw slack as if half-asleep. "I hear her."

Between the groan of the trees and the bellow of something

large and angry in the distance, my ears weren't picking up anything else. Elijah was being tricked, just like those missing children, pulled toward the tempting embrace of the woods by promises too good to be true. We had no time to argue about it. Voice or not, we had to go.

Daniel let out a small yelp as I reached out to tug on the waistband of his belt, unhooking the keys he had connected to his pants. His moment of surprise at my rudeness dissipated in seconds when he caught on to the plan. We each grabbed one of Elijah's arms, and while he struggled with an unwillingness to leave the forest's edge, we had no choice but to drag him away kicking and screaming. And kick and scream, he most certainly did.

The trees quaked and branches snapped, the fog swirling around our heels as it grew ever closer, quickly abandoning the limits of the woods. I shouldn't have looked back. I shouldn't have even considered it. But as I listened to Elijah's breath hitch and felt the resistance of his body trying to pull away from my hold, I couldn't help but turn to look over my shoulder.

I hadn't had the incredible honor of seeing Jennifer's decayed and broken corpse as Daniel already had, skulking and falling apart as she struggled with every limb to chase after him. That changed as soon as my head turned and I caught an instant glimpse of her ruined self. The way she walked made no sense. She was so broken, so torn that I was shocked she didn't fall to pieces just trying to hold up her own weight.

She had changed. In the crack of her neck where the skin was split, the beginnings of a fifth limb grew out of her open throat. She had another set of dark, doe-like eyes on her forehead, slightly askew as if a second face was trying to emerge from the side of her head. Mushrooms were sprouting from her chest, tangled in the open cavities between her ribs. I never really understood the word 'shambling' so well until I watched her desperately move in every awkward, jerking motion that would bring her to us as if she needed to get closer no matter what it took.

Elijah's face was washed out, his legs and arms going limp as he was forced to take in the view of the woman he once loved now in a state of utter decay. Her whispers and croaks, her white orb-like eyes, and the way strings of her hair tangled between bits of exposed scalp and bone would be the last image he ever saw of Jennifer in the flesh. It would be mine as well.

I was the first to race up the stairs, with Elijah right behind me and Daniel pushing against his back to force him upward. Finn was waiting at the top, yelling for us to hurry the fuck up. He had already been attempting to pick the lock on his own. But as he moved aside, I unlocked the door as quickly as I could and threw it open, leaving the keys dangling on the outside. We all filed in one after the other, slamming the door behind us.

I wasted no time rushing to the desk, flipping my microphone on to give the emergency broadcast. The music had paused— of course it had. This place was getting better and better at making its own decisions all the time.

"There is a fog warning in effect for the village of Pinehaven. I repeat, fog warning for the village of Pinehaven. Please remain inside and lock all doors. Stay away from your windows. Stay tuned for further instructions, everything is under control."

It would take a few moments for the frequency to drive off the fog, but I hoped to God that we hadn't been too late. Buttons were pressed, my headphones were slipped on, and I got the music started once more. As it filled my ears, I breathed out a shaky sigh, knowing that relief was soon on its way. All the while, I watched the mass of gray mist outside the window with caution. Elijah was there, half-stumbling toward the glass, visibly shaken to the core and holding his breath.

From out of the fog bank, I could see a trace of pallid skin taking slow steps toward the window. She had crawled up the fire escape. Elijah, his legs shivering and knees buckled, put a quaking hand against the cold surface of the glass where there was pressure from the other side as well. Her hand, missing most of its fingers and long blackened from decay, was pushed against the glass as if she knew who stood on the other side. Obscured partially in the mist, the white glow of Jennifer's eyes and the open gape of her mouth were visible just inches away from where he stood.

If she was this close already, there was no telling what else was out there. We didn't have time to find out.

Elijah would have to say his goodbyes very quickly.

I jumped from my seat, unwilling to wait. The instant option was our *only* option. When Daniel saw me move across the room, he was already taking off his hearing aid, tossing it onto the table before it had a chance to go haywire. Without a moment's hesitation, my palm slammed down on The Bell with a satisfying push. Nothing happened, but that's how it always was. Just because we didn't hear it didn't mean the creatures didn't.

Jennifer's rotten mouth went wider, her jaw cracking as a muffled scream left her throat. The pain from the noise caused her distress which I hoped would drive her away. And perhaps she would have left if she hadn't been dragged away first. Everyone in the room felt a sudden shake from the fire escape, which jostled one way and then the other, before Elijah stepped back with a startled yelp. A long, clawed hand reached for Jennifer's throat and pulled her back with enough power to break whatever bones weren't already shattered.

We all saw a glimpse of the Amalgamate: six distinct eyes, the points of huge twisted antlers, and a hulking body covered in blood-soaked fur. As the fog began to clear, the beast grabbed Jennifer in both hands and snapped her clean in half like a twig, opening its jaws and ripping pieces of her flesh with ease. As it devoured her, it shook the entire room with the pounding of its horned forehead against the glass. My fist smacked the button once again as if perhaps the first time didn't work. I did not want to imagine in a million years that this thing was stronger than the sound.

Finally, the beast shrieked in both pain and anger. The fog cleared. It tossed the rest of Jennifer onto its shoulder to save for later before leaping off the fire escape and back to the ground, its muffled moans of agony becoming distant as it sank back into the safety of the woods. The mist was gone, taking every unnatural thing with it, leaving us in a sea of broken twigs, snapped branches, and a still and sickening quiet.

God, my heart broke. There was a heaviness in my chest, one of fear and despair. I always thought Elijah was a god-awful prick, but he didn't deserve to see *that*. I knew what would happen to Jennifer now, and it was a fact that made my stomach tighten into knots just imagining it.

The Amalgamate would take her back to the mountain, tearing her apart and claiming the pieces it wanted while tossing the rest aside like garbage to be devoured by the other, smaller beasts who settled with its rejected scraps. Jennifer was no longer herself. She was just one of the many who had been claimed by the giant's need to grow. I wondered briefly what parts it would take: her limbs, her hands, her eyes?

If we ever saw her again, it wouldn't be in this form.

"Finn," I said softly, "can you drive Elijah home?" I looked up at our new recruit, who had nothing rebellious to say. He simply nodded to me, grabbing the stunned and silent man by the arm to drag him away from the window.

We didn't say 'goodbye' as they left, but there was no need. This wasn't a pleasant visit and it deserved to be over as quickly as possible, left as a nightmare or a shared delusion we'd all try to forget. As soon as Finn's car eased away, Dan joined me at the desk and scooted his chair a little bit closer, noticing the way I sat with my head against the surface.

"Hey, partner," he said quietly, putting a hand on my back. He did it softly at first as if testing the waters before that subtle hand became a full arm wrapped around my shoulder. He was warm and he smelled nice, but that slight hint of cinnamon in his cologne made my eyes sting with tears. "Do you wanna talk about this?"

I shook my head, face still hidden.

"You want me to leave you alone?" he asked.

I shook my head again.

I don't know how long we sat there in silence, listening to the quiet hum of the radio through our abandoned headphones and watching the wind move through the trees. I thought about her the whole time. I wondered if she felt pain at the end and if she *still* felt pain now. I wondered how much of Jennifer was left in that body and if she had any memory of the life she used to have or the person she used to be. Thinking about the way she laid her hand on the glass, it was as if she knew Elijah was there, but I couldn't tell if she wanted to reach for him or rip him to shreds.

I would almost rather imagine that she was nothing more

181

than a beast now, mindless and driven by bloodlust. It hurt less than the other possibility: the idea that she was still in there somewhere and there was nothing we could do to save her.

Finally, when the early afternoon arrived, Daniel stepped out just long enough to get us some burritos. When he returned, we ate our lunch quietly while listening to the next tape from Number 7's hidden stash.

Here's what he had to say:

This is Eric: Operator Number 7 from the 104.6 FM Emergency Broadcast Station. It's the second day of December. The folks up at the town hall still haven't found me a co-host. They aren't willing to spare any of the men from the rangers' division and when we asked if anyone was available from one of the other outposts around the mountains, we were told 'not to hold our breath'. Goddamn, it's getting harder and harder to find people willing to work up here. So for now, it's just me.

The isolation is starting to drive me mad. I can't go home, I can't visit my family, I can't even do my own shopping. You know, we used to be able to leave. The forest is learning new tricks all the time—the last time I stepped out for a half hour, I came back to find the door locked from the inside and everything unplugged. I had to grab the hatchet out of my truck to bust the door open. Still haven't fixed the damn thing, so I'm sitting here with my coat on, freezing my ass right off. There was nothing waiting for me inside the building, but I found a trail of human hair and leaves going up the staircase. There was a strange, dark sap on the desk as if something had come in just to touch everything. I think it was a warning.

So now, I can't leave the place without worrying the radio will shut itself off again. Last night, though, I had no choice. I saw something out there, crawling around near the tree line. We've had a couple of kids go missing lately—a young boy, about six years old, and his ten-year-old sister. So when I saw something small near the edge of the forest, I grabbed a light and rushed down there to see if it was just a child in need of help.

After all this time living in this place, you'd think I would know better.

When I got to the edge of the clearing, the kid ran. He was laughing like it was some sort of game. He couldn't have been more than six or seven years old, but I never saw his face up close.

That's when he got down on all fours and started to sprint like an animal. I froze. My blood ran cold as he slipped into the darkness, running like a beast while giggling and clicking his tongue. Jesus Christ, the way he moved was so unnatural, too quick for a human child but too awkward to be an animal. The sound of his laughter turned strange. It was like something trying to mimic the giggle of a child, but only barely getting it right.

I heard a second child crying—wailing terribly somewhere in the distance. A new chill entered the air around me, separate from the winter cold and the fresh snowfall. It raised the hair on the back of my neck and made my guts tie themselves into knots. I made the decision to turn right around the way I came.

I didn't look back. But that entire time, I heard that sharp laughter right behind me, paired with small footsteps following after my own. I don't want to know what I would have seen if I turned my head. I didn't want to know what would happen when I saw his face.

When the cassette popped out of the player, Daniel and I were both wearing expressions of grim unease. I was thinking of the children that had gone missing, of the faceless man seen standing at the edge of the forest, of the whispers near the playground. Once upon a time, I used to be one of those kids, playing on the swings near the woods and looking out into the trees.

I wondered if I ever saw something I couldn't explain. If I did, it was best not to remember, right?

"I'd hate to be a kid getting lost out there," I said as a shiver crawled up my spine.

Daniel chuckled. "I thought you grew up here. Not a big fan of hikes?"

"Eh, my dad was real strict about me not going in the woods alone." I shrugged. "Mom was overbearing too. As soon as she got remarried, she sold the old place and practically *rushed* us out the door and as far away as we could get."

It still hurt, remembering the day we left. I was angry about it. I remembered arguing and crying because I would miss all my old friends, Jennifer, my school, and visits to the fire station. I would miss the shed where my dad used to fix up old cars and the tire swing I would spin on until I got dizzy. The city was different. It was bigger and lonelier. It was harder to think, harder to breathe.

"What about you?" I asked. "What do you remember about growing up?"

"Noise complaints," Daniel said without missing a beat, then laughed. "I'm joking. Mostly. But growing up with three sisters in an apartment – it was restless. You know, I wished we had grown up someplace like this. Not the creepy part, but having space to run and play outside."

I wore a little smile, looking out the window at the gentle breeze that shook the pines. Somehow, the fact that Dan was the eldest sibling didn't surprise me at all. He certainly acted the type. One moment he would be fussing over a papercut and chasing me around with a bandage, and the next we'd be smacking each other with clipboards for fun.

"Am I gonna meet your sisters at the wedding?" I asked, folding one foot underneath me.

"Oh yeah," Daniel said as he leaned back. "Elisa and Isabel are twins. Lilian is the youngest, she's—"

"The favorite?" I laughed, and Daniel nodded with a snort of his own. "Yeah, I've heard. Your mom wouldn't stop bragging about her the first time she called."

I liked talking about Daniel's family more than mine. His family was vibrant, energetic, funny, and *interesting.* They had their quirks and their stories, their silly little habits and inside jokes. It was weird the way I loved my parents dearly but found myself wishing I could have somehow transported myself into that little apartment where Daniel grew up instead. He may have envied me for growing up in the great outdoors, but I envied him for something even more valuable.

"Are you nervous?" he asked.

"About meeting your family or about leaving the tower?"

"Both."

My eyes went out of focus as I stared into the far distance

and mulled the question over in my head. I was nervous, yeah, but there was too much to think about. I didn't even know where to *start*. I was worried I'd make a bad impression, I was worried Daniel would regret taking me with him, I was worried I wouldn't know how to behave like a normal human being.

"A little," I shrugged. "I just hope your family doesn't have high expectations."

Daniel gave me that shit-eating grin he loved so much. "I'll just tell 'em I found you crawling around on the side of the road and decided to bring you along," he said.

"Go one step further, tell 'em you found me in a ditch."

"Sewer?"

"*Perfect.*"

As we sat and talked the afternoon away, just chatting about useless things, the heartbreak and terror of the day started to subside. It wouldn't go away entirely. I knew it would be visiting me again that night when I tried to sleep, coming back full-force in a wave of tears and restless dreams. For just a little while, though? We could pretend it didn't happen.

I'm pleased to announce that an old friend has returned. As Daniel and I listened to the cassette tapes, Bartholomew appeared and hopped up to the window. He didn't stop tapping on the glass the entire time.

CHAPTER SIXTEEN: LIFE GOES ON
Daniel

Finn always kept true to his word.

Days after Elijah showed up and the fog rolled in, our lives had slowed down to a sort of 'mellow weirdness'. One night, I saw shadows on the stairs, floating up and down beneath the tower. The day after, we got a call from old Luke Marshall—a guy who owns a cattle farm outside town. He said he shot a two-headed coyote right between one pair of its eyes, but the thing ran back into the woods with its dead head just flopping around. He wanted to ask if anyone else in the area had seen something similar, and no less than seven callers dialed in to say, "Oh, that's just Two-Headed Larry". I didn't question it.

As for Finn, he stuck around to check on things and deliver Evelyn's groceries once a week. He collected audio logs and videos from the security cameras to take back to the rangers; it was some part of their study on how the forest worked. And then, on a Friday evening, he showed up one more time to take Evelyn's keys and free her from the weight of her constant vigil. I'll never forget the relief on her face as the keychain fell out of her hand and into his, finally passing the torch of responsibility. It was only for a weekend, but it was a start.

Until that day, I had never seen Evelyn really *breathe.* Her feet hit the ground and she gazed up at the sky, her tired, heavy blue eyes wide with comfort. She looked lighter already. I wondered how long it had been since she felt alive.

"Last time I stepped out, I was getting *arrested,*" she laughed, shoving her hands in her pockets as she kicked a bit of gravel.

"Bad time to tell you I'm an undercover cop?" I joked, pointing a pair of finger guns her way. She put her hands up with an expression of mock fear. "So, where are you staying tonight? Need a place to crash?"

"I've got enough for a motel," she said, patting her ass to check for her wallet for the tenth time. "There's that one downtown on Parker Street. It'll put me close enough to the shops to find a dress to wear tomorrow."

I laughed, unlocking the car doors. "I thought we were getting matching tuxedos?"

Evelyn snorted as she climbed into the passenger side of my car. "If I can find two in both of our sizes, I'll let you know."

Very briefly, her eyes flittered down and I noticed the way she tried to avoid looking at the duct tape on the seats and the missing button on the stereo system. I wasn't exactly proud of my 'starving artist' phase, but Evelyn was either too understanding or too polite to mention how junked this old thing was.

She leaned back in her seat, buckling in and giving the tower one last look out the window before the wheels crunched against the gravel road. We began the slow, winding journey through the trees and out of the forest, back to the road where the air seemed lighter and smelled fresher.

I glanced in the rearview mirror, taking one last look at our workplace before we turned onto real, proper pavement. I had left so many times before, but it took me this long to realize that Evelyn had never left *with* me. There were no weekend lunches, no dinner parties, no nights playing darts at the bar with locals. I wished we could do this more often.

"What do you want for dinner?" I asked, scratching my chin and reminding myself to shave before morning. "I'll buy. We could get takeout and go to my place, maybe watch a movie?"

Evelyn was visibly thinking it over, her lips scrunched to one side of her face. "Maybe we can go to lunch tomorrow instead," she offered. "I think I just want to sleep right now."

I didn't push. She didn't need an excuse. I knew she deserved some time to herself that wasn't spent in the broadcast tower, sleeping in a *real* bed even if it was covered in a few mysterious stains and smells. "Yeah, that's fine," I told her, distracted by the annoying blink of the turn signal as we entered town. "I'll pick you up at noon tomorrow, how's that sound?"

"Sounds like a plan, my man." She stretched and her back gave a loud snap.

The rest of the ride was quiet, brief, and with a few small intervals of conversation when there was something worth talking about. Now and again, Evelyn would point out an old store that had shut down or tell me which houses her elementary school friends used to live in. She told me about the diner on Main Street and how it had been there since her parents were kids. *"They haven't remodeled since the Vietnam War,"* she said.

As much as she claimed she hated this place, the freedom of leaving the radio tower seemed to awaken a new appreciation for it. As we turned onto Parker Street and pulled up to the old Heritage Motel, she was leaning her head against the cold window.

She unbuckled herself from her seat, nothing on her person but her wallet, her phone, and the clothes on her back. She gave me a crooked smile, her freckled cheeks pulled into a grin as her hand fell on my shoulder with a hard clap.

"Call me before you pick me up, okay? I sleep through alarms."

"Will do, boss," I assured her. "Now go get some rest. And a shower. Oh, and see if they've got a free hair brush you can steal."

Evelyn turned up her nose at me, tongue sticking between her teeth. One playful swat later, she grinned and got out of the car, pushing the door shut behind her before tripping over the curb and straightening up again. She looked from side to side to see if anyone noticed. Then, she passed through the doors while giving one last pat to her back pocket to check for her wallet.

···‖··‖·‖‖·‖‖··‖‖···

I spent that night the way I spend a lot of nights. I went home to my apartment, locked the door, and grabbed some leftover cold pizza from the fridge. Back when I lived in the city, the world outside our windows was still alive when the sun went down. There was always the sound of traffic, people walking late at night, bars and clubs open late. Pinehaven was like a ghost town in comparison. I stood near my window on the second floor, looking across the way as little shops closed up for the night and the neighbors settled in.

The worst part of it all? I never realized I was lonely until I got here. Back home, all the noise made my little world feel lived-in. I could watch strangers stumbling home at night and imagine that I knew them. I could ride the bus for no reason and listen to gossip about people I'd never meet. Things were different here. Here, every-one knew everyone—except for me.

I was just a voice to them.

For a split second, I considered texting Evelyn to ask how things were going before I remembered that she was safer now than she ever had been. I'll admit there were many times when I sat awake at night and wondered why the hell I went back. Thinking about Lyn set up in the motel, both of us free from the broadcast station, made me wonder how we'd get away with just *leaving*. It would be so easy, wouldn't it? We'd just get in the car and drive. We could divide our money to get as far as we could, sleeping in the back of the station wagon if we had to, roughing it under the stars.

It felt wrong, though. To give up a burden we chose would just push it onto someone else. Finn would be the next on the list, sitting alone in the tower just like Evelyn and Number Seven and everyone who came before. I don't claim to be a perfect person, but I don't think either of us are that heartless.

As I lay down in bed, taking off my hearing aid and putting my phone on the charger, I saw the glow of the screen light up in the dark. I squinted at it, almost expecting some late-night spam text, but I was surprised and amused to see a row of messages from Evelyn instead.

Holy shit, they have REAL coffee in here! And it's not ducking gasoline!

Fucking, not ducking.

Autocorrect can kiss my ass.

I laughed, tapping away in response. **Save it for the AM, weirdo. Go to bed and you can tell me all about it tomorrow.**

And she did. At noon, just as I promised, I stopped by the

motel and parked at the curb just as she was dragging herself out the door. She had a department store bag full of wrinkled clothes in one hand and a to-go cup in the other. I tried hard not to laugh as she approached the car. She had found a simple green dress – plain yet attractive – but the part that made me chuckle was that she still wore the same pair of oversized, dirty old boots underneath it.

That aside, she looked neater than I had ever seen her before, somewhat rested and with her hair combed and falling in long waves. Her short, stubby nails were painted with black polish. It looked as if she had made some small attempt at makeup on her eyes and mouth, but there were patches of red skin where she had rubbed it off and tried several times to apply it again. Still, she looked good. She looked different.

"Hey, Dan. Look at you! We're gonna be the fanciest ass-holes at the diner." That was the first thing she said to me, and at that point, I knew that the change in appearance did not change the person. I was glad about that.

"You look nice for a change," I complimented. "And here I thought you'd find a tuxedo."

Evelyn smirked as she buckled herself in. "I was going to buy one, but I didn't wanna *outshine* you. Besides, I can't tie a tie."

"That's okay, me either." I glanced down at the blue tie at my collar, pinching the top and pulling it off the shirt in one motion. It was a clip-on.

Once we arrived at the diner, I felt fully immersed in real Pinehaven culture. Evelyn had been completely right about the out-dated furniture, but not even that could be as nasty as some of the looks we got from the locals. This was that 'small town paranoia' I had heard so much about. I hadn't lived in the village long enough to be considered a local, but from the glares of townsfolk sitting up at the bar, I got the distinct feeling I never would.

A white-haired, elderly waitress brought us coffee and Evelyn was being very precious with her cup so as to not spill on her new dress. As we waited for our orders, she glanced around but avoided looking at any one person for too long. In little towns like these, everyone knew one another. Everyone knew who moved in, who left, who came back, and who got into trouble. From the way people whispered and cast their eyes toward her, I got the feeling that Evelyn may have still had a reputation.

"What's the bride's name?" she asked. I felt like such an idiot then. I had mentioned her to my family dozens of times but hadn't even told her the name of the couple getting *married.*

"Her name's Adriana," I said. "She's sweet. You'll like her." I hummed for a second, going through the mental list of who all would be in attendance. "You'll get to see my parents, my aunts and uncles, my sisters ... Grandma only speaks Spanish but you'll meet her too."

Evelyn nodded. "Don't try chatting with grandma, got it."

"Oh, no, she'll still talk your ear off," I said. "Just smile and nod and pretend like you know what she's saying." I actually made Evelyn laugh that time—a *real* laugh, not one of her fake, polite little huffs that sounded like an angry hedgehog.

We saw people come and go through the diner, tables filling and emptying and then filling again. We talked the whole time about anything other than work or the woods. I talked about that time I worked at a movie theater, and she told me about breaking her ankle sliding down a fireman's pole as a kid. We shared stories of the worst dates we'd ever been on. We talked about college and our weirdest former roommates, then complained about how terrible the nachos were while simultaneously trying to get one another to eat an entire hot pepper in one bite. It was almost two-thirty in the afternoon and we were fifteen photos deep in a mobile album of my parents' dogs when we realized we weren't alone anymore.

A group passed by, made of four older men all dressed in eerily identical denim jeans and trucker hats. The last one spotted us out of the corner of his eye before he backed up a step, his eyes traveling from Evelyn's face to mine with a frown hidden somewhere in a bushy gray beard. He stopped next to our table, hands in his pockets, and spoke to us.

"I know you two," he said with a low, dry grunt. "Recognize your voices. I've been hearin' ya' over the radio."

Evelyn glanced over at me before an uncomfortable smile stretched across her face—it was more like a grimace than anything else. "Hey, thanks, I'm glad to hear someone actually listens to—"

"It won't do any good," he interrupted. It shut Lyn up in an instant. "Nothin' in this world is gonna stop it. We've been tryin' for a century, you'll be tryin' forever ... Tryin' as long as you last."

It was amazing how quickly everything seemed to dim, like life had been sucked out of the room. The old waitress stopped what she was doing and watched us from the corner. A family on the other side of the room put down their forks and knives, looking down at the table in silence.

"Bad weather's a-comin'," the man continued. "The cows have been actin' up, dogs howlin' day and night. Wind's been changin' directions. Y'all watch yourselves up there and start countin' your good days. Ya never know how many you've got left." He took a deep breath and looked out the window at the cloudy sky. Then, he tapped the front of his cap and nodded in farewell. "Good luck."

As unpleasant as that was, perhaps the distraction was a good thing. It was getting into mid-afternoon now and we had a couple of hours on the road to look forward to. Evelyn in particular didn't seem to mind the prospect of getting out of the village limits no matter how long it took.

After getting in the car and passing by the last rest stop before the winding road began, that easy feeling was coming back. We rolled down the windows to feel the mountain breeze, thick with static and the scent of incoming rain. I sang some classic show tunes and Evelyn complained. She counted road signs until she got to sixty-nine, at which point she laughed proudly and refused to count anymore. We kept the radio off the whole way.

It really was a wasteland. As soon as we left the village and rounded the mountain range that separated our little piece of civilization from the rest of the world, there was nothing to see for miles and miles. We passed a tiny rest stop with one gas pump, the inside of the building bathed in darkness and the door hanging off its hinge. We saw a barn that had been crushed in a landslide and a few abandoned homes left to rot into the ground. After that, it was just an endless expanse of forest.

All the way there, I couldn't help but wonder if anyone spotted strange things on *this* side of the mountain.

The sooner all traces of Pinehaven disappeared, the better.

Evelyn was talkative, but in a nervous sort of way, asking if I thought my family would like her and if they'd try to get her to drink any champagne.

"Don't worry," I assured as we pulled up to the building, several familiar faces already making their way in. "I'll make sure you stick to orange juice tonight."

It was oddly refreshing to sit through the ceremony, not only because I got to see my loved ones, but because it was a reminder of how life went on for the rest of the world. My cousin and her new husband looked happy. The children attending were whispering and rough-housing in their seats before their parents hushed them. My abuela was *loudly* crying in the front row, which made Evelyn snicker even though I could see a trace of her own heartfelt smile. None of that reminded me of the woods or of the radio tower. None of it scared me.

The normal world was still there and it wasn't as far away as I thought it was.

The reception was a whirlwind. Eventually, we left the pristine beauty of the church and filed into the back yard where tables had been set with heavy weights on each end to keep the white cloth from flying away in the wind. There was a live band playing, kids running amuck, and *everyone* wanted to talk to me and Evelyn. Now, to be fair, my family is naturally energetic and chatty, but it hit us like a brick wall as soon as we arrived.

Everyone wanted to know where I had been, who she was, and why I left home. Poor Evelyn was stark-white and stiff as a board while getting ambushed with another hug from a family member who assumed she was my significant other, and that was when I decided it was time to find a place to sit.

"Your family is sweet," she said once we had a second to sit and take a breath. I laughed, knowing what she meant by 'sweet'.

"Sorry, I know they're a bit much. I only told them good things about you."

"Oh, really?" She had that devilish grin again. "Did you tell them about my terribly crude language and all the highly infectious diseases I'm carrying?"

"Oh, yeah," I nodded. "And I warned them about the smell, too."

She punched me in the shoulder and we had a good laugh before my mother decided to make an appearance at last, recognizing Evelyn by association. At first, it looked like my poor coworker was about to have an allergic reaction to all the love in the room, but eventually, that socially-exhausted smile started to turn into a real, genuine one.

While my mom was asking Evelyn a million questions, I stepped away for a moment to grab a couple of drinks. I came back with champagne for myself and a cup of orange juice for her. I wasn't one to take back a promise.

Before the night was over, I learned a few things. I learned that I'm not the biggest fan of champagne, that jokingly calling Evelyn *'La Llorona'* is a quick way to get smacked by my grandmother, and that neither of us had any rhythm for slow-dancing. She graced me with one dance near the end of the reception, stepping on my toes at least a dozen times. I didn't complain. We both left with a smile and every sore toe and scuffed shoe was worth it.

My parents walked us out to the car, giving us so many hugs that I thought maybe they suspected I'd never come back. Abuelita wasn't far behind, pinching Evelyn's freckled cheeks and calling her a 'good, sweet girl'. The poor old woman had no idea.

Before we left, my sister Isabel reminded me to start calling our parents more often.

"At least once a week," she told me with a laugh and a cigarette between her teeth. "Mom keeps calling *me* asking if you died."

"You wouldn't get that lucky," I said. It was a joke, but in the back of my mind, I couldn't help but wonder how they would react if something *did* happen to me. All this time, I had been shielding them from the reality of what happened up there in the forest. I didn't want them to know. But could I really keep it a secret forever?

The drive back to town was a long one, but it started off on the right foot. We listened to some of the old, classic cassettes I had tossed in the glove box and laughed about my family's antics. We stopped at a gas station to load up on sugar and potato chips and afterward, Evelyn put her feet up on the dash and sipped her soda while pointing at cows and horses as if she'd never seen the damn things before. She was a different person outside of the tower; I felt as if I had found a new level of her highs and lows. I wished that I could put that feeling in a bottle for her.

We watched wildflowers rush by and saw a red sunset bloom over the river valley. And as Evelyn stuck her hand out the window to ride the breeze while singing along to Johnny Cash, it was one of those moments when I realized that we were actually friends.

Things felt different the moment we remembered where we were headed. When the sun disappeared and we found ourselves weaving down a dark path flanked by trees, the gloom started to creep back into the car. I watched Evelyn lean her head against the window, staring thoughtfully into the shadows of the pines. It wasn't until the mountain range came into view that the full weight of our return began to eat away at the glow of a genuinely nice evening.

Looking back, if I had known better, I would have turned around and taken Evelyn right back to the city that night.

CHAPTER SEVENTEEN: BLOOD SACRIFICE
Daniel

Before long, we were at the outskirts of the village, passing a little Christmas tree farm and a green pasture full of sleepy cattle.

"I don't want to go back yet," Evelyn said, still staring out her window. "Not until morning, at least."

I knew that if I had my way, we wouldn't go back at all.

"Wanna crash at my apartment?" I asked. "I'll let you have the bed. Hell, I'll even make you breakfast. I make a *mean* scrambled egg."

Evelyn considered it for a moment, fidgeting in her seat. She was doused in the red glow of the only stoplight in town. Her gaze followed the passing cars, the crack in the windshield, the rear-view mirror ... anywhere but my face. Finally, she cocked her head to the side, a new idea sparking in her eyes.

"No," she said, "let's go to my place instead."

I'll admit, I was confused but still curious. We passed the apartment building, the residential district, and the shops. I was driving slowly, expecting her to tell me to stop or take a turn, but she never did. She waited until we were driving by the old elementary school to point out the window at a small stone driveway near the park.

"Here," she said. "Let's pull in here."

I did as she said, putting the car in park right in front of the school playground. It was empty, as to be expected, but the swings were swaying gently on their own with a sharp, spine-tingling creak. It was eerie in the dark, one flickering street lamp flooding the park with a dirty yellow glow. Beyond the faded plastic playground equipment was a gentle hill that met the thick, dreary tree line.

Evelyn gave me a look, her eyebrows raised as she nudged her head toward her door. She unbuckled herself and stepped out, stretching her legs after the long drive and giving her back a good few snaps. I followed behind her, shoving my keys into my pocket.

"So, this is–"

"My last residence," she said without hesitance, stepping up on a curb stop and then hopping back down on the other side. She kicked a bit of gravel out of the way and began to step toward the border between grass and wood chips. It was summer vacation for the students now and the place was getting overgrown with weeds and black-eyed Susans.

"I went to school here as a kid," she continued. "I played here with my old friends. Dad would put me on the swings and pull me back as far as he could to see just how high I could go ... When Jenny and Elijah kicked me out, I slept underneath the slide for a few weeks. So, this is it. This is my place."

The sudden change of direction hit me like a brick wall. While Evelyn passed under the monkey bars, lifting a hand to gently tap the metal above her head, I stood still and just watched her move about the playground like a ghost. The paint was chipping, the swing's bars were slightly bent, and the merry-go-round shrieked as the wind turned its rusted gears.

I looked at the slide, which was made of bright yellow plastic that had faded in the middle from years of use. Underneath was a pile of wood chips, as well as a few stray pieces of trash from kids and teenagers who bummed around here after school. It didn't look like a comfortable place to sleep.

"I'm ... sorry," I said as I ducked under the monkey bars.

"Shit, man, don't say you're sorry," Evelyn laughed as she grabbed a swing, propping one foot up on the seat and then the other. She swayed back and forth slowly, both hands on the cold chains. "Just ... I dunno. Ask if the wood chips ever poked me in the ass. Make a joke about it. Laugh. It doesn't have to be awkward anymore, Danny."

I sat down on the swing beside her, giving her an embarrassed smile. Alright. If that's what she wanted, it wouldn't be awkward anymore. I pushed off the ground and gently drifted forward and backward, all the while wondering when she decided to start calling me 'Danny'.

"So, *did* the wood chips ever poke your ass?"

She cackled. "Oh yeah, all the time. You know what was way worse, though? Waking up face-to-face with a raccoon at, like, two in the morning. Or a kid poking me with a stick because he thought I was dead."

"In the kid's defense, sometimes I wanna poke you with a stick too," I joked, leaning to the side to evade her as she tried to give me a little kick.

She plopped her boots back down on the ground to properly take a seat on the swing, using one foot to slowly tip forward and back. I slowed to match her speed, listening to the squeak of the chains in unison. We were both facing the woods, a feeling that brought me discomfort and dread. I could only imagine it did the same for her.

"Finn told you about the abductions, right?" she asked, her eyes stuck on the tops of the trees. "He said the kids were being lured into the woods outside the school. You think he meant right here?"

A chill went up my spine and I chuckled in an awkward, reluctant sort of way. "Oh God, don't say *that*. At least wait until we leave to put that image in my head."

Evelyn made a spooky *'wooo'* noise and wiggled her fingers at me. This was how she did things. This was how we both did things. If we were scared or uncomfortable, we had to laugh about it or else we'd go mad.

We were swinging in silence for a few minutes before Evelyn began to slow, her foot nearly motionless on the ground as she drifted to a stop. I noticed the way she sat perfectly still, looking down at the wood chips beneath her feet. Her eyes were more glassy than usual.

"The wedding was nice," she said softly, a touch of sorrow in her tone. "Thanks for inviting me."

"Oh, sure, no problem. Well, technically my *mom* invited you, but—"

"Yeah, but I wouldn't have gone if you didn't agree to go with me." She looked up at me instead of at the ground. There was a sad, uneasy expression on her face as if the fake smile she wore caused her physical pain. I didn't know what to say to make it all better.

"You know," she continued, "I hoped I'd be going to Jenny's wedding someday. Maybe I'd be a bridesmaid, help her get ready, go to some stupid party with all her other friends that I would complain about for weeks." She gave a joyless chuckle and then sniffled. Her grief was still palpable. I could feel it radiating off of her, sometimes subtle and sometimes strong but never very far away.

"I know how Elijah feels," she said, "to miss someone so much that everything reminds you of them."

I had stopped swinging, leaning my head against one chain and quietly listening.

"I feel bad for the guy," I said. "Even if he did try to break my nose."

"You just have one of those punchable faces," she smirked.

Here we were again, in a situation that wasn't funny, still chuckling. In hindsight though, the moment I got out of my car and ended up getting leveled onto the gravel was kind of hilarious.

Evelyn kicked at the ground and began to swing again, leaning back to look up at the sky. When I copied her, I found it to be surprisingly dizzying. The sky was clear and the stars were brighter out here away from the lights of town. I could imagine they were even more dazzling at the tower, but I had never paid much attention. Maybe I should.

"I never saw stars like this in the city," I said, watching a distant plane blink as it crossed the sky. "I don't really know my constellations."

"I know a few," Evelyn closed one eye and stuck her tongue out in concentration. "You can usually see Mars this time of year. Here, gimme your hand, I'll show you."

Just as we were scanning the stars, the hunt for the red planet was cut abruptly short. Her eyes snapped to the tree line, wide and panicked. I adjusted my hearing aid and that was when I heard it too: the sound of footsteps through dry grass and leaves. They were taking small steps, moving quickly and clumsily. Evelyn was the first to stand, squinting up at the gentle slope of the hill.

I expected to see some abnormal creature crawling out from

the bushes, but what we saw instead was a little figure dressed in red pajamas taking those final steps into the forest. He was reaching for something—something tall and obscured by the shadows of the trees.

It was exactly as we feared.

"Did you see him?" she asked, but she didn't need to. I was already on my way, breaking into a jog while she ran beside me. "Was he following something? Oh, *goddammit, Dan.*"

We didn't wait around to come up with a plan. As we hurried toward the edge of the forest, we made that silent agreement that catching up with the boy was our only option. We could call someone, sure. But would they ever find him? Would anyone ever find him?

I got to the top of the hill first, stopping to grab Evelyn by the arm and pull her the rest of the way. Although she was out of breath, she was the first to rush ahead and break the tree line that separated our safe, normal world from one that was wild and blood-thirsty. In these misshapen blobs of shadow where it was difficult to tell the difference between a bush and an animal, our eyes were in constant search of a flash of red cloth, a hint of movement, or the glow of eyes.

This place was alive. The forest was echoing our steps. My one intact ear was ringing, but in that muffled mess, I could hear the deep, painful groans of unseen beasts. I could hear footsteps and crunching twigs. There came a time when I could no longer tell what sounds were coming from us and what sounds were coming from the woods, but twice Evelyn stopped in her tracks and grabbed my arm to keep me still. She was listening. I felt my own heartbeat racing out of control, so powerful that it hurt. I thought I could hear the distant cry of a child and little footsteps, sometimes running and sometimes walking.

Evelyn heard it better than I did. She held up two fingers: *two* sets of feet. We didn't wait around before breaking into a run once more, following the upward tilt of the mountainside.

"Where the hell did he go?" Evelyn grabbed a tree, panting for breath as she looked from side to side. I could no longer see the tree line or the lights of town. There was no telling how far we had gone. Shit, I couldn't even tell the *direction* we were facing anymore. I was terrified, but we would worry about finding our way out when we found the boy and not a moment sooner. He was so young, so small. I knew that neither of us could live with ourselves if we were the last ones to see him alive and we refused to do anything.

"I don't see him anymore," I said, my legs stiff and tired as we soldiered on at a slower pace. We had been staying quiet, speaking close and in hushed tones, but we were already lost and standing in plain view. There was no point in hiding now.

"Hey! Little boy!" I cupped my hands over my mouth and yelled. "We're here to help you! Where are you?!"

We both jumped as a small group of bats tittered and squeaked above us, abandoning their perch in the tree and flying away. Something small stirred in the long grass, making the bushes quake. All around us, an eerie silence took over and chilled my spine as if a ghost had just passed through my body. I felt goosebumps on my arms as Evelyn grabbed my wrist and pointed a finger into the distance.

"I heard crying," she said. "He's that way. *He's that way!*"

The constant, sharp ringing in my ear drowned out most of the noise, but when I paid close attention, I could make out some slight suggestion of a high-pitched, uneven sound. It was the sobbing, hiccuping voice of a child, moving further away from us until I could no longer hear him. But Evelyn could. She took the lead and guided me through a section of close-growing pines that scratched at my neck as we pushed their branches aside. They felt like claws. Some of them moved on their own but I didn't dare look.

We were running at full speed when we finally noticed a flash of red up above. It was on the ground, crumpled up in a heap. My heart sank, hoping and praying that the only red stain in my vision was the color of his clothes. As we grew closer, we saw the child move, rocking back and forth with his body hunched and little fists pounding into the dirt in frustration.

"Hey, buddy. It's okay. Shh, calm down," Evelyn dropped down to the boy's level, putting her hands on his back. He looked alarmed to see us at first, his tear-stained face flushed bright red and covered in dirt. He seemed ready to burst into terrified wails until he realized he was looking at two very ordinary humans. I didn't want to even imagine what he had seen already.

He didn't say anything, but it broke my heart to see the way he crawled toward Evelyn as if looking for someone to comfort him. *Anyone.* He had to be no older than three. Shit, this kid was barely old enough to upgrade from a crib. He could have been dead, and the sight of this tiny thing becoming prey to the forest was something I don't think I would ever recover from.

"Let's start walking," I said, offering Evelyn my hand. "We'll either find our way back to the road or we'll see the radio tower, one or the other." The little boy wrapped his arms around her neck, seemingly content to cling to her rather than walking on his own.

"Shit," she sighed. "He's shaking like a leaf."

I almost commented that maybe she should watch her language around a three-year-old, but it didn't seem like the time or place for that.

"Lyn? Have you been keeping track of which direction we've been going in?"

She grumbled. "No, I haven't. And I can't see a damn thing out h—"

She suddenly stopped, almost jumping out of her skin as the tree branches behind us shivered and branches snapped. For only a second, I saw a dark shape taller than myself moving quickly through the pines. It appeared and disappeared so quickly, darting from one side to the other and sinking back into the darkness. Evelyn held the little boy tighter to her chest as he whined and hid his face in her shoulder, his tiny hands taking fistfuls of her hair.

"Walk faster. *Walk faster,*" she hissed, taking quicker steps. The look of panic on her face was one I had only seen once before. It was the same face I saw the night the power went out, but this time, we were in enemy territory without a generator. This was their domain and we were lost in it, just three lambs leading themselves to slaughter. The creatures of Pinehaven Forest were already out looking for us, fog or no fog.

We heard a shrill voice. The little boy screamed, his shriek breaking through the quiet night air as he pointed into the darkness behind us. His little hand was shivering, gesturing to something I couldn't see.

We stopped, one last crunch from both of our feet bringing silence around us. And then, we heard another crunch, then
another, *then another.* It was moving at an agonizingly slow pace. I
hated to turn, but I had no choice. My mouth was as dry as sand and
my heart was racing the moment I glanced over my shoulder, seeing
a figure standing perfectly still just a few yards away. It was tall and
thin, facing us with a blank wooden stare. His face was gone, encased
in twisted tree roots that continued to wiggle and crawl over his head
like parasites. The clothes hanging off his body were torn to reveal
a skeletal cavity with vines and bark curling into his hollowed-out
corpse.

He creaked when he moved, joints snapping like the brittle
branches of a dead tree with each step. As he swayed on the spot as
if moved by the wind, I had the fleeting idea that perhaps the blind
creature wouldn't spot us if we stayed silent and still.

But then I blinked, and he was closer. The sound of cracking
twigs followed as he took long, awkward strides toward us on legs
that snapped with every step. He made no sound and had no voice
as if the human inside of the wooden mask had been eaten away entirely.

The little boy screamed and Evelyn and I both began to run,
her speed impaired by the weight in her arms. She was yelling at me,
her words drowned by the child's cries and the chaos of the forest
around us. Her screams were mostly curses of panic and rage, but I
distinctly heard her say, *"Don't look back."*

I didn't, but I still made the mistake of looking at her instead
of watching where I was going. Shadows swirled around us, dead
faces peering out from between the trees. My feet hit the edge of a
thorn bush and I was startled by the impact, faltering in my steps
and collapsing forward onto the forest floor. My forehead hit something solid and I saw a bright flash of swirling color in my vision.

Time seemed to go slower then. My arms felt numb and
cold, so weak I couldn't push myself up. It took me two attempts to
realize something was pressed against the back of my head, keeping
me trapped against the soil.

It was a blur of activity and noise. When my head hit the

ground a second time, a sharp pain sent an electric surge through my back. I felt something crack in my chest and the pain became so blinding that I couldn't help but scream. A heavy weight pressed down against the center of my body and I smelled the stench of dead flesh, leather, and mud. Twigs wrapped around my shoulders, but they weren't really twigs at all. They were wooden hands, flipping my body over until I saw the sky and the silhouette of the root-faced man looming over me like a curious beast toying with its meal.

I coughed and tasted blood. My vision began to swirl. The creature disappeared into the trees, but not before cracking his boot against the side of my head one more time. Seconds were stolen away from me as I drifted in and out of sleep, time moving fast and then slow and then fast again.

I heard the little boy crying. I heard Evelyn screaming at the top of her lungs. One moment, I was looking up at the stars, and the next, I was looking at her frightened face as she pulled me by the sleeves of my shirt while the boy clung to her hip.

"Danny, you have to get up!" Her voice was distorted, sometimes loud and sometimes quiet. "Danny, *please!*"

I felt her tighten her grip as she tried to lift me, but I was just dead weight. No matter what I did, I couldn't move. The best I could do was force the air through my lips to speak a single word: *"Go."*

She shook her head. Every time I blinked, moments were lost to me. Evelyn screamed at the boy, telling him to run in a hoarse, broken voice. An instant later, the warmth of her hold was torn away as she was ripped off of me and up into the trees. I could no longer blink. I couldn't move my head. I could only watch as the towering creature shook her and held her in the air by her throat while she struggled.

With long, wooden fingers, it rubbed her forehead, her cheeks, her hair. It pushed her bangs away from her face to inspect the look of terror that she wore, its sharp claws leaving scratches on her skin. She was flailing and kicking desperately for freedom, sobbing with the anguish of one who knew she was going to die. Paralyzed and half-awake, all I could do was watch.

The beast was tracing lines on her face, reading her like braille. That moment was so painfully slow until finally one finger found the top of her eyelid and pushed it up to reveal a frantic, darting eye. Evelyn was dripping with sweat, tears flowing down her face as she screamed for help; I couldn't even fucking *move*. I tried to. I tried so hard to stand. Even with my head spinning, there was no mistaking the scream that tore through her throat a moment later, nor could I ever forget the sound of sharp claws *digging* into soft tissue. The monster tilted Evelyn's head back and drove its finger into her eye socket slowly, bright red blood dripping down her face and into the grass. Onto my clothes. Onto my skin.

She cried. Oh, dear God, she cried with a wail that hurt more than anything else. I watched the beast give one strong tug, a spray of red flying just before he dropped her onto the ground, where she writhed and squirmed from side to side in misery. One hand covered her face, but even in the darkness, I could see blood pouring through her fingers.

The root-faced man brought his hand up to his own chest, putting a mass of blood and flesh into his body cavity as if it were a pocket. Evelyn was still crawling, one of her red-stained hands finding my shirt. She nudged me, but I couldn't reach for her—she probably thought I was dead.

I blinked and the beast was gone. I blinked again, and suddenly a dark shadow loomed over me, swaying and cocking his head one way and then the other as if looking for signs of life. I watched as he tilted his head upward, and from the center of his neck, a single blue eye opened and focused on my face.

I only saw it for a split second. Then, the smell of leather and the pain of impact sent everything back into that quiet, cold darkness.

Like being in a dream, nothing was linear. Nothing made sense. I no longer heard Evelyn's sobs, but I heard the distant voice of a man, so distorted and strange that I wasn't even sure if it was real. My sparse hearing picked up the pop of gunshots, the terrible screech of the monster, and heavy steps through the leaves and twigs.

Then, all I knew was pain. I was being dragged through the grass, drifting in and out of consciousness while the view of a starry sky swirled above my head. Sometimes, I could see a glimpse of heavy black boots and a pair of denim jeans. I could see limp strands of long red hair and a body tossed over a broad shoulder.

The final time I closed my eyes, they wouldn't open again for a good, long while.

···‖‖···‖·‖‖‖‖·‖‖···‖‖···

I didn't dream. I floated in a strange place, drifting back now and again just long enough to hear my mother's muffled voice or to feel cold hands touching my face. When I finally felt real again, the sharp scent of disinfectant was the first thing I was fully aware of. Underneath me was a stiff but warm mattress, and my fingers were touching smooth wires and cords. It was a chore to open my eyes, but when I did, the room was too bright to see. I blinked into the light until my vision began to clear, and suddenly, I was looking up at a white ceiling and a halo of machines.

I glanced down at my body and saw bandages peeking out from the neck of a blue paper smock. My chest was wrapped. I could feel the irritation of stitches and medical tape on my forehead. Before I had the chance to speak out into the open room, a faint voice greeted me from my bedside.

"Hey ... Can you hear me?"

"Yeah," I whispered, too low to even hear myself. My tongue and throat were dried up and my lips were cracked. I turned my head with effort and pain until I could finally see Evelyn sitting in the chair beside my bed, curled up with her knees against her chest. She was leaning her head on one arm of the chair as if she had been sleeping. She wore a hospital gown two sizes too big and a paper bracelet on her wrist, a large bandage covering one eye.

"Lyn, what day—"

"It's Wednesday," she said. "It's good to see you, Danny Boy."

I could say the same. Before being plunged into a near-comatose state, my final thoughts were all regrets. I couldn't save her, I couldn't save the little boy, I couldn't save myself. We could have all died. Maybe we did.

"Where's the kid?" I asked.

"He's okay," she sighed. Her words washed me with relief. "He's okay, Danny ... Finn found us. He chased the thing away and the rangers brought us back. The little boy wasn't hurt."

I was suddenly struck by the impulse to hold out my hand and I did so without even thinking. Evelyn looked down at my open palm for a moment before putting her hand in mine, our arms creating a bridge. She was cold and shaking. She looked smaller than before.

"W-we were afraid you weren't gonna wake up," she said with a sniffle, turning her eye up to the overhead lights to blink away tears.

"And miss out on pestering you? Never," I said with a weak little smile, my cracked lips stinging when they stretched. I found myself staring at her bandaged face, inspecting the hint of surgical tape peeking out from behind the patch.

"Can they fix it?" I asked. "Your eye?"

It was a stupid question. Evelyn just shook her head slowly and spoke in a hoarse croak, a heavy frown pulling at the corners of her lips. "He took it," she said. "The whole thing."

"Fuck ..." I looked for the right words, but there weren't any. "Evelyn, I'm so sorry. ... I-I'm so sorry."

She had no witty jokes, no sassing, no crude humor. Her 'Evelyn-ness' was gone. As we looked at one another across the way, my head on the pillow and hers on the arm of her chair, I remembered this moment as it happened once before.

She was lying next to me on the floor of the radio station. My ears were burning and the scent of blood was pungent in my nose. Evelyn's voice was far away, but I saw her mouth the words:

"Wanna sleep on an actual mattress?"

This time, I was the one to say it. I watched her stone-cold expression falter as a stiff lip began to quiver, and after a moment of hesitation, she nodded her head and wiped away a tear. Our hands slipped away from one another as she pushed herself out of the chair gingerly. That was when I saw for the first time just how many bruises littered her shoulders, neck, and limbs. I gritted my teeth with discomfort in an attempt to move over a few inches, but it was enough for her in the end.

My coworker, who once upon a time wouldn't even shake my hand, crawled into the bed beside me and laid her head on my chest without a single word. Her pale hand, spotted with freckles and with fingernails bit right down to the quick, rested over my heart where she could feel my pulse.

She closed her one remaining eye and I closed mine, drifting off to sleep while hoping that this would be the last blood sacrifice either of us would ever have to make.

CHAPTER EIGHTEEN: NATURAL ORDER
Finn

It wasn't often that Sheriff Jacobs would honor the emergency outpost with his presence, but at nine o'clock in the morning on a Thursday, he did just that.

I saw the way his eyes grew dull as he entered the building, the stern frown on his face turning weary as if he had aged ten years just by looking at the damn place. He observed the computer monitors, the security cameras, and finally settled his gaze on the main lookout window that pointed up at the largest ridge of mountains. Pinehaven Forest was quiet that morning.

"I don't miss coming up here," the sheriff said with a heavy sigh. "How are you settlin' in, Finn?"

"Just waiting for it to all be over," I responded, getting out of my seat to give the sheriff's hand a heavy shake. "Any news on how our Operators are doing up in Beckley?"

Andre put his hands in his pockets, taking a few steps toward the lookout. From up here, we could see all of Pinehaven. The door was ajar, letting in the humid summer air and the sound of very distant church bells ringing out the time.

"McKinnon's doing alright," he said. "They sealed up the eye socket. No infection, thankfully, but she's real ornery about the whole thing. Piss and vinegar, that one. As for Esperanza, he finally woke up last night. A bit of physical therapy and I reckon he'll be up and down those stairs again soon."

"We should put in an elevator," I joked, leaning against the desk on my palms. "Even I had trouble getting up here this morning."

The sheriff laughed—it was a low, hoarse laugh that I rarely heard from him. "That's because you're gettin' old, my friend." Big talk from a man with more gray hairs than a timber wolf. "Listen, all jokes aside, you and I need to have a conversation about that."

"What, my last will and testament?" I scoffed.

"No, smartass," Andre pulled out a chair and sat at the edge of the desk, one ankle crossed over his leg. "We gotta talk about what the hell we're gonna do with you. Now, we've got some young folks joining up with the rangers but none of them have had the kind of training you've had. They could use a mentor, someone who can really—"

I scratched my beard, already shaking my head before he even finished. "Andre, you know how I feel about goin' back into the woods," I said, sitting down across from him with both arms resting on my knees. "It hurt like hell to turn my badge in, you know that, but I can't go back. I can't stomach it yet. Maybe one day, but it ain't gonna be today, I can tell you that much."

Andre nodded. He seemed to expect exactly what he got.

"I understand," he said softly. "That's why I've got another idea. How do you feel about staying up here for a while?"

I was pulling my lighter out of my shirt pocket, flicking it open and closed out of habit. The boss would kick my ass if he saw me smoking up here, but I had to do something with my hands or I'd start to go crazier than a shit-house rat.

"You want me to stay on as an Operator?" I asked with a smirk at the corner of my lips. "I ain't no radio host, Andre."

"Neither are the majority of folks who have sat behind this desk," he said as he patted the surface with a rough hand. "But can I be honest with you for a moment? Man to man, in confidence?"

I grabbed a toothpick from my pocket and stuck it between my teeth, biting down with a soft crack.

"Shoot."

Andre ran his tongue along his teeth, giving another glance to the window before he spoke. "These two aren't gonna last," he said. It was matter-of-fact, his tone cold with disappointment. "I had high hopes for McKinnon, given her father's good name, but she's an apple rolled too far from the tree. She's reckless. Esperanza ... well, he's a decent broadcaster but we never expected him to stick around. After last weekend, I'll be surprised to see him come back at all."

I was looking down at the floor now, tapping my foot impatiently.

"You're already lookin' for a Number Thirty."

"Yeah," Andre nodded. "Yeah, I am. I know it ain't your dream job, Finn. It ain't what you trained for. But the way you handled that situation over the weekend was just about as clean as could be—I don't know many folks who can handle pressure the way you do."

I couldn't help but flinch. I knew McKinnon and Esperanza had done their best to keep that little kid safe—if they were better prepared and had a little firepower on their side, they may not have needed my help.

"I saw folks in trouble and I did something about it, that's all there is to it," I argued.

"And that's enough," the sheriff said, clapping his hands on his knees before standing up and circling around the desk. "You did well out there, Finn. You don't have to keep being modest about it. Now, I've got to get back to the station, but I'll call and let you know as soon as I get more news from Beckley."

As he stood, I followed suit, giving his hand one last firm shake.

"I'll make sure this place doesn't fly away, don't worry. Do me a favor and send someone out to feed my dogs, will you?"

"I think I can manage that," he said, putting a hand on my shoulder. "One more thing. Keep your head on straight. This place is going to try to get to you. Don't let it, alright?"

After growing up in Pinehaven my whole life, I didn't think there was much in this world that could get to me. But I would be the first to admit that the tower was a whole different story. Up there, trapped in a box with the wind whistling through the wooden beams, I felt like a newborn bird looking down from the nest for the first time. Everything was so much bigger from up here. The worst part of it all? When I looked out over the pines and into the deep, dark forest, I knew something was looking back.

In the mid-afternoon, it began to rain. It was one of those refreshing summer rains, breaking the heat just enough to take the

211

stickiness out of the air. I spent that time listening to the pitter-pat-ter against the window and cleaning up the mess of files sitting on Evelyn's desktop. I'm no expert with technology, but the way she refused to put things in order was enough to make my head spin.

Calls were coming in every day. Folks in town wanted to know when Evelyn and Daniel were coming back, why police vehicles were parked at the edge of the woods, and why the elementary school playground was blocked off with yellow tape. I didn't like having to lie to people, but I remembered what Andre had been telling me for years. *"Plenty of people around here already know the truth,"* he would say, *"but most folk aren't ready."*

For now, the story we were running with was that McKinnon and Esperanza had been attacked by a wild animal on their way back into town. Most people accepted it at face value – a few even sent in cards or kind letters. Others had questions.

"I heard screamin' from the trees." A young man who works at the corner store called in right before five o'clock. "It was Sunday night, I think. Real late. I took my dog out and he was hollering like mad, his back all bristled and everything. That's when I heard it ... A woman, I think. It was the kind of sound that curdles your blood."

It was a mistake to take that call live on the air, because he wasn't the only one. More people dialed in after that, telling their own tales of what they heard the night our Operators came back to town. A mother of two living near the school said she heard a child crying, but knew better than to follow the sound. "My pa always told me not to follow the cries that come from the woods," she said. An old man walking home from the bar that night saw a flock of crows circling over a spot in the forest. He said he knew something was wrong from the red ring around the moon and something he called 'the ill wind'.

I got one more call right before the sun went down.

"This is Finn at 104.6 FM, I've got you on the line. What can I do for you this evening?"

"That young boy isn't ever going to be the same, is he?" It was the voice of an older woman, soft and frail. As sweet as that voice was, something about it tickled the inside of my ear like a cold finger trying to dig into my brain.

"I'm not too sure I know what you're referring to, ma'am," I said to her.

"You do, my darlin'," she said kindly, voicing a small giggle. "That sweet little boy in the red pajamas. He's going to remember that night for the rest of his life, maybe not in the way the others will but in his own particular way. He'll think of it when he drifts off to sleep. He'll wonder if it really happened or if it was just a recurring nightmare he's had his whole life. He won't ever look at the forest again without thinking about it."

An instinct beckoned me to turn around and I did, glancing into the darkened corners of the room. I saw nothing except the creeping shadows that filled the empty spaces and the subtle flicker of the light over my head. Still, I didn't feel alone.

How did she know his pajamas were red?

I turned off my microphone. "I don't know where you got that information from, ma'am, but there's plenty of rumors going around that—"

She laughed, and the tone of her voice began to change. It fluctuated, neither old nor young, male nor female. Then it settled back into that sickly-sweet, elderly tone.

"Finn, you know exactly what he's going through, don't you?" With every word she spoke, the air around me felt colder. "You've been there too. Eight years old, right? Your daddy took you hunting for the first time. *Building character,* he said. What did you see out there, darlin'?"

I was holding my breath. Although I knew exactly where I sat, a part of me was afraid that taking in the air would bring the scent of blood and decay with it. Her words began to summon images I had long forgotten: too many crooked limbs, a rotten human face, a massive jaw unhinged to feed on the tangled remains of an animal I couldn't recognize. I remembered the way it looked at me in the dark of early morning, its eyes pure white.

I remembered the way its head split in two when my father aimed his shotgun at its nose and how it still tried to get up and follow us afterward. Its head dangled in two pieces like an eggshell cracked in half, but still, it didn't die. I don't think they ever really die.

Suddenly, I found myself thinking of something my father used to say. Every time he took his shotgun out to the woods, he'd come home and tell me, *"it was a good hunt"*. But he always came home empty-handed.

I hung up the phone without another word, putting my headphones down on the desk. The unease didn't leave when the old woman's voice was gone, however. I could still hear something: a hoarse, chilling whisper. It was muffled and quiet, coming from the other side of a door. Evelyn's closet. And although I didn't turn to look, I could imagine the drag of dirty fingernails down the old plywood surface and a rotten hand jiggling the doorknob.

Whether or not anything was in there, I didn't have any interest in finding out. Instead, I pocketed my keys and turned off the alarm, propping open the fire escape so that I could stand by the railing and smoke a cigarette. Andre said this place would try to get to me, and it was certainly doing its best.

Something far worse happened just after sunset, however. As the sky turned purple and the first stars began to twinkle above the trees, I saw headlights pull into the long gravel driveway. I was on my second cigarette, flicking the ash over the side of the railing and watching it disappear with the wind. I heard music blaring as a car door opened and then slammed shut, the doors locking with a series of beeps. There was a dark blue pickup truck parked next to the tower and I braced myself for the grating voice of the man who had just stepped out of it.

"Thought I was losin' my mind, hearing you over the radio!" my father yelled, old and cranky as ever. He stood at the bottom of the tower, smacking the staircase with the end of his cane.

I sighed and whispered under my breath, "You done lost your mind a long time ago, ya' old bastard." I straightened up and began the long walk to the bottom, flicking my cigarette butt into the gravel as I did.

"What brings you all the way out here, pa?" I asked, tensing up as soon as we stood face-to-face. My father—old Clayton, as I preferred to call him - was smaller and more crooked in his age than he used to be, but he still had the kick of a stubborn mule even with a cane at his side and a chin covered in white hair.

"Why, I came up to see you, stupid," he said with a hoarse laugh. "I thought you was in the police force still. Then I was drivin' up to town to meet with an old fishin' buddy and heard you on the radio. You must'a done somethin' awful squirrely for them to banish you to the tower."

"Nobody banished me to the tower," I said with a sigh, pulling out my cigarette case and offering him one. He took it, then held it between his teeth while I passed him a lighter. "Our Operators are laid up. I volunteered to take over, just for a little while."

"Yeah, yeah, I saw that in the papers," he said. "Homely redheaded gal and that Mexican feller, gettin' drunk and fightin' a bear? Strange folk you got workin' here, son, I tell you what." I rolled my eyes and held my tongue as Clayton leaned against one of the wooden beams, taking a long drag from his cigarette and blowing out a puff of smoke that was carried by the warm breeze. I could hear the cicadas, as big as rats, screaming from somewhere out there in the woods.

"You ain't much better," I laughed. "I was just thinking today about you goin' off into the woods, making a nuisance of yourself."

"You ever do any huntin'?" Clayton asked, gaze still fixed on the tree line.

"No, pa, I don't go out there much anymore," I said, sitting down on the edge of the stairs. I picked at an old stain on the knee of my blue jeans.

The old man chuckled. "Yeah, your ma didn't much like me goin' into the woods either," he said. "She believed in that, uhh, *natural order* of things, you know? Leavin' well enough alone? Didn't suit me right, though. I don't think the natural order applies on this side of the mountain."

There was a cloud of tension sitting with us at the bottom of the stairs. Neither of us wanted to look the other in the eyes, neither of us wanted to finish this conversation we started. We didn't talk about my ma. We didn't talk about the day Clayton left us, where he went, or why he only ever showed up when he needed something. Finally, I took a deep breath and swatted a mosquito away from my neck as I spoke.

"Why did you really come out here today, pa?" I asked. "It's a long drive 'round the mountain. So what's the deal, you need money? Are you in trouble?"

Clayton gave me a long, reflective look with pale eyes. "Nothin' like that. I reckon I just wanted to see you one last time," he said quietly. "You're my boy. It wouldn't sit right with me to leave town without sayin' goodbye."

I scoffed, tempted to take another cigarette out of the case but settling with a toothpick instead. "You're in good enough health, old man," I said. "You got a few years left in ya', I wouldn't be too worried about that just yet."

"I ain't talkin' about me, son."

Even in the summer heat, I felt that chill. It was a cold stab in my chest. When I turned my eyes up, I saw my father staring at me with a stern yet somber look that was uncharacteristic of him. He didn't elaborate. Instead, we shared that dismal gaze for the longest time until finally, Clayton dug his cane into the ground and took a step toward me.

He offered me his hand, old and wrinkled but still strong. I shook it as a last gesture of peace.

"I'll be listenin' in when I can," he said. "I hope to hear you again next time I drive through town."

"I'm certain you will," I told him.

My father toddled away back to his pickup truck, throwing the door open and tossing his cane in first before settling down in his seat. And as he prepared to pull away, his window rolled down, I stood up and hollered to him one last time.

"Hey, pa! You should, uh ... you should come around and see the old farmhouse sometime. I've been fixin' it up real nice."

Clayton smiled, one hand on the steering wheel and the other sticking out the window to feel the breeze.

"I'll consider it, son," he said. The long stare he gave me was sentimental and blue. "I know you always were good at fixin' other peoples' problems."

He was long gone before I even began walking back up to my station. Down on solid ground with a warm breeze against my face and the scent of pine, it was tempting to stay there. For a while, I just sat on the stairs, my ass getting sore against the hard metal surface. My lungs were happy to get a taste of fresh air.

For a moment there, things were alright. Things were calm. But then I heard that whistling again, the same one I hear outside the old farmhouse late in the night. It was random at first like a sharp sound just trying to get my attention before it began to form a melody. It was familiar: some old campfire song I almost remembered. I lowered my head and tossed my toothpick onto the gravel, trudging up the long winding steps before it wormed its way any deeper into my skull.

There was fog in the mountains that night. It hovered near the top like a pale blanket, beginning to drift down only when the heat and the humidity ebbed away. I kept the radio going all night, hand ready to slap the button on the wall whenever those waves of mist got too close. Eventually, it sat at the tree line, and the mist and I carried on a staring contest that lasted hours.

It was well after midnight when it finally started to roll back up to the peaks. Not everything left, however. Little gray feet were dangling from one of the trees, rotten and limp, blown around in a breeze that came from the south. I thought about that missing boy, Aiden. I thought about the little kid in the red pajamas.

As I stood at the desk, turning on my microphone to let the people of Pinehaven know that the threat had gone, I heard a miserable voice crying from between the pines. It sounded like a child. I knew it wasn't.

CHAPTER NINETEEN: HOMECOMING
Evelyn

elieve it or not, it isn't fun learning how to navigate the world with only one eye. Having depth perception one day and losing it the next is absolute bullshit. That wasn't the worst part of the whole ordeal, though. While I was in the hospital, jazzed on pain meds and being fussed over by nurses and Daniel's parents alike, I couldn't get any rest.

I woke up screaming the first night. I saw him in my dreams: that monster. I felt the pain all over again and that dread as I was dropped to the ground, shaking Daniel's body and finding him stiff and unresponsive. It didn't matter that we were both alive now. In those dreams, he was dead and I wasn't safe. Even when the doctor prescribed me something to help me sleep, I still went back to that place every time I closed my eye.

And sometimes, I wasn't myself anymore. Sometimes, it felt like that other eye was still open. When I had those dreams, I could never go back to sleep.

But, the city was nice. The people there were nice. One of my nurses—a young woman with a tattoo of flowers going all the way up her arm—would visit with me almost every day. We'd talk about music, she'd let me walk around, and sometimes she'd ask why I didn't have any visitors. Of course, Mrs. Esperanza fixed that problem pretty quickly, as she'd come to sit with me every time Daniel was in physical therapy. And between the bad soap operas on TV and rounds of Go Fish in the waiting rooms, I started to wonder what life would be like if I just stayed there in Beckley.

I'd be free from the tower forever. I'd never have to worry about the fog or the woods. But then again, I felt as if it would follow me. I'd never be able to go on a hike again, I'd never look at the morning mist without feeling terror, and I'd never forget the responsibility I left behind.

I remembered the day Daniel lost his hearing. He could have left and never returned, but he still showed up for work a day earlier than expected. Maybe I'm just stubborn, but I could not let a nerd like him show me up. I knew I'd never hear the end of it.

···||···|·|·||·|·|···||···

The day we were both free to go, we took a quiet, tired taxi drive back to the radio tower, facing the mid-afternoon sun the whole time It was dreadful, seeing the mountains and trees come into view: a solemn reminder that things were about to get difficult again. I spent most of the ride just looking out the window while Daniel spent it shifting uncomfortably and fussing with his bandages.

I may have lost an actual part of my body, but I'd argue that he got the worst of it. While he was still comatose, I begged the nurse to let me sit in his room, even though he didn't know I was there. His doctor said that he was lucky his back hadn't been broken. He had fractured ribs, bruises up and down his whole body, one hell of a concussion, and stitches on the side of his head. Meanwhile, the lost eye was the worst of my problems, aside from some bruises around my neck that made it look like I was into some seriously kinky shit.

When we arrived at the broadcast tower, we found Finn at the controls, looking tired but still relieved to see us. There was a hint of surprise on his face the moment we walked in. It was almost as if he didn't think we'd be coming back.

"You both look like garbage," he said. Straight to the point, honest, and brutal—I appreciated that about him. I watched Finn scrunch his brows together, looking at me before pointing to his own eye. "When can you get that bandage off?"

"No idea," I shrugged, then used one finger and a hollow cheek to make a popping noise out of the corner of my mouth. "Scooped it out like a melon ball."

"Sweet Jesus ..." Finn murmured, disgusted, as he turned back to the desk. At this point, I was just so sick of moping about my stupid eye that I had to laugh about it instead. If I didn't joke at my own expense, who was I anymore?

"So, did we miss anything?" I asked.

"A few things," Finn said casually. "The sheriff gave me a bit of lip for still carrying my old pistol, but seeing as it saved your asses, he's willing to slip that one under the rug. That ugly bird won't leave. There was an earthquake on Tuesday that caused a weird sink-hole out by the treeline and took down a security camera. I got it put back up. Oh! Local news wanted to interview you both about Bernard, but the police put their foot down on that idea, leaving it as a write-up in the paper about a bear attack or—"

"Who the hell is Bernard?" I interrupted.

"The three-year-old you two chased into the woods," Finn said, eyebrows raised.

I slumped down in my chair with a heavy sigh while Dan busied himself starting a fresh pot of coffee.

"Man, I feel bad for the little guy," I said.

"Why?" Finn chuckled. "He hardly had a scratch on him. You did good, kiddo."

"No, I feel bad because his name is *Bernard,*" I argued. "Have you ever *met* a Bernard who wasn't old, balding, and dressed like *Dan*? Or who fought in the goddamn civil war? Hey, let's ask this toddler if he remembers the industrial revolution. Oh, and don't call me *kiddo.*"

Finn pushed himself out of his seat with a laugh, leaving me alone at the controls while he meandered to the kitchenette. Before he left, he gave me a precious little pat on the top of the head like a pet.

"Good to have you back, kiddo."

I scanned the monitor in front of me. The security cameras were up and running with nothing to see except the trees. All of the tabs on the screen were minimized in a perfect grid and Finn had even timed every song perfectly to fit each 30-minute segment down to the goddamn second, ads and all. This guy was better at doing my job than I was.

"Are you going home?" I asked as Finn walked away. But instead of grabbing his things and heading out the door, he was just finding a place to lean against the kitchen counter.

"No, ma'am," he said. "I'm getting paid overtime to relax and drink coffee while you do all the work this afternoon. Let me have this."

I gave him a smirk. "I'd say you've earned it."

I wasn't going to say it out loud, but I appreciated everything he had done. He saved our lives, he took over for us when no one else would, and he kept this place under control. As far as I was concerned, Finn was a good son of a bitch. Cranky, sure, but so was I.

Daniel appeared in the doorway then, two mismatched coffee mugs in his hands. He passed one over to Finn with a grimace of apology.

"The water's rusty again. I put extra creamer in it though." He handed me the second cup. "Did I hear you two making fun of me?"

"I was telling Finn that you dress like a grandpa."

Daniel gasped in mock offense, biting down on his knuckles as if holding back tears. God, he was dramatic.

"Excuse you, I dress like a *sexy* grandpa, and it's not my fault if you can't see that."

I laughed, plucking at his argyle sweater vest.

"Oh, I can see it alright, that's the problem. Thanks for the coffee, pops."

I looked down into the oddly orange-tinted liquid with some hesitation before realizing I had probably had worse-tasting and more harmful things in my body before. I gave it a sniff and something about it made my stomach churn.

"It smells like iron," I said, taking the tiniest sip possible. "*Bleh,* it tastes like how biting your tongue feels."

Finn hadn't ingested even a drop from his own cup, giving it a scrutinizing look instead. He was pickier than I was.

"I should, uh ... check the plumbing, probably," he said, stepping back toward the sink with his rejected coffee cup in hand.

Daniel sat down in the chair Finn had been keeping warm. We were back to where we used to be, just the two of us dipshits sitting side-by-side in front of these headache-inducing screens, our headphones next to us and waiting to be used. The last few days had dragged on so long that it felt surreal to be back, almost as if we had been gone for months. I didn't like this sense of *newness* that it brought, like sitting down behind this desk for the first time all over again.

"We've got a little time to waste," Daniel said, setting his coffee cup off to the side next to his keyboard. It always made my heart drop right through my asshole when he put his drinks so close to our delicate technology. "There's quite a few of those cassette tapes to get through. Do you need a break from the creepy shit or do you want to put one in?"

My gaze left my coworker's face and wandered to the corner of the room, where the cassette player was sitting beneath the lookout window with the tapes stacked neatly around it. I sighed, pushing myself out of my seat. "We're never gonna get a break from the creepy shit," I told him, marching over to the pile and searching for the next recording on the list.

The tape was relatively short compared to the others, but no less interesting. Here's everything Eric—or Number Seven— had to say:

It's December tenth. The year's coming to an end. I've been told time and time again that we'll find a Number Eight soon so that I can get some time out of this goddamn tower, but it hasn't happened yet. I'm starting to think I'll be waiting around much longer than I hoped.

Someone from the police station stopped by today, giving me some more information about Number Six. After they brought his body down from the radio mast, the decision was made to never tell his family how he died. Instead, they told his wife and two children that it was an animal attack—not entirely untrue, I suppose—and that a swift cremation was preferable. Thankfully, they agreed. His family didn't have to see him and no one knows about the parts that weren't recovered, except for those of us here.

Our conversation was interesting for other reasons, however. The officer, who had been here for quite a while, was curious about my time working in wildlife conservation. In turn, he told me some interesting facts about this location and what it used to be for.

At first glance, I could tell that it was obviously a fire watch or a ranger's outpost of some sort. The building I'm sitting in right now is much older than the radio mast sitting beside it. The officer told me that there's been an outpost at this exact location for almost a century, even before the radio was built. He said that right after the big upgrade, this place was all fenced up and occupied by military personnel, but people got too curious. Kids would come poking around, people would ask questions, folks were getting suspicious. To keep the villagers from getting riled up, they decided to disguise the tower as something more simplistic. Something they would trust. A radio station.

According to him, the first known solution to our unique problem up in Pinehaven was an actual bell sitting up in a high tower. Members of the village council would take turns keeping watch and ringing the bell to chase off anything that came out of the woods. It sounds like a rotten solution to me, considering they'd have to ring it constantly to keep this place in check. I'm glad our technology is more sophisticated now, but still, I found it interesting how Pinehaven has adapted over time. I can only hope that in another ten years, it'll be even easier.

It's another foggy day. I'm prepared this time, thankfully. I don't intend on ending up like my former coworker. The only thing distracting me is this fucking bird sitting near the window. It's the same bird from yesterday, sitting almost in the exact same spot. Something about its dark, beady eyes makes my skin crawl. I hope by tomorrow, it'll be gone.

Of all the recordings, that one was probably the least traumatic of them all, but somehow the most useful. When it was over and the tape was left with nothing but empty white noise, I ejected it from the machine and put it back in its case where it belonged.

"You know, it makes sense," I remarked, eyes scanning the wall until they fell upon the big red button. "I guess that's why we still call it 'The Bell'."

Daniel chuckled. "And here I thought it was just a little nickname to be *quaint.*"

At that point, I was just about to put my headphones on and

get ready to broadcast our heroic return to the airwaves when heavy footsteps began to stomp toward us from the kitchen. I recognized Finn's various walks. Sometimes he marched around like an elephant and sometimes he was quieter than a shadow on the floor. This time, however, his feet raced toward us with more urgency and panic than ever.

He grabbed both of our coffee cups straight out of our hands, a sickly expression on his face. I lifted the headphones off my ears just in time to hear him babbling on his way back to the kitchen.

"What was that about?" I asked.

"The water's not rusty," Finn said. "You don't want this."

"What?" I put my headphones down on the desk with a clatter.

"I said, *you don't want this.*" I could hear Finn pouring the coffee down the sink, both cups at once. I knew that our kitchen sink had always been a little *eccentric,* and I should have left it at that. But curiosity tore me away from the comfort of my rolling chair and into the kitchen doorway where the sight of the mess made my stomach turn sour.

The sink was gurgling again. Large bubbles of thick red liquid popped and left splatters on the basin's edge, staining the countertops on either side. Finn's hands were covered in it, leaving fingerprints on the coffee cups and a sticky residue on the knobs and the spout. He turned to me, a scowl of disgust on his face, and showed me his red-tinted fingers.

"Smell the water," he demanded.

"... No?"

"I said, smell it."

"Yeah, actually, let me think ... *Fuck no.*"

Before Finn could further pressure me into inspecting the scent of the filthy sink, a large bubble popped and sprayed a dark red stain across the side of his face, causing him to squint one eye and grimace as a shiver went down his spine.

"It's not water," he said, wiping his face and blinking away the liquid sticking to his eyelashes. "It's blood. And it's *warm.* Have you ever seen your sink do this before?"

I didn't answer him, too busy wishing I could somehow

wipe the taste off my tongue. God, I *drank* that. I actually put that in my mouth. *My own, personal human mouth.* I was busy trying not to lose my lunch and all Finn could ask was if this had happened before.

Strangely, the answer was yes. That face made me want to rip the sink right out of the kitchen and chuck it into the woods.

"Ugh ... yeah. Yeah, it has," I said, gagging. "Once. It was the night I called you—when Elijah showed up the first time."

In September of the year prior, as I spent my first few weeks here in the tower, I wondered how on earth a voice had gotten into the pipes. It was Jennifer's voice specifically. At the time, I assumed it was some creepy parlor trick meant to scare me or a sick joke made by my own brain, but this brought it into a whole new light. I thought about where the water in our taps came from; I thought about those long, clanking pipes that snaked down from the tower and into the soil.

The ground beneath us, shared with the forest, was as rotten as the roots that squeezed the life out of my friend.

"We're drinking bottled water from now on," I announced, still shivering from disgust every time I tasted that hint of metal on my tongue. "Get the cheap shit. I don't care."

Was it ever any wonder why this place was making everyone sick? Sometimes I barely slept and other times I couldn't stay awake. I hardly ever ate real food, Daniel was collecting injuries like bottle caps, and Finn was gaining a silver hair for every day he spent up here. And now, the forest had taken a piece of me for its own. I knew for a fact that I wasn't the first person to feel like trash from spending too much time up here. I could only begin to imagine the former Operators: how many of them ended up dead, injured, sick, scarred for life, driven to drink?

The blood coming up into the water supply was just the cherry on top. God, this place was fucking *unlivable.*

I was sick of looking at this kitchen. I turned my back, ready to sit down at the desk and carry on with bullshit as usual when we were surprised by a very unexpected sound: it was a knock on the door.

Through the small glass window, just big enough to peek a face through, I could see someone on the other side. Elijah was back, just when I thought we'd never see him again.

"Oh shit, it's him again," I said hoarsely. Finn was standing in the kitchenette still, inspecting a partially-bruised tangerine. He put it back on the counter to peer around the corner and caught a glimpse of our visitor from behind the glass. Elijah knocked again, making eye contact with me through the window.

"Finn, stick around in case he tries any more bullshit," I said with a sigh. "Dan ... just try not to get punched in the nose again, buddy."

Daniel was already moving to the other side of the room, taking that directive to heart. Before Elijah could raise his knuckles to tap the door again, I grabbed the handle and forced it open with a loud, rusty squeak. I didn't get a chance to even say 'hello' or 'what the hell do you want?' before he was inside the station and pacing back and forth, his hands dug deep into the pockets of his sweater.

It was July. He didn't *need* a sweater.

"I had to come back," Elijah said, voice trembling. "I-I can't stop *thinking* about it. I can't relax, I can't sleep. Every time I do, I-I see *her* as soon as I start to dream. I leave all the lights on, the television, the radio, *anything* to keep me awake so I don't see her face in the fog again."

He was speaking quickly, one hand pulled out of his pocket to gesture wildly with each word. He paced from one side of the room to the other, back and forth in front of the window again and again. As he passed by Daniel, I could see my coworker flinch and take a step back, but Elijah didn't even acknowledge him.

Finally, he stopped, standing next to the kitchen counter and leaning with both hands up to his head. His fingers tangled in his hair, which looked caked in grease as if he hadn't washed since the last time we saw him.

"Believe me," I said, keeping my distance. "Elijah, I wish I could forget too. But you need to go home and get some rest, okay?"

"It doesn't work," he responded, turning to the wall and pressing his forehead against it. "I look out my window and I see the woods. I see the trees. Every photo of her doesn't look like *her* anymore. It looks like ..."

He was unwilling to say it, but I knew what he meant. After

seeing Jennifer's corpse, it was hard to imagine her alive anymore. Even in my head, images of her rosy cheeks and her smile were gone, replaced with visions of that rotten skin suctioned tightly to her bones. All I could think about was the way her jaw hung open, limp, lopsided, and broken.

Elijah banged his head on the wall. I flinched when I heard the way his skull smacked against the wooden planks.

"Goddamnit, I can't even turn on the *radio* anymore without remembering it," he sobbed. "I hear this broadcast, I hear *you,* and the sound of it all makes my fucking brain itch!"

"Elijah," Finn spoke sternly, stepping forward to clap a hand down on the other man's shoulder. "You need to relax. You need to talk to someone about this."

Elijah laughed. He shook his head as he pulled away from Finn's grasp, resuming his quick stomp around the room until he was pacing in front of the lookout window again. His laughter was hysterical and unhinged, tears flying off his face.

"I am!" he shouted. And when he did, he threw both hands in the air. Inside his pocket, he had been carrying a pistol, which he waved above his head as he yelled.

"I'm talking to you," he pointed the gun at Finn. "And you, and you!"

He turned it toward Daniel and then at me before centering back on the former officer, who had suddenly changed his mind about stepping forward to grab him.

The three of us were frozen in place as Elijah's eyes darted, waiting to see which one of us would move first. I wasn't going to. I wasn't stupid enough to get closer knowing that I couldn't defend myself against a fucking *gun.* However, I was stupid enough to open my big, dumb mouth.

"Elijah, you're acting like a fucking *idiot!* Now please, put that down!"

A tone of voice that I thought was demanding only earned a bitter laugh from him.

"I'm the fucking idiot, huh?" he said.

It was chilling, the way he managed to laugh, cry, and grimace in pain all at the same time. His tired eyes were wet and red and his hands shook when he pointed the gun at me, both hands wrapped around it with a white-knuckle grip.

"I'm the idiot because I'm the one looking for justice? I'm an idiot because I still care about Jen? How much did you *hate* her, Lyn? Enough to let her die and then sit up here as if it never happened? We don't even have a body to bury anymore and you've been up here with your new buddies talking about the weather like everything is *just fucking peachy!*"

As soon as his finger began to twitch near the trigger, I could see Finn begin to move. He was side-stepping across the room from one end to the other, both of his hands up. Even as he inched closer to the lookout window, Elijah didn't take the gun off of me. I felt Daniel creep closer, one of his hands squeezing mine in a painfully tight grip.

"I didn't hate her," I said, tears in my eyes. My voice trembled and my chest began to burn with a sob that was being held hostage. "How could you *ever* think I'd want her to die? *How?!* I m-miss her so goddamn much, you don't even realize! I *live* here. I have to look at the place where she died every fucking day! Elijah, *I* want her back too."

His trembling finger began to steady. As his shaking hands settled, the gun was pointed steadily at my face and Elijah's lips pursed into a thin frown of concentration. He was glaring unblinkingly, taking heavy breaths through his nose.

"Then act like it."

As he said those words, I expected the next sound I heard to be a single shot. Instead, an ear-piercing alarm cut into the air, shrieking in the cramped space and making all three of us jump. The gun went off, a single shot ringing as a bullet flew into the wall a foot above me and dangerously close to Daniel's head. I covered my ears and Dan fidgeted with his hearing aid.

Elijah's concentration was broken long enough for him to drop the weapon, his palms against both sides of his head.

Finn had been circling the room with a purpose. While Elijah was focused on me, he had pushed open the fire escape door, which sounded the blaring alarm now tormenting all of our ears. As the siren continued, I watched Daniel leave my side and race across the room, kicking the handgun until it rested at Finn's feet.

He stooped to pick it up quickly, releasing the remaining ammunition and shoving the now unloaded gun into his belt loop. Moments later, he was pulling out a ring of keys, using one of them to disable the alarm next to the door.

"Get out," Finn said, gesturing toward the fire escape. "You're going to sit on the stairs, you're going to put both hands on the railing, and I'm going to *watch you* until the police get here. If you so much as move two *fucking feet* down that fire escape, I will have this thing loaded and aimed at you before you reach the first landing. Now *go.*"

Without his weapon, Elijah's confidence seemed to drain. It was like watching dirt wash away under a warm tap, there one moment and then gone the very next. He had no words, only a tremble in his breath as he followed Finn's orders and left the room, all of that pent-up anger turning into shame, embarrassment, and maybe disappointment. I watched him put both hands on the railing and face the woods, his head down.

A warm hand rested on my shoulder. "Lyn, you okay?" Daniel asked, his fingers trembling.

I sniffled, feeling a tear roll down my cheek. I hadn't realized how afraid I was until it was all over. "Yeah," I said as I wiped my face. "Yeah, I'm okay. You okay?"

He offered me a lopsided smile and pointed to the brand-new bullet hole in the wall. "He almost took my semi-decent ear," he joked, but I could see anxiety in his eyes. I could see the way his chest heaved, pulse still racing. I put a hand over his and squeezed his fingers, but he quickly turned his attention away from me and toward the man now sobbing on the fire escape.

"Wait, wait," Daniel jogged away from me and over to the door, slipping through the crack just before Finn was about to close it. Finn and I exchanged looks of confusion just as Daniel stepped onto the fire escape, easing himself down on the landing next to the man who had just pointed a gun at his head.

As I joined Finn by the window, he pointed a thumb toward the two.

"Your part-timer is a dumbass," he said.

And I agreed.

Finn had propped the door open with one of our chairs, leaving to make a phone call at the desk. Meanwhile, I stood nearby, feeling the warm breeze and watching a hazy orange color spill into a late afternoon sky. Elijah was holding onto the rail tightly, his eyes squinting as he looked out across the treetops.

"I'm sorry," he said softly, glancing at Dan out of the corner of his eyes. "I-I didn't want to hurt anyone. I just hate this place so much. I hate everything it's done and I ... I can't stop thinking about it."

Daniel didn't attempt to touch him or even sit close, but there was compassion in the way he looked at him and patiently let him speak. We both understood, I think. Sure, the part with the gun was a little over-the-top, but at the end of the day, Elijah was feeling a lot of pain. He was haunted by this place, the same as us.

"What's keeping you here?" Dan asked.

I saw Elijah shrug his shoulders after a moment of thought.

"I don't know," he sniffled. "It's where we lived together, it's where we grew up, where I've always been. I don't know anything else, I guess."

Daniel shook his head.

"No, no, that's a shit reason," he said. "If you hate it here and the memories just hurt, there's no good reason to stay. You can take the *good* memories with you, you know. No one ever said you had to leave those behind."

Elijah rested his chin against the railing, his glassy eyes focused up at the fluffy clouds. They were tinted pink and yellow against the setting sun as a dusky purple haze began to rise over the mountains. It really was a beautiful day.

"You need to get out of town, Elijah," Daniel continued. "You can leave. You don't have to come back."

My eye drifted over to the silhouette of Pinehaven, tucked between the trees about a mile away. Sometimes, I think living in a small town makes it seem impossible to leave. You forget that there's more to the world than your own village limits. Those long, endless roads flanked by corn fields, deep dark woods, and abandoned barns actually *go* somewhere.

We were sitting in a world of complete isolation, but it wasn't forever. This loneliness only reached so far.

Elijah wiped his face, a few tears collecting on his cheeks. One hand dug into his pocket and he pulled out a box of handgun bullets, which he slapped onto the floor of the fire escape.

"Keep these," he said, sliding the box toward Dan. "And keep the gun. I ... I don't need it anymore and I don't want it, but you might."

Daniel's silent 'thank you' came in the form of a slow nod as he picked up the box, setting it in his lap. Moments later, Finn was at the doorway again, pushing past me and standing next to Elijah while offering him a hand to help him back to his feet.

"I made the call," he said. I expected him to follow it up with a warning for Elijah's arrest. "I told them the alarm went off by accident. No one's coming out. But you have to leave, Elijah, and you cannot come back to this tower. If I see you around here again, I'm not covering for you. Do we have a deal?"

Elijah stood, his hands dropping away from the railing where he left imprints from his sweaty palms.

"Yeah," he said, glancing toward Daniel and then toward me. "I don't think I'll have a problem with that."

The gun and bullets were stored safely in one of the desk drawers between our chairs. Finn walked down the metal staircase with Elijah by his side, leading him to the driveway and making sure he got back in his car. They shared a few hushed words and then Finn gave him a pat on the shoulder, standing there in the tall grass and summer thistle as the car disappeared down the long gravel road and through the trees.

I stood outside, enjoying the fresh air against my face. I realized something then. This was probably the last time I'd ever see Elijah again. He was just a small piece of my life with Jennifer and now he was disappearing, off to someplace where I couldn't follow. I hoped he would listen to Dan. I hoped he would find something different—something *better* and very far, far away.

But now and then, I really wish he could have taken us with him.

CHAPTER TWENTY: THE MISSING PIECE
Evelyn

Danny was right when he said there were more stars over Pinehaven than anywhere else. After the sun went down and Finn left, I sat on the fire escape, watching the moon rise over the mountains. It had been nice keeping the door open all day, feeling the mid-July breeze. I sat with my chin against one of the bars and my feet kicking back and forth as I looked down at the fifty-foot drop.

I heard the crunch of gravel under a set of tires. Daniel's car was pulling back into the driveway, his headlights flooding the long grass that sat between our tower and the edge of the forest clearing. I got up and started to make my way down just as he was struggling to get two cases of bottled water out of the back of his station wagon.

I met him at the bottom step, grabbing the cases from him with a decisive tug.

"You should have waited," I said, disgruntled. "I would have grabbed 'em. You're not supposed to lift anything, remember?"

Daniel leaned against one of the tower's stilts, stretching out his sore back. I heard something crack and I winced.

"I'll be fine," he said. "I'm not a quitter."

"No, but you're a dipshit," I chuckled as I put the cases down on the stairs and jumped back to the bottom. "Don't break your back, okay? I can't carry you all the way up the stairs. Now come here, give me a hug, and then get your ass back home and go to bed."

"I thought you didn't like hugs," Daniel said with a stupid grin. I had already reached my arms out, but then I slapped them down at my sides with an immature scowl.

"Well, now I don't want one anymore if you're going to be a

dick about it—"

Dan rolled his eyes and put his arms around me before I could whine anymore.

"Ohh, so *grumpy,*" he teased.

His hugs were usually the kind that would snap my spine and lift my toes off the ground, but this time it was just a gentle little squeeze. I patted his shoulders, avoiding his bandages and trying not to think about the fact that he would be leaving me alone for the first time since before his cousin's wedding. Before that night in the woods ...

"Drive safe, buddy," I said, giving him one last squeeze around the shoulders.

As he pulled away, I watched him turn his eyes up to the tower. "Are you sure you don't want me to—"

"Stay?" I finished the thought for him. "You always ask the same thing ... No, I don't want you to stay. Get the hell out of here, Danny Boy. I'll see you in a couple of days."

He held out his fist and I gave it a gentle bump with my own before he walked away, getting into his car and slowly moving down that long, curving road. It was colder than usual for a July night. A strange wind was coming in from the north, bringing an eerie chill and the smell of smoke with it. I knew it must have been a burn pile from one of the farms by the roadside, but my mind wanted to see a campfire rising into the trees. I thought of the music, the taste of beer, and the voices of my old friends.

I didn't think about graduation as much as I used to, but when it came back, it always came back with a vengeance.

The smell made my skull itch from the inside. I left the fresh air and went back into the building, carrying those two cases of bottled water with me and closing up the tower for the night. The automation tools were right on schedule; "Wild World" by Cat Stevens was currently playing through my abandoned headphones like a whisper in an empty room.

I listened for a while, sitting cross-legged on the floor by the window. The forest was alive that night. I could see the motion of something huge between the trees, weaving a path and sending birds scattering. Through the drafty walls, I heard it: a deep, beastly bellow mixed with the sharp cry of an elk echoing together in the darkness. The Amalgamate was on the hunt again. He was always on the hunt.

When I settled in to sleep for the rest of the night, I stared at the wall for almost an hour as my mind wandered relentlessly. I was afraid to sleep–afraid of the dreams I would have when I did. I could only stare at a crack in the wall for so long before I began to drift.

My body isn't mine anymore. From my head to my toes, every-thing is pure pain and rage. I can see the forest floor and the maggots and worms that wriggle at my feet. They're inching away from me as if they, too, are trying to escape. I can hear a labored breath, purring like a beast's final death rattle. And as I stumble through the trees and the thick ferns, I know exactly where I'm going.

Nothing in the forest gives me any sense of fear. When I spot the glow of eyes between the leaves or rotten hands reaching out of the soil, I run past them with a singular purpose—to hunt, to grow. My body shivers against the wind and my joints creak and snap with the stiffness of tree bark, and yet every single step brings me absolute agony.

*If I manage to feed, this pain will go away. If I can only grow stronger, it won't hurt anymore. I know this. I **need** this.*

When I saw the lights of town, my rough, solid flesh begins to burn. My head is pounding as the most disorienting, terrible noise floods my ears–it makes my skull throb as if it's about to burst into pieces. I feel such fury; the tower, that's where it all comes from. That's where this misery lives. I can't step any closer to the tree line, but I'm always just close enough.

I see her: a young girl, perhaps fifteen years old, standing per-fectly still at the edge of the woods. She's smoking a cigarette in the park where her parents can't find her. No one would find her.

In an instant, she's running between the trees with frantic, bumbling steps and I'm right behind her. I like the chase. I like the challenge. She shrieks when she sees dead faces watching her from between the branches, their mouths open in permanent screams and dripping dark ooze. Their gray, decaying limbs reach for her as vines snake around her ankles, pulling her down and dragging her on her stomach. Her nails leave claw marks in the soil.

I grab at her. Wooden hands and long fingers wrap around her throat and hold her in the air. She kicks and she screams and she begs for mercy the whole time, but the hand–my hand–will not let her go. I squeeze her even tighter, choking the breath from her body and cracking her brittle bones. I feel them snap. Her face turns purple. And for just a moment, her eyes stare directly into mine.

My one, solitary blue eye.

I heard my own scream before I even bolted up in bed, sweat running down my forehead and sticking to my hair. I threw the blanket off and frantically began to pat my body. I had warm skin again, a pair of human hands, and blunt nails chewed down to the quick instead of long, wooden claws.

Nightmares weren't new. Almost every night, the beasts of Pinehaven Forest ripped me to shreds in my dreams. Sometimes I saw Jenny's body again, and sometimes I saw Daniel being snapped in half or eaten alive, but never had I been in the body of one of them ... not until that night after the wedding.

My stomach was sick. My mouth began to water and the taste on my tongue was sour as I lingered on what I had seen. That beast took my eye and now wore it as his own. I felt violated whenever I thought about it. That was natural, right?

But dreams were just dreams. Just because it scared me didn't mean it was real.

I tried to get back to sleep, but I couldn't turn my brain off. I kept thinking of that young girl's face and the way I felt her bones crack between my fingers. It was so vivid and so real—I didn't even know how my mind could conjure that kind of distinct, visceral feeling. I sat awake in the dark for a long time, the stickiness of the summer heat making my blanket cling to my legs.

I thought about texting Daniel. I almost did. When I looked down at our chat, tempted to start typing, I saw the last messages he sent me.

It's wedding day, ya lil bitch. I'm on my way.

That was right before he picked me up from the motel. Right before we had a great day that turned into the most awful night of our lives. I put my phone down, deciding to let him rest.

At that point, I probably would have tried to go back to bed if not for the series of sounds coming from the broadcast room. It started as a series of clicks: *tap, tap, tap* in a quick rhythm. Those clicks eventually turned into a voice, muffled through the door and crackling through an old speaker.

The floor creaked beneath my bare feet as I stepped out and toward the desk, following the glow of the screens in an otherwise dark room. Clouds were rolling overhead and the stars were hidden behind a stormy sky as it began to rain. The tapping sound I heard wasn't droplets against the glass. It was Bartholomew—that shitty little bird—clicking his beak against the main lookout window with his eyes locked on me the whole damn time.

I was uneasy the moment I realized that we had something in common now. Pieces stolen, pieces lost.

I could still hear a voice. It was coming from the cassette player, which was sitting on the floor and running on its own with a brand new tape in the machine. Number Seven's voice sounded tired, weary, and slurred. Never before had I been so convinced I was hearing the voice of a ghost.

It was an accident. I hadn't slept in days. I was so exhausted, so sick that I had no choice but to lay my head on the desk, and then … the phone woke me up before anything else. When I opened my eyes, all I saw were swirling clouds. Something enormous was out there, stomping through the trees and trying to bring down the radio mast, so I did exactly what I was trained to do. I pressed The Bell and I ran the broadcast.

It wasn't enough. The sheriff just about bit my fucking head off. The fog reached the outskirts of town, he said. Livestock was slaughtered, a farmer and his wife were found in pieces, the road was soaked in blood, cars were flipped upside-down and covered in ooze. We don't know what to tell people.

We've been seeing weird folk hanging around here lately. Military vehicles. I joked to the sheriff that maybe they're gonna lock us down like Area 51 and he didn't seem to find that very funny. He just looked me in the eyes and said, 'There are problems in this world bigger than what bombs can handle'. I don't know what he meant.

When do I ever? Lately, I feel like we're all in the dark, giving our lives for a cause without really knowing what we're fighting for.

All I know is this: I haven't seen my family in weeks. I've been paying a guy from the drugstore to bring me cigarettes and booze just to get through the day. Number Eight isn't coming. That bird is still out there. I think it's waiting for something. I think my time is almost up.

Those last few words were garbled and distorted as the cassette player popped open, the reels spinning rapidly until the tape became tangled. I rushed forward to grab it, pulling it out and gingerly trying to twist the tape back in place without ruining it. The cassette was cold to the touch with an odd stickiness to it, something dark and tacky rubbing off on my fingers like a viscous ink.

Whatever was on my finger began to burn my skin, the stinging discomfort traveling up my wrist. I wiped it against my shorts, but the pain didn't go away. That tacky, hot feeling against my fingertips sank in even deeper, setting my nerves on fire.

Just as I was getting up to rush to the bathroom, the floor trembled. All hell broke loose in an instant.

The closet door began to slam, opening and shutting again and again. The desk was shaking and screens were flashing with red and purple lights. I could hear a sound coming through the speakers. It was Daniel's voice, repeating a broadcast from earlier in the day. But something about his tone sounded darker, more menacing, utterly unlike *him.*

"We're just about to end your day here at 104.6 FM and Evelyn and I just want to remind you all to get ready for some extreme weather. It's going to be a stormy night, folks, so remember to close up your windows and be careful on those roads. Get ready for—be careful—Evelyn—be careful—be-care-ful ..."

The voice started to slow, growing deeper and more distorted until I couldn't make out the words anymore. Eventually, it was just noise. It was one low, demonic-sounding drone in this chaotic room full of flickering light and shivering floorboards. The bulb over our desk began to swing, the kitchen sink began to gurgle and spit dark red droplets over the countertops and the walls. As it did, I could hear those cries again, only they were different now. She choked, sobbing and coughing as if her life was being strangled from her throat.

Like a mouth full of twigs and leaves ...

I could smell metal in the air. The kitchen sink wasn't the only thing acting up – the bathroom tiles were covered in red stains as every pipe seemed to overflow with steaming, bubbling blood that pooled across the floor. The smell was intense, like roadkill after its gut ruptures in the sun. In the neon red glow of the screens, I looked down at my hand. That black stain on my fingertips was beginning to raise welts, the pain stronger than ever. Soon enough, whatever shit I had touched would eat through to the bone.

Disgusted and gagging, I stumbled into the kitchen with bare feet slipping against the blood-covered floor, grabbing for a case of bottled water. As I tore at the plastic, I felt warm droplets spray against my back, wetting my hair and my bare skin. The smell was enough to make me lightheaded. I grew so dizzy and disoriented that it took me a moment to notice the cold, wet wriggling that I felt between my fingers.

Maggots were crawling up my hands and my wrists, creeping up the length of both my arms. I staggered back with a startled screech, my spine tingling as I frantically wiped them away. It was no use. The maggots began to burst, streaks of blood and gooey pale flesh running down my arms from their fragile bodies. I could taste sour nausea on the tip of my tongue the whole time.

Stepping backward toward the desk, my feet hit something soft and wet. *Warm.* I looked down in time to see chunks of crimson, pulsating tissue squish between my toes. The floor was soaked from corner to corner. Something was *wiggling* within the sea of blood—bits of flesh, muscle, and blinking eyes that all formed some shapeless mass of organic filth. I was stepping on top of a living thing, like a creature with its parts all spilled to the outside.

The light above the desk flickered on and began to spin violently, shining a red light that traveled from wall to wall. As it did, I could see them: dead faces stretching through a layer of muscle and flesh, gnashing their teeth and trying to bite their way through. This was a dream. *I was still dreaming.*

An alarm broke through the noise. It was the fire escape door, bursting open and letting the cold wind and rain in. As the siren blared, I ran for the exit, tripping as tendrils began to stretch from the floor and around my ankles. When I fell, that terrible scent of rotten meat hit my nose full force and I felt the warm, wet ooze touch my skin. It stained my clothes, my hair. It dug under my fingernails and splattered my face and neck.

The cold wind drew me near and I crawled for the door, throwing myself out into the rain. As it washed over me, I sat on the fire escape with my knees dug into the metal and watched the red stains drain away. Like a river, the blood slipped off my body and down the stairs, dripping over the sides of the building to drop fifty feet down into the soil below.

I looked up at the sky, panting for breath and choking back nausea. The stars were hidden behind the clouds but lightning flashed over the forest and lit up the whole world. I saw the way the pines shook, tossed from side to side by the wind and other, stronger things. The violence of it all made it look as if the mountain itself moved in waves. The alarm was still blaring. I didn't even think about it.

Minutes passed and I didn't want to leave the cleansing shower of rain still pounding down against my shoulders. I only dared to move when I saw the flash of police lights slowing to a stop near the base of the tower.

"Operator Twenty-Eight!" One of the policemen, an umbrella covering his head from view, shouted up from the bottom of the stairs. "We're comin' up! Is everything alright in there?"

My mind was still catching up. I pushed wet hair out of my eye and finally saw the faces of the two men now marching up the metal steps.

The blood was gone. The black stain on my fingertips had disappeared and it took the pain with it. Chest still heaving from the panic, I turned and looked through the wide, open door to see the broadcast room looking completely and extraordinarily normal.

"Operator, is everything alright?" the man repeated when he and his partner had gotten up to the top steps. One of them held a hand out to me and I took it shakily, standing up with wobbling knees.

"Yeah," I said. "Yeah, everything is fine, fellas."

"And the door alarm?" he asked.

I wrung the rainwater out of my hair as I stepped back into the building, my bare feet making wet prints on the otherwise clean wooden floor. I was relieved to feel solid ground.

"It was an accident," I lied, holding my arms close to fight the chill that was sinking down to my bones. "I-I, um ... I guess I was half-asleep still. Sorry, I should have disabled it before you came all the way out here."

Both officers gave the room a quick scan with their eyes before turning back to me. One of them looked me long and hard in the face as if trying to read me like an open book; I think they knew something was wrong.

"Alright, well, just be more careful next time, alright?" the second officer said. "Need us to take a look around the place?"

I shook my head, arms still crossed in front of my chest. My tank top and shorts were sopping wet and my hair was dripping all over the floor around me.

"No," I said. "Thanks, but no."

It wasn't long before I was alone again. I watched the headlights disappear down that long, winding road as the two officers went back to town. Dawn was still a couple of hours away and the rumble of the storm hadn't left yet. Once there was a time when the sound of thunder used to lull me to sleep. The patter of rain against the windows was like a rhythmic lullaby that calmed me down and made my blankets feel even warmer—*safer.*

But now? I simply sat on the floor and watched the clouds roll overhead, afraid that going back to sleep meant slipping back into the eye of the beast.

That piece it took from me wasn't really gone, was it?

·‹‹||‹··|·|||·||‹··||‹··

When morning broke, I got a call from the police station. It was the sheriff, sounding tired and weary from a very long night.

"We need you to run a news bulletin this morning," he said.

"Run it again this afternoon if we don't have any updates. I'll keep in touch if anything changes."

I was already grabbing a pad of paper and a pen, sitting cross-legged in my chair and preparing to take notes.

"Sure thing, what do you need?" I asked. His answer made my blood run cold.

"Sixteen-year-old girl went missing last night," Sheriff Jacobs said. "Rachel McKay. White, average weight. Long, dark hair, nose piercing, about five-foot-three. She was last seen wearing a baseball cap, jean shorts, and black canvas sneakers. Her friends say they last saw her at the park, but she stayed behind to smoke a cigarette. Never came home."

I was in the middle of writing the girl's name when my hand stopped. My fingers were shaking. In my head, I could still see her, down to every last detail. She had grass stains on her shorts and a white t-shirt. Her fingernails were painted black but mostly chipped. I could smell the cigarette smoke in the air and I could feel that horrible, burning pain that the radio tower's hum drilled into my skull.

No, not *my* skull.

"McKinnon, you there?" the sheriff's voice tickled my ear through the phone.

I took a sharp breath and nodded, blinking my one remaining eye until my vision cleared.

"I'm here," I said shakily. "Rachel McKay. Dark hair, five-foot-three. Got it. I'll, um, I'll let everyone know."

And I did. At nine o'clock in the morning, I gave a brief weather update to the Pinehaven area and included a description of Rachel McKay: what she had been wearing, where she was last seen, and who to call if she was found. I knew she wouldn't be found. Clear as day, I could see those long fingers wrapping around her throat, cracking her bones until blood began to trickle from the corners of her lips.

It hurt more now that I knew her name.

The afternoon sky was dismal and colored a flat charcoal gray. The rain hadn't let up since the day before, deep puddles forming in the driveway and the clearing around the tower growing soggy with mud. I cracked one of the doors for just a little while when the showers were calmer, letting the cool air come in. It smelled like worms and mold.

He was out there again: the Amalgamate. I could hear its low, ghostly groan in the wind and I could see the tremble of the trees as it made a path up and down the mountain. God, I was way too tired to think about him. I closed the door, sick of hearing his bullshit, and went back to my desk. At three o'clock, no news had come in about Rachel McKay. I gave the announcement a second time, feeling like a royal piece of shit for getting anyone's hopes up about a missing girl who was already long gone.

I thought about the gun in the desk drawer.

That night, I had another dream. This time, there was no violence, no bloodshed, and no missing children, but it wasn't unicorns and rainbows either. I stayed awake as long as I could, hoping that maybe I could wait to fall asleep until Danny was there to hit me with a rock if things went south in Dreamworld. The exhaustion took me before the sun came up.

I can see the tower from the tree line. I can see the blinking red light atop the radio mast and the glow coming from the broadcast room window. The pain is stronger here, like a throbbing headache that sets every nerve in my body aflame. For hours, I've been standing here, just watching and waiting as the rain patters down and slides off my shoulders and down my arms. My breath is a low, rotten rumble that quivers within my wooden chest, the air passing through bone and bark.

When the sun comes up, still hidden behind the clouds, I see the lights of a car pull near. A man is stepping out, tall with black hair and carrying a red umbrella. I know this man. I can still feel the crack of his bones beneath my shoe and I can smell his blood as fresh as it was the day I tried to break his spine in half.

Pain erupts in my chest. Something is wriggling inside me, trying to fight its way out through my ribs and these twigs that encase what remains of my rotten human parts. I can hear the little screams and cries of children, like a lullaby that eases my constant hunger. They're reaching for the man with the umbrella, begging for escape.

He can't hear them. We took his ears already. I want to take so much **more**.

"Hey Lyn? ... Lyn? ... *Evelyn!*"

Daniel's voice dragged me out of the dream like a lasso around my neck. I jolted upright and immediately hit my forehead against his skull with a loud crack before falling back down onto the mattress again.

"Ah! Fuckin' balls, man," I groaned, a hand against my head as an angry red bump began to form.

"Sorry," Dan wasn't any better off, rubbing his sore nose. "Dude, you've got a hard-ass forehead ... You slept in. It's six-thirty. You feeling okay, champ?"

I blinked up at the ceiling. For a moment there, I still felt like I was in a dream. But as my brain began to thaw and I fell back into my body again, I nodded my head, pulling the blanket up to my chest to chase away the chill of early morning.

"Yeah, I'm fine," I said, wiping the crust from my eye. "I-I was just dreaming."

Dan gave me a gentle smile and ruffled the top of my head, making a mess of my already ratty-looking hair.

"Get dressed and brush your teeth. I'll get coffee started, okay?"

"With bottled water?" I asked.

"No, with mud," he snorted. "Yeah, dork, with bottled water."

Danny Boy brought some much-needed levity to my morning, but it didn't undo the anxiety I felt any time my eye wandered to the tree line. That creature had been standing there all night, watching from the border. You know, I would have been perfectly fine going the rest of my days not knowing what went on while I was asleep, but now that I knew that this fuckstick was out there stalking the tower while I was sawing logs? I couldn't get it out of my head.

I was distracted all morning. I hadn't touched my coffee

until Daniel remarked how cold it must have gotten, at which point I chugged it all in one go while flipping him the bird just to assert dominance. I stumbled over the weather forecast. As Daniel and I were riffing back and forth on-air about our favorite summer vacation memories, I stuttered and lost my focus more than once. It wasn't like me to lose my cool when the microphones were on.

By early afternoon, I had the jitters something awful. I was on my fourth cup of coffee with an otherwise empty stomach and Daniel, astute as always, had been watching me for at least an hour trying to figure me out.

"You're acting weird today," he said. "Not your normal level of weird either. Like ... an *edgy* weird. Are you sure you're feeling alright, dollface?"

He went to put his hand on my forehead and check my temperature, but I wiggled away in defiance.

"I just didn't sleep well," I said. "I've been having bad dreams since the incident. You know how it is."

"I have 'em too," he admitted, wearing a sympathetic and forlorn smile. "Do you wanna talk about it?"

I had kept a lot of secrets from Dan during our time together. I knew I had a problem when it came to opening up and telling people the truth—the *entire* truth, that is. But there comes a time when you experience enough shit with someone that you have no choice but to trust them. Almost dying in the woods had put that into perspective.

"I'll tell you my dreams if you tell me yours," I offered.

Daniel chuckled and gave a heavy sigh, squinting up at the ceiling as he tried to catch a wandering thought.

"Last night, I had a dream about a, uh ... a big *hole.*"

I tightened my lips in an attempt to resist a joke, but I couldn't hold it in. "Tell me more about your big hole," I snickered, and Dan immediately cracked me on the head with a clipboard in response.

"Oh, fuck you," he laughed. "Come on, Lyn, I'm being serious. It was like ... a crevice. A split in the ground. I heard something down inside of it: like, hundreds or thousands of voices all growling and screaming. Just this big pit to hell."

"What happened after that?" I asked, shuddering as I tried to imagine the intensity of the sound he described.

"Nothing," Dan said with a shrug. "That's probably the worst part. I was just stuck looking down into it, standing there for ages while slowly going mad. When I woke up, I felt nauseous so I ran to the bathroom." He lapsed into silence for a moment, looking down at his fingernails before glancing at me again. "I've never had nightmares that made me sick before."

"You've got a lot to be sick *about,*" I said with a sympathetic smile, giving his arm a little squeeze. "I mean, you got chased through the woods by a monster, you watched me get mutilated, you almost *died.* You had a rough night, Danny Boy. I think it would be unusual if you *didn't* have the worst nightmares of your life."

He gave a little chuckle, looking down at the desk with a lazy, tired smile. "You're right. I guess it'll get easier in time," he said, letting out a deep breath. "So what did you dream about?"

I hesitated for a moment, my eye stuck on the tree line where I knew the root-faced man had been standing.

"I had a dream about the missing girl, Rachel," I said softly. "I had a dream about what happened to her."

"After what happened to *us,* I don't blame you for thinking about it again."

"No," I shook my head, staring at the floor. "No, this was ... different. It wasn't the first time."

A grave silence fell between us. I didn't want to look at Danny, even though I could feel his gaze like a target on my forehead. He waited quietly as I steadied my breath, my fingertips gently touching the bandage that sat over the shredded remains of my right eye.

"Whenever I fall asleep, I'm in the woods again," I said. "Sometimes, I'm not myself. Before I even knew who she was, I saw that girl standing in the playground, smoking a cigarette ... Moments later, she was suspended in the air by her throat. That monster squeezed her neck until her bones *crunched.* She's dead, Dan. I saw it. And I saw you too. He watches you from the tree line. He remembers you."

I felt a warm, wet tear roll down my cheek and I wiped it

away with the edge of my sleeve. The dream was still so vivid. More than anything, though, I was afraid; if this happened again, what else would I be forced to see? Would it ever end?

"Are you sure you aren't just having these dreams because you're ... you know, *traumatized?*" Daniel asked. The way he said it didn't sound condescending or argumentative.

"I'm sure," I said with a nod, wiping my nose. "It was real. And it'll keep happening if I don't do something about it."

Dan gave me a look. It was resolute, endlessly encouraging, and supportive as always. His brows lowered as he gave me a steadfast nod.

"Then we'll do something about it," he said. "What do you have in mind?"

A sadly optimistic warmth bloomed in my chest. You know, anyone else in the world probably would have called a doctor or tried again to convince me that these nightmares were just the product of a troubled mind. Daniel was different. At the end of it all, he was just as much of an idiot as I was, willing to do something stupid if it made someone else happy. Sometimes, we all need an enabler.

Still, I couldn't help but notice how bold he had become since we first met. This was the guy who was terrified of bumblebees, after all.

I glanced down at the desk and tugged at one of the drawers between us. As I opened it just a crack, a box of ammunition shifted and a loose bullet rolled across the plywood bottom. Elijah's gun was still there.

With a shaky breath, I picked it up, letting my finger slide against the trigger.

"I'm getting my eye back."

CHAPTER TWENTY-ONE: A GOOD HUNT
Evelyn

As we watched the sun go down through the lookout window, I thought to myself: if this was the last night of my life, it was a beautiful one. The clearing was abundant with wildflowers, thriving in the humidity and enjoying the summer rains. The sky was painted with strokes of red and yellow that burst from over the mountain road, while the peaks over Pinehaven were bathed in purple. It would have been a picture of serenity if it didn't remind me of a wildfire rising up from the trees.

Maybe that would have been preferable to what it really was: a long, dreadful night on its way. The damp air was thick with electricity, putting my nerves on edge. The storm was gone, but I could still feel the lightning.

Daniel and I were getting our things packed: a compass, flashlights, batteries, Elijah's handgun, and all the ammunition we had. As we filled our packs, we decided to tune in to one more of those cassette tapes from Number Seven. Deciding to rush to the end of his tale, we bypassed the audio journals in the middle and went straight for the final recording.

We should have expected what we heard.

It was a different voice. After a minute of crackling white noise, a woman spoke to us with soft, austere professionalism.

It's February 10th. My name is Victoria Lang and I am Operator Number Eight from the Pinehaven Emergency Broadcast Station. I'm afraid it is my unfortunate duty to announce that we have lost Number Seven. Eric reached an impressive three months of service here in the tower before his death, mere days after my arrival as his co-host. I regretted that I knew him for such a short while, and

247

I am even more regretful that I had to be there when he was killed.

They warned me about this place. They told me that the creatures from Pinehaven Forest liked to take parts from their victims to grow their own mutations, but I was still unprepared to see how savagely they ripped him to shreds.

The only thing left was his head in the end. Even then, his eyes were gone. Both of them were ripped clean from the skull, the rest of his face left in a perpetual scream.

I might be losing my mind already. I swore I recognized those eyes again, but it was just this strange-looking bird that's been hanging around near the broadcast room window all day. Weird how an animal can somehow look so ... familiar. It's been tapping on the glass ever since the police took Eric's head away.

Even when it's gone, I still feel watched. I'm so sorry, Number Seven.

The recording sent a chill up my spine. Maybe several. Daniel must have seen the look on my face as I listened because both of his hands found my shoulders with a tight, encouraging squeeze. I was thinking about the day the police dragged me out of the tower and that long, agonizing medical exam they made me sit through. It would seem that most people who lost a piece of themselves to the forest didn't live to tell the tale.

Unfortunately, I wasn't interested in sharing my eyes any longer.

"I can't live with it," I said as I grabbed a glorified fanny pack out of the closet and clipped it to my belt. I shifted it to the side so I didn't look like a tourist. "Even if I *wasn't* having fucked up visions, I still don't like the thought of my eye being *out there,* belonging to something else."

Daniel shook a box of ammunition, making sure there was enough in there to get us by. "So this is a necessity *and* a revenge mission,"he teased.

I looked up at him, lips pursed in a frown.

"Yes," I said bluntly, and I fuckin' meant it. "Listen, you don't have to go with me if you don't want to. After the last time, I'd completely understand. This is my fight."

Dan didn't say a word at first. Instead, he looked me straight in the eyes as he laced the strap of his bag around one shoulder, securing it tightly. With one last peek at our computer monitors to check the music, he gave me a singular, assertive nod of the head.

"I'm ready when you are," he said. "Ready to ... go shoot a fuckin' tree, I guess."

I chuckled, dry and humorless. If this didn't work, he would have been ready to die. I didn't dare say it out loud. There was no need to acknowledge what he already knew—what he understood the moment he agreed to my stupid, foolish idea.

Our steps down the metal stairs had never echoed the same way they did that night. The sound was sharp and oddly uniform, like the tap of drumsticks in a funeral march. When our feet hit the ground and the summer air came washing over us, it was humid and dense. I heard the crickets and frogs, the sound of my boots kicking up dirt, and the squeak of bats as they hunted for mosquitoes.

If I focused really hard, I could have imagined that I was still at my childhood home, reading a comic book on the porch swing at night while mosquitoes ran into the bug zapper. Maybe I was drinking a beer outside my college dorm, listening to the muffled music from a party a few doors down. I imagined myself anywhere in the world but here.

The last rays of sunshine disappeared and the sky became the darkest it would ever be. As Daniel and I approached the edge of the clearing, the gentle rhythm of crickets and frogs stopped. It was unnatural, the way they buzzed one moment and then went quiet the next as if the night fell so thick around us that it choked the sound out of every living thing.

"Do you want to carry the gun?" Daniel asked, pointing down at his bag. It was a generous offer, but perhaps not the wisest.

"I don't think my aim is what it used to be, Danny Boy," I joked, pointing to my single eyeball, which was currently struggling to carry the weight of the world after the loss of its twin. "I'll trust you with it for now, okay?"

Those first few steps into the forest were dizzying. There was energy out there, but I don't mean some kind of vague ghostly bullshit. It was teeming with *too* much life, even when there was none to be seen. When the branches above our heads cracked and shifted, the groans of those old oaks sounded like voices. When little animals ran through the overgrowth or scaled the sides of the trees, I could feel them watching us and whispering to one another. Even the mosquitoes, which were eating the shit out of Dan's neck, were busy and agitated.

This place was crowded, unhealthy, and sick.

I stopped for a moment to listen, and Daniel did me the courtesy of standing still as well. From somewhere deep in the forest, I heard a low bellow, distant but weary and pained. Immediately, I imagined some old dragon being awoken from its ancient slumber. I just hoped that it wasn't as big or as angry as it sounded.

"Think the root man only shows himself when there are kids around?" I whispered to Daniel, who was squinting in the darkness to see my lips move.

He shrugged. "He seemed content enough with you and your eye."

"Yeah, well, next time he wants to take a chunk, he can take one of *yours.*"

Dan snickered. "Just don't make it something I'll miss," he said. "I've got a wisdom tooth he can help himself to if—"

He paused. One of his hands stretched out in front of me, stopping me in my tracks. In the darkness, I could see the whites of his eyes set on something between the trees; he was watching and waiting. My heart skipped a beat when I heard it. A faint cry echoed on the whistling wind, muffled as if struggling to breathe.

Both of our lights scanned the branches. We stepped forward, our feet digging into the mud from days and days of heavy rain. I felt the dampness against the bottoms of my jeans, caking onto the sides of my boots and making them heavier. There was an awful scent that came up from the ground, and immediately I thought of the water supply again and the lake of blood that lay beneath this forest. The graveyard.

The smell was coming from aboveground, too. Daniel's flashlight caught something bright and reflective. It was an eye. One of the nearby oak trees was *looking* at us, its trunk covered in eyes that all blinked independently and followed us with an almost human curiosity. I was disgusted by the sound its eyelids made as it blinked: wet and sticky, with strings of sap between the folds of flesh. Its eyes were all different colors.

We avoided the tree, easing around it and making some distance to evade its penetrating gaze as if it were a spy. We were headed in the right direction. I knew it as soon as I heard the cry again, and this time I recognized it better. It was a girl's voice, young but not as young as Bernard. Her sobs were interrupted with small, pathetic whimpers, sad and scared.

Daniel was the first to take a step back in disgust. His light scanned a nearby tree from the bottom to the top, revealing tight, rotten flesh the color of clay. The girl was there, trapped in the roots with her torso and her arms wriggling to escape. Her legs were wrapped up in vines and twigs, her neck was snapped, and her head was loosely dangling to one side on a partially-torn stump.

"It's Rachel," I said, a horrible rotten taste entering my mouth when I spoke. The poor girl was almost unrecognizable if not for the white t-shirt still hanging off her body in tatters. Her face was encased in fungus with mushrooms sprouting from her ears, nostrils, and her open mouth, her skin covered in mold and moss. Her cries were distorted behind a mouth full of oyster mushrooms and thin, wiggling parasites. They crept out of her eye sockets, the holes in her skin, and between her teeth: hundreds of long, white worms.

It was far too late to save her.

But even if her eyes were gone, she knew we were there. As soon as I said her name, her head snapped up and she faced us, her sobs quieting in an instant. She made a rattling sound as her broken throat filled with air. A puff of rotten dust escaped a hole at the base of her neck, a sickly moan slipping between her exposed, shivering vocal cords.

Daniel and I took a step back, watching in horror as Rachel slammed both hands against the trunk of the tree and began to push herself out from between the twisted roots. The bark cracked around her torso, the vines snapping as she tore them away. She began to make a low, guttural sound that didn't come from her mouth, but instead from the holes in her throat.

"Is it gun time?" Dan asked, fumbling with his bag.

I shook my head, pushing him by the shoulder.

"No, just move," I told him urgently. "Don't waste your bullets on her, j-just run before she gets *loose.*"

She was almost there. As we turned and began to race in the opposite direction, further up the mountain, Rachel had already freed one leg from the roots and was pulling the other one up. Something else was bound to hear her, I realized. Our steps weren't quiet in the least, two pairs of feet stomping through the woodland paths and cracking twigs as we went. Eventually, those two sets of steps turned into three. Rachel was out, and she was staggering after us with surprising speed.

Daniel grabbed my hand and pulled me in another direction, zig-zagging through the trees at random. I think I understood his aim. As we made a turn and began heading back down the mountain, he pushed me toward a dip in the earth where an old, rotten tree had fallen, creating a hole where its roots were now dangling.

I rolled into the pit, covered in more mud than before, a foul stench rising up from the ground. Daniel followed after me, huddling close in this cozy fort made of dirt, bugs, and stinky, diseased sap.

"Turn off your light," he whispered close to my face. I did as he said, plunging us both into darkness. We were silent, waiting for the shoe to drop as the sounds of the forest engulfed us. Somewhere, a fox was screaming. An elk cried out, sharp and haunting like a ghost up the mountainside. And still, I heard that rattling breath as Rachel's broken body shambled toward our hiding spot with clumsy, quick steps.

I put both of my hands over my mouth and nose, trying to hold my breath as my lungs began to burn. Daniel hid his face in my hair, as if not looking would make the fear go away. I saw Rachel stagger by, dragging a large tree branch behind her like a weapon. She was *sniffing* for us, hunting us with every sense except for her sight. Those little parasites wiggling out of her mouth and nose suddenly looked more like feelers tasting the air.

I was finally thankful for the stench of the swampy, muddy water collected around us. I don't think Rachel was able to catch our scent, as she only stalked around the trees for a few moments before running off in another direction—going the way we originally came. She would find our trail again and it would lead her right back to where she started, tangled in the roots next to a tree with hundreds of eyes.

Daniel crawled out of the hole first, reaching down to help me slip and slide my way up the muddy slope. We sat on the ground together for a while, checking our supplies, making sure the moisture hadn't damaged anything. The gun was fine. We lost a couple of bandages and a few loose bullets had fallen into the mud, but it was better than getting beaten to death by a walking fungal infection.

"Ugh, fantastic. I've got mud inside my boots," I complained, wiggling my toes and cringing at the moist feeling.

"I've got mud in places I don't even wanna talk about," Daniel said with a tiny chuckle. "At least we blend in with the forest stench now."

I leaned back against the grass, taking just a moment to gather my strength. As I looked up into the trees and the night sky, the moon looked different from here. It had a murky green hue as if the air around us was stained. There was a subtle mist in the air. Above us, an owl was looking down from a branch and turning its head upside-down with a curious click of its beak. It had four eyes and was about half my height.

"We should move," Daniel said, giving my leg a nudge. "We don't know what will find us if we sit around too long."

Groaning as I sat up, I winced and felt mud caked into the end of my braid. While standing, I tried to wipe my hands on my pants but found that every part of me was just as dirty as my palms. It felt hopeless, like the forest would never get off of me.

I slammed my flashlight against my hand a few times, trying to bring it to life.

"Damn thing must have gotten wet," I sighed as I opened up the cap at the end and let the batteries slide out of my hand. I was wiping them off and putting them back in just as Daniel stopped in his tracks once more.

"Did you see that?" he asked, pointing between the trees. I shook my head.

My flashlight finally came to life, illuminating the grass at our feet and huge, fat centipedes that were all crawling away in the same direction. I followed them with my light, my spine tingling as they crawled over the toes of my boots and between my heels. They were trying to escape.

I jumped when I heard the crack of a twig. My light shot up to eye level just in time to see a shadow move between the trees, quick as lightning and too blurry to see. My heart skipped a beat. The figure passed behind one of the pines and disappeared completely, but not for long. Seconds later, I heard the crack of twigs again and rapid, heavy steps raced behind us—something was *circling*.

Daniel's hand found my arm and squeezed it tightly, *painfully*. It was hard to breathe. The air around us was filled with a rotten stench that reminded me of toxic gas bursting from something that had been left to bloat in the summer heat.

I could hear him: the croak of old wood and a death rattle trapped in old, mummified flesh and bone.

"*Gun,*" I mouthed the word to Daniel. "*Take out your gun.*"

He was already digging in his satchel. His hands fumbled and I wanted so badly to be annoyed at him, to tear that bag out of his hands and get the gun myself. But even in the dark, I could see his hands shaking. Everything was shaking. That shadow was lurking nearby, circling around us. It wasn't a curious gesture like the owl in the tree, just trying to get a better look at something it had never seen before.

This creature was moving rapidly and in random directions, appearing a little closer each time. Daniel and I stood back-to-back. I felt the tension in my chest knowing that if one of us took our eyes off of him for even a moment, he could bound toward us easily and *quickly*.

"Fuck!" Daniel almost dropped the gun as he tried to load it, distracted by the movement between the trees. "Goddammit, come on, *come on ...*"

I heard a click. Daniel readied his stance, the weapon trembling and rattling in his hands. His head turned one way and then the other, waiting for the creature to stop in his sight. The shadow never sat still for more than an instant, always jumping from one tree to the next or crouching low to the ground as it circled. In the dull light of the moon, I saw the whites of Daniel's eyes dart back and forth while his face sank with worry and fear.

I found myself thinking exactly what I thought the day Daniel came back to work after losing his hearing, and again when he joined me in the forest to find Jenny's body. He didn't need to be here, but he chose to. He didn't need to put himself in danger again, *but he chose to.*

Goddammit, Danny Boy.

A single gunshot pierced the air, way too close to my head for comfort. I covered the ear that got the worst of the sound, but any words I may have exclaimed would have been drowned out by the gargantuan bellow that shook the ground beneath our feet. The moan of an angry beast came from up the mountain, haunting and resonant. It was low and high-pitched all at once, like several voices trapped in the same throat. It came from far away, but even the distance made the insides of my ears pound and my head throb.

Birds abandoned their nests, the buzzing flies grew silent, and the root-faced man retreated to the shadows during the chilling silence that followed. I watched Dan flinch, a hand twitching as it raised to his ear by pure instinct.

All this time, I wondered about the final sound he ever heard with perfect ears. I considered that bellow to be an answer.

"What the *fuck* was that?!"

I turned to squint my remaining eye toward the tops of the trees, horrified by the distant movement that I saw. Something was bending the pines further up the mountain, pushing them aside with ease.

"Danny, *what the fuck was that?!*"

"I don't care, but we're leaving."

He sounded urgent. With the gun still held in one hand, he reached the other out to grab the sleeve of my shirt, tugging me along. We were ready to give up our entire mission. Did I still hate the idea of that creature having my eye? Was I still dreading my next dream, knowing I would be forced to see things that would traumatize me for life? You're goddamn right! But I had the very distinct feeling that if we waited any longer, the forest would have far more pieces of ours to call its own.

255

We headed downhill, not knowing where we'd end up. I heard the call of crows and the hoot of owls, fleeing as we got close. I heard the whispers of lost souls and I saw the eyes of the trees following us, blinking in the moonlight.

But it wasn't the pale, rotten flesh of hanging bodies or the sounds of animals that made my blood run cold. It was the pitiful sound of children, sobbing together somewhere down the path. This wasn't Rachel's voice. These voices were tiny, young, and muffled as if trapped. In an instant, I knew I had heard them before.

We were wrong to think that the earth-rattling bellow of the beast would truly chase away the creature we had come out to find.

The crack of twigs and the rustle of leaves followed us. A shadow darted to my left, then disappeared when it crossed in front of us, leaving Dan and I both stopping in our tracks. The son of a bitch was trailing after us, even when the distant rumble of giant steps became not-so-distant anymore. Two things were gaining on us, one large and mysterious and the other tangible and *close.*

But just as soon as he was there, he was gone. The woodland stretched out before us, thick with vegetation but empty and still. I shined my light up into the trees, where I saw nothing but the eyes of bats and the glistening dew stuck to the moss.

We heard a crack behind us. His footsteps were slow but with a purpose.

I heard a rattle of breath, like a gasp trying to struggle out of dry, withered lungs. Daniel and I turned just in time to see him. The man had no mouth, but I could see a puff of dust leaving an empty cavity between his exposed ribs. He had grown since we last saw him. The worn and ratty clothes he once wore were now gone, but where he would have a naked human form, the forest had sought to replace his flesh with vines, thorns, and a gaping hole full of pale, thin, *tiny* hands.

Dear God. They were crying. They were flailing as if trying to escape.

The little hands were half the size of mine.

We moved before he did. Daniel gripped the gun tightly, saving his ammunition and resisting the urge to shoot at anything that moved. I don't think I've ever been able to run so quickly in my entire life, fueled by adrenaline and the fear of certain death. And yet, no matter how far we thought we ran, it never seemed far enough. We still heard those pounding feet behind us. We saw his shadow dart between the trees from one side and then another, back and forth again and again as if taking huge strides. He was playing a game with us.

And somewhere up the mountain, we couldn't outrun that angry bellow. It only grew louder as the earth began to shake.

We didn't know which way we were running anymore. In the darkness, every tree looked the same as the one next to it. My light would catch the glow of an eye or the bared teeth of a bloated and rotten face, but none of it mattered. Even the dangling feet of some dead thing swaying in the breeze didn't stop me. Finally, one thing was unfamiliar.

My eye caught the straight edge of a wooden sign. The words were so old and chipped that I couldn't read what it said, but I almost tripped over huge, rusted nails in the process. The sign was sitting before piles of wooden planks, a stack of stone, and discarded metal tracks. The railway moved into a deep cave, surrounded by old, crooked beams and a path that sloped downward.

"Shit! *Shit, shit shit!*"

I skidded to a stop, grabbing the back of Daniel's shirt before he had a chance to stumble into the dark and lose his footing. We were standing at the top of a steep downward drop, which had likely been a smooth path before the ground began to shift and reclaim it. A track that once led into the Pinehaven mines was now being swallowed by several decades worth of moving earth, mudslides, and utter neglect.

As we moved to race around it, I felt the earth shift under our feet. The ground didn't feel safe—it didn't feel *sturdy*, and those few moments of hesitation were all that it took.

The rattle of bone and bark sent a chill through my body, but nothing in the world froze my blood the way the glimmer of a single eye in the darkness did. It darted, searching until it finally focused on me. *My very own eye* was sitting nestled in the center of the creature's throat, staring unblinkingly forward as he staggered toward us, one noisy step at a time.

Those tiny, pale fingers in his chest were reaching out, clawing and flailing as if trying to pull something in. When the creature moved closer, I moved back, my feet faltering against the loose dirt. There were only so many steps we could take before we fell into the darkness of the mines.

I heard a click to my side. Daniel raised the gun he had been waiting all this time to use, holding it shakily in both hands as he pointed it at the root-faced man. I could hear my own heartbeat in my ears. I could hear ... something else as well: the crack of branches from a nearby oak, the huff of breath through a dust-filled snout.

The footsteps of a giant.

CHAPTER TWENTY-TWO: DAYBREAK
Evelyn

A single gunshot rang out and I could see bits of wooden splinters scatter in the air. Dan had hit his mark, the bullet wound spewing bits of bone, rotten flesh, and dry plant life. The root-faced man staggered back, one arm hanging at an impossible angle. Another bullet followed, this one hitting his chin and tossing his head back with a puff of dust.

The eye was staring straight at us, wide and furious.

Dan was preparing for a third shot, but before he could, a high-pitched shriek cut through the night. In a split second, a shadow bigger than anything I had ever seen fell down from the trees, taking branches with it and snapping a thin birch tree in half as it landed. The ground shook and mud splattered in all directions as Daniel and I struggled to keep our footing.

The Amalgamate had changed. It always did. For the first time, I saw the beast in full. The giant had four hooves on the ground and two in the air from legs sticking out of its sides. Its rib cage was exposed, the bones now sharpened into a second gaping mouth that rippled and dripped like a blood-filled cavity. It had the coarse, long fur of a gray wolf but the face of an elk, covered in eyes and with mismatched fangs that stretched from ear to ear in a Cheshire cat grin.

Enormous antlers, curved and wrapped around one another, cracked against the tree limbs as the beast grew to its full height, long arms reaching all the way to the ground to drag its claws through the mud.

Those were the same claws that busted the roof of the shed. They were the same claws that tickled the back of my neck when I was first trapped in the fog. And now, those claws were reaching out to grab the root-faced man around his waist and snap him in half like a tiny twig.

The way the smaller beast screamed made my blood run cold. A dry wheeze escaped his chest cavity, but I swore that somewhere in that twisted body of plant and human bone, I could hear small, pathetic, *frail* whimpers...

The Amalgamate tore him in half with one powerful snap, ripping its prey into two pieces. The bones and thick pieces of bark cracked in half with ease. The beast threw the bottom half aside, leaving the forest floor to reclaim it, while the cavity in its chest opened to welcome the rest. It *ate* him alive, swallowing his body piece by piece until the arms, hands, roots, and that one singular eye were all absorbed, finding new homes in the Amalgamate's own form.

Two of the small arms broke through the skin near the beast's shoulders, dark putrid blood dripping from the open wounds. Another arm crawled its way out of its chest with several others, all wiggling and flailing like tiny antennae compared to the massive creature. I suddenly became aware at that moment of just how many pieces had been taken: bones, hooves, claws, teeth, extra limbs the beast didn't even *need*. I could see so many human parts in just one glance, but I wasn't going to count them. I didn't want to know.

The creature blinked, six eyes glimmering through the dark all at once. Then, a seventh blearily opened on its forehead for the very first time.

If this thing had it, I was never getting it back.

"Oh, *fuck this!*" Daniel yelled as he pointed the gun upward. The Amalgamate charged toward us with the confidence of some-thing that knew we could never outrun it. But this time, Dan didn't hesitate. I heard one gunshot, then two, both of them aimed at the head of the monster. The first shot grazed an antler, which agitated the beast but didn't seem to injure it. But the second?

The howl the creature made was utterly ear-splitting. I felt as if my brain were melting inside of my skull, my head ready to burst as both hands rushed to cover my ears. Danny had hit his mark. A stream of dark blood fell into the grass beneath the monster's hooves, dripping over its snout and sticking to its fur on the way down. How on earth the son of a bitch managed to hit that thing directly in the eye, I'll have no fucking idea for as long as I live.

The Amalgamate stomped around the forest floor, flailing its massive head in anger as blood poured from the center eye socket. It was a small injury compared to this thing's massive size, but goddamn if it didn't piss it off. Daniel and I stepped back, and every inch we moved made the earth shift. Those stomping hooves, that *weight*—the beast was going to cave us all in.

"It's okay," Dan suddenly gripped my wrist with a white-knuckle hold and took a large step back. The soil shifted again, this time crumbling into the dark pits of the mine behind us. I looked back and couldn't even see the floor. I was struggling to breathe, my heart pounding as I tried to choose one flavor of pain over the other: death in the jaws of the Amalgamate or a fall into the abyss?

"It's okay," Dan repeated. "Just take one more step. Trust me. Lyn, *it's okay*."

I finally looked at him. In the dim light of the moon, his face was bathed in equal parts confidence and panic. Finally, I nodded, and he began to count.

"On three," he said. "One ... Two ..."

He didn't get to three.

The Amalgamate flailed its antlers one final time and then began to charge, but those first two steps were enough to crack the ground and send the earth crumbling at our feet. The shock of falling back into the unknown was cold and sudden, like the surprise of falling into freezing water.

I finally remembered the tile on the bathroom ceiling of that little apartment where I used to live. The design was hideous, made up of all these random scratches and shapes against dingy yellow. If you stared long enough, they would start to take form, turning into faces or letters or the shapes of animals. It was like watching clouds.

As I dipped back into the bath water, I stared up at a shape above my head. It took the face of a man with a big, bushy beard and a kind smile.

I thought it would be the last thing I ever saw. My eyes closed and I let out my breath, sinking down into the lukewarm bath. The sound of my own pulse mingled with the rushing of water around my ears. I was calm, drunk, and sleepy—I felt content knowing that the end of my life would be quiet.

But strange voices were in the room with me. I heard a woman screaming, a man speaking sternly, and footsteps racing back and forth. A heavy hand clapped against my back and I choked on cold water, my face pressed against the bathroom floor and my body frozen and naked. Jennifer was crying, asking 'Is she alive?' over and over. Paramedics draped a blanket over my body and held back my hair as I gagged.

After that day, no matter how long I stared at the ceiling, I could never find that face in the tile again.

There was no water this time, but the stone poking into my back was painful and cold all the same. I opened my eye to the dim, jagged opening above my head and a silhouette blocked the moonlight.

It wasn't Jennifer this time. Daniel was panting for breath, clutching his chest with one hand as the dust cleared around us. I had only been out of my mind for a few seconds.

"Shit, Lyn, are you okay?" he asked, holding my face in both hands as he inspected a wound on my forehead.

"My back hurts like hell," I said, wriggling atop the stone. "B-but yeah ... Yeah, I'm fine."

He looped his arms behind my shoulders gently and helped me sit up, letting me lean against him as I caught my breath. I squinted up to the light above us, dust and dirt clouding my vision and filling my stinging eye with particles. Somewhere up there, I could hear the heavy steps of the Amalgamate's hooves pacing around the forest path as if trying to find a way in.

It hadn't fallen in with us, thank God.

"I didn't kill it," Daniel said, disappointed. In the pale sliver of moonlight we were offered, I could see his dirty-covered face, brown skin now turned red with bloody scratches and glistening with sweat down in the hot, humid cavern. He wore a scowl. "... I'm sorry you won't be getting your eye back."

I wiped my face, smearing the dirt and blood already on my

cheek.

"It's fine, Danny Boy," I laughed. "Don't think I would have had a use for it anyway ... We should see how far this mine goes, I guess. It's only a matter of time before Frankenfuck up there finds a way down."

He was pulling his flashlight out of his bag, while mine was surely lost somewhere in the mud or kicked down into the mine shaft in pieces at this point. When the yellow glow hit the ground, the sight was unpleasant. I expected stone and coal, but at first glance, all I saw were roots. The trees above us had taken over, fighting their way through the dirt and wooden beams until they wrapped around every inch of this place like veins. They *pulsated,* dripping a thick, stinking ooze.

An old mine cart was tipped on its side, cocooned in the roots of a tree that had grown over it. Vines wriggled and slithered across the floor in no real pattern, reminding me of how worms moved in the dirt.

We walked quietly, tired but with a purpose. Any desire I had to investigate this place was long gone, but a shuffle of sound from my right made my heart skip a beat. I gave Daniel's arm a shove and he turned his light to the wall of the mine shaft.

Roots covered every inch of the stone and soil, but somewhere in there, we could see the movement of something half-formed trying to break through. There wasn't just one. If I looked closely, I could see the parts of many different animals all trapped in the bark, all in various states of decay but still moving. It was like seeing a graveyard from underground. Bones and rotten bodies, both animal and human, were stuck in a wall of soil as if they had been trapped for years and years.

Some of those remains were draped in bits of rotten old cloth. I felt another wave of discomfort as I recognized a fireman's coat, almost like the one my father left behind when he died. He used to let me wear it around the house all the time. It smelled like smoke and gasoline.

These coats were older. *Much* older. These were the remains of Old Pinehaven.

"What do you think caused all this?" Dan asked, flashing

his light on the opposite wall just in time to see a pair of white eyes looking back at him. He jumped in fear before realizing the mutated corpse was bound by the roots and unable to reach us. "What do you think made all of them start coming back to life, *changing* like this?"

I wished I had an answer.

"Honestly, I don't know," I shrugged. "Maybe nature just ... acts differently here. Maybe there isn't a reason."

Dan took a deep breath through his nose, but in the dim light, I could see him wince and scrunch up his face. It smelled awful down here.

"That's a terrible answer," he said.

"Yeah. I know."

The mines were full of twists and turns, sometimes splitting into forked paths that went in opposite directions. We got lost more than once, finding dead ends and turning back. Above our heads, we could hear the shift of the earth and the grumble of creatures both big and small crying out into the night.

"I can't tell if we're getting deeper into the mountain or not," I complained, stopping in place to look back at a long stretch of tracks. We had been leaving marks in the dirt with a stick, but we rarely came across our own handiwork. How many goddamn paths *were* there?

Daniel had a hand on his hip as he tapped his foot impatiently, deep in thought. I became aware of a squishy, wet sound beneath our feet. It was a mistake to look down.

I felt movement beneath the heel of my boot. Those centipedes were back, but these ones were fatter and longer than the ones up above. The size of ball pythons, they crawled over my shoes and up my jeans, all their tiny legs tapping against the denim with a damp sound. I shrieked and kicked them away, afraid to get my hands near for fear they'd latch onto my fingers and wrists.

Daniel, who *despised* bugs with the fury of a thousand suns, decided to put his big boy pants on and grabbed a stick, smacking me in the knees to crush the meaty fuckers before they could crawl any further up my body. The impact of a small branch against my shin wasn't *great* and neither was the soggy feeling of centipede guts spraying all over my clothes, but it was better than being eaten alive by fucked up worms.

"Oh God, I'm throwing these pants away when we get back," I whined, sticking my tongue out in disgust.

Looking down proved useful, though. If not for the insects, we wouldn't have seen the path they were taking. The centipedes were all moving in one direction, just as they had when the root-faced man was chasing after us. They were running from *something*.

Daniel shined his light down the path, illuminating the ground we had just stood on. The way was clear and silent, flanked by wiggling vines and old bones. But as we stared into the darkness, something stared back.

The hair on the back of my neck stood on end. I felt a chill run up my arms as a wheeze echoed through the tunnels. Slowly, the wet slap of bare feet began to stagger toward us, the sound bouncing off the walls. I recognized that voice …

It was the hoarse, dry sound of air and dust pushing through exposed vocal cords. It was the husky voice of a young girl, now twisted and overtaken by fungus and parasites.

"Move," I said, pushing Daniel with both hands. He led the way, his light bouncing from wall to wall as we raced down the unfamiliar path. We had already followed the mine for at least a mile. The twisting trails and the sharp corners all looked the same, but this time, they were alive. As if sensing another of their kind, the rotten bodies trapped behind the root systems began to wiggle and fight to escape, throwing their arms out and grabbing for us as we passed.

Clawed fingers caught the edge of Dan's shirt. He was pulled, his feet sliding on the ground as he fell flat onto his back. I watched his flashlight roll away, illuminating the ground as vines slithered around his ankles and held him hostage.

"Get up!" I yelled, pulling him by the arm. It was no use. Those vines were tight, pushing him against the ground until he couldn't move a muscle. One of them wrapped around his head, covering his mouth and silencing his labored grunts. Still, I could hear Dan cry out in pain as the life was squeezed out of him, those powerful tentacle-like appendages taking a deadly grip on all four of his limbs.

We didn't have time. *We didn't have time.* Rachel was staggering closer, a shriek coming from her broken neck as her blind form shambled toward us with single-minded speed. I could see her rotten, gray legs in the glow of the flashlight. Without any other choice, I reached into Dan's satchel and pulled out the gun, struggling to load it with unskilled fingers.

When I finally had my finger on the trigger, I aimed for her leg first. One shot was enough to tear through the fragile flesh, her skin ripping and the bones crunching, releasing a puff of toxic spores and foul-smelling liquid that oozed all around her. As she fell, I saw her face, half-consumed by fungus and wiggling worms.

I shot again, this time aiming for her nose. It was an easy, close mark to hit. Her head burst like a balloon, spraying dark fluid all over the ground and sending chunks of fungus erupting in all directions. Her skull was split open, the top separating from the bottom. Inside, I could see clusters of mushrooms where her brain used to be, covered in tiny spores and white specks that wiggled and crawled their way out of the wound.

Jesus H. Christ. The forest really did infect her from the inside out.

The vines that once held Daniel slithered away and began to surround Rachel's carcass instead, rushing to soak up her rotten blood like carrion birds flocking to a meal. She still twitched, half alive and trying to pull her pieces together.

"Quick, we gotta go," I said in a hoarse whisper. Dan gasped for breath as I pulled him to his feet. He looked paler than before, as if his life had just flashed before his eyes. He said nothing as we staggered down the path, slow at first and then picking up speed once his lungs had filled and his head stopped spinning.

It felt like we had been in the tunnels for hours. When we finally saw a glimmer of red light, Daniel and I gazed at it as if we had never seen the sun before. Our tired legs moved quicker, eager for escape as the end of the mines appeared at long last. The glow of a summer sunrise signaled the early hours of the morning, but the fresh air was the most welcoming thing.

As soon as we stepped out, I took in a deep breath and coughed, tasting ash and rotten air in my lungs. I dropped to my knees and Daniel dropped next to me, one of his arms draped around my shoulders as he laughed in near-hysterics.

I looked like shit. I felt like shit. I probably smelled like shit. But seeing the sun and the nearby tree line would have been worth ten times as much blood and dirt caked into my body.

When we stepped out of the forest, we found ourselves standing near a paved road that stretched around the mountain. It was the same road we took when we left Pinehaven and the very one that brought us back.

"Ah, piss," I said quietly, crossing my arms and looking out over the edge of the mountain. We were by the cliffs, staring into an abyss of forests and winding roads that went to nowhere. "Where the *fuck* are we?"

"What's a few more steps?" Daniel shrugged, already trudging down the side of the road with a limp in one leg and his arms hanging tiredly by his sides. I groaned in exhaustion and followed after him, looking like two feral adults covered head to toe in mud. It must have been a sight to see for any vehicles that passed. I didn't blame any of them for driving on, picking up speed a little at the sight of us.

But finally, after a half hour of trying and failing to signal for someone to stop, a rusted pick-up truck pulled off to the side of the road and an old man with a long beard signaled for us to jump in the back.

"Well, ain't you two lookin' like a gawdamn mess?" the old man laughed, husky and low. "Musta' had a wild night, huh? Where y'all headin'?"

"Just outside Pinehaven, if you don't mind," Daniel said, sticking his head through the window in the back of the pickup while I still struggled to get my stubby legs into the bed of the truck. When I finally did, I laid flat on my back and let my head flop to the side as if playing dead.

I heard the old man chuckle. "I was just headin' that way," he said, changing gears and pulling the vehicle back onto the road. "Heard about a decent farmer's market on the radio. Now hold on, you two, this old clunker likes ta' shimmy and shake a bit down these rocky roads."

As the truck started to weave around the mountainside, I heard the muffled sound of the radio playing from the old man's speakers. The familiar jingle for 104.6 FM hit my ears with a sharp, all-too-familiar sound, followed by the sweeter tones of Dolly Parton. And as "Jolene" began to inch her way into my ears, Daniel joined me on the rough metal surface, his head on my shoulder and his eyes gazing up into the sky.

"It's a nice morning," he said with a smile. "Don't you think?"

The sky was a pretty purple, dusted with hints of red and orange. Fluffy clouds were stained pink with a yellow shimmer from the sun's powerful, warm rays. I could see the distant sparkle of the river and the shadow of a hawk flying overhead. Danny was right. It *was* a nice morning.

"It's perfect," I said, leaning my cheek against the top of his head. "It's really perfect."

···||᳴·||·||||·||·||·||·||᳴···

The old man dropped us off at the edge of the gravel driveway that Daniel took every morning and the same drive where I had been dropped off on my very first day of work. Back then, I had no idea what this life would become. I expected that when I saw that tower again, I'd feel a heavy sense of regret and dread.

I didn't. When everything else in this forest was a thousand times more dangerous, the tower actually felt like ... *home*. I found myself missing the broken coffee maker, the leaky faucets, the lumpy mattress and its mysterious stains. I missed the squeak of my rolling chair and the sound of Finn's heavy boots against the wood floors.

Luckily, I didn't have to wait very long to get it all back.

Finn was waiting at the top when we arrived, looking like a disappointed dad who had been waiting up for us all night.

"You know," he started, "I had *just* been starting to think that maybe you two had one brain cell between you, but now I'm pretty sure I'm working with the biggest dipshits this world has ever seen."

"Not gonna argue with you," I said, leaning against the wall and sliding down until my ass hit the floor. "Nice to see you too, Finn."

"We had good reason," Daniel tried to argue. "It's ... a long story."

My co-worker *told* that long story, sparing no details. After an hour of Daniel repeating every single twist and turn of our harrowing journey, Finn seemed happy just to have us back. Hell, he even congratulated Daniel on getting a shot in, telling us that they could hear the beast screaming all the way from town.

As I sat there, watching my mud-covered friend excitedly share his account, I wondered if we really *did* anything. It seemed like we didn't accomplish much. In the end, we didn't get our revenge on the root-faced man and we didn't kill that antlered fuck, whom we've decided to call Big Boy from now on. We didn't figure out why the forest is the way it is and we didn't make anything better.

But like all things in life, it was a learning experience. Daniel learned that he's pretty good with a gun and I learned that I hate centipedes. But jokes aside, I think this tower and this forest have taught me a lot more than that. They've taught me about what I'm really afraid of, what I care about, and what I need to let go of.

They've taught me about hope and the people who make it all worthwhile. Life is hard. It sucks ass sometimes, sure. But when I sit down and I think about everything that's happened since I arrived at 104.6 FM, I stop counting the things that have gone wrong and I count the things I'm thankful for instead. I'm thankful for my new friends, for every laugh we manage to share even in the darkest hours, and for every fear that I've faced.

Maybe there was a time when I wished I would have died in that bathtub. But if I did, I wouldn't be here, watching my best friend covered head to toe in mud and performing a one-man show about a fungus monster. And *that* is something to be grateful for.

Finn mentioned in passing that there's been whispers of a new project among the forest rangers—something about 'trapping and removing' creatures that are already in the woods, hoping that maybe putting them down off-site will keep them from coming back. We were standing in the kitchen, talking about the likelihood that he would get placed in the new division. I poured some bottled water into the coffee maker and it hissed to life.

"You think we'll ever get this place under control?" I asked.

Finn wore a far-off look, his eyes on the window.

"Sometimes you can't fight to win," he said. "You just fight until you can't anymore."

That was a bit of lukewarm optimism I could get behind.

With two cups of coffee in hand, I stepped out onto the fire escape. The weather was pleasantly warm and the door was left propped open, the alarm turned off to let the breeze in from the west. The air was filled with the sound of sparrows singing and frogs gathering near the forest pools. I could smell the sweet scent of the dusty pink flowers that spread across the grassy hills and the leafy, wet aroma that drifted in from the bogs.

"Here." I handed Dan a cup, which featured a cool picture of a horse in front of an American flag. "No blood this time."

He just smiled and scooted over a bit so that I could sit next to him. We let our legs dangle over the side, his long and lanky and mine hidden beneath a pair of baggy, torn jeans.

"You know," he began, "we've got our Number Thirty now."

"Yeah?"

"Yeah. We could go on that vacation we talked about."

I leaned my chin against the railing for a second, but the hard metal made my jaw ache. With a sigh, I decided that maybe resting my head against Dan's shoulder would be a bit more comfortable. I was right.

"Where do you wanna go?" I asked, shifting the hair out of my eye to peer up at him. "Tropical island? The big city? The Alps?"

"I don't know," he sighed wistfully. "Somewhere far away. *Really* far away."

"How about Mars? I hear it's pretty nice this time of year."

Daniel scrunched his nose at me, then gave me a stupid-looking smirk. His tongue was sticking between the gap in his two front teeth.

"Do you have a rocketship?" he teased.

My laugh came out as a snort. "Yeah, you bet. It's in the

shed."

Letting the coffee cup warm my hands, I took a long glance out at the tops of the trees, wondering how on earth we'd actually relax if we ever left this place behind. Even if we drove miles and miles, would our thoughts stay here? I had a distinct feeling that Pinehaven would forever be in our blood—occupying our minds, running through our veins. It was both a blessing and a curse.

I think, even if we left, we'd never forget it. And maybe that wasn't the worst thing.

My gaze caught the flutter of wings. A familiar face decided to show up just then; Bartholomew the bird with his hazel, human eyes landed on the tree closest to us and hopped around on the branch. I watched him pick at a nest of twigs and grass that he must have been working on overnight.

There was something in that nest. It was black and square, a little scratched, and made of plastic. I could see smudged black marker and the number '15' half-faded on one side. Eric's last words.

"So that's where that missing cassette tape went," Daniel said with a chuckle of surprise.

"Good luck getting it from him."

I stared at Bartholomew, that shitty little bird. Then, I broke contact to blink my one remaining eye.

He winked back with the *same* eye.

"They're not all bad," Daniel said. He took a sip of his coffee but kept his shoulders still so as to not disturb me. "Yeah, most of them are downright nasty, but ... some aren't out to hurt anyone, right?"

The bird hopped away, off to grab more material for his nest. I glanced up at Dan again with a weak little smile before settling my head back down. "Yeah, I guess they're not all bad."

I don't know if I was still talking about monsters anymore, or people.

Some of them may have just been people.

This is Evelyn McKinnon at 104.6 FM. And on behalf of everyone here at Pinehaven Radio, thank you for tuning in.

Kel Byron

Milton Keynes UK
Ingram Content Group UK Ltd.
UKHW050728200624
444399UK00010B/616